# DAVID
# MARK
# TAKING
# PITY

MULHOLLAND
BOOKS

HODDER

First published in Great Britain in 2015 by Quercus

This paperback edition first published in 2017 by Mulholland Books
An imprint of Hodder & Stoughton
An Hachette UK company

1

A CIP catalogue record for this title is
available from the British Library

Paperback ISBN 978 1 473 66889 8
eBook ISBN 978 1 473 66888 1

Printed and bound by Clays Ltd, St Ives plc

Hodder & Stoughton policy is to use papers that are
natural, renewable and recyclable products and made
from wood grown in sustainable forests. The logging and
manufacturing processes are expected to conform to the
environmental regulations of the country of origin.

Hodder & Stoughton Ltd
Carmelite House
50 Victoria Embankment
London EC4Y 0DZ

www.hodder.co.uk

For Police Constable 72, Michael Duck.
Much admired, sadly missed.

Self-preservation, nature's first great law,
All the creatures, except man, doth awe.

*Andrew Marvell*


Out of suffering have emerged the strongest souls; the most massive characters are seamed with scars; martyrs have put on their coronation robes glittering with fire, and through their tears have the sorrowful first seen the gates of Heaven.

*Edwin Hubbell Chapin*

# PROLOGUE

## 29 March 1966

John Glass tips his head back, as though draining ale. Gulps down some of the late evening sky. Sees faces form and shift in the storm clouds: unfolding like crumpled, dirty lace and drawing a veil over a full, yellow moon.

'You still don't belong, John . . .'

Though not quite drunk, he is edging towards a maudlin, philosophical state of intoxication. These wide-open spaces still trouble him. He is a city man in city clothes, masquerading as a part of this place. He feels like a wrong note. He is a discordant presence; an intruder. This is a landscape of greens and browns, of straw and earth. He is a speck of blue. Fancies himself as a bluebottle, buzzing ineffectually against dirty glass . . .

He feels his starched collar rub at the back of his neck.

'Sober up, John. Sort yourself out.'

He scratches at the sore patch at the top of his spine with cold, clumsy knuckles and takes the top off a scab. Grunting, he raises his fingers to his face and catches the whisper of his own blood. He doesn't like it. Drops his hands and adjusts

1

his clothing. Winces as he feels the white material of his shirt absorb the tiny crimson droplet.

He breathes deep.

Shivers, unexpectedly, as he drinks down the night air with its tang of pulverised crops and churned earth.

'Another beautiful night . . .'

He lets the weather do its work.

Feels the soft kisses of falling snow. Feels a harsh wind chewing at his exposed face and hands. Feels the pleasant haze of alcohol give way to the cold grumble of sobriety.

He gives a little shake. Centres himself. Swallows a burp of beer and pickled egg.

Stares up into a sky the colour of dying flowers.

Turns back to the car, trying to warm his hands on the shit-streaked bonnet without actually touching the metal.

'End of the bloody world,' he says, softly, leaning on the open door of the vehicle and gesturing with a sweep of his arm. 'Furthest you can go without getting wet.'

The driver of the vehicle leans across: his big, round face all benevolence and bewilderment.

'You say something, John?'

Police Constable John Glass screws his eyes up again. Hopes that when he opens them he'll be somewhere else.

'Just thanking my lucky stars, Davey. Just enjoying the view.'

Glass reaches back into the vehicle and picks the torch from the passenger seat. As he does so he leans on his tie; the knot suddenly bunching around his Adam's apple and bringing a chill wave of nausea up from his gut.

'Should have stayed in the pub,' he says, though he has said it several times already.

He feels a smoker's tickle in his lungs and gives in to a fit of coughing, punctuating the outburst with curses as he slithers his tall, jointy frame back out of the dirty farm vehicle. Takes a deep breath. Tries to cleanse his nasal passages by sticking a finger into each nostril and inhaling. Fills himself for a moment with the smell of Woodbines and salted peanuts.

'My own fault for enjoying myself . . .'

It only took the pair of them a couple of minutes to drive here from the alehouse but it had been long enough for him to absorb a whole cloud of heavy agricultural smells, and for most of Davey's sheepdog to attach itself to his navy-blue trousers. Despite that, it took an effort of will to get out of the vehicle. It had seemed warm and harmless in there. Had felt like a pocket of metal certainty in this vast flat sea of crops and earth. He pulls himself back out of the vehicle. Looks at the open gate. At the darkness beyond. PC Glass scratches at his short hair. He rubs his fingers at his temples, dislodging his cap with the big blunt end of the black torch. The hat slides halfway down his face and he has to make a grab for it before it falls into the thick mud. Makes a mental note to take his shoes off before he drags it through the house when he gets home.

He fastens his tie.

Buttons his collar.

Pulls a packet of chewy toffees from the deep pocket of his long blue coat.

Switches on the torch and sweeps it downwards to illuminate the patch of mud which is sucking at his shiny black shoes.

He points the torch back towards the car. Notes that the silly bastard has squashed a little patch of flowering snowdrops under the back tyre. Makes a note to tell Davey off when he gets back, then decides he probably won't bother. The lad's done him a good turn. He would have hated to have cycled down here. Not at this hour. Not in these conditions. Not to this place, beneath a sky heavy with darkness and snow.

'Howay, lad,' he tells himself. 'Get job done.'

PC Glass is thirty-one years old and a decent enough copper. He's done an adequate job looking after this patch of rural East Yorkshire. The locals tolerate him. He knows the villains. He's only taken a couple of punches since he left his native north-east and they were thrown while in drink. He is a person first and a policeman second. He accepts people for what they are. Their vices tend to mirror his own. He likes a few pints after work. Likes a grope of a pretty girl and knows that if he gets a slap he has gone too far. Likes avoiding the taxman now and then on the odd box of imported cigarettes and brandy. He does what he's paid to do. He stops trouble. He keeps the peace. He enforces the law, if it's helpful. And he sometimes leaves a pint of bitter on the bar so he can go and attend a report of gunplay at a half-abandoned church in the middle of bloody nowhere.

'Bloody spooky, lad. Go canny.'

Glass is muttering to himself as he approaches the gate of the small, grey-brick church that has stood on this patch of ground for more than six hundred years. In this light it gives off little air of majesty. It is a squat, angular building surrounded by a low wall made of stacked stones. At its front is a long, stained-glass window, which looks oddly liquid against the stone. To the rear is a copse of woodland; all charcoal branches and spindly limbs.

'Christ.'

4

Glass bunches his fists and shakes his head as the gate to the churchyard creaks. Above him, something large and feathered rustles the uppermost branches of a tall tree, then beats at the air with a sound like skin on skin.

'Hello,' he says, more to himself than to anybody else. 'Police.'

Glass swishes the torch. His feet have found the shingle path to the wooden front door of the church. To his left, the beam illuminates a flash of colour. He glances at the snowdrops and daffodils that spring from the thick grass around a rectangular tomb. Sees lichen on grey stone. Sees old iron railings, punched deep into soft, wet earth.

'We know it's you, Peter. Don't worry, you're not in trouble. But this can't go on . . .'

Glass's words are met with silence. He sighs. Flashes the torch to his right. Sees newer headstones, fresher pain. Reads names and dates, chiselled into granite, and lets his torch beam linger on the soggy and bedraggled posies nestled against cold, unfeeling rock. 'Peter?'

From the rear of the church, Glass hears the soft, whispered chink of stone on stone.

'Peter? You're not in trouble, I told you . . .'

Glass means his words as he says them, even though he cannot rule out giving the simpleton a clip around the ear before sending him home. He's had to deal with the lad before. Given him warnings, tellings-off and a couple of rough shoves in his efforts to get him to act a little more civilised, and a lot less of a prat. He thought he'd been making headway. Thought the slow-witted farm-boy may have turned a corner and started behaving himself and working hard. No such luck. Glass had been halfway down his fourth pint when word reached him.

5

Peter bloody Coles. Taking potshots at aeroplanes from the grounds of St Germain's Church out at Winestead.

Glass scowls as he pictures himself not twenty minutes before, perched on a bar-stool in his civvies, supping ale and telling Colin the barman that Jimmy Greaves was no certainty come the World Cup and that Jack Charlton could keep his temper and do a job in defence if he was managed the right way. It had been a pleasant enough bloody evening. He'd planned another pint, then home to Enid and the boy. She'd promised toad-in-the-hole with onion gravy for his evening meal. Was going to cut the accompanying white bread and margarine into triangles to make it posh. Would probably have come and sat on his lap once the nipper was in bed and let him press his face to her ample bust until his legs went numb. Then the big bloke in the army boots had tapped his shoulder and told him what he'd heard at Winestead.

Shots.

More than one.

Said he knew it was a farming community and that it was probably nothing important but thought he should tell the authorities or he wouldn't be able to sleep . . .

Glass had got young Davey to run him home. Changed into his uniform and splashed cold water on his face. He could have gone in his street clothes but the Chief Constable would have a field day if word got back to him.

*Curse of the rural bobby*, he had said to himself as he pulled on his shiny black shoes and slipped half-heartedly into his tie. *They always know where to bloody find you . . .*

He coughs. Adds some authority to his voice.

'Peter? I thought we were past this, son. I've told you, haven't

6

I? It's not me. It's not even your gran you should be thinking of. It's the bastards at the RAF base. They'll come down on you like a ton of bricks. What if you hit a plane, eh? Or put a window through in the church? Peter . . .'

As he talks, Glass finds his feet leaving the gravel. His shoes sink into springy grass, speckled with fallen snow.

'Peter?'

The young man is sitting with his back against a gravestone, chucking pebbles at a tomb. A shotgun lies uncocked and dog-legged across his knees. He looks up at Glass's voice. Holds up a hand to shield his eyes as Glass raises the torch beam.

Through a veil of tumbling snow and gathering darkness, Glass sees the dirt on the young man's hands. Sees, too, the splattered colour upon his face. Across his neck. Upon his lips.

Glass feels his chest tighten. Smells his own blood inside his face; behind his nostrils, in his mouth.

'It all went bad,' says Coles, softly, looking down at the floor. Then he raises his face and tries to catch a snowflake on his tongue. He looks straight at Glass, then past him, to the dark tangle of trees. 'Am I going to prison?'

Glass follows the young man's gaze. Squints and raises the torch.

The body is draped over a half-fallen gravestone, arms dangling to brush the longest blades of grass that push upwards from the corpse-fed ground.

'Oh, sweet Jesus . . .'

Steam rises like a freed soul from the holes in the back of the corpse's head.

Glass raises a hand to his mouth and fumbles with the torch. It drops to the ground, and rolls, gently, down a slope of wet

7

grass. Its beam exposes the second body. This one is female. Young. Shapely. Half dressed, and with her blouse ripped open and bra pushed up.

Stumbling, slipping, Glass reaches the corpse. Her face is in shadow, and it is only as he retrieves his torch and shines it upon her that he sees that most of her head is missing.

As he recoils, he smells blood and gunsmoke.

The girl's body is only a signpost to the next dead. In snow and blood and darkness, PC John Glass staggers from one body to the next.

Veiled by tumbling snow, the world turns dark.

'Does it matter if I'm sorry?'

Peter Coles's voice is quiet and childlike against the night-time silence.

John Glass is too consumed with the blood rushing in his head to hear the boy's repeated question. But in the darkness of the sheltering trees, his words are heard by another.

Tall, powerful, the figure watches, silently, as the policeman slips and falls over first one body then the next; his clothes matted with dirt and blood and brains.

His answer, when it comes, is little more than a breath.

'*Sorry* doesn't matter. This is how it had to be.'

He slinks back between the dark trunks of a forest nourished by bones.

Fades into the snow and the night.

# Part One

Part One

# Chapter 1

Monday morning, 10.14 a.m. A meeting room in the Charing Cross Hotel.

The heart of London, and a long way from home.

It's a place of comfortable, high-backed chairs. Expensive carpets. Pictures of ships in chunky frames. Tartan curtains framing windows made murky by a hard rain; thrown down from a sky the colour of rancid meat. The whirr of a dozen laptops and the distant swish of tyres through dirty water. The honk of angry motorists and the soft thunder of trains rattling through the station next door. The rattling breath of smokers and the unsubtle glug of liquid down the throat of a buxom, dark-haired and middle-aged woman in biker boots and a black dress . . .

Detective Superintendent Trish Pharaoh lowers the cup. The coffee tastes of cigarettes and perfume. Extra-strong mints and vodka. Cardboard and sweat. It tastes of her mouth.

She wipes lip gloss from the plastic lid. Sits her takeaway latte down on her sheaf of papers and reaches over for a china cup filled with strong tea. Grabs a Jammy Dodger from the plate in the centre of the long, varnished table. Curses, under her breath, as it crumbles around her bite. Brushes crumbs from her face and her damp clothes with a hand that smells of cigarettes. Of cold coffee. Of gin.

'Trish? Anything to add?'

Pharaoh turns her gaze on the man opposite. Soaks him up for an instant.

His name is Detective Superintendent Nick Breslin and he's high up in the Met's Specialist Intelligence Service. He's younger than her. Slicker. Maybe six foot tall. Slim, but with muscle definition beneath his smart checked shirt and plum-coloured suit. He looks box-fresh. Clean. Looks like he's thought about every inch of his appearance, from the simple gold wedding band to the frameless spectacles. Looks like a man who will be Chief Constable before he's forty-five. The sort of man who insisted she be at Grimsby train station at 6.10 a.m., shivering her arse off and facing a day in a city she hates. This 'symposium' is his baby. It's a 'meeting of minds'. A chance to share information. A place to 'push the envelope' and do some 'blue-sky thinking'. Pharaoh hasn't seen any blue skies in years. The only envelope she wants to push is a big square cardboard one – right down Breslin's scrawny throat.

She turns her head back to the image on the big pull-down screen at the far end of the room. Looks upon injuries she has seen too many times before. Looks at the face of a man who died in agony. Flicks her gaze over congealed blood and fingers curled inwards in pain. Studies black ink and purple bruising. Absorbs the tar-black ruination of the dead man's chest and the stripes of bone that peep out from behind the churned, burned flesh.

'There's no doubt,' she says, softly. 'Our boys. Our bastards.'

Breslin nods and sucks his cheeks. Gives her some twinkle.

'I believe you refer to them as the Headhunters?'

Pharaoh meets his gaze. Manages a smile in return.

'One of my officers came up with it. It kind of sums them up. That's what they do. They talent-spot. They look for people on the up and they recruit them. It's run like a business. Like a consultancy.'

Breslin nods. Looks down at the folder in front of him and makes a note with a ballpoint pen.

'To use your corporate analogy, it seems they have their eyes on a lot of hostile takeovers.'

Pharaoh wonders if he wants a gold star. Of course they're fucking expanding. They're branching out, moving up and taking over. That's why she and all the other poor bastards are here.

She looks around the long, high-ceilinged function room. Rolls her eyes at the other senior officers who have been dragged away from catching killers and rapists to sit eating biscuits and drinking coffee in a hotel she could never afford to stay in. They all look similarly bedraggled. All soaked through and pissed off. They have better things to be doing. They all run CID units the way they choose to and have been around long enough to remember when a meeting such as this would have been conducted through a fog of blue cigarette smoke and to the sound of whisky glasses hitting stained desks. To Pharaoh, this all feels too polished. Too anodyne. Too far removed from the nature of what they do. She wants somebody to swear or shout or break wind and laugh about it. She wants to feel like she's in a room full of coppers who use words like 'bastards' when talking about the bad guys and 'poor bitch' to describe a victim.

Breslin steeples his fingers and looks at the dozen men and women who sit around the oval table. He gives a politician's smile. Turns to his left and whispers something in the ear of the woman sitting next to him. She hadn't introduced herself when they were doing the meet-and-greet at the start of the session. Breslin had simply said that 'Anne' was here to help. She had a 'watching brief'. She was a 'great asset'.

Pharaoh considers her. Young. Short brown hair. Looks classy and sexless in a round-neck, long-sleeved shirt and cream jacket. Her scarf looks expensive. Her jewellery too, though it's subtle and not designed to catch the eye. There's an intelligence to her gaze, and Pharaoh fancies that this is somebody she wouldn't want to be playing poker against.

Breslin looks down at his notes again. 'Arthur. You had something you think may be relevant?'

A stocky, fifty-something man with luxuriant white hair and a blue suit gets to his feet. He gives a nod and the image on the screen changes. It shows a strip of shingly beach on which a male forearm, wrapped in cling-film, is sitting next to a yellow evidence-marker.

'This is Lloyd Moore,' says Detective Superintendent Arthur Blowers, in a broad north-east accent. 'Or, it used to be. Lloyd's been the face of villainy in Newcastle for the best part of twenty years. His dad, Dermot, had the honour before him. Crime family in the proper sense. Old-school. Didn't court the media, but those in the know knew his name. Lloyd had a bit about him. Relatively fair man, provided you didn't upset him. Done a few minor stretches but it was always a bitch to pin anything on him. Witnesses tended to scarper or lose their bottle. Evidence would disappear. Plenty of other people intruded on his turf over the years but they never lasted long.'

'Muscle?' asks a short, stocky woman with a grey perm and glasses whose accent ensured she hadn't needed to tell anybody she was from Birmingham during the introductions.

Blowers sucks on his lower lip. Gives a smile that suggests a grudging respect and affection for the man he is about to describe.

'Well, that's the thing,' he says. 'Lloyd may have been the public face, but those with long memories may remember this chap.'

A new image flashes up on the screen. It's a shot from the 1960s. Black-and-white. It shows a squat, bulldog-looking man in a double-breasted pinstripe suit and a flat cap. He's been captured on camera coming out of a brightly lit building with two tall, intimidating men in black suits and ties. The two men look so similar they could almost be twins.

'Is that . . . ?'

Blowers smiles. 'Yep. You know all those stories and urban myths about the Geordie gangsters turning away the London boys at Newcastle station? It's bollocks. This man let them in. Then he did a deal with them. And he's been top dog ever since.'

'And he is?'

'Francis Nock. He's eighty-one years old now and we haven't had anything tying him to organised crime since the seventies, but that may well be because he's very good at it. We've had people in his operation before. We had one in Lloyd's outfit until recently. And from what we can tell, Nock has been the man who says yes or no, live or die, since the sixties. To all intents and purposes he's a retired property developer. Suffers with arthritis and diabetes. Looks forward to his daughter's visits from Spain. Holidays in Panama when he's well enough.

But he's the one who Lloyd has been reporting to all these years.'

'And you think the Headhunters bumped Lloyd off to send a message to this old boy?'

Blowers shakes his head. 'No, I think your Headhunters approached Lloyd and offered to back him. They wanted him to turn his back on the old man. I think they offered to give him the crown. And I think Mr Nock found out about it. And Lloyd ended up an arm on a beach.'

There are exhalations from around the table.

'And who does Nock's dirty work?'

This time Blowers gives a proper smile. He clicks a button on the laptop and nods, appreciatively, as the screen fills with a prison mugshot. It shows a handsome man in his late twenties, with thick hair swept back from a face with cheekbones so sharp they could slice the breeze. He's looking at the camera with soft, inquisitive eyes, and has the appearance of a big man afraid he might hurt somebody by accident. It's a look that Pharaoh recognises.

'This was Raymond Mahon in 1971. He was arrested following an incident in a pool hall, for which no charges were brought. Handsome devil, isn't he?'

Blowers clicks the laptop. Enjoys the change on everybody's faces as the image on the screen morphs into something new.

'This is the same man in 1976, when he began a lengthy stretch for blowing the face off a man in a Denton pub with a double-barrelled shotgun.'

The assembled officers give a chorus of curses and grimace at the image on the screen.

'He served seventeen years. Other pictures were taken but we

16

don't have them any more. You can probably thank Mr Nock for that. Further images were taken upon release and during his interactions with his probation officer, but they, too, are no longer in our possession. He's clearly camera-shy. You can see why.'

The image is hideous. One whole half of Mahon's face looks as though it has been torn away. A glass eye pokes out from inside a cave of tangled, livid skin. His hair looks like it has been burned off on one side and grows patchy upon the other. His lower lip is missing a chunk and his teeth are exposed in a grisly mockery of a smile.

'What the hell happened?'

Blowers shrugs. 'Lots of urban myths. We've heard he did it to himself while strung out on LSD. Another story goes that it was done to him in prison by some southern hard man while he was asleep. We know he's alive. He's not such a mess now but you won't see him on the front cover of *Men's Health* any time soon. We know he's a killer. And we know that at the moment we can't locate him or Francis Nock.'

'And you want to talk to them both about Lloyd?'

Blowers looks at Breslin as though he's a toddler. 'Yes, sir, that would be very helpful.'

After a time, Breslin waves Blowers back to his seat. He flicks through his notes again. Tries to find the right facial expression. Leans across to Anne and gets no reaction to whatever it is he whispers in her ear.

'Fucking hell,' says Pharaoh, under her breath, but with enough gusto for it to be heard by all.

'So, just to recap . . .' says Breslin, looking at each of the officers in turn. His gaze lingers for a moment on a haggard,

17

round-bellied Detective Chief Inspector from Nottingham. The man is still sweating off last night's ale. He's an unhealthy green around the edges and has a whole spaghetti loop crusted onto the lapel of his supermarket suit. His name's Melvyn Eades and he's a bloody good thief-taker. He's also a man with a temper, a limited vocabulary and a pathological hatred of southerners. Pharaoh likes him. His presentation to the other officers had been quick and to the point. Two bodies on his patch. Both tortured almost to death. Hands nailed to their knees and a blowtorch used on their bare chests. Finished off with a nail to the temple. The bodies were thrown from a moving vehicle in the early hours of the morning. Dumped, like rubbish, on a quiet cobbled street near the entrance to the city's castle. Both men had ties to Andy Hadrian, who had been looking after the city's cocaine and firearms needs for as long as anybody could remember. Hadrian had played the hard man in the interview room. Given them nothing. But Eades had a man on the inside and a bug in the bastard's phone. Hadrian wasn't just rattled. He was fucking terrified.

Despite his presentation being cut short by an unhappy Breslin, Eades had at least managed to give the little symposium its first bit of positive news. Something was causing the Head-hunters a little disquiet. Rumour was that they had recruited somebody to the firm who was doing things very much their own way. Somebody was refusing to follow instructions. They had stopped listening to the voice at the end of the phone. They were causing the organisation a little upset. And that could only be a good thing.

Eades rolls his round head on his fat neck and sniffs, noisily.

'To recap, sir, you're on the money. They're taking over

existing firms. They're looking at which outfits make money, and then they're telling the man at the top that he now works for them. He can pay them a cut of his profits, or they'll go to his number two and make the same offer. They'll give demonstrations of what they can do. Andy Hadrian's not an old man. He's got years ahead of him. He's got kids. He wants to live to have grandkids. He can keep his lifestyle and his life if he just bows his knee. I think he'll do it. He'd rather have these people on his side than against him.'

Breslin whispers to Anne again. Nods. Turns back to Pharaoh.

'And we're certain they started out in Humberside?'

'East Yorkshire, actually, Nick.'

'Sorry?'

'No such place as Humberside.'

'But you're with Humberside Police . . .'

'Yeah. Stupid, isn't it?'

Damp, tired, hungry and hungover, Pharaoh wants this meeting to be over. She wants to tip the rest of the Jammy Dodgers into her handbag and run for the train. She wants to get home. Back north. Back to her four daughters and semi-detached house. Back to catching killers and putting an arm around those who need it. Back to her shitty bloody life and all the things she's good at.

'We don't think that perhaps they were operating elsewhere but your team were just the first to come into contact with them?' asks Breslin, with a little more steel to his voice.

Pharaoh sighs. Takes a handful of her hair and wrings it out onto the carpet.

'It started in Hull. Or at least, that's where they got good. We reckon it was no more than a year ago. Couple of blokes turned

19

up at a cannabis plant run by the Vietnamese. Held a phone to the foreman's ear and he got the message from his boss that they now worked for somebody else. Next thing, every dealer who got their supply from anybody else was finding themselves on the wrong end of a nail gun. The new firm recruited. Picked some rising stars. Couple of serving dealers. Some muscle. Even got a big name in the traveller community to join them. We had some successes. Put some away. But we haven't scratched the surface. They're too well-connected . . .'

Breslin holds up a hand. Looks down at the papers in front of him.

'I understand one key prosecution had to be dropped following allegations of assault by one of your senior officers.'

Pharaoh bites her cheek but can't keep the sneer from her face.

'That's not strictly true, Nick. DCI Colin Ray was suspended following an accusation from a suspect. The CPS were still debating the merits of bringing charges when the other incident took place. Fortunately for all concerned, that suspect is no longer an issue. Or a person.'

Pharaoh keeps her eyes on Breslin's. Forces him to look down. Counts to ten in her head as she waits for the next question.

'The suspect in question is now dead, yes?'

Pharaoh rubs a hand across her face. Takes a sip of tea then a swig of cold coffee. Remembers, for a moment, the phone call that shattered everything.

'Yes, Nick, he's dead. So's a civilian. One of my officers may never come back. A good man lost everything that mattered. But yeah, the little bastard's dead. We'll miss him.'

Pharaoh throws herself back in her chair. She's breathing

hard. Thinking of Roisin McAvoy. Of Helen Tremberg. Of the poor dead bitch who took the full force of a hand grenade blast to the chest. Of her sergeant and friend, Aector McAvoy. Of what he has become in the four months since he left the hospital and returned home to charred masonry, broken timbers and dried blood.

Breslin seems about to speak when the woman beside him leans in. Her lips brush his ear as she speaks. He seems to like it.

Through an awkward smile, Breslin suggests they adjourn for a short break. It's met with considerable enthusiasm from the assembled cops.

Pharaoh is first out of the door, reaching into her handbag for her little black cigarettes and lighter. She thunders down the wide spiral staircase, knocking over ornamental tea-lights with her clumsy feet. She's already inhaling nicotine as she barrels across the broad, tasteful lobby and out through the revolving door into the rain and smog of a city that doesn't give a shit if she lives or dies.

She leans against black railings and watches two black cabs try to nudge a bus into a bicycle lane. Listens to the British flag flutter damply above her head and drip water onto the feet of the homeless man in the sleeping bag curled up by the wall. Watches pedestrians skip through puddles and between cars, clutching takeaway coffees and mobile phones. Watches the commuters pour in and out of Charing Cross station. All individuals. No conversation. All headphones and iPads and paperback books. No new friends. No neighbours.

Christ, she wants to go home . . .

'Trish. Could I have a moment?'

21

Pharaoh spins and finds herself facing the mysterious woman from the meeting room. The woman's not panting. Not damp. She looks poised and cool, and appears to be holding back a smile. She gives the impression of having followed Pharaoh into the revolving door and emerged first.

Pharaoh turns her head to avoid blowing smoke into the woman's face. Gives her a wary look.

'Don't worry,' says the woman. 'Breslin. I think he's a prick as well.'

Pharaoh leaves it a whole half-second before breaking into a smile. 'He's just so . . .'

The woman whom Breslin had called 'Anne' finishes the sentence for her. 'So oily?'

'Oily,' says Pharaoh, mulling it over. 'Yeah, that would do it. I'm sure he's very good, but . . .'

'He's not,' says Anne, dismissively. 'Not good at what you do, anyway. He's good at the media and public appearances and coming up with information-sharing working groups like this bullshit, but I can't imagine him holding back a dozen rioting Millwall fans, can you?'

Pharaoh gives Anne a more considered appraisal. 'You're a cop?'

Anne shrugs. 'Sort of.'

Pharaoh runs her tongue around her mouth. 'SOCA?'

'I'm on secondment.'

Anne nods in the direction of the Thames, vaguely indicating the general direction of Westminster.

'Home Office?'

Anne smiles. 'Can I have one of those?'

Pharaoh is about to retrieve a cigarette from her bag when

22

Anne takes the one from Pharaoh's lips. She sucks on it deep and breathes out through a broad grin.

'Gasping,' she says, by way of explanation.

Pharaoh pushes her wet hair back from her face. Lights herself another cigarette.

'I think I like you,' says Pharaoh, nodding.

Anne shakes her head. 'You won't soon.'

'No?'

'We need a favour.'

'We?'

Anne nods in the direction of Westminster again. In the direction of Parliament. In the direction of a viper's nest full of people like Breslin.

Pharaoh holds Anne's gaze.

'I thought you were here for Breslin's symposium,' she says at last. 'Thought you were making sure we hadn't missed anything obvious, like bodies on the lawn or a surge in nail gun purchases.'

Anne sucks half an inch of the cigarette and lets her smile drop.

'No, I'm here for you. You and McAvoy.'

Pharaoh seems to freeze. Every protective instinct in her being comes rushing to the surface.

'He's on sick. Will be for as long as he wants to be. What he's been through. What he's done . . .'

Anne nods. Looks at the floor.

'We understand. We also understand the situation he's currently in. The financial problems. We don't need very much. Just somebody thorough to check that somebody else has done their job right. It might be good for him. It would be very good for you.'

23

Pharaoh stares at her, hard.

'Tell me,' she says at last.

Anne grinds out the cigarette beneath an expensive heeled boot. 'Can you imagine spending nearly fifty years in prison for something you didn't do?'

'Well, I'm married. So, yeah . . .'

'Can you imagine spending fifty years locked up without a trial?'

Pharaoh winces. 'I bet the press could fill in any mental gaps.'

Anne nods. 'A test case is coming to court. Home Secretary has a personal interest. A certain man has been locked up under the Mental Health Act since 1966. And now his doctors say he's sane. So the Home Secretary wants him tried for a mass murder committed back in the days when England could still play football.'

Pharaoh scowls, confused. 'But the law doesn't work like that . . .'

'We just need a case building on the off-chance our Minister gets his wish. We need to show we're doing what he wants and that if it comes to court, nobody will end up looking silly. We need to know everything was done right.'

The two don't speak for a moment. The rain continues to fall. A businessman marches past shouting the word 'cunt' into a mobile phone. An attractive black woman thrusts leaflets into the hands of some passing tourists while eating a pot of cold salad and trying to send a text message.

'I can't promise anything,' says Pharaoh, at last. 'What he's been through. If you saw him. He's living out of a suitcase. He's broken.'

Anne traces the outline of her mouth with a finger. Purses her lips. 'Would be worse if his sick pay was withdrawn.'

Pharaoh's face seems to turn to stone.

'You couldn't do that.'

Anne simply nods in the direction of Westminster.

Pharaoh grimaces and looks at the ground.

'He's good, this McAvoy?' asks Anne, quietly. 'His file could be read in one of two ways.'

Pharaoh lights a fresh cigarette. Holds the smoke in her lungs until stars explode in her eyes.

'Good?'

'A good detective, I mean.'

Pharaoh closes her eyes. Says nothing and just lets the rain fall upon her face. She remembers the day when the call came through. McAvoy had been found, half dead, with a serial killer cuffed to his wrist. Ambulances on way. And then, moments later, the call from Hessle Police. McAvoy's home destroyed in an explosion. People trapped inside. At least two dead . . .

Pharaoh has wanted him to come back to work for weeks and he has pushed and pushed to be allowed to. But her duty as a friend has outweighed all other desires and she has insisted he be a father first and a policeman second. His wounds still weep when he exerts himself. He is suffocating under the weight of death and separation. Can't seem to find the strength to put a kiss on the end of his text messages any more. Can't seem to find the strength for much more than holding his son and squeezing him until they seem to fuse.

She will agree, of course. She will do the Home Office their favour. She will let McAvoy loose on a case full of ghosts and long-dried blood. She will do so for many reasons, but more than any other, she will agree so she has a reason to call him. To visit him in that hellish place. To give him the hug and the kiss on

25

the cheek that sustains her in a life where the only love and affection she receives is from her children.

To remove her guilt for robbing him of his wife and child.

Pharaoh looks at the other woman and wonders whether she knows. Wonders if the Home Office and the various intelligence services know of the threats to Roisin McAvoy, and the way Pharaoh broke the rules to spare her sergeant's heart.

She pushes out a lungful of smoke and nods her assent. Then she turns on her best smile.

'I'm going to need a favour . . .'

# Chapter 2

McAvoy's sigh paints a patch of condensation on the window. It does little to change the view. It simply makes the wet car park and the pewter sky a little more fuzzy around the edges. For a moment the scene appears in soft focus. It takes on the appearance of a soggy watercolour: hung on the wall too early and reduced to puddles, trickles and smears. Then his breath clears and the scene returns.

Drab

Soulless.

*Home.*

It is 8.06 p.m. and McAvoy is leaning against the window in the largest bedroom at The Lodge, a few miles west of Hull. It has been home for more than three months. Were he to use a mirror on a stick he would be able to see the Humber Bridge. Would be able to watch the waters of the estuary ripple and pop beneath the teeming rain, as though millions of fish were rising up to feed. But the only window in this small, rectangular room faces the car park and the most exciting thing he has to look at is the arse-end of a Transit van. It has at least given him the faintest of smiles. In the dust on the double doors, somebody has written, 'Please overtake quietly – refugees asleep'.

The Lodge is a squat, red-roofed, cream-painted building that backs on to the dense woodland of the Country Park. It offers easy access to the foody pub, a hundred yards away across the patch of rutted tarmac he has come to think of as his front garden.

He used to like it here. Used to come here with his wife . . .

He shakes the thought away. Fills his head with the first memory he can think of. Finds himself remembering this view during the summer months. He had gone to sleep to the sound of laughter and chinking glasses during the brief spell of warm weather. He may have gone to sleep in tears, but the sounds that bled into his nightmares had at least been cheerful ones.

Summer has come and gone. The leaves have turned and begun to fall. Black clouds hang heavy over a city the rain never seems to wash clean. On a grey, miserable autumn night, the car park is home to only a dozen cars and most of them belong to the staff. McAvoy has got to know them pretty well these past few weeks – the employees and their vehicles alike. Has heard life stories over his daily cooked breakfast. Has learned which duty manager will make a fuss if he fills a carrier bag with bread rolls and fruit from the buffet table. Has made friends with the dumpy little chef who works two nights a week and who hasn't made up her mind whether she wants to mother him or ride him like a racehorse. Whatever her motivations, she has yet to run out of excuses for making him and Fin an evening meal that they haven't paid for whenever she's on duty.

McAvoy turns from the window. Looks at his son, asleep in the bed they share. Fin is five and the double of his father. Big for his age. Red-haired. Soft brown eyes and a wary smile. A look of worry on his face when in repose. He's a handsome lad, with pale, freckled skin, unsullied and perfect. That is where father and son differ. Detective Sergeant Aector McAvoy has scars. A livid furrow runs from his left eyebrow to his cheek, bisecting a faint, jagged line that travels from the corner of his mouth to disappear into the permanently damp hair at his temples. Fire has made its mark upon his back. A blade has carved a trench into his clavicle. The puncture wounds upon his shoulders still need to be re-dressed each morning and night. He's six foot five, with limbs like railway sleepers and huge, broken hands. He looks the way his people have for generations. He may be a crofter's son from the banks of Loch Ewe but it would not take much effort to imagine him wielding a broadsword and cutting soldiers in half.

While McAvoy hates the image he projects, Fin finds his father's appearance fascinating. Even got himself into trouble at school for drawing a particularly accurate portrait of his dad when his class were doing a project on heroes. He'd told his teacher his dad was a detective. A knight in shining armour. And he'd used a red crayon to show the gruesome toll that such work has taken upon him. McAvoy hadn't told the boy off. Had been too busy blushing at being thought of as a hero.

McAvoy readjusts the covers around Fin's sleeping form. Brushes his hair back behind his ear and breathes the boy in. These are the hardest moments. After tea. After Fin's shower. After a story and a kiss and some memories of Mammy. By 8 p.m., Fin is always softly snoring and McAvoy is alone with his loneliness.

Several months ago, McAvoy's new home was partially destroyed in an explosion. Roisin's best friend, Mel, took the brunt of the blast. Blameless, guileless, she had done nothing to deserve the destruction wreaked upon her slim body by the shrapnel and flames. Roisin had been concussed by falling masonry and suffered gruesome wounds to both legs. Despite that, she had managed to crawl to their baby daughter Lilah, and had been cradling her among the smoke and flame when the fire crews pulled her out of the wreckage. She'd bitten one of the paramedics to the bone when they tried to take Lilah from her grasp. The firefighters found Detective Constable Helen Tremberg too. Her wounds were worse. It was touch and go whether she would survive. Touch and go whether she would ever wake up to explain why she had been in McAvoy's home, or accept his pitiable sobs and embraces for saving his wife and child.

McAvoy was a patient in the same hospital as the survivors. He'd needed a blood transfusion and microsurgery on the nerve damage to his shoulder and neck. Had needed to be told on half a dozen different occasions what had happened at his home. Had collapsed in the same heap of snot and tears each time Trish Pharaoh explained that his loved ones were OK. They were going to be fine. But they couldn't come home . . .

McAvoy tears his gaze from Fin and takes up his position in the corner of the room. He should probably have said no when the insurers told him they had found him accommodation fewer than five hundred yards from the ruin of his family home. Should probably have left this place when the insurers began to find fault with his policy and warned him he was almost certainly not covered for the damage. McAvoy should probably find a low-rent flat for himself and Fin. Somewhere with a bed long enough for his body. Somewhere with a kitchen and a bath. But to do so would suggest that he was starting a new chapter. That he was putting down roots as a single father. That the way things used to be was dead and buried. So they stay in their little room. They live out of carrier bags. McAvoy washes their clothes under the shower-head and he ensures Fin eats a good complimentary breakfast each morning over at the pub. He goes hungry himself. He's still paying the mortgage on a house that structural engineers have condemned. He's still on sick pay from work but is drowning in debt. He can barely afford the petrol for the school run. Has begun to experience migraines brought on by the discomfort of sleeping in too small a bed, and lack of sugar.

Looking up at the small, wall-mounted TV, McAvoy catches a glimpse of his own reflection. Tracksuit trousers. White trainers. A crumbled lumberjack shirt and unshaven, hangdog face. He closes his eyes. Reaches out for the remote control. Lowers the volume and checks that Fin is comfortable and undisturbed.

For an hour, McAvoy flicks through the six free channels that the TV offers. Learns a little about an artist he had never heard of and salivates over an advert for a new cookery programme. He tries to close off his senses to the adverts offering Payday loans. Quick. Simple. Effective. A few hundred quid would tide him over. But paying it back the next month would tip him into genuine penury. The problems are getting too big. The postman knows where to find him and every letter is a request for money. Unpaid utility bills on a house reduced to a shell on his second day of living there. Council tax. Credit card bills for presents he bought Roisin back when it seemed that a new leather jacket and a necklace were worth declaring himself bankrupt for.

31

Predictably, slowly, McAvoy's eyes begin to close. This is his routine. He will climb into bed next to Fin in a little while. Will say a silent goodnight to Roisin. Will kiss his baby daughter in his mind. Will fall into a fitful sleep, waking every time he rolls onto his back and the tears in his flesh sing with pain.

There is a soft, policeman's knock at the door to his room. McAvoy sits bolt upright. Rubs his face with rough hands. He doesn't know what he fears. Criminals? Debt-collectors? Knows simply that it has been a long time since a knock at his door meant anything good.

'Hector. You decent?'

The door handle turns and there is a thump as the body on the other side puts their weight against it. After a moment's silence a boot hits the wood.

'Hector!'

McAvoy doesn't know whether to pretend to be asleep or leap up and hug the person beyond the wood. He hates her seeing him like this. Feels sudden shame that he allows his son to be raised here when he thinks of it as too pitiful a place to welcome guests. And yet, she helped put him here. It was she who took the phone call. She who heard from the plummy-voiced man at the end of the unregistered mobile phone. She who told him of the threats to Roisin's life. She who said that Roisin needed to be taken somewhere safe. She who said that Lilah's place was with her mother. She who dictated there was no time for goodbyes.

McAvoy hauls himself up. Runs a hand through his hair and uses the hem of his shirt to polish his front teeth. Wishes, for just a moment, that he could afford a hotel with a receptionist and an escape route.

'Hector, it's pissing down.'

He opens the door a few inches. Looks into her scowl. Streaks of black hair cling to the lines in her forehead. The red lipstick at her mouth has been applied within the last few moments. She smells of expensive perfume and her little black cigarettes. As she raises a hand to push her hair back from her face, her gold bangles jangle beneath the cuff of her biker jacket. He can't see her little convertible car but she looks as though she may have driven here with the top down.

McAvoy is incapable of rudeness so greets his boss with a weak smile. Puts his hand out as if to shake, then bends down for a clumsy, awkward kiss. Pharaoh rolls her eyes. Reaches up and takes this big bear of a man in a hug that takes the air from his lungs.

And then she is inside the room. Picking up clothes and sniffing them. Hanging towels on radiators. Straightening the row of shoes at the foot of the bed. He feels like a teenager whose mum has had enough. She opens a window and cold air floods the room.

'He gets a bad chest . . .' says McAvoy weakly, gesturing at his son.

Pharaoh looks scornful. 'It's fresh air, Hector. It's good for people. You should try it.'

'We go for walks . . .'

'Yeah? Does he make you wear a collar or are you allowed off the lead?'

'Could we use indoor voices, please, guv? He's a light sleeper.'

Pharaoh points at the snoring child. 'Does he know that?'

They stand, a few feet apart. McAvoy's mouth twitches and then he lets himself smile properly. It's a nice feeling. He feels almost immediately guilty for it, but for an instant it's a simple, uncomplicated pleasure.

'Can I make you a tea? There's some fruit, in a bag. Oh, it was London today, wasn't it?' he asks, agitated and gabbling. 'The Met's symposium?'

Pharaoh mimes cutting her own throat.

'Nothing earth-shattering to report on that score,' she says, with the air of somebody who expected nothing and got less. 'It's what we thought. Headhunters are moving up. Hopefully they're moving out. The Met's going to liaise with Interpol and all the big boys to see if the nai gun and blowtorch thing has been used overseas. Bloke from Liverpool reckoned he'd heard about something similar in Eastern Europe, years back. They're checking it. Anybody with informants inside the major gangs is getting their palms greased to listen twice as hard. A lot of scary people are feeling scared, which is no bad thing. The Head-hunters may have picked a few bad apples who are causing them headaches but other than that we're no further on. I'm not running it. Never thought I would be. This prick Breslin from SIS had the chair. Seriously, you'd have loved him. Three different types of notepad and his ballpoint pen matched his socks. Reminded me of what you'd have become if I hadn't dirtied you up a little.'

McAvoy plucks at his eyebrows, listening hard. He is desperate for new information. Desperate for Pharaoh to tell him that the gang is about to be taken down, and that Roisin and Lilah are safe. It takes him a moment to register the faint praise in Pharaoh's words. He doesn't know what he would have become had Pharaoh not spotted his potential, shortly after taking over as head of Humberside CID's newly formed Serious and Organised unit. Before that he had been a pariah. He'd been the cop who helped push out Doug Roper: the slick, Machiavellian, cold-hearted media darling who had let murderers walk free and locked up any innocent upon whom he could pin a charge. Roper had been a popular man. McAvoy could never claim to be similarly appreciated. But at least as Pharaoh's right hand, he has earned back some respect. Taken his lumps and his broken bones and bleeding sores, and worn them like badges of honour.

'Were there awkward questions?'

Pharaoh holds her hands wide, as if hosting the Last Supper.

'Some shit about Colin Ray. Few questions about how we failed to capitalise on the info we got from our traveller friends. Some raised eyebrows about the way we let our big, brutish sergeants swan around like pirates, getting themselves stabbed. I told them the slogan's right: "It's never dull in Hull".'

McAvoy nods. Wonders if she's popped in just to keep him in the loop, or whether she's going to deliver bad news. The last time she came over it was to inform him that despite her best efforts, the Police Federation rep was refusing to put him and Fin into one of their rental properties. Apparently he didn't fit the hardship criteria. In truth, the rep had served under Doug Roper and was simply enjoying saying no to the man who had spoiled his comfortable life.

Pharaoh looks at her sergeant. At the state of him. He looks broken. Looks ill. Looks like he's had his heart torn out and replaced with cold stones.

'How are you coping, Hector?' asks Pharaoh, softening her gaze and perching her rump on the windowsill. 'Seriously?'

McAvoy looks as though he is about to say something glib in reply but he stops himself and sinks, slowly, onto the foot of the bed, eyes closed. He pushes both hands through his hair and when he withdraws them, his hair remains sticking up. Pharaoh cannot help herself. She crosses to him. Flattens his fringe. Takes his face in her hands and raises his eyes to hers.

'It won't be forever, Hector. It won't always be like this.'

McAvoy holds her gaze. Holds her scent in his lungs. Fills himself with the cigarettes and perfume, the mints and gin. Wonders how she would react if he pressed his head to her stomach and let her cradle him until the world made sense again.

'Auntie Trish?'

McAvoy spins around as his son struggles upright, rubbing his eyes. Pharaoh gives the boy a wide smile. They have only met a handful of times but Fin has fallen very much in love with his dad's boss. She's loud and naughty and she talks funny and doesn't mind him hearing when she swears. She also has four daughters who all think he's the cutest thing since baby rabbits, and her visits tend to presage the consumption of sweets.

'How the devil are you, my little monster? You driving your dad up the wall?'

'I'm being good,' says Fin, sleepily. 'Where's Sophia?'

Sophia is Pharaoh's eldest daughter, and Fin's favourite human being.

'She's at home, trying to find how many pairs of dirty knickers it takes to cover a bedroom carpet. It's important work. She's taking it very seriously. I've told her she should use mine. When we were poor they used to double as a tablecloth.'

Fin has no real idea what Auntie Trish is talking about but he finds everything she says hilarious so falls into fits of giggles. Pharaoh turns and catches McAvoy's eye.

'Shall we take a stroll? I've got something to run by you.'

McAvoy looks unsure. 'It's late. He needs to get to sleep . . .'

Pharaoh scoffs. She is an experienced parent used to being obeyed and believes that most children can be made to behave by the judicious application of chocolate bars and headlocks.

'He'll fall asleep the second we get back. That's right, isn't it, Fin? No moaning now. You can come for a walk with Dad and me but if you make a fuss when we put you to bed, I'm allowed to set fire to your legs, yes?'

Fin grins and nods. He looks at the window and the teeming rain.

'We have umbrellas,' he says, solemnly. 'Daddy can hold yours. If you hold his he'll have to walk on his knees.'

'You're a bloody genius,' says Pharaoh, grinning.

Fifteen minutes later they are heading west, taking the narrow footpath by the water's edge. To their left, the rain beats down on the still brown waters. To their right, the dense forest gives way to a train line and rough, stony wasteground. It would have been far more pleasant to turn left out of The Lodge but by unspoken agreement they avoided the sad ruin of McAvoy's abandoned home.

'Can you run on a little way, Fin? I need to talk to Daddy.'

Obediently, Fin splashes away up the track. He's dressed in wellington boots and a blue raincoat. It's not the sort of thing he would have worn if Roisin were around. She styled him with attitude and flair. But his clothes were ruined in the blast and Fin is now wearing whatever Daddy can afford.

For a few moments, neither McAvoy nor Pharaoh speak. They trudge in silence, McAvoy holding the umbrella. He's wearing his expensive coat with his trainers and jeans and looks like he has ram-raided a charity shop. He is a regular visitor to the thrift stores in the centre of nearby Hessle. He's bought himself a few shirts and comfortable trousers, discarded by the nice, middle-class types who live in these towns and villages to the west of Hull. Eight miles east, in the centre of the city, the charity shops sell clothes with knees so shiny they could double as a mirror.

At length, Pharaoh slips her arms through McAvoy's.

'She's OK,' says Pharaoh at last. 'Roisin. I couldn't get much more than that. Just that the injuries are healing and she's making a nuisance of herself. And she wants to come home.'

There is rainwater in McAvoy's eyes, but he can still feel the pricking of tears.

'And Lilah?'

'Missing her daddy. She's taking to the gadget. Loving music. Got a taste for reggae . . .'

McAvoy stops, the pain in his chest almost overwhelming. He stands with his hands on his knees while Pharaoh rubs his back. His daughter sustained damage to the inner ear during the blast. Will probably need the tiny hearing aid for the rest of her life.

'And she knows that's what I want, yes? That I don't blame her. If I could just talk to her. Just say I don't blame her . . .'

Pharaoh gives his shoulder a squeeze. 'She's being kept safe, Hector. That's all. The threat remains the same. She knows you want her. Knows you'd die for her. But right now, you have to live for her. I can't justify putting you in witness protection. There's been no threat to you. We're still off the books here. It's all still unofficial. I wish to God he would call again so we could get something more but for now we just have to wait until the threat to your family is removed.'

McAvoy purses his lips, as though biting back protests. The

image that was sent to Trish Pharaoh's private mobile phone had shown Roisin McAvoy asleep in her hospital bed. Whoever had taken it had got past the uniformed guard on the door. They'd pulled back the bedsheets and lifted her nightdress. Then they had slipped away. Had taken the time and trouble to digitally alter the image. The picture Trish had received had been too grotesque to show her sergeant but she can bring it to mind in an instant. She knows how McAvoy would react if he knew the picture showed how his wife would look after somebody had taken a blowtorch to her breasts.

The call had come later. It had been short and to the point. The Headhunters were split on the issue of Roisin McAvoy. There were those within the caller's organisation who believed she needed to suffer. The caller himself was more pragmatic. Even had a grudging respect for the tough, beautiful gypsy girl. But the Headhunters were run by committee. And a decision had been made . . .

McAvoy wants to tell Pharaoh that his wife and child would be safest with him. But experience has shown him that is not the case. He just wishes to Christ he knew where they were. Where Pharaoh had sent them. Who was taking care of them and making sure they didn't forget him.

'You're a bit of a mess, Hector,' says Pharaoh gently, as they begin to walk after the distant figure of Fin. 'If she came back tomorrow, what would she see?'

'I'm trying,' says McAvoy petulantly. 'Fin's warm and clothed and fed. We do his homework. I tell him stories. I try and be a good dad.'

'You *are* a good dad. You're just not taking care of yourself. Look at your knuckles.'

39

Like a child hiding chocolate-smeared fingers, McAvoy shoves his hands in the pocket of his long, cashmere overcoat. It's the only coat he has, and were he to hold it up to the light, he would be able to see the holes made by the scalpel as it was plunged into his back by a serial killer.

'You're boxing again?'

McAvoy shakes his head. 'Just keeping fit. Heavy bag.'

Pharaoh looks at him knowingly.

Abashed, McAvoy looks down. 'I use a tree.'

'In the Country Park?'

'Nobody can see. I know a place. Under the cliffs. Big, broad sycamore trunk. I take one of the blankets from the room. Twist it and tie it round the middle. It's just a workout.'

Pharaoh pulls a cigarette from her bag and lights it, making a tent from her jacket around her head. When she emerges, she has clearly made a decision.

'You can't go on like this,' she says firmly. 'I can't either. Can't watch. Can't feel the guilt. I don't like guilt, Hector. It makes me cross. And I feel like shit that you're all alone and hating yourself and beating up fucking trees in your spare time. I wasn't sure I was going to agree to what they wanted. But seeing you . . . Christ, you need to be a policeman again.'

McAvoy feels lost. He's cold and wet and hungry. His hands hurt. There's a clamminess to his skin and a dull ache in his forearms. Whatever Pharaoh can give him, he'll take.

'You can't come back properly,' she says, through a mouthful of smoke. 'Not to the unit. Not yet. With you off, and Ray still suspended, and Helen out of action, I'd love to be able to put you back in the front line, but Human Resources will go bloody mental.'

'So what can I do? With school times and picking up and dropping off and stuff, I can't even go full-time . . .'

Pharaoh waves him into silence, her cigarette a conductor's baton between her fingers.

'Home Office has asked for you. They said they wanted the best I had to offer. Said they wanted you.'

Despite himself, McAvoy feels a smile twitch at his lips. A tremor shoots through his hand and the umbrella twitches, spilling water down Pharaoh's right arm.

'Aye, I told them you were a bloody genius,' she says, wiping herself down with a soaking palm. 'Anyway, it's a job where you can set your own hours. Just something to ease yourself back in. A bit of digging. A bit of fact-checking. All the stuff you like. It won't be too much of a headache and I've managed to arrange a bit of a discretionary supplement to your sick pay. Won't be much but it might help.'

McAvoy shivers. Hopes his boss will put it down to the weather.

'And if I do an OK job . . .?'

Pharaoh shrugs. 'It will be hard to let you be involved in the Headhunter investigation. Not when you're so connected.'

'But not impossible?'

Pharaoh grins. Looks up at him from under the umbrella they share. 'Just keep out of mischief. Don't dig up more bodies than you have to.'

McAvoy watches his son in the distance, swishing a stick at the thistles in front of the railway line. He straightens his posture. Pushes his hair back from his face. Feels himself spark into some semblance of life.

'Will I have my warrant card?' he asks. 'Is it police work? Will I be a policeman?'

Pharaoh rolls her eyes and gives him an affectionate kick on the ankle.

'Yes. You'll be a policeman. Tomorrow, I might let you be a fire engine.'

McAvoy nods. 'With a siren?' he asks, from behind a tiny smile.

Pharaoh lifts her face to the rain.

'That's my boy.'

# Chapter 3

9.18 p.m. Ninety miles north.

A patch of woodland, five miles inland: buffeted by stiff winds and transformed into a charcoal sketch by darkness and rain.

A great bear of a man, wrapped up against the chill, moving through the trees without a sound.

Mahon's face is barely visible in the gap between his black scarf and flat cap. His tinted sunglasses reflect the light from the half-moon. The lenses rarely leave his face, no matter how dark the sky becomes. The incident that destroyed his face wreaked devastation on his vision. One retina was irreparably damaged, leaving him unable to see bright colours. The other, perhaps in sympathy, lost its ability to distinguish between shades of dark. It left his world sepia-tinted, streetlamp yellow.

'Like honey?' the doctor had asked, when he removed the bandages.

'Like piss,' he had replied, with bleeding gums.

Mahon is a big man. Tall and broad. It seems as though he is wearing several layers of clothing beneath his heavy leather jacket, but he's not. It's all him.

Light, agile, straight-backed and purposeful, he strides across a carpet of wet leaves and rotten twigs to the little house that hides among the high trees and bent branches. In this light it has the appearance of a fairy-tale cottage and Mahon is the Big Bad Wolf come to snarl at the windows. It is made of big grey stones and has been here for a long time. The windowsills are painted white, and patterned with roses. A small garden sits at the front of the property, which will be rich with snowdrops and scillas in February, but is colourless now.

Home.

Mahon opens the unlocked wooden door and steps onto the concrete flagstones of the hallway, followed by a swirl of wind, rain and leaves. He shuts the door against the darkness outside, but it does little to stop the sighing of the wind and the fingernails of rain on the glass.

It is cold in the house. It seems to grow colder with every step.

Mahon switches on the hallway lamp, and the yellow of his vision becomes more pronounced. He turns and walks to the large, farmhouse-style kitchen, and fills the deep sink with water from the cold tap. He removes his sunglasses, hat and scarf, and places them on the wooden work surface. Behind him is a large granite-topped table. It supports a vase of bright yellow roses. In the corners of the room, drifts of dead rose-petals pile up like dunes of autumn leaves. Their vivid colours have faded to brown and black, their scent a sickly-sweet decay, heavy on the air.

Looking up, Mahon catches a glimpse of his reflection in the dark window.

He has spent endless hours under the surgeon's scalpel but there are still moments when he sees himself as almost inhuman. One side of his face is still a hairless mess of white and pink flesh; a butcher's window of raw and rotten meat.

He looks away.

Mahon places his hands in the icy water and leaves them there until the splashes of blood begin to lift from his skin. He has done this many times in his long life, and knows the process cannot be rushed.

Slowly, the water turns red. It is a gradual transformation, like milk being poured into strong tea, one drop at a time. Eventually, he rubs his fingers together, scrubs at his wrists, and removes his hands from the rose-red water. He dries them on his trousers, and walks across the concrete flags to the lounge.

For a time, still in semi-darkness, he busies himself by the slate fireplace. Twisting kindling, stacking logs. Then he strikes a long-nosed match on one of the rough bricks of the mantel-piece, and touches it to the dry paper. A soft warm light grows into a red and yellow blaze as the kindling is devoured, and the wood begins to crack. Satisfied, Mahon stands up, removes his coat and sits down in the armchair facing the fire. He closes his eyes and settles back, retrieving an untipped cigarette from a crumpled packet and igniting it with the cheap plastic lighter he has taken from the pocket of his black jeans.

The room takes on the appearance of a cave. The light of the fire flickers and dances, pushes inwards, then retreats like a tide. It exposes the drabness of the sitting room. Pale walls, mottled with damp, and patterned with patches of pink wallpaper that the scraping brush could not remove. A solitary standing lamp. Three-seater sofa, with only one flattened cushion. Wooden floors, stained and unvarnished. Almost black in the places where the blood has dried.

The breeze hurls handfuls of leaves and twigs at the thick, old-fashioned windows. It is utterly black beyond the glass.

'Feeling better?' asks Mahon.

The thing on the floor was a man just a few nights ago. He was handsome and poised, well-perfumed and elegantly dressed. Tonight he is a collage of bloodied silk and frayed flesh.

Mahon leans forward and puffs some cigarette smoke into the man's face. For a moment he is wreathed in mist; a demonic, half-made thing.

The man on the floor tries to push himself into the ground. Wrestles with the blade that holds his arms still and only serves to further expose the tendons in his palms, bisecting the open wounds.

Mahon has not bothered to gag the man. Was content to let him scream and shout and beg. Let him holler himself into unconsciousness while he went up to the big house and gave Mr Nock a report on the day's wins and losses. Mr Nock hadn't asked whether the slick bastard in Mahon's house had talked yet. Both men know that it is only a matter of time.

'Wake up, bonny lad. We've got to have another wee chat.'

The man is still dressed in the designer clothes he was wearing when Mahon took him. His black suit and purple shirt are streaked with blood and piss but Mahon has allowed him to keep his dignity and chosen not to strip him. He's searched him, of course. Taken the man's two mobile phones and the expensive leather wallet. Took his switchblade too. Used it to pin the man's hands to the hardwood floor of the cottage to keep him still while Mahon set about levering up floorboards and gathering stones.

He has used this technique before. It's messy but effective.

'Pressing, it's called,' says Mahon, conversationally, pulling a sleek black mobile phone from his pocket. 'I'm sure you know that, of course. You look like a clever man. Not as clever as you think you are, otherwise you wouldn't be here, but you've obviously got a bit of something about you. Guile, I think it's called. Ambition, maybe. Some people might say you were bloody stupid to think of going behind Mr Nock's back. I'm not so sure. I understand the temptation. He's old. Had things his own way a long time. Outstayed his welcome at the party. The thing is, though, bonny lad, it's his party. He can stay as long as he wants. And he's got one or two bouncers who don't like gatecrashers. You understand? Now, I'll ask you again. The passcode for this phone. What is it?'

On the floor, the man gives a cough and spits out blood and swear words.

Mahon shakes his head. He reaches down and picks up a big white rock from the pile beside the fire. Lightly, he tosses it onto the floorboards that are laid horizontally across the man's chest. It lands among the bricks and boulders already crushing the man down onto the sharp stone Mahon has wedged between the vertebrae at the small of his back.

The scream is lost in the rain and the wind.

'You're being awfully silly,' says Mahon, whose voice wavers with the slightest sibilant hiss around the letters that require his tongue. 'Tell me who you report back to and I won't even

47

bother with the phone. I know who you represent, of course. Your people have got a lot of folk running scared. But I would love to put a face to a name. Now, tell me who asked you to come and rock the boat. Who told you to approach our man Lloyd? Who decided that would be a good idea?'

Through snot and tears, the man manages more venom, shaking his head from side to side and opening fresh wounds on his chin as he rubs his flesh against the splintered wood that pins him down.

'The French have a name for this,' says Mahon, sitting back and holding a fresh rock in his lap. '*Peine forte et dure*. I'm no linguist but I think that's right. Only been to France once and never got a chance to use the expression. Hope I've got it right. Protestant bastards used it on Catholics who refused to recant. Was a famous case in York. Beautiful city, York. You ever been? No? Was a lady there called Margaret Clitherow. Decent, well-liked, normal sort of woman. Authorities arrested her for her beliefs. Ordered she be pressed to death. Laid her on a stone the size of a man's fist then placed a door on her chest. The town sheriffs were supposed to load the door with rocks but couldn't bring themselves to do it. Couldn't persuade any townsfolk either. Ended up paying some beggars. What that woman must have endured, eh? But she wouldn't recant. Stuck to her beliefs. Some people even say that her final words were "More weight". I admire her for that. She cared about something so much she was willing to endure whatever it took. The thing is, son, you're not protecting a faith. You're not standing up for what you believe in. You're just being a silly, obstinate bastard. You might get your orders through a mobile phone.

You might not know who the next man up the chain is. But you know the passcode for your mobile phone. And if you don't tell me, you're going to spend the rest of your life in a wheelchair, shitting in a bag. And I tell you, nobody's going to think you're a saint.'

The man on the floor opens his mouth. His breathing is ragged and strained. A blood vessel has popped in his right eye and the wounds to his palms from the switchblade are big enough to pass a coin through.

'Please,' he manages, and red tears run down his face. 'No more . . .'

Mahon is about to indulge himself with a smile when his own mobile phone rings.

'Sergeant,' says Mahon, brightly, into the phone. 'This going to be expensive?'

For the next few moments, Mahon doesn't speak. He just listens and stares at the shadows on the wall, as if the flickering shapes are players on a stage.

'Thank you,' says Mahon, at last. 'Usual amount, plus a bonus. And your loyalty is appreciated.'

Mahon ends the call. Looks at the broken human being on the floor at his feet.

'Painful memories,' he says, rubbing his jaw. 'Haven't thought about that place in years. Bad business. Mess, it was. Cost me a lot, that night. People can't control themselves, can they? Just have to act like animals. And then people like me have to pick up the pieces.'

Mahon drops the rock on the man's chest. Listens for the sound of bone turning to powder.

He turns away from the riot of screams and looks out of the small window at the dark forest and the tumbling rain. He drifts into remembrance. Lets his mind drift back almost half a century. Remembers gravestones and blood, snow and gunshots. Remembers the girl and the smell of innocence lost. He has no wish to revisit that place. Nor to remember that night. But circumstances dictate he has to rebury a ghost.

McAvoy can only afford one cup of coffee and fancies that he will need to use the internet for longer than it will take him to drink it. So he orders the drink in a takeaway mug and walks with it through the soft rain and grey air to his car, parked directly outside the Costa coffee shop that sits on this little retail park to the west of Hull. From his vehicle he can still access the shop's wi-fi but he won't feel compelled to get up and leave as soon as he drains the last sip of his gingerbread latte. This way he can take his time and won't sweat and blush himself insensible each time one of the nice young ladies asks if they can get him another.

He opens his laptop. Takes a sip of the sweet, frothy drink. Wipes foam from his freshly shaved upper lip and rubs his back against the driver's seat. One of his wounds is finally scabbing over and itching so badly he wants to tear his skin off with a rake.

McAvoy is dressed in a way that would not displease the women in his life. He managed to find a supermarket suit in his size and looks passable in dark blue with a plain white shirt and old school tie. His walking boots don't look too incongruous and last night's rain cleaned the last of the dirt from his cashmere coat. He looks fine. Battered, and careworn, and a little dangerous around the edges, but he had still felt appreciative eyes upon him when he dropped Fin off at school this morning and said hellos to the staring mums.

McAvoy accesses his emails. There are some big files from Pharaoh. They were sent just after 8 a.m. and the originals carry government logos. He opens one at random. Flicks through the findings of a Mental Health tribunal. Closes it down and opens another. Scanned images of witness testimonies. Black-and-white photos. A shotgun, tagged and wrapped in polythene. A photograph of a footprint. Tyre-tracks on crushed snowdrops. He takes a deep breath. Opens up a search engine and types a name into the internet. He gets fewer hits than he had expected. But he still finds plenty to keep him going.

Over the course of the next hour, McAvoy's drink grows cold in the cup-holder at the front of the battered people-carrier. The laptop screen casts images onto his face. Fills his scarred features with the words of witnesses long dead. Fills his mind with images he will not soon forget.

By mid-morning, McAvoy feels ready to close the computer. He blinks hard. Rubs a hand over his face and drains his cold drink. He reaches into the pocket of his overcoat and pulls out a chocolate croissant, wrapped in tissue paper. He munches it thoughtfully. Wonders, for a time, quite what he should hope for. Were this a fresh case he would be giddy at the thought of taking it on. But these murders happened nearly fifty years ago and the tone of the correspondence between Pharaoh and her contact at the Home Office suggest that it is McAvoy's job just to make sure that if the case should ever come to trial, it can be tied up swiftly and without embarrassment.

The situation he finds himself in is the direct result of the new Home Secretary staying true to his word. Two decades

51

ago, while still a junior minister, the Cabinet member had met one of his constituents at a local surgery. She was a sweet woman. Timid but determined. A loyal party member. A regular voter. A pillar of the community and the sort of person who looked good in a twinset and pearls. She'd told him about her grandson. Peter Coles. Arrested back in 1966 at the scene of a spree killing and locked away under the Mental Health Act. Had been pretty much catatonic ever since. Wouldn't tell her why he had done it. Hadn't been a bad boy. Hadn't ever wanted to hurt anybody. Was it right? Could he be locked away like that, without trial, for all those years? She wanted to hear the facts. Wanted to know if he could be kept in a cell for decades without a proper hearing before a judge. Said her neighbours, the victims, had a right to know. The Minister had made a promise. Said he would do what he could. And twenty years later, a decade after the old woman's death, he remembered it. Set the wheels in motion and demanded that if Peter Coles was mentally fit to be so, he should be tried on four counts of murder. Caused his civil servants a succession of heart attacks. And they had approached Trish Pharaoh with a request for help.

*1966*, thinks McAvoy. *Bad year to be a Scotsman.*

McAvoy was not born until a decade after the events he has been tasked with investigating. His mother and father had not yet met. His dad was still working the family croft near Aultbea. Still not sure who or what he wanted to be. Never sure whether he should flee the croft for adventure, or stay and work the land where so many McAvoys had lived and died. Still a bit of a bastard and a bugger for trouble when the drink was in him. It

52

would be another few years before he met and fell in love with the wild, bright-eyed and very English student on a backpacking holiday in the Highlands. Still a few years until he became a father to two strapping sons. Still a few years until he had his heart broken by a woman who left him because his big, strong arms and his brooding intensity were nowhere near as attractive as her new lover's money.

McAvoy considers the man his father is today. He and his dad have little to do with each other. Haven't seen each other more than a dozen times since he left the croft at the age of ten and went to a boarding school paid for by his mum's new man. His dad sends Fin a letter each month, filled with details about life on the croft. Sometimes they include little pencil sketches of views that make McAvoy dizzy with nostalgia. He always asks after McAvoy's health and even threatened a visit during his stay in the hospital. But the visit didn't happen. Fin has still only met his grandfather twice. Lilah has never met him at all. Probably never will. Neither of them have met McAvoy's older brother or visited the low-roofed, tumbledown property that Aector owns in Gairloch or the snug, well-tended family croft a few miles away. McAvoy wonders what his dad was doing in 1966. Whether he watched England's triumph in the World Cup that year or spent the evening by the fire with a book, refusing to acknowledge the cheers from the English sailors who docked their warships in Loch Ewe and headed into the towns and villages like marauders.

McAvoy rubs crumbs from his fingers and ponders the name of the church mentioned in the top report. St Germain's. It seems familiar. Had he heard about this case when he first moved to the area a few years back? Had he taken a trip to the remote patch of Holderness with Roisin? Did it have some significance to his studies? His training?

He nods, pleased to have remembered.

*Andrew Marvell.*

When he moved to Hull as a uniformed constable, McAvoy had been single and lonely and had spent his spare time reading up on the area's history. Andrew Marvell was one of the city's most revered sons. He represented the city as MP for more than thirty years and became one of the closest confidants of Oliver Cromwell, before making himself equally invaluable to the restored monarchy under King Charles II. More than that, he was a poet who epitomised the metaphysical ideals. And he had been born at Winestead and baptised in St Germain's Church, where his father was rector.

McAvoy is pleased he has not had to say any of this out loud. Pharaoh makes fun of his ability to recall odd facts and dates. Reckons he would be a pub quiz champion if he would just let himself cheat on the questions about popular culture. Laughs at the idea he would be fine on the rounds about astrophysics and literature but would let himself down on *EastEnders*.

McAvoy winds down the window and breathes in the cold, damp air. He needs to order his thoughts. Needs to lay out every piece of paper on a bare wall and input every fact into a database. Needs to see which pieces of data are incontrovertible and which need to be reassessed and validated. But more than anything, he needs to feel a connection. Needs to see where this family met their deaths.

It will take him around forty-five minutes to get out to Holderness. Through the city and on into nowhere. He will learn nothing he can put in a database. Will find nothing of forensic evidential benefit. But he will at least feel something. For these past months the only pain he has felt has been his own.

He turns the key. Feels the wind on his face.

Drives, through the wind and the rain, to a murder scene built on bones.

# Chapter 4

9.18 a.m. The chain pub opposite Hull Crown Court.

Traffic nose to tail, turning the leaves in the gutters into a paste of orange and gold.

Solicitors and coppers, criminals and clerks, hurrying through the sideways rain; illuminated by the reds and yellows of headlights and streetlamps.

Detective Chief Inspector Colin Ray sits on one of the high bar stools, staring out through rain-lashed windows. Watches, as the driver of a white van beeps his horn at the tall black woman crossing between the motionless cars, dragging a briefcase on wheels that were not designed to deal with the potholes and cobbles of Hull's city centre. Watches as she jumps at the sudden noise, then gives a nervous smile to the fat prick behind the wheel.

He spoons up a last mouthful of hash browns and scrambled egg. Takes a sip of wine and wipes the grease off the rim of the glass with the end of his tie. Takes a look behind him at his fellow diners. It's mostly men. Old boys. Retired trawlermen with missing fingers and chapped faces. Workmen in luminous yellow jackets and steel-capped boots. A shaky-looking bloke holding a tall glass of gin and orange and leaning on the bar. His shoes are polished to a shine and his blue suit neatly pressed, but his right leg is shaking in a way that suggests he is due before a judge this morning and is sinking his drinks like somebody who is not expecting to get the chance to do so again for a while.

*No new faces*, thinks Ray. *Same shit. Same pricks and nobodies. Same friends.*

He takes in his surroundings. Up, at the exposed air-conditioning units, all coiled steel and polished copper. The walls, with their modern art and blocks of colour, their history posters informing him of the rich heritage of this old building, which served Hull as a post office for decades. Down, at the sticky wooden floorboards and blue carpet trodden flat.

He drains his wine. Takes his electric cigarette from the pocket of his crumpled black shirt and inhales. Scowls at the weak, anaemic hit the gadget provides. Wishes he could just flash his warrant card and tell them he wants a fag. A proper fag. Three inches of nicotine and tar, smoke billowing upwards in a greasy cloud, masking the stench of men.

He sniffs. The bar smells of damp carpet and clothes dried in musty rooms. It smells of brick dust and mud, mildew and spilled ale. It smells of stifled burps and cigarettes. It's a place where men in their eighties place their daily budget on the table in front of them and keep drinking until it's gone or the fruit machine pays out. It's a pub that caters to the sort of clientele who like their fried breakfasts with a whisky chaser. It starts serving pints at 9 a.m.

The double doors bang open, bringing in rain and wind and traffic noise. Two solicitors with a pretty little thing. One of them is fat and bearded, leading with his belly and looking around him like he is thinking of making an offer to buy the place. His colleague is a step behind; short and skinny, twitchy and beige. The blonde looks halfway familiar. She's got on a business suit and flip-flops and has mud streaked up her pale calves. She's wearing big spectacles and cheap jewellery. She looks fun. The trio order coffees to go. The blonde asks for a muffin. Says it with a giggle and a hint of innuendo and gets nothing back from her colleagues. Sighs, saying, 'Tough crowd . . .'

This has been Colin Ray's routine for the past three months. He has been suspended from work since slapping the piss out of some mouthy little prick in the cells. At fifty years old he should have known better, but he was goaded into it by a slimy bastard who knew which buttons to press. The victim is dead now but Ray still hasn't been invited back into the fold. He feels like an outcast. The police has been his life since he was twenty-one. He doesn't know how to be anything or anybody else. He hasn't the money to retire – his ex-wives see to that. His various families want little to do with him. He has a teenage son in Bristol whom he last met when the kid was still in nappies, and his last wife has gone back to Singapore with the daughter he gave her. That one hurt. He always did his best by the kid – right up until the point her mum closed her knees for good and sent him on his way. He misses that one. Liked looking after her. Liked the way she squeezed his face and did silly drawings and laughed when he swore. She'll be nearly ten now. Probably doesn't remember him. Probably doesn't know why she looks a bit less bloody foreign than her bitch of a mum.

'Can I take that, sir?'

58

Ray turns to the handsome young lad who is hovering by his stool.

'Your plate, sir? Can I take it?'

'No, lad, leave it a bit. There's something almost artistic about the way the bean-juice is congealing. I want to look at it a bit more.'

'Oh,' says the barman, acceptingly. 'No problem . . .'

'Take the fucking plate,' says Ray, pushing it away. 'Christ.'

The youngster looks confused but has enough experience of dealing with the breakfast drinkers to know that he shouldn't make a scene. He takes the plate and retreats. Ray sits back in his chair and returns his gaze to the scene beyond the glass. He can see St Mary's Church across the way. Its chimes used to wake him when he first moved to the city centre. Now he finds them soothing, like an infant's mobile, playing gentle lullabies over the grind and fizz of the city's soundscape.

'Getting poetic, Col,' he says to himself, with a twist of his lip. 'Be taking it up the arse next.'

He coughs. Sprays spit and undigested food onto his shirt front and the table top. Wipes it with the palm of his hand.

Behind him he hears the doors bang again. Turns around to see that the suits have fucked off. Probably on their way to a trial across the road. Probably going to make a fortune for pushing bits of shit around the judge's chambers like dung beetles in expensive shoes. He has no time for lawyers. Doesn't like the way they talk. Doesn't understand what would compel somebody to do such a job. Feels the same way about parking attendants, traffic wardens and prison guards. He has a lot of hate inside him. Reserves most of it for coppers who don't know how to play the game. Despite his own poor disciplinary record he considers himself to be a decent detective. He's not bent. Not on the take. He'll accept a few free pints or a bottle of whisky as a thank-you or a sweetener, but he would never make the kind of deals that some of his colleagues have done over the years. It was the head of the Drugs Squad who let the Headhunters take root in the city – exchanging a blind eye for good headlines and ready information. Ray can't abide that approach. He thinks of a villain as a villain. Hopes he has passed some kind of moral backbone on to the few protégés he has helped out over his long career.

That thought makes him contort his face afresh. Pictures his friend, Shaz Archer. She's been riding his coat-tails for years and he has enjoyed her company all the way. She's from money. From good stock. She's good-looking, fashionable and sexy as hell, though Ray has never entertained the notion of bedding her. He cares for her. Thinks she could make a good cop. Admires her tenacity and willingness to do whatever it takes to get ahead – even if that means undoing a couple of extra buttons on her blouse while interviewing reluctant witnesses. But she's let him down during his suspension. Fallen in love with some slick bastard she hasn't even had the courtesy to introduce him to. Left him lonely and ignored while she has been throwing her legs over her shoulders and making pretty eyes at some ponce from London. Silly cow should know better. She's got a case of her own that could be the making of her. Lorry driver, stabbed to death while on remand at Hull nick. She'd even known the prick. Had interviewed him months ago while the Headhunters were in the ascendency and got nothing more for her trouble than a cup of piss to the face. His status as prison hero didn't last long. Within six weeks he'd had his throat cut with a sharpened phone card and been left to bleed out in the urinals.

Colin watches the street. Tops up his wine and takes a sip. Wipes his nose with a knuckle and wonders why the fuck he still bothers to put on a tie when the most exciting thing he will do today is go to the market for a couple of slices of cold meat and a six-pack of beer . . .

His phone rings. He doesn't hear it at first. It doesn't ring very often so he barely recognises the tone. Finally, he pulls the old-fashioned, coffin-shaped phone from his trouser pocket. It's from a withheld number. He holds his breath. Reaches into his pocket for the knackered old pocket tape recorder. Begins recording even before he answers. Wonders. Sneers . . .

'Col Ray,' he says, settling back into his chair and putting the electric cigarette to his lips.

'Well hello, Detective Chief Inspector.'

It's a voice Colin Ray last heard months ago. It's accentless but refined. Posh without giving much away. It belongs to a man that Colin Ray has spoken to twice before. The first time it contained promises, and then threats. The second, it adopted a superior, mocking tone, and goaded him into taking a key-chain to a drug-dealer in the cells. Some people call him Mr Mouthpiece, but Colin files him under the mental heading of 'Gobshite'.

'Well I never,' says Colin, scratching his armpit with the edge of a laminated menu. 'I was just thinking about you. I had dog-shit on my shoe, you see, and my mind wandered . . .'

'Excellent, Detective Chief Inspector,' he says in reply. 'I'm pleased to see you have lost none of your spirit. That's commendable and remarkable, considering the sorry state of your

61

life. You would think, would you not, that if your colleagues really wanted you back they would have resolved the uncertainties surrounding your suspension. One would have expected you to be back at your desk, making a nuisance of yourself and providing me with the occasional, albeit almost infinitesimal problem.'

'I've missed you,' says Ray, blowing out a tiny puff of smoke. 'I knew you'd ring, like. Knew that eventually you'd have to have your say. I hear things are going well for you. Branching out. Expanding, I believe, is the word you would use. Hope you're staying on top of things, son. You must be having to recruit faster than you did in the beginning. You sure no bad apples are slipping in? I'm not fishing around for information, you understand. I'm being conversational. Truth is, I've heard the rumours. A lot of people have. You've made some mistakes, eh? Recruited some right dangerous bastards. You can't keep a shark on a leash, you know that, don't you? Comes as no surprise to a tolerable old twat like me. That's villains for you. Bad lads want to do things their own way. Nobody wants to take their orders from some invisible prick at the end of the phone. Charlie's Angels was a long time ago, mate. People like face-to-face these days.'

After a moment of silence, Mr Mouthpiece speaks again. There is an edge to his voice that Ray has not heard before.

'There are no problems within my organisation, whatever you may have heard. Any business enterprise suffers from the occasional recruitment miscalculation, but I assure you and your colleagues that steps are being taken to remove those obstacles.'

Ray sits forward. He had been stabbing in the dark. Had not expected to hit a nerve.

'That's the thing with villains, mate – they're not to be trusted.'

'I did not ring you to discuss the structure of my organisation,' says Mr Mouthpiece, sharply. 'I rang because I have been informed of the pitiable picture you currently present and wondered if you might at last see the good sense in receiving a regular stipend from my associates in exchange for occasional helpful behaviour and information. I hate to think of you sitting there in your shabby clothes, eating a fried breakfast, drinking wine, barking at the poor barman for trying to do his job . . .'

Ray looks around him. Takes in the sea of average men and women. Looks at table tops covered with crisp packets, empty glasses and the occasional mobile phone.

'You're watching me?'

'We watch everything, Detective Chief Inspector. A lot of thought has gone into this operation. We are expanding at precisely the speed we had planned. And as I have always tried to explain to your accommodating colleagues, we do not plan on being here forever. We are a temporary migraine for your officers. Turn a blind eye for a while and soon you can go back to catching the imbeciles and thugs who have run organised crime so ineffectually for so long.'

'Who you got watching me?' asks Ray, temper flaring. 'There's nobody in here would fucking dare . . .'

Mr Mouthpiece gives a little laugh. As he speaks again, the faint sound of a siren drifts from the phone.

'Can I presume then that whatever I say to you, you will persist in being obstinate? You will continue to bumble on with your shambolic existence just because you find the nature of

63

my operation so distasteful? Have I not been a better friend than an enemy? I have done what I can to keep bloodshed to a minimum. I have always kept my word. I have brought you good headlines and though you may not know it, I am actively taking steps to keep one of your number from serious harm. I would expect a little gratitude.'

'Expect away. I just think you're a knob.'

Mr Mouthpiece's next words are drowned out as an ambulance turns right onto Lowgate and whizzes past the window. Colin freezes in his seat. He heard that siren a few seconds ago, coming from the phone. It had passed Mr Mouthpiece.

*Fuck*, he's somewhere nearby!

Ray hears the line go dead. Realises that Gobshite, that most cautious of men, has just fucked up.

Ray plays back the recording. He's been waiting for that call for three months. Been carrying around a tape recorder like a fucking journalist ever since he spoke to the oily bastard and realised that a tape recording of his voice would be a hell of a good bit of evidence if it ever came to court.

He takes a huge sniff and swallows the last of his wine. Wipes a smear of egg from the table top and sucks his finger, thoughtfully. He's too old and knackered to start running around the block looking for suspicious characters. But the city centre cameras may do the job for him. And he knows a man who owes him a favour.

As Colin Ray begins scrolling through his phone for a number he should know off by heart, he finds himself beginning to feel like a policeman. More than that, he begins to feel like a man who just got a little closer to revenge.

•

Mid-morning. Heading east.

Through the city and past the docks. Past the prison and the neighbouring cemetery; the open graves of countless boarded-up factories. Past the abandoned shops and the burned-out taxi office. Past second-hand cars being flogged for cash behind chain-link fences and chipboard signs. Past the ferry terminal; the towers of the great vessels looming like shark fins above the towers and cargo containers.

McAvoy presses east, through towns and villages that cling to this wild, flat tongue of land. Through uncultivated fields and straggly patches of still-farmed land. Through air the colour of smoke and a listless rain that falls ceaselessly onto this torpid, half-deserted world.

Hedon.

Keyingham.

Otringham.

On the right, the sign to Sunk Island. McAvoy remembers reading about it when he moved here. Remembers being fascinated by the tiny hamlet that emerged as a large sandbank from the River Humber a few centuries before and which caused maps of the coastline to be redrawn.

On. Towards the coast. Towards dead seaside towns and villages that are slipping into the sea.

Towards a church where a family were killed by a boy they had never felt reason to fear.

McAvoy misses the gap in the hedge the first time he drives past it. Finds himself on the edge of Patrington and knows he's gone too far. Turns around in the car park of a pub and heads back down the winding road. Spots the church through a gap in the high privet and swings the vehicle left onto a muddy, rutted track.

McAvoy winces as the car jolts in and out of the deep grooves that other people's tyres have left in the sodden grass. Pulls up outside a white-painted gate and switches off the engine.

Takes in the view.

St Germain's Church nestles among a grove of trees, some hundred yards from the main road. It's a tiny, towerless construction: two rectangles of old stone and stained glass surrounded by a low wall. To the right of his vantage point an empty, grassed-over field stretches away towards the main road. The rear of the church is shielded by a straggle of denser woodland.

McAvoy kills the engine and gets out of the car.

The first thing he notices is the silence. A light rain still falls and the wind plays with the tails of his coat, but besides the rustling of the trees he can hear almost nothing. He strains his ears for the sound of passing traffic or the chatter of agricultural workers in the nearby farmland. Can't hear a damn thing. Just the low whistle of a harsh wind, breaking around the stone statues and gravestones that dot the church grounds.

He lays his hand on the flaking paint of the gate and enters the grounds of the church.

Despite the solitude, it does not strike McAvoy as an eerie location. It seems quite peaceful. The gravestones in this churchyard stretch back centuries. A vast tomb stands immediately to McAvoy's left; all black railings and angular blocks of stone. Around it, headstones jut at random angles from the spongy, deep-green grass. As he walks along the short, overgrown path, McAvoy sees a tall grey angel looking down at him; face serene and shiny with rain. It stands atop a square slab and seems to survey the grounds with an air of timeless ownership. It has

66

been here for at least two centuries. Those grey eyes witnessed the events McAvoy has come here to excavate and explore. They have seen gravestones sunk into black mud and watched soil patter down on coffin lids. They have watched grief in all its forms. Seen mourners come and go. Seen the bereaved lose interest in pulling up daffodils and weeds to honour their loved ones with hand-picked blooms. Seen the living forget the men and women beneath the ground. Seen graves turn green. Seen headstones crumble. Slip. Fall.

McAvoy walks to the rear of the church, past newer, shinier headstones decorated with the odd bouquet of half-dead flowers and the occasional sad teddy bear, saturated and rotting among shingle and dirt.

This is where it happened.

Here, at the rear of the church.

This is where they were found.

McAvoy pulls his notepad from his pocket and reacquaints himself with the names and timeline he jotted down in perfect shorthand as he sat staring at the computer screen. Looks at the little map he copied from the photographs in the file. Looks, with soft eyes, at the little crosses he has drawn upon the map of the graveyard, and the four corresponding names.

Nods.

Puts the notebook away.

Listens to the silence.

Tries to picture what happened here.

On the night of 29 March 1966, Police Constable John Glass was alerted in Patrington to shots having been fired from the church grounds in nearby Winestead. He had presumed that this was a troublesome young man from a nearby farm cottage whom he had spoken to before about using firearms without supervision. PC Glass and a resident of Patrington drove to the scene. It was dark, and beginning to snow. A short time later, PC Glass found the first body. Within moments, he had found three more. And then he saw Peter Coles, sitting on a gravestone, cradling a shotgun, and mumbling about how sorry he was. Glass had arrested the lad and instructed his companion to drive to the nearest telephone and alert his superiors. Uniformed officers and a team of CID men from Beverley Police were at the scene within the hour. By morning, Peter Coles had been charged. Following his initial statement to PC Glass, he did not speak again. A search of the house he shared with his grandmother led to some unsettling discoveries. A notebook beneath his bed was filled with scribbled fantasies about the blonde, pretty teen whose face he had just blown off with a shotgun. A search of an outbuilding revealed a cache of underwear he had stolen from his neighbours' washing lines. A series of interviews with nearby villagers revealed that Peter Coles had always been a peculiar, unhinged kind of boy whose mother had left him when he was just a toddler and who had been brought up by his grandmother in one of the cottages belonging to the nearby manor house. The manor house and the surrounding farmland had been owned and operated by local businessman Clarence Winn. And Peter Coles had just killed Clarence Winn, his wife Evelyn, his son Stephen and daughter Anastasia. Only the eldest son, Vaughn, had survived the massacre, having left a day earlier to return to the north-east, where he was working. Vaughn later provided identification of his mother's and father's bodies. His brother and sister were too disfigured by the shotgun blasts for him to be allowed to see them.

After being remanded into custody at York Crown Court, Peter Coles was quickly declared mentally unfit to stand trial. He was sent to an institution in Shropshire. He has been in mental hospitals ever since.

McAvoy pulls on the stubble beneath his lip and breathes deep. He looks around him at the attractive, peaceful scene. He finds it hard to picture what occurred here. In front of him is the low, mossed-over gravestone upon which Peter Coles sat and confessed. To his right is the sloping patch of grass where Clarence Winn was found with a hole the size of a pumpkin blasted from his back to his front.

Why had they been here? What had they been doing at this remote spot on a quiet, snow-filled night?

McAvoy opens his notepad again. Refreshes his memory. Flicks through the pages and pulls a face. He returns to the car and opens up the laptop, accessing the files of saved witness statements and photographs. He has only just dipped a toe into the investigation and already he feels that the info he has been sent is a little thin for a case of this size. Things seem to be missing. There are gaps. Entire witness statements seem to have vanished from the file. And the numbers for the evidence log are blurred and indecipherable. McAvoy senses he is going to go to bed tonight with a headache.

Slowly, reading as he goes, he returns to the rear of the church.

According to witnesses, Clarence was in the habit of taking a walk each night with his pet spaniel, Digger. Sometimes, his wife would accompany him. On this night, his children had clearly decided to come too. This was rare, but not unheard of. Stephen was sixteen years old; his sister two years younger. Still young enough to enjoy their parents' company and the thrill of a walk in the moonlight. And unlucky enough to stumble upon a deranged young man with a shotgun, out taking potshots at passing aeroplanes.

McAvoy leans back against the church wall. Closes his eyes and tries to see it. A family, wrapped up against the cold. Laughing. Sharing stories. Missing their older brother who had just said his goodbyes. Bumping into a dangerous, excitable boy holding raw power in his hands. Had they spoken? Were there pleasantries exchanged before he raised the shotgun and blasted Anastasia Winn in the face from a couple of feet away? Certainly the family knew him well. He had been raised alongside the oldest boy, Vaughn. Had been friends with him during their adolescence. Had even worked occasional shifts as a labourer on the farm and was a regular visitor to the manor house, where his grandmother would pop in most mornings for a cup of tea with Evelyn. There had been no bad blood between them. Clarence had even defended Peter to PC Glass when the boy had got in trouble for using his shotgun in the church grounds. Had that been the tipping point? Had Coles feared getting into trouble for letting down Mr Winn? Winn was a big man. Had he threatened the boy with a slap for being silly? Or had the sight of Anastasia set off something primal in the boy? Had the throbbing steel of the gun in his hands chimed in his troubled mind with the soft flesh visible between Anastasia's knee socks and her skirt? Had he simply wanted her?

There were plenty of theories and each were put to Peter Coles as he sat in the police interview room. But he kept his mouth shut. Whimpered once or twice, but refused to say another word.

70

McAvoy realises he does not know enough about the victims to be able feel anything other than a vague, ephemeral kind of pity for them. He wants to know them. To understand them. To feel them as individuals. As people. He looks at the laptop again and tries to find something in the witness statements that will help him get a sense of who they were. They have been dead so long that for a moment he wonders if there is any benefit to any of this. The boy's grandmother is dead. The manor house has since been sold and redeveloped. The cottage where Coles lived has been bulldozed to make way for a grain silo. The blood has long since sunk into the grass in the churchyard. There are no bullet holes in the stone. Time has healed this place. The bodies have been laid to rest two miles away in the grounds of St Patrick's Church in Patrington.

McAvoy chides himself for his lack of compassion. Fears, for a second, that he is becoming everything he hates.

Gets his brain in gear. Turns his thoughts to the survivor, Vaughn.

Vaughn was nineteen at the time of his family's slaughter. Almost certainly still alive. Definitely entitled to know what could be happening to the man who killed his family.

A sudden commotion in the treetops causes McAvoy to look up, startled. Two magpies are fighting with a crow in the top-most branches of the evergreen to his right. It is an unpleasant sound; all cawing and flapping feathers and falling leaves. McAvoy suddenly feels he has seen enough. He had half entertained the notion of walking deeper into the woodland at the back of the church, but the ground looks soggy and difficult to navigate and he is suddenly aware of just how very alone he feels. He wishes Pharaoh were here, to crack jokes and connect

71

him to the world. He senses that without her he would eventually disappear into an internal world of corpses and memories. He wants to call her. Tell her that he has begun. Wants to run some initial ideas past her. Wants to ask if she can spare a detective constable or one of her civilian workers for half a day to track down witnesses from 1966 and put him in touch with Vaughn. Wants to hear her voice.

McAvoy turns away from the landscape where four people lost their lives. The birds still squawk and flap and shake the branches as he walks back up the footpath to the gate. He's not sure how he's supposed to feel. Doesn't know if he should phone the vicar and ask to take a look inside. Services are still held here twice a month. Every couple of weeks a handful of parishioners gather within its thick walls and shiver in its cold, half-dark embrace. The font has been there since the twelfth century. Andrew Marvell was baptised within. It was erected when this part of Holderness was an important entry point to Britain and it has watched as the sea has nibbled the coastline and moved inland by inches. McAvoy doubts its embrace will bring him comfort. Nor will it help him better understand what occurred here.

The gate squeaks on stone as McAvoy leaves the churchyard. He takes a deep breath, his feet on muddy earth, his hands on the bonnet of the car. He imagines how PC Glass must have felt. Imagines this place in the darkness. Wonders if he would have kept his nerve and his head with moonlight and snow slashing patterns in a graveyard full of blood.

He climbs back into the car. Rests his head on the steering wheel. He feels cold. Soaked through, even though there is only a light veneer of rain upon his coat. He reminds himself what he has been tasked with. He has to check that things were done right. Has to check there are no embarrassing gaps in the established narrative. Peter Coles was here. He killed a family of four. And he admitted it.

McAvoy nods as he turns the key in the ignition. He has to keep it simple. Has to do what he has been asked and not let his gut take him in some unhelpful direction. He has always been a methodical, disciplined policeman. He takes the rulebook seriously and can quote official guidelines the way religious zealots can quote scripture. He knows that it would be unhelpful to start re-interviewing witnesses when they gave statements nearly fifty years ago and are no doubt in their dotage now. And yet he feels a need to reach out and touch these events from long ago. Policing was different then. Forensic sciences were limited. There was no DNA. Fingerprint analysis was a difficult and laborious process. He cannot help but think that something may have been missed. Already he feels himself forming a picture of Peter Coles. Instinctively, he feels compassion for the boy. Today, he would have been under supervision. Social workers would be watching. There would be pills and counselling to help him better fit into the world. He would be kept a long way from shotguns. Then he thinks of the Winn family. Two adults and two teens, shot to death and left for the crows. McAvoy doesn't yet understand this crime. Needs to get a sense of what it did to this tiny community. Needs to hear real memories and look into eyes that once looked upon a scene of slaughter.

He needs to talk to Vaughn. To PC John Glass. To the villagers who told investigators that Peter Coles was always trouble.

73

McAvoy comes to a decision. He has not been tasked with reopening the investigation – just making sure that it's watertight. He has been specifically told to be as low-key as possible. Media attention would be embarrassing for all concerned.

But to find justice for the dead he has to give a damn about those who died. And to do that, he has to understand them.

The car does a complicated, wet-wheeled U-turn on the patch of grass that will be rich with snowdrops before Christmas. It bounces up the track and through the gap in the hedge.

He heads towards the coast, knowing, despite himself, he is about to start making waves.

## Chapter 5

'What if he runs?'

Pharaoh looks at her pudgy, round-faced companion, as sauce drips from his sausage sandwich onto the patch of hairy belly that winks from between the buttons of his pale blue shirt.

'Then I should imagine he'll get away, Constable.'

Detective Constable Andy Daniells considers this for a moment and drops his head in anticipation of a telling-off.

'I should have got the sandwich on the way back, shouldn't I?'

Pharaoh shrugs. 'Doubt it would have made much difference. I don't think you're built for speed.'

'Used to be,' says Daniells, conversationally. 'Four-hundred-metre hurdles. Was quite good at school.'

'Yeah? Did they let you use a horse?'

Pharaoh and Daniells are traipsing across the wet grass of East Park. The rain has eased to a low drizzle and there are patches of blue peeking out from behind the low, concrete sky. To many, this is the heart of Hull. During the days of the trawling industry, east Hull provided the men and women who worked

75

the docks and made a living from fish processing. The west of the city provided the trawlermen. It has seen hardship but maintains a sense of pride and community with a more pronounced local accent than across the river. Every 'o' is 'an 'ur'. The joke goes that in east Hull, the residents believe a camera takes photos, and a sock takes five.

On a summer's day East Park swarms with families. The city council spent a few million on it some years back. Put in a miniature zoo and a decent swing park. Dredged the lake and bought a few rowing boats and pedalos. Scrubbed the graffiti off the stone walls and dotted the well-tended lawns with outdoor exercise equipment. Even built a little water park, though that seems to have attracted more geese than people. Despite fears that teens from the nearby estates would smash up the swings and abuse the wallabies, it's actually become one of the council's badges of honour. People like East Park. It's a happy place. The circus comes twice a year and there's a funfair in the summer. The occasional drug addict still turns up dead in the bushes, but nowhere's perfect.

'First time I came to Hull my old boss brought me here,' says Pharaoh, who was born and raised in the little town of Mexborough in South Yorkshire and has never spent enough time in Hull to appreciate its dubious charms. 'That was before they did it up. Some skinheads had taken to chucking anglers in the lake. Can't remember why I was here but I tagged along with Tom. Weird job, it were. Happened every Sunday morning, so these poor bastards told us. They'd come down to cast their rods in this grotty puddle of rubbish and rainwater. Then the skinheads would come down and chuck the anglers in. Then they'd climb out and go back to their fishing. Was happening regular

76

as clockwork. I couldn't work out why the anglers kept coming back. They said they had every right to and the skinheads were the ones in the wrong. I agreed. Just didn't understand why they kept coming back. Said it was because they always did this on a Sunday. Couldn't get their heads around doing something else.'

Daniells looks at his boss, waiting for more. 'And what happened?'

'Can't remember.' Pharaoh shrugs. 'I think the fun went out of it for the skinheads. I do remember we had to arrest some old bloke for trying to steal a duck for the Christmas dinner.'

'Seriously?'

'Honestly. Local sergeant said it was a problem every December. Families who were struggling to afford a bird for the table used to pop down to East Park with a carrier bag and nab something juicy.'

Daniells creases his round, merry face into a laugh. 'That still go on?'

'Dunno,' says Pharaoh. 'I reckon there will be one or two nippers sitting down to wallaby and chips this Christmas. Oh, hold up, lad, there he is . . .'

Bruno Fa'amasino is known by all as Bruno Pharmacy. His Samoan surname was not designed with the Hull dialect in mind, and the nickname he now goes by is appropriate, given his lengthy criminal record. He's served two terms for possession of Class A drugs with intent to supply, and another for GBH. The crimes he's been sent down for barely scratch the surface of his true criminal history. He's become a significant player this past year. Graduated from the petty shit into a better class of scum. And it's easy to see why he would seem an appealing prospect to any criminal enterprise looking to recruit muscle. He's a big man. Came to Yorkshire from his native Samoa when he was still a teenager. Had a brother who played rugby for Castleford Tigers. Got in with a crowd that liked being associated with a big, flat-faced bruiser with tattooed shins and shoulders. It didn't take him long to get a liking for steroids. Took him a little while to start paying for his own addiction by selling other types of pills. And by his mid-twenties he looked after a good chunk of the Hull drugs trade. After a few stretches inside, he came to the attention of the Headhunters. Oversaw the transfer of the crown by bringing a dumb-bell down on the head of his old friend and boss. And became number two to the slick little shit who blew up Aector McAvoy's house.

'He's going to go on about harassment, isn't he?' asks Daniells, acceptingly.

'I hope so, lad,' says Pharaoh, raising a hand in greeting. 'We are harassing him. I'm enjoying it. How about you?'

For the past few months Pharaoh has been making Bruno's life as miserable as she can. His prints were found at McAvoy's house and all over the burned-out taxi office that used to be his boss's base of operations. She can't make anything stick and the Crown Prosecution Service are being their usual unhelpful selves, so she is contenting herself with spoiling his every peaceful moment. Her team are doing their bit to make him unhappy. Even Shaz Archer is playing ball. She spent a month undercover, flirting with Bruno and wearing more perfume than clothes. Got him on tape showing off about his connections, but she had her cover blown before she could get anything concrete out of him. Pharaoh doesn't know how far Archer would have been willing to go for a decent collar, but has her suspicions. She doesn't like the girl but can't argue with her results. Were she to give as much of a shit about people as she did about her arrest record, she'd be a decent police officer. As it is, Pharaoh can't imagine a world in which she and Archer don't some day come to blows. Pharaoh's looking forward to it, as are most of the men in the station.

Bruno is busy grunting away on one of the pieces of bright yellow exercise equipment rammed into a large rectangle of cushioned asphalt. His big arm muscles are greasy with sweat as they poke out from beneath a sleeveless hooded top. He's doing chin-ups and pulling a face like an angry rodent as he pushes himself hard.

'Afternoon, big boy,' says Pharaoh, leaning herself against one half of a set of parallel bars. 'Your flies are undone.'

Bruno drops to the floor. Takes a look at his visitors. Closes his eyes and shakes his head. Swallows, like there's dog-shit under his tongue.

'You can fuck off,' he says, waving with an arm like a farmer telling kids to get off his land. 'This is harassment.'

Pharaoh pulls a cigarette from her handbag and lights it with deliberate slowness. She doesn't speak until her words are wreathed in smoke.

'Yes, Bruno. It is.'

The pair of them stare at one another for a few moments. It was the same in the interview room. Pharaoh pushed the big man's buttons brilliantly. Got him to explode so often there was a risk they would need to repaint the room. But he stuck to his story. Kept telling his lies. Pissed all over Roisin McAvoy's name and walked out of the station a free man.

'You know you've got nothing,' he says, wiping a big hand over a bigger face.

79

'Doesn't look like you've got much yourself. Struggling to get a gym membership, are you?'

The barb seems to cut him. Bruno may have expected to slide onto the throne vacated by his boss's demise but the Head-hunters seem to have cut him adrift. The taxi office he ran was torched within twenty-three hours of the blast at McAvoy's home, and the team of Eastern European drivers and drugs couriers he ran have scattered and vanished. Bruno is the only member of Adam Downey's old crew still on the scene. He's got nowhere to go. His movements are still restricted by the terms of his last probation agreement and he owns a house in east Hull that nobody seems keen to buy. He's adrift. Pharaoh has seen to it that he's lonely. None of the gyms he used to frequent want the trouble that comes with having him as a member. Every pub where he begins to drink is soon raided by uniformed officers acting on information received. He can't find straight employment. Every girl he meets soon gets a phone call warning them he's a nonce. Life is getting unbearable for Bruno Phar-macy. And Pharaoh is proud to be the architect.

'You're tremendously loyal, Bruno. Considering.'

'Fuck you, Pharaoh.'

'Just saying, son. You're being a good soldier. You're staying true to your personal code of ethics. I like that. But they've moved on, matey. They've forgotten you. I want to forget you as well. But you won't give me anything. You keep telling lies. You've got every policeman in the city pissed off and talking about you. You can make it all better, Bruno. Just talk to me. Make me happy. Make your own life that little bit less shit.'

Bruno turns away from her. Like all steroid addicts he has difficulty controlling his temper. Difficulty behaving himself at all. An ex-girlfriend told Pharaoh that he got his kicks by putting her in 'sleeper' holds. Used to grab her around the throat while she was reading magazines and squeeze her into unconsciousness, just to make himself laugh.

'You haven't got a clue, love,' says Bruno, reaching down and taking a towel from a sports bag. 'No fucking clue.'

Pharaoh and Daniells share a smile. These little jousts have become a part of their lives. This is what they do. They give him little jabs in the chest and shoves in the back. Despite what she has told the Assistant Chief Constable and Breslin's symposium, they don't know much more about the Headhunters now than they did a year ago. The organisation still controls the cannabis production. Bruno's old team sewed up the cocaine route pretty damn efficiently before the explosion at McAvoy's place brought them more heat than they could handle and shut up shop. Pharaoh doesn't doubt they have solved those problems now. The Headhunters will have fitted a new face. An ambitious young thing and some hired muscle will be making good money. Bruno is out of the loop. But he knows more than he is letting on. And the lies he told about Roisin McAvoy mean he cannot be allowed to slide away.

'Was it their idea?' asks Pharaoh, quietly. 'What you said about Roisin and her friend? Their little giggle, was it?'

Bruno turns and spits on the grass at her feet. Then he treats her to a wide grin, full of genuine glee.

'I just told you the truth, Pharaoh. Like you wanted. Me and Adam and a couple of the Turks met that gypsy lass and her mate in a bar. She asked us back. We had a good time with them both and left it at that. She's the one couldn't take it for what it was. Got obsessed with my mate, she did. Texting him, turning up at his house. Said her husband was a loser. Limp-dicked ginger prick. Wanted a repeat performance. She must have pushed Adam too far. Threatened him. I don't know how it ended up bringing the house down but she was the one who caused the problems. Some bitches just can't be cool about stuff though, can they? Can't enjoy the moment. That's her. You should tell me where she is, really. I'd like to send her some flowers. See if she's OK. Pass on my condolences about her mate. Horrible way to go, eh? Poor lass. Nice tits she had. Bit weird to think of them flying across the room . . .'

Pharaoh has spent her career knowing when to let her temper out and when to smile sweetly. Right now she just gives him a little wink and grinds her cigarette out in the little pool of Bruno's spit.

'You're on borrowed time, Bruno. Borrowed time.'

He snorts and pushes past her, stomping away over the wet ground in the direction of the main road. Daniells arrives at Pharaoh's side.

'I thought you were going to hit him, guv,' he says, regretfully. 'Prick, isn't he? Those things he was saying about Mrs McAvoy. Christ, does the Sarge know?'

Pharaoh turns a cold stare on the young constable. 'He knows what I tell him, Constable. If he knows everybody's talking about Roisin like this, he'll either fall to pieces or kill everybody in Hull and neither of those things are going to help the crime statistics, so let's just keep doing what we're doing.'

Daniells watches Bruno as he disappears through the park gates. After a moment he pulls his radio from the pocket of his jacket and with grease-stained fingers, releases a burst of static into the cold, damp air.

'Ben, he's moving.'

Pharaoh rolls her head on her neck and wonders whether it would be against a specific guideline for her to ask Daniells to massage her shoulders. The train journey yesterday has left her with aching bones and she spent last night asleep on the sofa with her neck wedged at a painful angle. She'd had no reason to go to bed. Has not had a warm body to press herself against since the colossal stroke left her husband unintelligible and bed-bound; a living ghost in their converted front room.

'He's rattled. He'll have to make a call eventually. He can't carry all this on his own.'

Pharaoh sounds confident. In truth, this whole operation is based on hope and bloody-mindedness. Right now Detective Constable Ben Neilsen is tailing Bruno. Detective Inspector Sharon Archer is spending most of her time in the upstairs bedroom of the house across the street from her target, listening carefully to the bugs planted all over his house by the unit's technical wizards. Bruno will have to make a useful call soon. Will have to get a visit from somebody. All Pharaoh wants is an opening she can push at.

'He's on the phone, guv. Sounds pissed off.'

Ben's voice comes through the radio and Pharaoh mulls over the new information. She has no listening devices implanted in Bruno's phone. If the big man is cracking and making a call for help, there is a chance she and the team will miss it.

'Stay close, Ben. Get what you can. But don't spook him. He might be doing this because he knows you're there.'

Pharaoh sighs and wonders if it would be wrong to have another cigarette. She feels tired. Feels like she's carrying too much weight on her back. Too much weight around her middle too. Feeling flabby and old. She has started leaving it a few extra days between shaving her legs and armpits. Can't see the point any more. Can't see her bikini line neither. This job was supposed to be the one where she made a difference. She's been a full detective superintendent for less than a year. Has overseen some key arrests and made significant progress in the scuffles with organised crime. But her days seem to be filled with spreadsheets and budget plans, report-writing and signing of expense forms. She doesn't feel like she has a chance to catch crooks. Isn't enjoying any of it any more. Hasn't since McAvoy went off sick. She wonders what he's doing right now. Hopes he's sitting in a coffee shop somewhere, using a highlighter pen and a ruler to check timelines and evidence logs. Doubts very much that he is.

'Guv?'

Pharaoh realises she has been lost in her own thoughts. Daniells looks at her expectantly, gesturing at the exercise machine Bruno has recently vacated. There is a low buzzing sound emanating from the base. Pharaoh crosses the asphalt and squats down. A cheap, white, pay-as-you-go mobile phone is ringing. On the screen, the caller's name is displayed. It says 'Answer me'.

Eyes closed, heart slowing, Pharaoh takes the call.

She recognises the voice immediately. Feels light-headed as her memory floods with images. The mock-up of Roisin's corpse. The words of warning. The promise of further cooperation provided she was a good girl and did what she was told.

'Detective Superintendent. How wonderful to hear your voice again. Might I ask that you hold the line for one moment? Thank you.'

Pharaoh listens as some muffled words are spoken. She fancies she hears the word 'now'.

84

Before she can respond, Ben Neilsen's voice is buzzing in the radio.

'. . . big bloody car, guv! Fuck, there's blood coming out of his head. He's dead, guv. It just splattered him and took off . . .'

Andy Daniells starts to run towards the road. Runs towards the screams and the sound of screeching tyres.

Pharaoh turns and walks away across the grass. She already understands. Already knows.

'One last job, was it?' she asks, quietly. 'Bet he thought he was back in your good graces. And all he was to you was a demonstration.'

For a moment there is silence, then the softest of laughs.

'No, Detective Superintendent. He wasn't the demonstration. He was a way for you and I to be alone. I have a proposal for you. It seems that life is being a little unkind.'

In her handbag, Pharaoh's own phone beeps. She retrieves it and looks at the image on the screen. It is, unmistakably, a photograph of the room where Breslin's symposium took place. The projection screen at the end of the table is filled with an image of a severed arm.

'Impressive,' says Pharaoh, grinding her teeth. 'Do you want me to give you a round of applause?'

Pharaoh is rewarded with a quiet laugh. 'No, Detective Superintendent. I want a favour.'

'You're fucking joking.'

'One favour, and perhaps Roisin McAvoy can come home.'

Pharaoh can contain herself no longer. She lashes out with a boot, aiming a kick at nothing.

'After what you made Bruno say? After what your man did to

85

her home? After everything you put Hector through? You want me to help you?'

The man at the other end of the line seems to be digesting all of the questions.

At length he sighs, softly, into the phone.

'Detective Superintendent, I am merely asking you to provide some information. And in return, I may be able to redress some of the damage caused to yourself and the good sergeant these past few months.'

Pharaoh chews on her lower lip until she tastes blood.

'What do you want?' she asks, hissing the words through locked teeth.

'A location. A little background. Some suggestions.'

Pharaoh shakes her head. 'And who exactly can you and your bloodhounds not find?'

'A man past his prime. A man who should have taken the offer that was made.'

Pharaoh chuckles. 'People not cooperating?'

'Not yet. But he will. Once his monster is put down, he will listen to reason.'

Pharaoh narrows her eyes. 'His monster?'

'Yes,' says the man, in a voice somehow laced with both respect and disgust. 'Francis Nock. A certain Mr Mahon. We need to find them. And our regular sources are proving, shall we say, unhelpful.'

'You mean people are as scared of them as they are of you? Delighted to hear it. So what makes you think I know where they are or want to tell you?'

'Check your phone,' says Mr Mouthpiece. 'And allow me to apologise in advance for the crudeness of the image.'

Pharaoh looks at the screen and watches the picture fill the screen. Looks at Roisin McAvoy. Bandaged. Bruised. Pale. Staring out of the window of the second-floor flat where she has been staying with plain-clothes officers for the past twelve weeks.

Pharaoh ends the call. Lowers herself down onto the damp grass.

Puts her head in her hands.

She wants to stay here. Isn't sure she can face wandering over to the road and looking on the broken body of Bruno Pharmacy.

At length, she makes the call she knows she must. When it is answered she wonders whether she is acting out of goodness or ambition.

And, for a second, knows how McAvoy must feel all the time.

Softly, under her breath: 'Poor bastard.'

# Chapter 6

Autumn has come early in this part of Holderness. A patchwork quilt of mottled browns and golds obscures the neat front lawn and carefully tended borders at the front of Audrey George's home on Bydales Lane in Winestead. The quiet road that winds past her front door is mouldy with mushed foliage and tyre-grooved mud. The last of the summer nettles are folding inwards and dying in the shadow of a field maple, its roots stretching far under the compact, pebble-dashed property.

*Acer campestre*, thinks McAvoy. He screws up his eyes, thinking of his dad, and the lessons they used to share at the kitchen table. His father would know a use for the tree. How best to cut it back and what colour smoke it gives off under flame. Roisin would know how to use the nettles. Would have a recipe for an ointment or a tea. He has a sudden flash of memory, picturing her chewing on a nettle leaf, oblivious to the stings, then spitting green gunge onto Fin's red-rashed legs. Taking the pain out of his stings in a moment. Shrugging off her own pain with a smile and a cuddle: her lips fuller, redder, like crushed fruit.

He sits in a high-backed floral sofa and watches the birds

flit and flutter to the wooden feeder in the centre of the lawn. He's already had a good look around the living room. Drank it all in. Ornaments behind glass. Magazines stuffed in a pink, well-upholstered footstool. An ornamental gas fire sitting unlit in the space where a real fire should be. Pictures of country landscapes and a pleasant pencil sketch of a church in Lancashire. It's a nice room. As nice as the old lady, busy pottering about in the kitchen and promising she doesn't need any help with the tray.

McAvoy stands. Ignores her protests. Stoops as he enters the kitchen and takes the tray from Mrs George's hands. She aims a playful slap at him then grins, showing two sets of perfectly false teeth.

Audrey George has lived in this area all of her life. She's seventy-eight years old. Was born in an old farm cottage that used to belong to the manor house and has called this neat semi-detached her home for last few years. Lived here with her husband, Anton. Scottish, she'd told McAvoy as he'd introduced himself. You might have known him . . .

'Sugar, I presume,' says Audrey, settling herself on the sofa and beginning an elaborate dance with teacups and saucers. 'The flapjack's home-made.'

McAvoy is feeling more comfortable than he has in some time. Mrs George had welcomed him like some favourite nephew. Had already known what he wanted before he got to the end of his explanation for being here. She lives here alone and doesn't get many visitors. A chance to chat to a nice young detective represents a good day.

'Horrid day again,' says Audrey, nodding at the window and settling back in her chair. 'I know they say us old buggers always

89

look at the past with rose-tinted glasses but it seems like it's been miserable forever, doesn't it? I try to keep the gardens nice but my son plays merry hell with me for it. My back, you see. Aches if I do too much bending. And he won't come and do the weeding, will he? He's a busy man. The grandchildren could do it but it's a bugger to get to Winestead if you haven't got a car. That used to be its biggest asset, of course. Out-of-the-way kind of place. Just seems a bit lonely now. There's only a dozen or so houses and I don't know half the people other than to say hello to. Shame, really. Still, there's the WI in Patrington and I still get days out now and again. Life's what you make it, isn't it? That's what I always say.'

McAvoy is coming to the conclusion that Audrey always says a lot of things. She has barely stopped talking since he arrived.

'That's wonderful flapjack,' says McAvoy, after demolishing a slice in two bites. 'My son would love it.'

'Oh, you take some with you,' says Mrs George enthusiastically. 'Will just go to waste if not.'

McAvoy is about to outline which part of the ACPO guide prohibits him from accepting gratuities. Then he realises it's just a flapjack and tells his conscience to grow up.

'I would have called first,' says McAvoy apologetically. 'But I was in the area and the computer said you were still local.'

'Don't you worry,' says Audrey, brushing crumbs from her neatly seamed navy-blue trousers. 'I don't get scared answering my own doorbell. We don't get many door-to-door salesmen up here. And the Jehovah's Witnesses haven't found me yet.'

McAvoy smiles and drains his tea. He pulls his notebook from his pocket. Audrey exclaims as she sees the shorthand squiggles that line each page.

'Ooh, that's fancy! I always wanted to be a secretary. No opportunity for it up here though. You didn't get the same chances then as now. Never known a man who could do it though.' She claps her hands, delighted. 'Aren't you a man of many talents!'

McAvoy doesn't quite know what to say. Just smiles and tells her it's a useful skill. Then he reads though his notes.

'Mrs George, I understand . . .'

'It's Audrey, Sergeant, please.'

'Audrey,' says McAvoy, a little more firmly. 'As I explained, we're making a general review of a sample of old cases and as part of that review, we're examining the deaths of the Winn family in 1966. I have a witness statement you gave the police at that time. Now, I appreciate it's a long time ago, but I just wondered if you could recall precisely what you told police on that day.'

The old lady gives a conspiratorial little snigger. 'You mean you want to see if I'm some crazy old bat who will look silly giving evidence if Peter Coles ever comes to trial?'

McAvoy colours. He'd been quite pleased with his cover story. Hadn't expected to be shown up by his sweet companion.

'I'm sure nobody could doubt your faculties, Audrey,' says McAvoy, with a dusting of charm. 'It's just that anybody's memory would be questioned after all this time.'

Audrey sits forward and puts her cup down. 'I don't think I'd be your star witness,' she says, thoughtfully. 'But I can tell you what I said. And as much gossip as you fancy!'

'Please do,' says McAvoy. 'If my maths is correct you'll have been around thirty years old at the time of the shooting.'

'And quite the looker,' says Audrey, happily. Then her face falls a little, as she looks inside and begins to remember the

91

night of the killings. 'We lived in one of the farm cottages at the manor house. My dad had worked for Winslow Royce, you see. His family had farmed the land for nigh on a hundred years before he sold it to Mr Winn. We were all a bit concerned that when Mr Winn bought it he'd boot out all the men and women who had worked there before, but he barely got rid of a soul. Kept everybody on. We kept the house.'

'And you lived there with your mother, father and husband, yes?'

Audrey nods. 'Cosy rather than cramped. Anton was away quite a lot. Worked on the barges, you see. Was a sod for him to get home. Had to cycle as far as Hedon, then get two trains just to get to work. Amazing we had time to start a family. But he got on well with my dad and there wasn't as much fuss then about needing your own space. I was happy enough, and Anton was happy if I was.'

McAvoy enjoys the look on Audrey's face as she smiles at the recollection of her husband. He wants to ask her what happened to him but fancies it will take him an age to steer her back to answering his questions.

'You knew the Winn family?'

'Well enough,' says Audrey. 'Nice lot, for incomers.'

'How old were you when they bought the house and farm?'

'Maybe ten,' she says, shrugging. 'War hadn't long finished. Mr Royce was no spring chicken any more. Mr Winn had made some money making things for the army. Don't ask me what. Could be bullets or Spitfires for all I know. His wife, Evelyn, was a Hull woman, as far as I can remember. You know how badly Hull got it during the war, don't you? Second most bombed city in the UK behind London. Knocked the stuffing out of the place.

You can still the scars. I think it affected Mrs Winn's nerves. Word was that Mr Winn bought the farm to give her somewhere peaceful to lay her head and start a family. I didn't get the impression he had much desire to be a farmer and landlord.'

McAvoy's pen scratches at the page. He finds himself recalling black-and-white photographs of Hull during the Blitz. Crumpled homes and blackened beams. Fallen stones and smoking craters. Finds himself suddenly hot beneath his clothes as the images merge with his own more recent memories. Digs his fingernails into his legs and tries to concentrate.

'How well did you know the family?'

'You get to know most people around here pretty quickly,' she says. 'Was a small place. Didn't look like it does now, neither. The copse of trees at the back of the church was bigger. The manor house and the cottages were all still there. Did you know there used to be another manor house on that spot, centuries ago? Belonged to the Hildyard family, if you've ever heard of them. Great old sprawl of a place. Medieval times. Lord of the Manor had the place demolished after his son died in the moat. Sad, really. Sometimes it seems like even the prettiest places have seen too much tragedy. Didn't stop us playing there, mind. If you look at the back of the church you can still see the moat. Cross over that and you're in the woods. Beautiful, it was, when we were kids. Used to be some rough lads from Patrington and Withernsea would cycle there sometimes, but my little gang loved it. And when we were a bit older, it was a popular place for courting couples, if you know what I mean.'

McAvoy returns Audrey's happy, wide grin. Makes a note.

'The night of the killings, Audrey. Please, tell me what you remember.'

Audrey looks down at her feet. She is wearing slippers and begins pressing one toe into the carpet, as though digging for something troublesome.

'It was never any surprise to hear shots,' she says, quietly. 'This is a farming community. Was then, anyways. The sound of a shot just meant a rabbit for the pot or somebody practising for a pigeon shoot. We wouldn't look up. Didn't this night, neither. Just heard a few shots. That was that. Sounded close, but sound carries on flat land like this so we didn't think nothing of it.'

'You were all at home?'

'No, just me and Mam. Dad will have been in Patrington having a pint or two. That's why I was a bit surprised to hear the knock at the door. Big Davey. Standing there all soaked through and white as a sheet. I thought something had happened to Dad. Felt faint, I did. But then he got his words out. Said there had been an accident. Or worse. Bodies, up by the church. He wasn't making any sense. I got him a drink of water and then he said John Glass had told him to go phone for help. He remembered Dad telling him we had a phone. Had a piece of paper with a number on it. He was gabbling, and a right mess, but we showed him where the phone was and I got my boots and coat while he phoned the police or the ambulance or whoever it was. Then he was begging us for a drink and we had to give him some of Dad's best bottle.'

McAvoy continues to write. Looks up and nods, telling her she can go on.

'He said he didn't want to go back there. But I told him he couldn't stay. Told him he needed to sort himself out and show me what was going on. I bullied him out the door. I don't really know what was going through my mind. I suppose I thought

94

somebody had had an accident with a gun. Shot themselves or a friend. Anton wasn't due back but he had surprised me once or twice by wangling a lift from somebody and maybe I was getting panicky that he'd taken a short cut across somebody's land and scared the landlord into firing a warning shot. I don't know. But Davey drove us back to the church. Snow was falling heavy by then. Coming down thick. John Glass was waiting at the gate of the church. He had Daft Pete with him. Had him tied to the gate with his tie, if you can imagine that. Hadn't brought his cuffs, had he? Had to tie him up with his own tie! Next thing, John's telling me not to go into the churchyard. Says there are bodies in there. He's looking like death and there's a shotgun leaning up against a gravestone and it's too dark for me to see anything, but first thing I asked him was who it was. He looked all shaken up and scared. I mean, he was a policeman and all that, but he hadn't been prepared for anything like what he saw. And he came out with it, all of a sudden. He recognised the clothes. Was the Winn family. Man, wife and two bairns.'

McAvoy finds his right leg jiggling as he writes. Has to slow his breathing as he scrawls blue ink on the page. Feels, for a moment, like he can see the whole scene in front of him. Can smell gunpowder, blood and snow.

'I asked what Daft Pete was doing there,' says Audrey, her face flushed. 'Why he was tied up. I don't know why I asked, really. Looking back, it seems obvious. But I was in such shock that I was gabbling too, like Big Davey. I asked Pete if he was OK. If he'd been hurt. He didn't reply. Just stared like a dead fish.'

'You thought Pete might have been a victim?'

'It didn't cross my mind he was the one who'd done it. He was just a big daft lump. Everybody knew Daft Pete. He was

95

a bit of an odd one but it never seemed there was any harm in him. So when John Glass told me Pete was under arrest for killing them all and that he'd just confessed, my feet just went from under me. Was a night I'll never forget. Wasn't long before it was all ambulances and blue lights and coppers asking questions and tyres getting stuck in the mud. But in that moment it was just the four of us and it didn't seem real.'

McAvoy pauses. Rubs a big hand over his face.

'What did you know of Peter Coles before that night?'

Audrey shrugs. 'He lived in one of the other farm cottages with his gran. His mum had been a silly, flighty soul who kept falling in love with every bloke who showed an interest. Went off with an airman, if I remember. Left little Peter at home. He was never a bright lad. I suppose you'd have to say, looking back, the other kids were a bit mean to him. He was years younger than me so I'm probably not the best one to ask, but I got the impression school wasn't much fun for him. He was happiest on his own, I think. Used to walk miles, away in his own little world. Loved those woods behind the church, I remember that. I think it was when he was a teenager and he started getting those, you know, *urges*, that he went a bit off the rails. His gran got a few knocks on the door from local blokes who said he'd been watching their wives. I would love to stick up for him but I know for a fact he was a bit of a peeping Tom. Definitely had a good ogle through our bathroom window a few times. And stuff used to go missing.'

'Stuff?'

'Underwear,' says Audrey, shyly. 'Off the line. These were the days when you didn't even like to hang your bra on the line in case somebody thought you were a hussy. But there were days when the wind was blowing hard you could get your laundry done in an hour and you'd take the risk. That's when they'd vanish.'

'And people thought it was Peter?'

'There weren't many other suspects. And when they searched his room they found plenty, didn't they?'

McAvoy rubs one hand over the other, thinking.

'Did you have any reason to believe he had any problems with the Winn family?'

Audrey rolls her head to the left and makes a face, as though struggling with an uncertain thought.

'You know the oldest girl was a looker, don't you?' says Audrey. 'Anastasia. Pretty as a picture and very clever. She didn't go to school around here at first. Was off at some boarding school. Had lovely manners and real poise. I think the other girls were pretty jealous. Heck, I was jealous myself and she was half my age. She wasn't flash with it though. Just a nice, sweet girl. And I think Peter didn't quite know how to deal with the fact he liked her in a certain way.'

McAvoy nods. He would rather form his own conclusions, but can't help asking the question. Can't help finding out what the local line is on a tragedy that shook the whole community.

'What do you think happened, Audrey?'

She raises her arms, palms up. 'Peter used to like going up to the church to read the gravestones and play with his gun. He'd been told off for it before, of course. These days the police wouldn't let him anywhere near a gun. But this was a rural community and he was a farmhand and the local blokes didn't see any reason to object to him having a shotgun, provided he kept it under lock and key. Seems crazy now, looking back. But he was a hard worker for Mr Winn. Wasn't exactly one of the more popular blokes but people tolerated him and at least he was working. A shotgun kind of came with the territory. He would just have these moments where he'd do something silly, like taking potshots at passing aeroplanes.'

'And you think he was doing that when Mr Winn interrupted him?'

Audrey digs her toe into the ground again. 'Could be. Mr Winn liked to walk in those woods. Sometimes the family would go with him. It was a nice night before the snow started. Maybe they were walking off dinner. Maybe Peter panicked. Maybe he shot one of them by accident and killed the others so nobody would tell. That's the kind of thought I can imagine him having. It's just so horrible. Even now, thinking about it, I get goose pimples.'

Audrey rolls up the sleeve of her cardigan and holds the limb out for inspection. The grey hairs upon her flesh have risen like sails.

'I know it's hard, Audrey, but do you think you can remember anything else from that night which may help?'

She looks away, out of the window at the damp green fields and the carpet of dead leaves.

'You'd do well to speak to Vaughn,' she says, quietly. 'Oldest boy. Done well for himself, despite everything. Took a long time for his money to come in from the sale of the farm, of course. His solicitor's still alive, though he's about a thousand years old. Lives up the road there. Did a decent job for Vaughn. Wasn't easy to sell. Nobody wanted to buy the place for years. Took its toll on this little community, Sergeant. I'll never forget when

Peter's grandma came back from his first hearing at York Crown Court. She'd aged about twenty years. Was hard for her, after that. She'd been quite close with Mrs Winn. She was the one who persuaded Mr Winn to give Peter a job on the farm. She felt like she'd made it all happen.'

'She accepted Peter's guilt?'

Audrey cocks her head again. 'That's a harder one to answer. These days you'd say he was probably ill and give him pills to make him better. In those days she was just the grandma of a weirdo. And when he got sent to the funny farm she was left all alone. We assumed there would be a trial at some point, but after a few years we all kind of put it in the past. Mrs Coles moved away. I think she got a new lease of life after a few years and started putting the past behind her too.'

McAvoy keeps his mouth closed. Mrs Coles did find some renewed zest for life, but it took the form of harassing her local MP and demanding answers over her grandson's continued incarceration.

For a spell there is silence in the room. McAvoy settles back in the chair and looks up at the ceiling, where a crack runs from the chimney breast to just above the door. Audrey follows his gaze.

'Subsidence,' she says, tutting and rolling her eyes. 'If I ever sell this place it will get me about £1.50. Needs a lot of work doing. It's what some of the houses are built on, you see. Funny old place is Holderness. You know the saying about building on shifting sands, don't you? Could have been written for this bit of coastline. I'm a Holderness girl and even I feel like a stranger here sometimes. It comes with nobody knowing you're here. Unless you're from nearby you think the coast stops at Hull.

We're this little bit that's stuck on afterwards. Miles and miles of not a lot. Gives you a bit of a chip on your shoulder. Puts a bit of wildness in the eyes.'

McAvoy smiles as Audrey does an impression of having psychotic eyes.

'Anton said it was a hard place to get used to. He wasn't wrong. Loved it in the end, though. We had his ashes scattered in the front garden. Didn't know where to put him that meant more to him than here, with me.'

'Did you go to the funeral?' he asks, quietly. 'The Winn family, I mean.'

'It was a quiet affair,' she says, still looking at the garden. 'Would have been held at St Germain's but that would have been too horrible. Was held at St Patrick's in Patrington. The Queen of Holderness.'

'The Queen?'

'It's true. That's what it's known as. The "King" is St Augustine's in Hedon. St Patrick's is the "Queen". Stunning building. Was on a list in the Sunday newspapers as one of the most beautiful in England. The spire's nearly 200 foot tall. Looks a bit out of place in a little town like Patrington, but this used to be a big important place, centuries ago. Everybody knew the Queen. Quite a thrill to say you were married there.'

'You and Anton?'

She smiles, warmly. 'Beautiful day. 1962. I think that was the last time it was sunny.'

McAvoy lets his eyes travel back to the crack in the ceiling. He finds himself beginning to worry that one slam of the door will bring the roof in on Audrey George. She seems to read his mind.

'I'm no spring chicken, Sergeant. Whatever will be will be.'

'I could have a look at it, before I go,' he says, rising. 'Might just need the gable end repointing . . .'

Audrey puts out a hand to stop him. 'If you did everything today you'd have no reason to come back, would you. And I hope you do.'

McAvoy stays where he is, half risen. He feels like he is trapped midway into a curtsy. He straightens his back and readjusts his clothes, trying not to tower over the seated Mrs George.

'If you did ever need to give evidence in a trial . . .'

She shrugs. 'It would be something to do with my day,' she says. 'I can tell them all I've just told you. I told it all to half a dozen different policemen back when this all happened. Nothing ever came of it. Peter never really got dealt with properly. The ashes of the two Winn children are still blowing across this land, aren't they? Their parents are still rotting in the ground. You seem like a nice policeman, but I do think this was done a bit shabbily. It made life difficult for John Glass afterwards. He got the mick taken out of him a lot after that. For panicking. For not having his cuffs. And the detectives were not the nicest of people. He was supposed to be our community policeman and there were people thought he rolled over and let the men in suits say and do whatever they wanted. I always thought that was unfair. Anton did too. He and John were never exactly close but I got a lovely letter from John when Anton died. Not everybody was so thoughtful. Vaughn Winn was though. I'd only ever spoken to him a handful of times, but when he sent money for the new roof at St Germain's, I sent him a letter of thanks and he must have remembered me.'

McAvoy takes his eyes from the crack in the ceiling. 'Vaughn Winn? You're still in contact?'

'Well, not exactly contact, no, but there are people in Patrington who have a lot to thank him for. He's sent money for a few goodwill projects. Good of him, really, considering what this place cost him emotionally.'

McAvoy purses his lips and breathes hard, like a racehorse at the end of a gallop.

'Do you have his contact details?'

Audrey grins. 'If I give you them, do you promise to come back?'

McAvoy eyes the remaining flapjack on the plate.

'Promise.'

# Chapter 7

Colin Ray's face has taken on the same characteristics as the sky. He's grey, damp and there's a good chance of thunder.

He sniffs, almost from his toes. Something lumpy rattles its way from his lungs to the back of his throat and he turns and hawks it against the wall of Hull City Hall. It clings like a limpet.

'About fucking time,' he says, wiping the rain from his face with a grimy hand. 'Freezing me bollocks off.'

Inspector Phil Batty grins as he reaches across and opens the door of the patrol car. Ray pushes off from the wall of the building and ducks into the warm vehicle without a hello.

'Another lovely day in the city of sunshine – eh, Col?'

'Fuck off.'

Batty grins and eases the vehicle forward a few yards until he finds a suitable parking space. They come to a halt outside a clothes store selling the kind of jeans that makes teenagers walk as though they have just soiled themselves. It's all dayglo and thumping techno beats and Ray struggles to imagine he will ever be a customer.

'Used to be a record store, that place,' says Batty, taking his seat belt off and turning to face his passenger. 'Local institution. Bloody shame.'

Ray shrugs. He moved to Hull for work. He has little affection for the place and can't abide the accent. His own roots are vaguely West Midlands but he has little in the way of dialect. His words are all bile and sneer.

'Coffee shops and travel agents, that's all we've got left,' says Batty, waving a hand at the quiet shopping street framed by the rain-spotted windscreen. 'Was always heaving with people when I was a kid. Couldn't move for shoppers . . .'

'Shite,' says Ray, unable to let it go. 'I've seen pictures, Phil. Place has always been a shithole.'

'No, seriously, Col,' says Phil, earnestly. 'Hull used to be a great place . . .'

'Shite,' says Ray, picking at a crumb on the leg of his trousers. 'It's a hole in the ground. You can't build a city on fish without it starting to stink somewhere down the line.'

Phil seems about to offer a riposte but gives in to a smile. He's spent his whole career with Humberside Police and has a nice uniformed job that rarely takes him away from the station. He's a good ten years younger than Ray but his sedentary life means he looks a little flabby and unfit. He's well liked by his team and largely ignored by the brasses, which for a good chunk of the area's coppers is the ultimate dream. He's also a man who remembers a favour.

They sit in silence for a moment. Watch the rain and the mist on the windscreen, and the steam rising from Colin's wet clothes.

'They're missing you,' says Batty at last. 'The lads. It's shit you have to stay away.'

Ray is gratified by that. He coaches the force football team and is missing his interaction with the boys far more than any other aspect of his day job.

'You're taking care of them? I heard we let in a real soft one against those wankers from the tile warehouse.'

'They just need to concentrate. Keep their eyes open and not drift off. We'll do fine. Finish mid-table, I reckon.'

Ray grunts and nods. He'd be happy with that sort of finish. He wants Batty to do well in his absence but would hate for him to be seen to do a better job.

Above them, the streetlights suddenly flare back into life. There was only an hour or two, around midday, when they were switched off. It's not yet 4 p.m. but already evening is settling on the city centre; falling as ash from a sky of woodsmoke and rain.

'Shaz keeping you informed of developments?' asks Batty, resting his head against the window on the driver's side. 'Plenty going on. You'll know what happened to the Scotsman's house, eh? Gypsy bitch. I never even knew he was married. You can't imagine it, can you? Bet she's the sort to stop taking the pill and not tell you about it. Probably trapped him with a nipper.'

Ray swills his spit around his mouth, tasting cigarettes and pastry. He looks at Batty with a hard stare.

'You know that's shite, Phil. Was fuck all to do with his wife. That lad Downey was a villain. He wanted to show he was hard man. Picked on the first copper he could. Cost the Jock his house. She's left him, last I heard. Took the baby too. He's having a miserable time of it. Came out of hospital to find his life ruined. His missus had never even met the fucker who did it.'

Batty shrugs. He doesn't really mind which story is true but the one about McAvoy's pretty wife having affairs on the side is the one that's more fun to talk about over a pint with the lads.

'Shaz was the one who told me,' says Batty, a touch petulantly. 'Gave me plenty of details too.'

'Shaz doesn't know a fucking thing,' spits Ray. 'Silly cow's all loved up, isn't she? Fallen for some slick prick from London.'

'Aye, she was looking like something from a Disney movie when I saw her the other day. All bluebirds and bunny rabbits and twirling her skirts. You know him?'

Ray shakes his head. 'I haven't had the pleasure. Smelled him on her, though. Shaz and me had a drink a month or so back. Could smell his aftershave on her when she kissed me. Must bath in the stuff. Must be an estate agent or something.'

'He's not a copper then?'

'I didn't ask. Just know he's got money and he smells like a poof. And Shaz is so cock-blind that she's forgotten who got her where she is.'

He says the last with venom, turning away so Batty doesn't see the hurt in his eyes when he talks about his protégée. For ten years he and Shaz Archer have been inseparable. Every job he has taken has been on the proviso she comes as his number two. He had been expecting to run the Serious and Organised unit alongside her before the job went to Trish fucking Pharaoh. He's pissed off that she has abandoned him when he needs somebody to buy him drinks and tell him none of this shit is his fault.

'Pharaoh's got her hands full,' says Batty, and grins. 'This shit with the new villains has gone national. She's up and down to London every five minutes. Hard to tell if she's making progress. Hard to see whether she needs to, to be honest. Ninety per cent of the people these bastards hurt are bastards themselves. Let them get on with it, I say.'

Ray shrugs again, not really caring what inroads Pharaoh has made. He reckons he's doing better than she is, whatever she's got.

'You going to give me something useful, Phil?' he asks, turning his gaze back on his friend. 'Tell me you've got a pretty picture for me.'

Batty's face falls a little. The news is not going to be good.

'I've had two uniforms and one civilian checking every camera within three square miles,' he says, sounding put-upon. 'You know how many lies I had to tell to requisition them? They played a blinder though. Even called in some favours from the traffic lads.'

'And?'

'At that exact time, we saw eighteen separate individuals talking into mobile phones within the network of streets you asked for. Of those, ten were female. That leaves you with eight . . .'

'I can do the fucking maths, Phil.'

'Of those, two were teenagers, which leaves you with six.'

'Piss off.'

'And here are the six.'

Phil pulls an A4 page from his inside pocket, folded into quarters. He hands it to Ray, who looks at six blurry images. Men, phones held to their ears. A bloke in a tracksuit. An old boy outside a bookies. A security guard, outside the coroner's court. A bloke leaning outside the wall of Courts Bar on Land of Green Ginger, swigging from a bottle of milk. The *Hull Daily Mail* salesman in his booth at the bottom of Whitefriargate; a finger wedged in his ear. And the owner of the Manchester Arms on High Street, in animated conversation on a mobile while the delivery driver who brought the wrong wine sits on a beer barrel.

'Any takers?' asks Batty.

Ray sighs, crumpling his face. He can taste something vile at the back of his throat. Suddenly needs a cigarette and a pint.

'Nobody fits.'

'Shouldn't judge a book by its cover, Col.'

'Yes you should. These are just blokes, mate. I'm looking for somebody with swagger. Somebody who would piss me off and not worry about it.'

Batty gives a little shrug. 'I did my best, mate. I'm sorry if you were expecting more.'

Ray turns away wordlessly. Watches a group of raindrops dribble together and trickle down the glass. He hadn't known what to expect but he had known what to hope for. He wanted a photo of a man in expensive clothes and sunglasses, smoking a cigar and smirking into a state-of-the-art mobile phone – preferably with his name and address embossed on a designer leather jacket.

'Maybe for the best anyway,' says Batty, making conversation. 'You're suspended, remember. Maybe best not rock the boat. I'm sure you'll be back at your desk in no time anyway. I mean, the lad's dead. What can he do? You're best just taking it easy. Kick your heels a bit. That's what the tall lassie's doing, I'd say. Brave girl, that one. Deserves a rest . . .'

Ray coughs and swallows down the results. He'd forgotten about Detective Constable Helen Tremberg. Good lass. Decent brain. Hard worker. Nowt to do . . .

'She match-fit?' asks Ray. 'I know she took a bad knock . . .'

'She's home, I know that much. Wasn't in hospital as long as the Jock. Malingerer, that one. How long's he been on the sick now? Shouldn't even be in the job after what he did to Roper. Give me five minutes in a room with him, that's all. Christ, it was a scalpel he was stabbed with, not a samurai sword . . .'

Ray isn't listening. He waves a hand at Batty: his gesture of thanks. Then he lets himself out of the vehicle and steps back into the drizzle and the cold grey air. He stamps away, heading for the Punch Bowl, passing the impressive Victorian frontage of the City Hall. Posters for comedians he hasn't heard of and operas he will never see are trapped behind the glass display posters nailed to the big grey walls. The only paving slabs in the city not be turned mud-brown by the rain are those beneath the big balcony jutting out above the columns and double doors.

Somebody has spat on the front wall.

Ray pulls his old mobile from the recesses of his coat and scrolls through until he finds the number he is looking for. It doesn't occur to him that she will say no. Doesn't occur to him she may be traumatised and ill and too broken to start looking for the bastards who did this to her. She's a copper, after all.

She answers on the fourth ring; quiet and wary.

'Helen,' he says, pushing his way into the warm embrace of the pub. 'Got a little job for you . . .'

4.12 p.m. Flamborough Head.

Mahon's feet sink into mud and sodden grass as he walks quickly along the clifftop. He's leaving footprints and is quite enjoying it. The rain will come again soon and remove all trace he was here. He is free to make an impression. Free to enjoy

109

the salt and spray of the ocean. Free to accept the screams of the whirling seagulls and the caress of a gale which cuts to the bone.

Mahon is making for the lighthouse. Hasn't seen the place in years. Has pleasant enough memories of the last time that he and the old man took a little time for themselves and popped down to this untamed and ragged stretch of coastline. Mahon had needed to have a word in the ear of a couple of likely lads who had held up the local boozer after hours. They hadn't known that the landlord had friends. Hadn't known just what was coming after them. That must have been ten years ago, at least. Mr Nock was still pretty nimble. Still had it all upstairs. Had even managed to squat down to help clean up the mess without needing help to stand back up again.

He stops for a moment and admires the view. Squints through the driving rain at the distant exclamation mark of the light-house and wonders whether he should carry on to his destination or turn around now. He's left Mr Nock on his own. Has to think of his own physical limitations. He's going to need his strength in the coming days. Has to eat and sleep and save what he's got left. He's feeling his age. Feeling a pressure on his chest and noticing the odd bit of blood in his piss. His good eye aches after too much close reading and sometimes when he coughs he finds himself vomiting something ghastly and brown. He can't take unnecessary risks with himself. Mr Nock likes to tell him he's invincible and laughs whenever Mahon tells him his fingers are aching or his back is playing up. As far as Mr Nock is concerned, Mahon remains the scariest and most brutal bastard he has ever met. And he has met them all.

Mahon turns his gaze to the ocean. The sea, beyond the cliffs

110

and the shingly, oil-streaked strip of beach, seems to have been drawn in muddy grey, then striped with the frothy white chaos of rolling waves. Nobody would take a picture of this scene and put it on a postcard, but there is a kind of rugged, wild beauty to it which Mahon enjoys. He looks through the amber filter of his ruined eyes and surveys the ocean. Stares down at the jagged limestone and quartz-seamed boulders of the cliff. Remembers. Pictures his first meeting with the man who would become his benefactor and his friend, his keeper and confidant. Looks inside himself at the memory of a young man. Twenty-something and formidable. Polished and dangerous.

Mahon sees . . .

*The cell door opening and a young man standing in the green light of the hall, a pocket of dark inside the frame of the door. A half-smile on his face, as though he's the best dressed guest at a cocktail party. Dark hair slicked back and clean-shaven. Prison overalls somehow cut to look like a designer pale blue suit. Slipping the screw a few notes, as if he's a bellhop at a posh hotel. Staring in, at the creature on the lower bunk. Thinking. Nodding. Extending a hand, rigid as steel, smooth as silk. Clasping Mahon's shovel of a fist in his.*

*'Nock,' he'd said. 'Francis Nock.'*

And so it had begun. More than fifty years later Mahon remains loyal and irreplaceable. He remains the reason that Francis Nock lives and that he hasn't seen the inside of a prison cell in decades. Together, they have ruled the north-east from the shadows. They have stayed in business when partners and rivals got caught and died. Nock is in his eighties now but has managed to get old without losing any of the drive or ambition that first won him his empire. He's not an imposing physical specimen any more, and there are moments when his mind

111

seems to wander, but Mr Nock looks like nobody's sweet old granddad. He took care of Lloyd personally. Pulled the trigger with a liver-spotted hand and didn't blink as the blood sprayed on his face. Sat there with a cup of tea while Mahon bled the body and cut him up. Took himself to bed and slept eight hours; got up to a breakfast of toast and marmalade, then let his pretty, black-skinned nurse run him a bath and tug him off. He's still the boss. Still the man who holds Mahon's collar. They have been friends for half a century but Mahon is still a little afraid of his employer. Still can't look him in the eye without experiencing a chill. It's just the *certainty* of Mr Nock that unnerves him. All his life he has believed himself to be right. Believed himself *entitled*. Believed himself within his rights to take what he wants and end lives with a nod. Mahon cannot fathom what made Lloyd embrace disloyalty. He would have liked to have asked him. Would have liked to hurt him until he knew every last detail. But Mr Nock had been too busy shooting him in the face to ask questions.

Pleased as he is to be away from the north-east for a few days, Mahon is mildly disquieted by the chain of events that has disrupted his routine. He has had to deal with many interlopers and threats during his years beside Mr Nock, but there is something too calculated and disciplined about the new organisation which has so many of his outfit's allies and competitors running scared. Mahon has seen pretty much every type of criminal organisation over the years. The Headhunters are a new breed. They seem unencumbered by the kind of petty territorialism that has undone so many crime families and syndicates. They do not trouble themselves with boundary disputes or staffing issues. They simply take over existing firms. They come in at the top, promise resources and reward, and demand that those in command bow down, or end up nailed to their own knees. Those who fight back lose. In those cases, underlings are approached with a similar offer. Eventually they find somebody willing to play along. It is a merciless, brutal and very corporate way of running a criminal enterprise and Mahon half admires them for it. In another couple of years he imagines they will be running the north-east in Mr Nock's place. But for as long as the old man is alive, it is Mahon's duty to protect what he owns.

Mahon turns his back on the lighthouse and heads back the way he has come; walking in his own bootprints and obscuring his own tracks. He hasn't been gone too long. Mr Nock will be happy enough. He'll be sitting where he left him, drinking tea and watching the waves, lost in memories and schemes. He lives inside his own head. Doesn't watch TV or read books. Just sits and thinks with that little half-smile on his face, as though he is listening to a radio show playing in his head. He's doing it more of late. There are moments when he almost seems to have disappeared from himself. There are times his body looks like an empty suit. Sometimes he'll mutter a sentence from a conversation he had twenty years ago. Sometimes he'll take an extra couple of moments to remember where he is. Mahon worries that such incidents are signs of old age, but as soon as he gets himself together, Mr Nock is quick to reassure him.

*Never been fitter, Raymond. Never felt more alive.*

It was Mahon's decision to get Mr Nock away for a time. He has been left perturbed by his interrogation of the man who turned Lloyd's head. The man held on for a long time before giving up the information Mahon had pressed him for. And Mahon has no doubts that the organisation will be displeased to have lost somebody who is clearly a key player. He has no doubts they will come for Mr Nock. It will be easier to persuade some ambitious young lad from Newcastle to represent them if the spectre of Mr Nock has already been removed. Mahon is not afraid of the people who will come but there are other matters that require his attention and he doesn't trust anybody to look after Mr Nock in his absence. So he has brought the old man with him. Here. To this wild, ragged bit of coastline with its screaming gulls and feasting puffins and clouds of kittiwakes. Here, where gannets drop as stones into water the colour of earth.

They are perhaps an hour from Hull.

A little further from the church Mahon hasn't seen since he was handsome.

Winestead, he thinks to himself, as he traipses back along the clifftop. Then under his breath: 'Flash bloody Harry.'

Mahon has had decades upon which to think of that night. Remembers every second of it. The snow. The gunsmoke. The wet branches that slapped his face as he made his way through the woods. The sight of the girl's pretty, delicate foot in the gravel and the broken bones. The way the skull disintegrated in a tornado of shot and stones.

That night cost him dear. Cost him his looks. Changed him, inside and out. He'd known his decision would come at a price. He simply hadn't known how high.

'Y'all right?' says Mahon, in greeting, to a woman walking a little terrier and who is trying manoeuvre herself out of the way of the big, lumbering man in sunglasses and a scarf. 'Not much of a day for it.'

The woman is in her seventies and seems as nervous as the

114

shivering creature that leaves muddy paw-prints on her legs as it leaps up and asks to be carried.

'We get worse,' she says, trying to be conversational. 'Sea air's good for you, apparently. I like it when it's bracing.'

Mahon gives her a nod and moves past her. Doesn't look at her too closely. He knows that he unnerves people. Frightens them, even. He doesn't want to frighten her. She seems pleasant enough. He doesn't like to cause displeasure to people who don't deserve it, though he would happily cut her head off with a big fucking knife if Mr Nock insisted. Mr Nock used to mock him for his scruples. Would call him a soft shite, and roll his eyes. But he indulged his monster his conscience. Used to give some of the less palatable jobs to loyal men who didn't share Mahon's peculiar code of ethics. Mahon wishes that had been the case in 1966.

It was always going to end in bloodshed, of course. Mr Nock was an established name. He had the area sewn up. He'd greased the right palms and broken the right skulls and ran the city in a way that everybody could tolerate. He didn't need extra muscle or men from London with big ideas. He should have said no. Should have done what the papers said he did and seen them off at the station when they dared set foot on his turf. But Mr Nock had liked the brothers. Liked their London swagger and the way their men responded to them. He offered a hand of friendship and extended the freedoms of the city to the two tall, dark-haired cockneys who had such big plans. It had been fine, at first. No areas of conflict. No ill-feeling. Sometimes the brothers would send a couple of men north to assist Mr Nock with a job that required an unfamiliar face. Sometimes that favour would be returned. It was all fucking peachy, for a while. Then one of the brothers had lost the plot. Took an insult personally and put a man in the ground. Started himself a war with another London gang. It all got out of hand. Bullets, and blades, and pigs growing fat on flesh and bone. The brothers had reached out. Asked Mr Nock to provide a safe haven for one of their boys. A good boy, who needed to keep his head down for a while. And Mr Nock had agreed. Handed the job of keeping his guest happy over to the new boy, Flash Harry.

Savile Row suits and Mr Fish ties.

Ruffle-fronted shirts and a lacquered pompadour.

A dandy, with pretty-boy looks and eyes like a dead fish.

The young lad whom Mr Nock wanted to groom for the future and who hid the fact he was a psychopath right up until the moment he stuck a knife in the London boy's guts and ripped it up to his throat.

The man whose mess Mahon is still cleaning up, all these years later.

Tomorrow Mahon will go and say hello to an old copper he hasn't seen in years. He'll make sure that memories remain hazy and lips remain sealed. If necessary, he'll close them forever and open a new mouth in the man's throat. He won't take Mr Nock. He'll leave him to enjoy the sea air and the view. Let him listen to the radio show in his head and leave him a note with the times to take his pills.

Mahon will do what he has always done. He'll take care of it. Then he'll take Mr Nock home, and prepare for what the Head-hunters have planned.

Giving the sigh of a tired old man, Mahon lets himself in to the tiny, one-bedroomed chalet property that clings to the rain-pummelled, wind-scarred cliff. He shouts a hello to his employer and goes into the kitchen to make tea. As the kettle boils, he pulls a phone from his pocket. It belonged to a slick piece of work who is still dying, hundreds of miles away, on Mahon's living-room floor. The device is too complicated for him. It does things he thinks of as positively science-fiction. But he knows how to read the messages it contains. Knows a code when he sees one. And he can press the 'play' button in the video messages.

He wonders who the girl is.

She's pretty. Dark-haired and tanned. Has a gypsy look about her. Hoops at her ears and gold at her throat. There's a sadness in her eyes, despite the red-haired, big-eyed baby that she holds in her arms: rocking gently, from side to side – framed in the window of some ugly apartment in a city Mahon doesn't recognise.

He wonders, idly, what she has done to become the focus of the Headhunters' attentions.

Hopes that, if he watches the video enough times, he will eventually see her smile.

Mahon fancies that the girl must be beautiful when she grins.

He shudders at the thought of how she will look when they are through.

# Part Two

Part Two

# Chapter 8

McAvoy sits on the damp grass, feet dangling over the wall.

He watches the pea-green channel marker sit on the motionless water. Turns his head to watch the car headlights flash by on the bridge that towers up into the cloud to his left. Squints as he tries to make out the flag of the cargo ship slowly making its way towards the docks.

There's not much of a moon tonight. What little light it gives off forms a maze between the clouds. From below, it seems the sky is scored with scars and jagged lines: reflecting back in the still, black surface of the Humber. A low easterly wind ruffles the leaves of the trees in the dark, shapeless forest to McAvoy's rear. He has promised Fin they'll go in there one night. Have themselves an adventure after dark. He has not yet found the time or the courage to make good on his word. Bad memories lurk inside the forest's embrace. He was hurt there. Hurt badly. His blood has soaked into the mud and leaves of the forest floor. He has no desire to walk past the spot where it happened. No desire to tell Fin that it is not ghosts or shadows that he needs to fear in the darkness, but bad men of flesh and blood.

A bad man died today. A big, thuggish drug-dealer. He was thrown fifty feet by a big estate vehicle and was dead before he hit the ground. The driver didn't stop. Was never likely to.

McAvoy thinks about Bruno Pharmacy. He hadn't known the man's name when they fought. Had just seen a brute attacking his family. McAvoy had put him down. Put his friends down too. And one of those friends came back and blew up his house.

Pharaoh broke the news with a phone call around teatime. She'd sounded quiet. Had spent a couple of hours waterproofing her team's stories and trying to cover her own back. Bruno had been under police surveillance, and yet nobody had managed to get a look at the driver or glimpse more than a couple of letters of the registration plate. Ben Neilsen needs a blood test, having tried to give unprotected mouth-to-mouth to Bruno's battered corpse. Sharon Archer has subtly suggested to the top brass that Pharaoh had deliberately been winding Bruno up and that it was his aggravated state of mind that caused him to walk out onto Holderness Road without spotting the vehicle that turned him inside out. It's a shit-storm. But she had still made time to call McAvoy. Still made time to tell him that one of Roisin's abusers was dead.

McAvoy doesn't know how to feel. He never wishes death on anybody. But Bruno put his hands on Roisin. And Roisin has been absent from his life ever since. His only hope is that Bruno's demise will somehow remove the threat to her life and that she can be allowed to come home. He had suggested as much to Pharaoh and been rewarded with a sigh. She said she was working on it. To trust her. To carry on with the Peter Coles case and to hope for the best.

He looks down at the laptop that balances on his knees. He

can get a decent signal here as the landlord never switches the wi-fi off. Can do what he needs to do without losing sight of his room, where Fin is sleeping contentedly after polishing off a double portion of complimentary shepherd's pie. They had a good chat tonight. Fin told him what they had learned at school. Asked him if he knew who Henry the Ace was and whether he knew he had six wives. McAvoy had gently educated the boy. Told him what had happened to some of Henry's brides, only to find that Fin was already well aware. The conversation had taken a turn. Fin had asked his father if he had ever seen some-body have their head chopped off. Asked if Henry was arrested and sent to prison for murder. Whether a policeman was better than a king. Asked him what he would do if somebody cut Mammy's head off. Drew a picture of a corpulent king holding a big, blood-soaked axe over the head of a stick figure with black hair. McAvoy had steered them away from the subject. Told him the names of some Scottish heroes and a few stories about his granddad. Tucked the lad up in bed not long after eight. Sat himself down on the floor and waited until the thud-ding waves of panic and nausea subsided. He'd known, in that instant, just how much he missed his father. Had known that the arguments between them could be remedied with a phone call. But he had known, too, that he did not have the courage to make that call. McAvoy's father had angered his son beyond forgiveness when he refused to attend his wedding. He believed that Aector's teenage bride could not be trusted. He'd called her a gypsy bitch who was no better than the mother who abandoned Aector and his brother when they were children and who came and bought them back when she married money. McAvoy misses his dad. Knows, too, that the old man will feel like the worst kind of bastard for being so wrong in his estimations of his new daughter-in-law. But the McAvoys are stubborn men, and neither will break first.

For the last hour, McAvoy has been working. Going through the witness statements. Cross-referencing evidence logs. Double-checking dates. On the computer screen before him, the timeline is taking proper shape, but there are still peculiarities. Some of the witness statements are signed by policemen whose names appear nowhere else in the report. And worse, he is having difficulty locating the actual physical evidence. An email from HQ explained that the shotgun used to wipe out the Winn family was moved from its previous repository some years before, when the various police forces merged, and has since disappeared. The lack of the gun could scupper the case before it begins. Prosecutors will need to make the gun available to the defence team for independent analysis. They would also want to see the clothes worn by the victims on the day of their deaths. They, too, have not yet been unearthed by the civilian custodians who look after the evidence store.

McAvoy isn't really sure how he feels about the assignment yet. He has enjoyed today, in a peculiar way. Liked asking questions and building up a picture. He has heard of detectives who hear the voices of the dead as they search for justice in their name. McAvoy does not. He simply feels pity for the fallen. Mourns the waste of life. What drives him is a need to know. He believes in justice, of a sort. He is finding it hard to think in the same way about the events of 1966. In this case, half a century has elapsed. Peter Coles's loved ones are dead. Those who do remember him will not thank the Home Secretary for tearing open old scars. McAvoy wonders if it would not be best simply

124

to email Pharaoh's contact and ask them exactly what they would like his report to say. He won't do it, of course.

Did Peter Coles kill these people? It certainly seems so. Is there enough evidence to secure a conviction? He isn't sure. There are witness statements aplenty, but in many cases the people who gave them are no longer alive to be cross-examined in the witness box. If he were to put together a watertight case he could hand over to the Home Office it would do his reputation and prospects no harm. He should spend his time doing what he has been asked to, and simply check the facts for oddities and anomalies that would be embarrassing if put before the court. And yet he feels a compulsion. Feels a familiar disquiet. He has a picture in his mind of the young Peter Coles. Has a vision of that place, with its bodies and its corpses between the graves. Something about the two pictures seems awry when placed together. Could he truly have taken the time to reload? To kill two family members and then stalk the others? Why did they not fight back? What order did they die in? And why the hell did he do it?

McAvoy blows air through his nose and rubs a hand across his face. He flicks a key on the laptop and opens up an internet browser. He's becoming quite familiar with the history of Holderness. Spent a good hour reading about its notable people and places. Has taken a virtual tour around the inside of St Patrick's Church and seen for himself why it is held in such royal regard. Has read about the RAF base in Patrington and the men who were stationed there. It was built during the Second World War, when the coastline was of strategic importance. For a decade it served as a radar station and base for ground-controlled interception. In 1955 it moved to nearby Holmpton. Its former servicemen still return to Patrington for celebrations and anniversaries. To coincide with one recent get-together, the *East Riding Mail* published a special 'Bygones' supplement about wartime in Holderness. It revealed just how important the area was to Churchill's war effort. Told of the network of bunkers and hideouts that would have been used by a special local militia in the event of German invasion. McAvoy had read the story twice and been amazed at the units' sophistication, complexity and secrecy. They were known as Auxiliary Units and were dreamed up in 1940 by a Colonel Colin Gubbins. These highly secretive units were trained in all aspects of guerrilla warfare. They were taught to kill and disappear. To make and detonate bombs. And they were made up of local men hand-picked from the Home Guard. Of farmers, butchers and bakers. Of men too old to fight in the front line. They signed the Official Secrets Act and trained for a battle they would never fight. McAvoy wonders whether his grandfather knew about their existence. There was an Auxiliary Unit in the Western Highlands. How the hell did people manage to keep secrets like that? These days, anybody asked to dig a secret bunker for the government would be updating their Facebook status on their smartphones before their shovel even bit the dirt.

McAvoy checks the time on the corner of the laptop screen. Looks at his phone. Gives a sigh. He hates people being unpunctual, even if he always manages to make good excuses for them in his head. Starts counting backwards from a hundred, just for something to do . . .

His phone rings. A foreign number, complete with a lot of zeros.

'Detective Sergeant Aector McAvoy. Serious and Organised.'

'G'day, Sergeant. How you going?'

Vaughn Winn's voice is chatty and very Australian. He's in his late sixties now but his words come out bright and sparky. His email, too, had been amiable and light. He'd responded to McAvoy within half an hour. Promised to ring when he got out of his morning meeting and had a bit of time to himself. Apologised for the time difference and asked if it was OK.

'I'm very grateful for your returning my call, Mr Winn. As I explained, we're—'

'It's just Vaughn, mate. Mr Winn was my dad.'

McAvoy stops. Doesn't quite know what to say.

'You there, mate? Is this line all right?'

McAvoy takes a breath and starts again. Outlines what he is doing. Promises to get some answers for the family. Can't guarantee a conviction but hopes the older man realises how seriously Humberside Police take murder, even after all these years.

When McAvoy stops talking there is silence at the end of the line.

'You reckon it's worth it?' asks Vaughn eventually. 'After all these years? They've talked about this in the past, mate. Never came to nothing. And people's memories get hazy after a few years. I mean, I appreciate it and all, but I reckon you've got the shitty end of the stick.'

McAvoy chews on his lower lip. He had been hoping Vaughn would give him some encouragement. Tell him he is doing the right thing.

'Well, as I said, we are only doing some preliminary work to gauge the likelihood of securing a conviction against Peter Coles . . .'

127

'But he's locked up already, isn't he? I mean, why move him from one cell to another? What would be the point?'

McAvoy watches the channel marker move slightly on the waters. Watches a crooked smile of moonlight ripple on its surface. Wonders how to make a decent argument when you don't agree with your own opinions.

'We have no idea what the outcome of these investigations will be, sir. I contacted you out of courtesy and I personally believe it's important for justice to be seen to be done. He killed four people, sir. Perhaps he should be sentenced for it.'

Vaughn makes a musing sound, as though mulling it over. McAvoy can almost hear him shrugging.

'You got new evidence or something? New techniques?'

'No, sir, we believe the initial investigation was handled effectively. I'm just double-checking the case that would have been brought against Peter Coles had he not been declared insane.'

Vaughn clears his throat, noisily. In the background, McAvoy can hear the squawking of some unpleasant-sounding bird. Tries to get a picture of where the other man may be sitting or standing at this moment. He knows that Vaughn owns several properties in Queensland. Has his main residence at a little place called Noosa Heads, an hour or two from Brisbane. McAvoy has found a handful of images of him online. He's a good-looking older guy, with a full head of hair that turns up at the front in a luxurious quiff. His skin is tanned and teeth a bright white. In each of the images he looks fit and healthy: all linen suits, deck shoes and designer sunglasses. He's made a decent living since moving to Australia in the wake of his family's death. Opened a business transforming unused or sub-standard grain from the area's giant breweries into animal feed. Won some big contracts and eventually supplied half the coast. Mixed up some special batches for the equestrian community and won an endorsement from a national showjumping star. Made a mint and put his cash into houses and good causes. Sends money home to Holderness whenever a charity needs a boost. He seems a good man. A hard worker. Single and childless, according to what McAvoy found, but seemingly happy enough.

'Daft Pete was always a nutter, mate. Long before that night. You know we were mates, don't you? Well, near as dammit, anyways. I knew him pretty well and he always had a screw loose.'

'Did you ever fear for your family's safety?' asks McAvoy, sensing an opportunity to hear the words that would make him feel better.

'Nah, he was just a bit of a nuisance,' says Vaughn conversationally. 'Never grew up, I suppose. Liked to play in the woods and shoot rabbits and talk about racing drivers and look at mucky books. I didn't think there was any harm in him. My brother was a bit younger than him and a lot cleverer than me and he'd mentioned a few times that he thought Daft Pete had what people call a personality disorder nowadays. Maybe he did. I just know that when I heard they had been killed, Daft Pete wasn't the first name I thought of.'

'Who was?' asks McAvoy, softly.

Vaughn gives a little laugh. 'I thought it must be random nutters. Burglars. Somebody waking them up in the middle of the night and it all turning bad. That at least made some sort of sense. Dad wasn't poor. He kept a lot of money in the house and we had a lot of valuable things. I sold most of them when I moved and it came to a decent sum. And with the house so out of the way it made sense that somebody would have tried to rob them. I could imagine Dad fighting back. My brother too. Even Mum was a scrapper when her blood was up. Then they told me the full story. About where they were found. About Daft Pete. I felt like the ground was caving in, I really did.'

McAvoy takes a breath. Holds it. Tries to order his thoughts.

'How many people knew that your father kept money in the house?'

'No idea, mate,' says Vaughn. 'It was a big posh house. You'd see it and presume, y'know. And we had people in and out of there all the time. We had the tenants in the cottages. There was always people coming to see Dad. He never felt afraid in his own house, though. He was a formidable man. And he had a shotgun of his own. Ironic, really, eh?'

McAvoy cradles the phone between shoulder and neck and starts typing words into the laptop. He's recording the call but finds that taking notes helps him put bookmarks in the swirl of his thoughts.

'How did your father feel about Peter Coles?'

'Felt sorry for him, I reckon. Like I say, Dad was formidable but he had a kind side. He came from poor stock, you see. Made his money as a young man. Did what I did, I guess. Buying and selling. Hard work.'

'Am I right in thinking he made armaments during the war?'

'You are,' says Vaughn. 'Money to be made all over during that time. I hadn't come along yet, of course. He was still young and free. But he had an eye for a profit. Knew what he wanted. That's what Mum said about when she caught his eye. He was down from the north-east for some job or another. You know how badly Hull got a battering, don't you? He made a fortune in scrap after that. Anyways, Mum was just a normal Hessle Road girl. And he was a right flash soul. Whisked her off her feet. Fell for her in a big way. Gave her everything she wanted. And what she wanted most was a quiet life in the middle of nowhere. So he got her that. Became Lord of the Manor. That's why he tried to help Daft Pete, mate. Just liked to spread the wealth.'

'Vaughn, there is a good chance I will have other questions for you as the investigation progresses. Would it be possible for us to remain in touch so I can keep you up to date with the investigation?'

Vaughn makes an affirmative noise that goes up at the end. He betrays few of his East Yorkshire roots in the way he speaks.

'Thank you. I think we can leave it there.' McAvoy is about to terminate the call when he remembers something. 'Oh, Vaughn, just to be certain, can you confirm your own movements in the few days surrounding the date in question? I seem to have a couple of conflicting reports on what day you returned to Newcastle.'

Vaughn makes a clucking noise, flicking his tongue against the roof of his mouth. 'Was so long ago. I'd been home, I remember that. Seen Mum and Dad. I was working away, you see. Doing some office work for an old friend of the family in Newcastle. Only got home now and again. I'd brought some new shoes for Annie. Anastasia, that is. My sister. Bit of a present from her big brother. Was there a day or so, then had to get back. It was at least a day after they were killed that anybody got in touch with me. Can't remember much other than that. It was a crazy time. I didn't want to be there. I didn't know what to do with myself. Couldn't even face the funeral. I suppose that's why I've spent so much money on the church – because I was too much of a coward to go back. The headstone's beautiful. Have you seen the engraving I got them on the floor of the nave? I know it doesn't make up for it but I can't go back, can I?'

McAvoy is nodding. He's listening but is suddenly feeling sleepy. Can almost feel the warmth of the Australian sun upon him. Tells himself off for not paying attention. Not engaging with this man's pain. Sits up and makes the right noises.

'Perhaps we can make amends now. If we get a conviction. Get the full story. Get the truth.'

Vaughn seems about to say something, but a sudden burst of conversation at the other end of the line cuts him off. McAvoy hears a female voice. Mumbled words. Tries to make them out but hears nothing but static.

'Vaughn? Sir?'

'We'll see, eh, Sergeant?' says Vaughn, sudden and too loud. 'I don't know how I feel about any of this. But I appreciate the call and will help however I can. Just try not to dig up more than you have to, eh? I buried them a long time ago and I still hear their voices in my dreams. I've put 13,000 miles between us and I don't think it's far enough.'

McAvoy is about to reply when the call cuts off. He stares at his phone and slowly puts it away. He lowers himself back onto the grass. A sudden gust of wind rushes in from the river. The clouds change shape.

McAvoy feels the first drops of rain on his face at the same moment as he watches the star wink out.

He stands and walks back through the downpour to the room where his son sleeps. Opens the door and lays down beside the boy, fully clothed, and damp, front and back.

He strokes Fin's hair back from his face.

Feels his eyes grow heavy.

A whisper, in the dark.

'Sweet dreams, Roisin.'

He kisses the air.

Falls asleep staring at the ceiling through a veil of tears.

# Chapter 9

It's the look in Downey's eyes that Helen Tremberg can't forget. She can't remember the colour. Couldn't say whether the terror was inked on a canvas of green, blue or brown. But she remembers what they contained. Remembers gazing into absolute certainty: seeing the look of somebody who knows that hell is just seconds away.

He was a bad man, of course. He'd helped take a life. He would have taken hers if he could. But in the instant that he knew he was going to die, he suddenly looked very young, and very scared.

Helen can't shake that image. Can't help wondering if she looked the same. Whether her own eyes were wide and teary as the grenade hit the floor and she threw herself in the first direction that felt like 'away'.

She shakes it from her mind as she crosses Ferensway. She's eating a cinnamon pretzel from the shop in the train station to her rear and wishing she had a coffee to wash it down with. Her lips are sugary and her fingers sticky. She pushes in the last mouthful, then scoops up some standing rainwater from the top of the metal barriers in the centre of the busy road. Washes her hands and dries them on her jeans. Pushes her hair back from her face and straightens her jumper, scarf and purple woollen trenchcoat. Brushes the crumbs from her front.

Colin Ray is waiting for her outside the department store on the corner of Jameson Street. He gives her a nod as she approaches and holds out a takeaway coffee for her. It's an oddly generous thing for him to do, but Helen is nothing if not well-raised and takes it from him gratefully.

'It's got a flavour in it,' he says, ill-at-ease. 'Thought you might like it.'

Helen sips her drink. It tastes of vanilla and isn't at all bad. She gives a thin-lipped smile and considers her senior officer. He looks like he's made an effort. He's wearing cords and his work shoes, with a battered linen jacket over a striped polo shirt. He's got his raincoat on; darker at the shoulders than below the waist. He's been here, in this rain, for a while.

'We said ten, didn't we? I'm not late . . .'

'It's fine, pet. I had nowhere to be.'

Helen doesn't know what to say, so just sips her drink and wonders what the hell she is doing here. These past weeks have been hard. When she left the hospital she spent a few weeks living with her parents, and that experience alone had made her determined to get better as soon as possible. She has been back in her own little bungalow for a month now. She's eating properly. The stitches have healed and her stomach wall seems to have repaired itself without the need for the surgery the consultants feared when she was first brought in. She suffered puncture wounds and lacerations. Took a bad blow to the back of the head and the top of the shoulder as the ceiling fell in.

Even the paramedics who found her had used the word 'miraculous'. But she feels well enough to return to work – whatever that work may be. The past couple of weeks have seen her climbing the walls with boredom and frustration. She has been desperate to pick up the phone, call Trish Pharaoh and demand to be allowed to resume her duties. But Helen isn't sure she will ever be able to call herself a policewoman again. She has made mistakes in her life. The Headhunters have something over her that could cost Helen her career and even her liberty. She needs them brought down. And while she considers Colin Ray to be a vile and dangerous specimen, she had agreed to meet him without a second thought.

'You heard from him since yesterday?' asks Colin, producing a cup of tea from the windowsill behind him and taking a sip. 'Mr Mouthpiece?'

Helen shakes her head. She hasn't heard from him since she left the hospital. And the flowers he sent had gone straight in the bin.

'He's fucked up,' he says, as if to reassure himself. 'You're young. You know all this technical shit. We must be able to trace where he was when he made that call. I mean, he was within spitting distance. I heard the ambulance. I heard it.'

Helen spreads her hands. 'I said when you called, sir. I said that Dan in Tech Support could do all kinds of marvels. We can trace phones and with the agreement of the service provider we can ping people's phones and find out where they're at. You've got the number he rang you on, but if we ping that phone we both know it will be like all the others – ditched. They know what they're doing. He changes his phones after every call. We've tried all that, sir.'

Ray wipes his nose with the back of his hand. 'He was somewhere nearby. Here, listen.'

He pulls the recording device from his pocket and hands it to Helen. His eyes take in the scar to her wrist. She can see him wondering whether it was caused in the blast or whether she has tried to bump herself off. The wound is older than her most recent injuries. It was put there by a killer and Helen wears it with a degree of pride.

She listens to the recording. Tries not to shudder as she hears the voice of the man who set her up, manipulated her, and who in all likelihood still possesses a video clip that would end her days in the police if ever released.

'He hasn't changed his patter,' she says, handing the tape recorder back. 'Still talks more than he listens. Still seems to be charging by the word.'

'He's a prick. What we don't know is whether he's realised he's fucked up. He hung up almost the second the ambulance came past. You heard him cut the call. None of his preamble. If he'd kept talking I might not even have realised what it meant.'

Helen finishes her coffee. Ray takes the cup from her as if she were a child. He does it naturally, and Helen finds herself wondering whether he has any children. She curtails the thought before she can picture what his offspring would look like.

'And the ambulance came past the pub a few seconds after he cut if off, yes? You heard it faintly where you were but loud at his end of the line. We should be able to work it out then. I mean, if we had enough people in different spots, each with a mobile, we could surely see how far away from you he was at the moment the ambulance came past.'

Ray shakes his head. 'Too much fuss, love. Not enough people.

And we don't need all that science shite. We can sort this together.'

Helen listens as Ray explains that he has already found out that the ambulance on the previous day had been dispatched from Hull Royal Infirmary and was making its way back there with an elderly patient who had tripped and grazed her shins to the bone while getting into a taxi near the Rugby Tavern, a quarter of a mile away. It had travelled down Alfred Gelder Street and turned right into Lowgate, where it had passed Colin Ray. That meant the call had been made somewhere on Lowgate, or one of the little streets nearby. And Colin had an idea for how to narrow it down.

Ten minutes later, Helen is standing outside the Burlington Tavern. She's near the rear of Marks & Spencer, facing the hideous office buildings that block the broad green expanse of Queen's Gardens. She can hear Colin breathing in her ear.

'Have you got the right table?' she says into the phone. 'Right sort of conditions?'

'Shush,' he says. 'It will be past in a moment.'

Helen listens out. Takes the phone from her ear and hears a distant siren approaching from her left. She raises the tape recorder and presses play. The ambulance flies past her a few seconds later and she hears the tiny tinny sound of Colin Ray swearing and shouting 'No'.

'This is about as scientifically exact as astrology, you realise that,' she says, feeling like an amateur. 'They could be going at different speeds. There could be more background noise today . . .'

'Don't whinge, Detective Constable,' he says, unfairly pulling rank. 'We're doing the best with what we have.'

A few minutes later, Helen has deposited herself in a different part of Lowgate. She's on the other side of the road, leaning against the imposing façade of the old Magistrates Court. It's a wasted space these days but plenty of infamous prisoners have passed through its doors. Some of the women at Hull City Council refuse to go down there for fear of prisoners' ghosts jumping out and spooking them. Helen doesn't believe in ghosts. If she did she wouldn't be able to sleep as soundly as she does – even with the painkillers and anxiety tablets the doctors insist she dose herself up on.

'Is there anybody in Hull doesn't owe you a favour?' she asks, as the driver of the ambulance gives her a thumbs-up and cruises past in silence, returning to the Ruby Tavern for another circuit. 'Is he not going to get into trouble?'

'He's helping the police with their inquiries.'

'You're suspended and I'm on sick.'

'But he doesn't know that. And besides, you're the one who caught the bastard who killed that ex-paramedic a few months ago.'

'No I'm not,' she says, indignant. 'I just—'

'Take the credit, you silly cow. He doesn't know how to use credit. Make sure you do.'

Helen knows whom Ray is referring to. She has a sudden vision of her sergeant. Sees the pitiful gratitude in his eyes as he thanked her for saving his family. Saw him fighting with himself, struggling to keep it all in. She doesn't know how Roisin could have left him. Doesn't like to entertain the disloyal thoughts that sometimes creep up on her as she considers the prospect of McAvoy as a single man.

'Right, play it again . . .'

On the fourth circuit, Ray shouts 'Stop'. Helen lifts the phone to her ear again. She is soaked to the skin, cold and goose-pimpled. Her injuries are starting to hurt and her short bobbed hair is beginning to look like it was cut with a knife and fork.

'Where are you?' asks Ray, excitedly. 'There. It was wherever you fucking are now.'

Helen steps back and looks up at the building. She's almost back where she started. She's between Silver Street and the Burlington Tavern. This is where the solicitors have their offices. It's a place of briefcases and suits, water fountains and yachting magazines discarded on polished coffee tables.

'Well?'

Helen gives him her location. He tells her to wait. A minute later he appears, running arthritically and splashing through puddles.

'Wilde and Machale,' he says, reading the brass nameplate. 'Conveyancing and Consumer Law.'

He looks through the glass. Sees nothing of interest. Steps back and stares up.

'Three bloody floors,' he says. 'And solicitors on all of them. Should we just bomb it?'

Helen gives him a look that suggests she's still not ready for jokes about bombs and Ray has the good grace to wince.

'A lawyer,' he says, biting his lip. 'Fuck, I'm an idiot. The way he talks; the bullshit. All those bloody vowels.'

'Sir, I don't really know what we do with this.' Helen looks around her. 'I mean, what have we got?'

Ray isn't listening. He steps onto the polished tiles of the entrance hall and walks into the front office of Wilde and Machale. Helen sighs and hurries in behind him. She walks into his back. Ray has stopped short in the reception. He is smiling at the girl behind the desk.

Helen follows his gaze. Sees a face she recognises. She's kooky. Dressed like a student with an eye for a bargain. Fruit-pastille earrings and a nose-ring, sweat-bands on her wrists and plastic beads at her throat. Her hair is tied up with a pencil and her glasses are worn halfway down a cute nose.

Colin Ray saw her yesterday, ordering breakfast with two lawyers in his local pub. A few minutes later, Ray had taken the gloating call.

Helen Tremberg knows her from another case. Knows that she has blossoms tattooed on her back and butterflies on her wrists. Knows she nearly died at the hands of a pleasure-seeker.

Suzie Devlin smiles at her visitors. Recognises Helen and gives a wave.

'Hello,' she says, brightly. 'You're a friend of Roisin's, aren't you? Have you seen her? I've been calling.' Her face falls. 'Oh, I'm sorry, it was you, wasn't it? You who saved her ...'

Helen turns to Colin, whose smile almost reaches his ears.

'Take the credit,' he whispers, then turns his back and walks out.

Helen knows what he wants. Wants her to manipulate this girl's gratitude. Wants her to be a detective – whatever that takes.

'Yes,' she says, walking towards the desk, all smiles. 'I suppose so. I was wondering, could you do me a favour ...'

'Do you think she planned the layout with graph paper and a ruler? That's a thing of beauty.'

Trish Pharaoh is admiring the structural engineering skills of a twenty-stone woman who has taken the 'all-you-can-eat' offer at the West Bulls public house as a personal challenge. Her breakfast is a magnificent construction. A nest of beans, bacon, eggs and sausage, divided into separate floors by a supporting wall and ceiling of fried bread.

'You could put that in a gallery,' says Pharaoh, open-mouthed. 'You could put the woman in as well. Jesus, she's getting another hash brown . . .'

They serve a decent breakfast at this pleasant chain pub on the edge of West Hull. It's only a five-minute drive from the police station on Priory Road and Pharaoh is a regular visitor. She woke up on the sofa again this morning. Her youngest daughter had thrown a blanket over her and taken off her boots. Returned in the early hours to pour the last of the red wine down the sink and bring her a fresh orange juice and two paracetamol. They were sitting there when she woke – two eyes in a sad cartoon face.

Pharaoh is still wearing the same clothes as yesterday and put her deodorant and perfume on as she drove the kids to their various pre-school clubs. She did her make-up in the rear-view mirror as she headed towards the Humber Bridge. Flicked a V-sign at the Volvo driver who flashed his lights at her for talking on a mobile while driving. She'd made it in to work by 8.40 a.m. And after reading her emails, necking a coffee and shouting at her computer screen for half an hour, she got back in her car and came for breakfast. She's feeling human again after a decent feed, though she is conscious that there will be a line carved into her middle when she takes her tights off.

The air is greasy with the scent of cooked fat and burned toast. A persistent rain beats against the glass and hammers onto the uneven tarmac of the car park beyond. Some easy-listening is tinkling quietly from the speakers, competing for aural supremacy with the sound of clattering knives and forks and the low murmur of half-chewed conversation.

'I think she's drinking Diet Coke. She is! That's brilliant!'

Pharaoh's breakfast companion is her old boss, Tom Spink. He's an elegant, sixty-something chap in soft cords and a collar-less shirt who now makes a living writing local history books and running a guest house on the crumbling Holderness coast. Chances are it will be underwater within a decade, but Tom doesn't put that on the marketing materials.

'Should we ask for her autograph?' he asks, smiling. 'She could scrawl her name in your notebook.'

'Could we get her to use a sausage?'

The pair drag their attentions away from the large lady, who is working her way through her breakfast in a manner that is both determined and workmanlike.

'Makes you proud to be northern, doesn't it?'

'I'm sure they have fat bastards in the south.'

'Yeah, but we take it more seriously. There's a pride in it.'

Tom sips at his tea and examines his protégée. She's done damn well. Risen higher than he ever did. Blossomed from a hard-as-nails WPC into a hard-as-nails detective superintendent. Tom is happy to admit he first took her under his wing because he fancied her, but twenty years on he thinks of her more as a daughter than anything else. He's proud to see how she's climbed the ladder, despite the old-boy network and the accu-sations she was sleeping her way to the top. Spink knows the truth. Knows that she was far more loyal to her husband than he was in return. Knows that every time she came back to the force from maternity leave she had done her prospects more harm, but she kept catching crooks until the men upstairs had no option but to promote her. Tom had had words in a few ears to ensure the job as head of Serious and Organised went her way, but she got the role on merit and has had some solid results, despite the best efforts of some of her underlings. She's a good copper. The best. He hates that her personal life is seamed with unhappiness. Her prick of a husband made some bad investments and went bankrupt. The stress of it all caused him a massive aneurism and he has been a living ghost in the lives of his wife and daughters ever since. Pharaoh and her family are crammed together into a nondescript semi-detached in Grimsby and what little money she has left over, after paying the mortgage and her daughters' various childminders, goes on paying back her husband's debts. It's no wonder she still has red wine in the cracks in her lips. No wonder she has started lighting one cigarette with the tip of her last one.

'Have you heard from him today?' asks Tom conversationally. 'Your warrior poet?'

Pharaoh sticks her tongue out at him and takes a slurp of coffee. 'He doesn't have to check in with me every five minutes, you know. I'm not his mum. Or his wife.'

'No,' says Tom, holding her gaze. 'No, you've squirrelled his wife away and won't tell him where she is.'

Pharaoh plays with the bangles on her right wrist and keeps her eyes on Tom's. 'I've not squirrelled anybody. I've responded to a legitimate threat.'

Tom nods. He enjoys needling her, but wonders if this may be a topic about which she does not have a sense of humour. 'How did he take the news about big Bruno?'

Pharaoh looks away. Rests her head against her coffee cup and closes her eyes, suddenly tired.

'He was quiet, I suppose. You know how he is. Just thanked me for telling him and asked if I was OK. He was never going to start cheering.'

'Did he ask about the ramifications?'

Pharaoh gives a little smile. 'That was precisely the word he used, yes. He wanted to know the "ramifications" for Roisin. What could I tell him? I don't know the bloody ramifications. We're going through Bruno's possessions and trying to access the hard drive on his home computer. We've got his mobile phone in the Tech unit. We're trying to make some sense of what we found.'

Tom finishes his cup of tea and wipes his mouth with a napkin. 'You think it was Bruno who took the picture of her in the hospital bed? You think he was the one who was making the threats?'

Pharaoh pushes her hair back from her face. 'You know I don't think that. I've never thought that. Bruno was muscle. He was a thug. He was nothing to the Headhunters. The message I got was clear. Roisin has got a bullseye on her back. Somebody wants her dead.'

'But a copper's wife? Why go to so much trouble?'

Pharaoh shrugs. 'Maybe because she's a copper's wife.'

McAvoy and Pharaoh have never had much of a conversation about how Roisin came to the Headhunters' attention, but Pharaoh has pieced it together. She took some money from one of their dealers when he threatened her friend. She embarrassed him. And when he came to exact vengeance he ballsed it up and blew himself to bits. That cost the Headhunters. It inconvenienced

145

them. It made them look amateurish. And for an organisation run like a business, it made for unacceptably poor publicity.

'So she can't come home until you've brought the whole bloody empire to its knees? At some point you have to come up with a Plan B, Trish.'

Pharaoh breathes out heavily through her nose. 'How did she take it about Bruno?' she asks. 'Roisin?'

Tom gives a smile. 'Bit more enthusiastic about it than her husband. Asked if Bruno suffered and seemed pleased to know that he had. Then she started asking about Aector. Usual stuff.'

For the past three months, Roisin McAvoy has been living in an apartment in Sheffield owned by a landlord friend of Tom's. Tom has been pretty much her only contact with the outside world. He takes food for her and baby Lilah. Takes them out for the occasional quiet and uncomfortable drive. Reminds her, daily, of the importance of keeping her head down and not contacting her husband, no matter how badly she wants to. Promises her, time and again, that Aector and Fin are OK. Missing her, loving her, but OK. And then he drives back to East Yorkshire feeling the worst kind of bastard.

'You could let her come home,' says Tom quietly, into the silence. 'Not every threat has to be taken seriously. You could put a uniform on the door for a couple of weeks. And Aector would be a decent guard dog, don't you think? He wouldn't sleep.'

Pharaoh gives a tiny nod. She knows that she can't keep Roisin hidden away much longer. She should either make the arrangement official and have her taken into witness protection permanently, or she should let her return to her husband. But Pharaoh believes in the threat to Roisin's life. There had been something unequivocal about the way it had been made. Somebody high up in the organisation wanted her dead. And even the posh-voiced man at the end of the phone had been unable to dissuade them. He had given Trish a chance to keep her safe. And she had taken it.

'How's he getting on, anyways?' asks Tom. 'Rob Roy. This old case he's on.'

Pharaoh rolls her eyes. Tom has a thing for nicknames. Has called her 'Nefertiti' ever since meeting the young WPC Patricia Pharaoh. He had refused to let her change her name when she married. Said it was far too fabulous a moniker to be meddled with.

'He's doing his thing, I think. Talking to little old ladies. Being polite and blushing a lot. Bumbling his way along.'

'Bumbling?'

'You know what I mean. He's too big to be unobtrusive. He's a bull in a china shop but he's an apologetic bull. He knocks stuff over and offers to pay for the damage.'

Tom grins. 'What do the Home Office really want, do you think?'

Pharaoh shrugs. 'They want him to say that the officers did a good job back in the bad old days, but with the passage of time the likelihood of securing a conviction without a confession is zero. They can tell that to their boss. He can feel better and salve his conscience. And Peter Coles can slip from memory.'

'They'd let him go?' asks Tom, surprised.

'He's never been convicted of murder. He'll go into some halfway house. Get a new name, no doubt. Social Services will keep an eye on him and as long as the papers don't get wind of what's going on, nobody will be any the wiser.'

147

'And if the papers do get wind of it?'

Pharaoh pulls a face. 'That could be complicated.'

Tom licks some butter from his thumb and straightens the dirty plates in front of him. 'So Aector's on a bit of a hiding to nothing. He can't really come out of it ahead, other than by giving them exactly what they want. He'll just have to hope that really is the truth of the matter.'

Pharaoh nods. 'It was nearly fifty years ago. People's memories get hazy. If Peter Coles didn't do it, whoever did will be probably be long gone.'

'That's still a bit shit for Peter Coles though.'

'Yeah,' says Pharaoh. 'But shitty stuff happens to people a lot of the time.'

'That's good enough for you and me, Trish. It won't be good enough for him.'

'For Peter Coles?'

'For Aector.'

They sit in silence for a moment. Pharaoh watches the other patrons of the large, single-storey pub and tries to identify with them. A group of mums with pushchairs and wriggly toddlers are juggling knives, forks, spoons and offspring as they chat and gossip and spoon scrambled egg into their tired-looking faces. Two workmen in blue overalls sit opposite one another reading matching copies of the *Hull Mail* and shaking their heads at some story on page five about further delays in the city's pothole improvement scheme. The fat woman with the tower-block of hash browns is looking at the dessert menu. Pharaoh doesn't see criminals and victims. She just sees people. Good, bad and indifferent. Any one of them could lose their temper and become a murderer. Any one of them could say the wrong thing at the wrong time and end up on a slab, tagged at the toe. She doesn't see any end to any of it. Doesn't know if there should be one.

*This is life*, she thinks. *And a lot of it's shit.*

'The photo of the meeting room in London,' says Tom. 'That took some balls. Have you shown it to Breslin yet?'

Pharaoh shakes her head. 'I need to think on it.'

'If he knows you've waited . . .'

'I'll get shouted at again. I get shouted at a lot. I shout back.'

'What are you thinking?' asks Tom. 'One of the other officers in the room? Any candidates?'

Pharaoh pulls an electric cigarette from her bag and takes a puff. She lets out her breath in a sigh.

'I think there's a north-east connection. But the lad from Newcastle seemed legit. I don't want to start slinging mud.'

Tom nods. It's a hard position to be in. Pharaoh phoned him last night to update him on her day and ask for some help following the phone call from the Headhunters. The message had come through half an hour after Pharaoh had hung up on their representative. She now knows what they want in return for keeping Roisin McAvoy out of the gunsights. They wanted to know about the assets of Francis Nock. Specifically, properties registered in his name and in the names of his associates. They would be very grateful. Tom worked in the north-east for a spell. He makes a living as a researcher and writer. He is also Trish Pharaoh's friend. He had been happy to agree to a spot of breakfast and a quick briefing on his knowledge of the old boy who has been the boss of bosses in his corner of England for fifty years.

'You think they're having difficulties? The Headhunters?'

Pharaoh smiles. 'I get the impression their usual modus operandi isn't working this time. You know how they work. They get into the lives of the coppers who are chasing them. They offer cash, reward or threat. We've seen what they can do. But if Mr Nock is really the legend I've been hearing about, then perhaps the cops up there aren't playing ball. Maybe they're saying no. That's why the Headhunters have come to me.'

'But why do they expect you to play ball?'

Pharaoh gives a joyless laugh. 'Because I'm losing, Tom. We've given them a few kicks but barely hurt them. They know we need to be seen to be making progress. They know my team is scattered to the four winds. They think I'll play nicely because not playing nicely is going very badly.'

Tom thinks it over. 'Could you even get them what they asked for? If there was any internal inquiry it wouldn't take much to find out who had been snooping and who hadn't.'

'I know,' says Pharaoh. She winces and looks at her friend. 'But a writer could make a few phone calls without it being seen as too out of order . . .'

Tom gives a bark of laughter. 'I've already got Roisin McAvoy hidden away for you, Nefertiti. I don't know how many more times I can lie to the missus about where I'm going. She already thinks I've got a fancy piece.'

'You?' asks Pharaoh, grinning. 'You'd wear out the knees in your cords. C'mon Tom, you know you're interested.'

The retired detective rolls his eyes and lets out a breath. 'You do know that Francis Nock is old-school, don't you? I mean, proper old-school. You hurt him, you disappear. You try to rob him, they find bits of your body all over the north-east. He doesn't mess around.'

'He's in his eighties, Tom. How much trouble can he be causing these people?'

'They tried to get one of his top men to turn on him and Nock found out. You told me they found the poor sod's arm! You don't think that's a bit of a warning to anybody else thinking of having their head turned by the new boys? Francis Nock used to dine with the big boys, Trish. He may have got old but he's never changed. And if he's still got his monster . . .'

'Mahon,' says Trish, nodding. 'They mentioned him at the briefing. I looked him up on the PNC. Interesting record. Not much of a looker.'

'No,' says Spink. 'Only met him the once when I was up in Newcastle. I was a detective sergeant. There had been a glassing at a snooker hall. We went to speak to the owner and Mahon was there. I'd never seen a face like that on a human being before. And his skin. Jesus. It looked like pink meringue. He was very polite. Very quiet. Just told us that the previous owner was no longer working at the establishment. Didn't have a forwarding address. Asked me for a card and promised to pass on my details. I had to crane my neck to look up at him and then it was an effort not to look away. He was a terror, Trish. I don't scare, y'know that. But he chilled you to the middle.'

'The snooker hall belonged to Mr Nock?'

'No,' says Tom, shaking his head. 'It belonged to a city councillor. On paper, Nock was nothing to do with the place. But it was clearly under his protection. Mahon was that protection.'

'And the manager?'

'Never did track him down. He'll have been removed from the picture. Shouldn't have allowed trouble in a place under Nock's supervision.'

151

Pharaoh takes another puff on the electric cigarette. 'So we're not giving up a saint if we give the Headhunters what they want,' she says quietly.

'But you must know why they want it.'

'Of course I do,' says Pharaoh, in a hiss of temper. 'They want to find the old bastard. They've tried to have him removed politely. They sent one of their boys to turn Lloyd's head and he's gone AWOL. Lloyd's dead. They've got internal problems and they like things to run smoothly. Now they want to get rid of him the old-fashioned way. They just don't know where to look.'

'And you'd give them a place to start? Truly?'

Pharaoh looks away, angry and frustrated. 'I don't know. It would just be a list of properties. Half of it would be in the public domain anyway. You could ask a few old pals. Tell them you're doing a book on the time the Geordies turned away the London gangsters, or something. Play to their egos. Get a bit of juice.'

Tom sucks on his lower lip. 'Word would get back to him. He'd know people were trying to find him.'

Pharaoh opens her arms, palms exposed. 'Exactly! So if we can trade a bit of information for a bust or two and some harder information on the threat to Roisin, we use it. And Nock's people know to move him somewhere not on the list.'

Tom has bent a few rules in his career. He's a pragmatist. Doesn't hold too much of a moral code but knows right from wrong. This doesn't feel terribly wrong, in the grand scheme of things.

'You couldn't tell him,' he says quietly. 'Your prince. If it led to her coming home, he could never know the cost . . .'

Pharaoh looks down into the bottom of her empty coffee cup and gives a sad smile.

'He'd agree,' she says, with a conviction she almost believes. 'For her, he'd do whatever it took.'

Tom shakes his head, uncertain. 'But what about you? You're the straightest copper I've ever met. You've never left yourself open like this, Trish. This could cost you . . .'

She meets his gaze, then looks away. Thinks of the way her reflection swims in McAvoy's big, sad eyes and how it would feel to be protected in those huge arms.

'I'd do whatever it took as well, Tom.'

'For her?'

'For him.'

153

# Chapter 10

McAvoy arrived early for his chat with John Glass. Early enough to be considered rude. Left his car on the opposite side of the wide, green space and walked, as slowly as he could, towards the swings and slides at the far end of the park. Spent a minute watching a squirrel fighting a magpie at the base of a knobbly tree. Managed to step in a puddle that soaked his left foot up to the ankle. Watched as a Polish family sat and shivered in the rain; the children slipping from the wet climbing frames into the soaking woodchips as their parents silently passed a sandwich back and forth.

He leans against the railings. Shakes more water from his sock. Pushes his damp hair back from his face and looks up at a sky that looks like muddy snow.

He's still got a few minutes to kill. Doesn't want to hang around the park for too long. It's a nice enough area, on the edge of the Avenues. It's the sort of place where residents will ring the police to report a suspected paedophile rather than just chasing him down the street with a stick, but McAvoy could do without having to deal with either option.

He walks around the duck pond. He was last here a year ago. The water was frozen over and a group of teens were daring each other to run across it. Fin had asked Daddy whether he was going to tell them off. McAvoy had been mulling over whether it was his duty to save them from themselves when Roisin sprinted across the surface of the ice without leaving a footprint. She gave a bow as she put her feet on the concrete. Got a round of applause from the teens.

McAvoy plods past the little brick hut that sells ice cream in the summer months. Watches leaves fall from the high syca-mores. Kicks through a carpet of gold and brown to the grey footpath and checks his watch again.

Pearson Park is only a mile from the city centre, in an area that prides itself on being a little more sophisticated and cosmopolitan. It has wine bars. Some decent restaurants. The pubs sell olives and nibbles and put together charcuterie plat-ters on big wooden chopping boards. It's an area where people take their recycling seriously and dinner parties are competi-tive things. The Liberal Democrats do well here. Students and immigrants take the flats in the grand Victorian properties that line the nearby streets. Web designers and marketing consultants take the houses. Children with names like Emily and Frederick sit down to evening meals of tagliatelle in home-made pesto.McAvoy looks around him. At the properties that ring the park. No two are the same. They've been adapted and extended, pulled down and redesigned. Some have been turned into apartments and others remain detached properties, hiding behind leylandii trees and big, gravelled drives. The poet Philip Larkin lived at number 32 while librarian at the University of Hull. He wrote of the 'palsied old step-takers' and 'hare-eyed clerks' who jerked erratically around the park as they shrugged off the toad of work. McAvoy fancies that the great poet would have something equally unpleasant to say about those who inhabit it today. He wonders what Larkin would make of him. Mincemeat, probably.

McAvoy's steps take him towards the far end of the park. A squat, rectangular building looms to his left. It's an ugly construction, at odds with the faded Victorian splendour of its surroundings. It looks like it was built in the 1960s and designed by an architect on a tight deadline. It's been John Glass's home for the past twelve years. He's lived alone since his wife died.

McAvoy presses the buzzer on the outside door. Waits for a moment until a dry voice crackles through the intercom.

'You the copper?'

'Yes, sir. Detective Sergeant—'

McAvoy is buzzed in before he can finish the sentence. Makes his way to apartment two. The door wings open as he approaches.

Glass is still tall, for his age. He's withered a little, but still stands with a straight back. He has one knobbly and liver-spotted hand on the door-jamb. His thin wrist protrudes from a woollen cardigan with a harlequin pattern, which he wears over a plain shirt and vest. He's wearing grey trousers with a neat seam and comfy Velcro plimsolls. He still has some hair on top, but it is thin and perfectly white and looks as though it will stand up on a light breeze. He's not smiling, but his gaze is far from aggressive.

'John Glass,' he says, as McAvoy approaches. 'Christ, you're a big bugger.'

McAvoy takes the man's hand. He's careful not to crush it. Enfolds it as he would a frightened mouse. He's surprised to feel

Glass's grip is harder than his own. Feels strength in those old, bony fingers.

'Come away in then. I'll get' kettle on.'

McAvoy follows him down a short corridor and past the entrance to a neat and tidy kitchen. Glass shows him into the living room and tells him to make himself comfortable.

'Have a snoop, if you like. I know I would.'

As Glass disappears into the kitchen, McAvoy crosses to the window. The view is mostly of the hedge at the bottom of the garden, though he can see a little of the circular road that rings the park. The view back into the room is better. It's a comfy, homely place. Blue cord carpet and cream walls. There's an imitation log-fire against the far wall and a soft, suede-effect sofa against the other. A rocking chair, complete with doughnut-shaped cushion, is angled to face the boxy TV that sits on a glass unit beneath a large framed print of a racehorse. The other decorations in the room are pastoral in theme. Land-scapes and haystacks, tumbledown farmhouses and ducks on a rippling pond. There are no photos on the wall but a stack of leather-bound albums are at the side of the rocking chair. McAvoy considers picking them up but decides it would be too invasive. Better to wait.

'Mug OK?' asks Glass, handing him a tea brewed strong. 'Not really a cup-and-saucer person, me. And you couldn't get thon big fingers into a cup handle, could you?'

McAvoy smiles and sips his tea. It's got sugar in it. The old man guessed right.

'Is that a hint of Geordie in your voice, Mr Glass?' asks McAvoy, sitting down on the sofa as Glass lowers himself onto the rocking chair.

'Aye, Long Benton was the old stomping ground. Haven't been back up for years but you can't shake an accent, can you? Listen to yours! You sound like that fella. The one that used to sing about the bonny, bonny banks of Loch Lomond. You're further from home than I am, I'd say.'

McAvoy finds himself liking John Glass. He's got character. Seems still to have more than a trace of copper about him in the way he controls the conversation.

'Mr Glass, as I explained on the phone, I'm here to talk to you about . . .'

Glass shushes him with a wave of the hand. He sips his own tea and looks at McAvoy with blue eyes that swim on rheumy, yellowed lenses.

'I've not been a copper since 1983,' he says, conversationally. 'That's a long time to get used to being a civilian. You know how many times a detective has been to see me about some old case I worked on? None, that's how many. I left the job without any unfinished business. Nobody could say I left loose ends.'

'Nobody's suggesting that, Mr Glass . . .' begins McAvoy.

'Shush, lad. Let me speak. I'm saying that it always came as a surprise to me that nobody came asking about Peter Coles. I always expected a judicial review or some charity busybody stirring up the press. I always thought it would come back and cause me a headache. But it never did. Thirty years since I retired. Fifty years since it happened, near as dammit. It was almost a relief when you called. Another couple of years I'll be struggling to remember my own name. Or dead, like as not.'

McAvoy waits a moment to see if it is his turn to speak. Gets a tiny nod from the old man.

'You do remember that night, then, Mr Glass? I have your

original statement here. It would be very helpful if you could run me through your events of that night to see if they still tally with the written record after all this time.'

Glass sucks in a mouthful of breath. Seems to be thinking. Taps his hands on the arm of the chair and jiggles his left leg.

'I said I was home, didn't I? That's crap for a start.'

McAvoy sits back in his chair. Decides to just let the old man talk.

'We had a new boss, you see. Stickler for the rules. Made up a few of his own as well. Ran us like it was the army, and plenty of the lads responded to it well. For me, I reckon he lost sight of what we were really there to do. Got caught up in worrying about how shiny our shoes were. But he had the power to make our lives miserable if we didn't do what he wanted, so a fair few statements got a little bit of a polish. I'm sure you understand.'

McAvoy nods. Smiles. Doesn't endorse the policy but doesn't cause offence either.

'I weren't at home when I heard about the shots being fired at the church. I were in the pub. Having a few jars. Don't ask me how many because I don't remember. I know the last thing I wanted was to have to go out on another call, but that's a rural copper's life. Wasn't easy, fitting in out there. Not with an accent. You'd know all about that. Marks you out as an incomer every time you opened your gob. But I reckon they warmed to me and the missus. And people knew where to find me if I wasn't in the police house.'

'You were in one of the pubs in Patrington?'

'Aye, usual routine. Was always the same faces and a few strangers. People would come to see the church or visit the airbase or stop in on their way to a caravan in Withernsea or

159

whatever. It wasn't the Wild West. We didn't stop playing the piano when an out-of-towner came in. That's what the bloke was. Definitely an out-of-towner.'

'The bloke?'

'Big man. Good-looking. I reckon he was from the same part of the world as me, though I couldn't tell you the exact words he used. Just asked me if I was the local bobby and apologised for interrupting me. Said he'd heard shots fired out at Winestead. Knew it was a rural community and probably didn't mean anything but felt it was his duty to pass it on.'

'I don't think I saw a statement from that person in the file,' says McAvoy, reaching down for the bag at his feet.

'We never got one,' says Glass. 'I went home to get changed into uniform. Got Big Davey to give me a lift out to the church. That's when we found them. And after that it went crazy. By the time I had my wits about me and we were doing things properly, he'd moved on.'

'Were efforts made to find him?'

Glass puts his head to one side, a little pityingly. 'We didn't have CCTV and traces on people's phones in those days, lad. It would have been nice to have a statement but we already had a man in custody and the four dead bodies were the priority. And after the first night I was pretty much excess baggage anyways. Len Duchess oozed his way in and my job was little more than fetching and carrying and apologising to the locals for the fact he was a dickhead.'

McAvoy pulls his notes from his bag. Finds what he's looking for.

'Len Duchess was the detective inspector who led the investigation, yes? I saw his name on several statements. I've requested

160

his personnel file and run some checks to see if he's still on the scene, but nothing's come back.'

'It won't have,' says Glass, with a dry little laugh. 'Wasn't exactly a poster boy for policing after the crackdowns in the seventies. Always was a slick bastard and it caught up with him in the end.'

McAvoy puffs out his checks. He realises his knowledge has gaping holes in it and gestures to the old man that he is willing to be led by the hand until the situation is remedied.

Glass takes a final sip of his tea, wetting his mouth to talk.

'Len Duchess was a southerner. London lad. Not exactly Mr Popular with the lads who worked for him but very much a star in the eyes of the men at the top. Strictly speaking, he should never have been anywhere near the investigation. The inspector from Beverley CID should have got the nod. But Len Duchess happened to be having a drink with the Assistant Chief Constable when the calls started coming through about what had happened and the ACC graciously told Beverley they could borrow the expertise of his specialist murder squad detective. Len was on the scene before the Winn family were cold. Stamped his mark on it and took over. Until then, Peter Coles was playing nicely. Wasn't saying much that made any sense but he was sitting quietly and willing to give us what we wanted. Len steamed in and wound the kid up. We were sitting in one of the cottages on Clarence Winn's estate at that time. Can't remember who it belonged to. I still had the lad tied up with my tie. I'd forgotten my cuffs, you see. Silly of me, I know, and believe me I paid for it. But it was all I could think of to do at the time. Len came in like a bloody demon and started screaming in the lad's face. Pushing him about. Scaring him half to death. Peter just

161

clammed up. Didn't speak again. Len was always one of those coppers who leaned on people. He did it to everybody. Was the same with every witness he went to see. They signed their statements just to get him out of their houses.'

'Do you think anybody signed anything they would no longer consider to be entirely truthful?'

Glass smiles and rubs one hand with the other. 'They'd have sworn they had two heads if he was looming over them. He wasn't a big guy but he had that look. Even the farmhands and men like Big Davey were a bit intimidated by him.'

McAvoy looks at his notes and the statements poking from his bag. He's beginning to wonder how he should start his letter to the Home Office. *Dear Sirs, Following detailed investigation I have concluded that the sixties was a great time to be a criminal . . .*

'Are there any statements or particular witnesses who suggested to you they had given false information? Anybody you think may have been in two minds about the guilt of Peter Coles?'

Glass is silent for a moment. He stares out of the window at the damp hedgerows and miserable sky.

'Len ended up on Nipper Read's squad. Did you know that?'

McAvoy thinks for a moment. 'The man who took down the Kray twins?'

'Very same. They went in hard, did Nipper's boys. Len was a perfect fit.'

'But you mentioned the seventies . . .'

Glass nods. 'Anti-corruption purges. A lot of high performers were put to the sword. Stings all over the place and all the boys who had been accepting envelopes to turn a blind eye were rounded up and booted out.'

'Len Duchess was among them.'

Glass looks like he wants to spit. 'Should have been, from what I'd heard. But he saw the writing on the wall and scarpered before anybody could put the cuffs on him.'

'And now?'

Another shrug. 'Happy ending to the story is that he's living in a nice little villa in Spain with some fat lass feeding him paella. That's not the version of the story I believe. I reckon he ended up in somebody's fried breakfast.'

McAvoy gives a quizzical look.

'Was a favoured disposal method, lad. One particular firm in London. Had a pig farmer on their payroll. They got rid of unwanted personnel for them. You seen what a pig can do to a human body? Can munch the whole lot down. Bones and teeth and everything else. I've never seen it happen but I wouldn't want to neither.'

McAvoy swallows. Tries not to let his thoughts stray or let the pictures in his head become too clear. He looks out of the window, breathing slowly.

'They've given you a right shitty job here, ain't they, lad?'

McAvoy turns back and gives a sigh that turns into a smile as he catches Glass's eye. 'It's proving a little awkward to get specifics,' he says, as tactfully as he can. 'The one thing that seems certain is the culprit. Nobody has suggested anything to the contrary, which is almost a relief. But in terms of building a viable case . . .'

'What do they expect, eh? They should have looked into this years ago. I was the one who found the poor bastards and even I don't think somebody should have been locked up without trial for half a century. And that night cost me a lot. I wasn't in

Patrington for more than a couple of months after that. When the merger came through I ended up in a police box on Myton Bridge in Hull. Spent my days dealing with drunks and scrubbing puke off the door. Dragging people out of that mud by the River Hull. Breaking up fights in the Old Town. Was a bloody treat to retire. And I'm pleased to say I've had more years on a police pension than I gave to the job. Feels like a victory, that.'

McAvoy is looking at the floor, brooding. He's wondering about Len Duchess. Trying not to imagine the sound of pig teeth crunching through a shin bone. Wondering whether he will have to paint John Glass's actions in a negative light when he writes his report for the Home Office.

'There's no real chain of evidence,' says McAvoy, gesturing at his paperwork. 'Half of the crime scene photos are missing. I don't have a single image of the bodies *in situ*. The post-mortem is completely missing and I don't know where to start looking for that. And all I really have is a list of people saying they thought Daft Pete was a bit of an oddball but not really capable of murder. I think this needs more than just me, Mr Glass. Or it needs nobody at all.'

Glass nods. Slowly, he reaches down beside him and retrieves one of the photo albums. He opens it at a page marked with a Post-it note and hands it to McAvoy, who takes it with a puzzled expression.

'Dug it out when you rang,' he says. 'Winter, 1963. Coldest for fifty years. That's the Winn family. And that daft bastard's Peter Coles.'

McAvoy peers at the black-and-white image. A young, slim-hipped man is in the foreground, shovelling thick snow from one pile into another. Behind him, a tall, broad-shouldered man in an expensive woollen coat is standing up to straighten his back. A middle-aged woman in furs is wincing into the cold as she steps across a newly cleared path carrying a tray on which a teapot and six cups sit alongside a silver milk jug and sugar bowl. And in the far right of the picture, an adolescent male in blue overalls and a flat cap is talking to a dark-haired lad in a Harris tweed overcoat and a pretty girl wrapped up against the chill in pale fur.

'Clarence,' says Glass, leaning forward and touching his finger to the older man in the foreground. 'His missus. His youngest, Stephen. Vaughn, Anastasia and Peter. Wouldn't credit it, would you?'

McAvoy looks closely at the picture. There is nothing sinister within the image. Nothing to suggest that the lad with the dungarees would kill four of the other people the camera caught that day.

'You took this?' asks McAvoy.

'The wife. We were new to the village. Trying to make friends. She took photos of everything, she did. Was like a human camera. Cost me a fortune in film. She'd love those new digital cameras. Died before they were invented, poor lass.'

McAvoy would normally offer condolences, but is too lost in the image to make any comment.

'Clarence Winn looks a strong man,' he says speculatively.

'He was. Hard worker. Good man, if it's possible to be such a thing when you're rich.'

'That's what I find hard to understand,' says McAvoy, locking his hands and tapping his thumbs together. 'Without the post-mortem report I can't know whether he fought back. And Coles must have reloaded. So how come nobody tackled him? I know

165

it must have been terrifying, but if he just stumbled into their paths in the wood and killed them so he wouldn't get into trouble . . .'

'. . . Then how did he get them all? I know. I asked.'

'And?'

'Coles hasn't spoken much at all since Len Duchess slapped him about. You should ask him yourself.'

'Coles?' McAvoy looks instantly unsure. 'I don't know how that would be received . . .'

'I can imagine,' says Glass, sympathetically. 'Have yourself a look through the albums if you like. I've got no others of the family, but you might find something interesting. Wish I had a better one of Vaughn for you. Did you say you'd spoken to him? Give him my best if you speak to him again. Doubt our paths will ever cross, but he was always a charmer and he's done well for himself. Nothing if not deserved. Anyway, I'm going for a piss.'

Glass hauls himself from the chair and makes his way towards the living-room door. McAvoy is left alone in the silent room. He drops his head to his hands. Finds himself thinking not terribly charitable thoughts about Trish Pharaoh for landing him with all this, and instantly chides himself for disloyalty.

He begins absent-mindedly to leaf through the album. Sees pictures of a young John Glass with wife and child. Holidays on Bournemouth beach interspersed with candid snapshots of Patrington village life. McAvoy wonders what happened to the child in the photos. Whether they're still in touch with their dad. Whether they ever heard him whimper in the night as he suffered nightmarish recollections of what he found in the grounds of the church that snow-filled night in 1966.

McAvoy examines smiles and changing fashions: Crombie

coats and colourful flares. Watches heels shorten and hemlines lengthen. Watches a couple grow old.

He turns to the final page. Recognises the image. St Germain's Church; shot with the stone angel in the foreground and a watery sun behind.

It seems out of place. Incongruous. Seems almost to have been stuffed in, while the other images are neatly placed behind the clear cellophane.

McAvoy pulls on his lower lip, confused.

Why keep it? Why retain an image of a place with such terrible memories?

He looks at the date, written in black ink on the pale blue sky. 1983. The same year Glass retired from the police force. Had he really used his retirement to make a pilgrimage back to the place where he saw such atrocities? Did that not speak of a man who felt he had unfinished business? Or had he simply taken a photograph of an attractive building while visiting old friends on the remote strip of land he once called home?

McAvoy slides the image from the photo album. Holds it by the edges so as not to leave fingerprints on the surface. Turns it over.

There are four neat crosses, set out in a random constellation.

Three words are written underneath in a shaky, old man's scrawl:

*Count the bodies.*

McAvoy looks up as Glass shuffles back into the room. He locks eyes with the old man. Raises an eyebrow and looks down at the photo in his hand. Glass gives the tiniest of nods. McAvoy puts it in his pocket, and feels the hard thud of his heartbeat as his palm touches his own chest.

'Thank you so much for your time, Mr Glass.'

The old man gives a sad smile. 'I ain't got much of it left, son. Seen the morgue enough times to know when a body's on the way out.'

'I'm sure you're fighting fit, sir.'

'There's no fight in me, Sergeant. Wish there was.'

McAvoy takes a business card from his wallet. Takes one of Pharaoh's too. He leaves them on the windowsill and turns back to Glass. He shakes the old man's hand. Something passes between them. Were McAvoy asked, he would not be able to describe the feeling. But as he makes his way to the front door, he feels as though a fresh weight is settling on his chest.

He doesn't want his thoughts to move in the direction they are drifting. But he cannot help it. As he walks through the rain and across the damp grass, McAvoy finds himself thinking of Peter Coles. Finds himself overlaying the image of the old man in a mental hospital with the young, dull-eyed lad in the photograph. Was it possible? Could he really have been robbed of fifty years? Or was he seeing secrets and lies, shadows and conspiracies, in the place of a simple truth?

McAvoy's head spins with thoughts of corrupt coppers and forced confessions, intimidated witnesses and the crunch of bone. He smells rain and damp earth, crushed leaves and wet wool. He turns the three words over and over and tries to make sense of the strange, cryptic message that seems to be forming into a fist in his shirt pocket.

McAvoy doesn't feel the gaze upon him.

Doesn't sense himself being watched by the one, amber-tinted eye of a man who has inhaled the last breaths of countless dying men.

Doesn't sense Mahon, as he stands in John Glass's living room and stares through the gloom at his dwindling shape.

Doesn't look around at the monster who is burning fresh holes in his broad, scarred back. Doesn't see Mahon scoop the business cards from the windowsill and slide them into his wallet.

Doesn't see him turn back to John Glass, and smile.

# Chapter 11

Mahon doesn't like this city, with its wet, chilly air: its heat-haze of some undefined gloom.

'Itching for home, I am,' says Mahon, turning away from the window. 'Nice to get away but always better to get back, I always say. Mr Nock does too. Or at least, he used to.'

John Glass is still sitting in the rocking chair. His lips are pressed tightly together. It looks as though he is biting down hard on an expression of fear. His eyes betray him. Terror has turned his pupils to pinpricks.

'He's a big bastard, isn't he?' says Mahon, jerking a thumb over his shoulder at the retreating figure. 'Little on the inside, though. Couldn't hear half of what he said. I was expecting some sort of sergeant-major voice. Came as a shock, it did. And at our age, John, we don't need shocks.'

'I played along,' says Glass, with a dry wheeze in his throat. 'I had to give him something. It would have seemed like I was being awkward. Everything I gave him he knew already and the other bits were just to show willing . . .'

Mahon holds up a hand to stop him. He bears John Glass no

ill will. He even feels for the poor old sod. Lost his wife. Living in a faceless apartment all by himself. And now, in his dotage, answering the door to a man he hasn't seen in fifty years. A man willing to do harm.

'You did fine, John. Don't worry. We've always thought of you as reliable. You were worth every penny, my friend.'

Glass screws up his face. 'I don't . . . What money? I never took a penny from anybody.'

Mahon pauses for a moment. Then he barks a laugh.

'Cheeky bastard! That Len was a card, wasn't he? I almost wish the crooked fucker was still alive. Would give me a chance to kill him myself.'

Glass clears his throat but the cough bursts a dam and for almost a full minute he is racked by wet, hacking sounds. His face turns red and his eyes run. His hands begin to shake. Mahon goes to the kitchen and returns with a glass of water, held in a large, gloved hand. Glass takes it gratefully and sips, only to cough the liquid back onto his chin.

'Jesus, John. Take it easy. Breathe slowly, mate. In through the nose, out through the mouth. Relax, yeah? Relax.'

As Glass's breathing begins to slow, Mahon drops onto the seat that McAvoy vacated. He sinks a little into his clothes.

'Len really never slipped you a bob or two? Crafty bastard.'

Mahon stares at the picture above the fireplace. Gives a shake of his head. Len Duchess earned good money. He had never needed to swindle Mr Nock or any of the other firms who lined his pockets. But some people are corrupt to the bone.

'He said you understood,' says Mahon. 'Said you were on board, bonny lad. Said he'd given you a couple of packets to salve your conscience. I am sorry, John. This must feel even more unfair, given you've never seen a penny.'

Glass has taken on the appearance of a scared old man. He seems smaller since McAvoy left. What strength he had was used up keeping the anxiety from his face as they chatted. Mahon had been in the next room, listening at the door. Glass doesn't recall seeing a gun. Nor a blade. Mahon hadn't even threatened him, really. Just stood there at the front door and given his grotesque, scarred smile. Glass had known immediately. Known, since the copper called him the night before, that the events of fifty years ago were about to be brought back into the light.

'You're him, aren't you?' says Glass, wetly. 'From the pub . . .'

'I was prettier then,' says Mahon, with a smile. 'Wasn't sure you'd recognise me. Thought I'd have to go through a whole rigmarole of threatening you and telling you what would happen to you and your loved ones if you suddenly decided to succumb to honesty. But you're still on the ball, aren't you? I'm pleased you're on my wavelength. Makes things easier.'

Glass says nothing. His chest hurts and his legs have started to jiggle of their own accord. He needs a piss. Couldn't squeeze a drop out when he excused himself to give McAvoy a chance to read the note he had hastily scribbled on the back of the photograph when the doorbell rang and Mahon had slipped into the next room.

Mahon looks the older man up and down. He can still see the young cop in the sack of skin and bones before him. He has a good memory for faces. Seems to recall that Glass was a bitter-drinker. Had looked positively pissed off when he sidled up to him that night and told him he'd heard gunshots out at the church.

172

'You must have had your doubts, John. Over the years. You weren't a proper city cop. You didn't have murders on your doorstep every day of the week. You must have had the odd sleepless night wondering what it meant. The smell. The odd drop of blood. C'mon on now, mate, unburden yourself.'

Glass closes his eyes and turns away. He should never have gone up to the manor house. Should have gone straight to the cottage. But his mind had been all over the place. He'd just found the bodies of four people he knew. He was speckled with blood and brains and mud. He'd needed to see. Needed, just for a moment, to knock on the door of the big house. He'd known the squire wouldn't answer. Had known he was lying dead in the graveyard of St Germain's. But he'd had a few moments before the masses arrived and needed to extinguish his one last flicker of hope.

'I saw nothing. No matter what Len said, I saw nothing.'

Mahon smiles, kindly. Dabs his face with his handkerchief. 'You let yourself in.'

'Only for a moment.'

'What did you see?'

'Nothing!'

'What did you see, John?'

A shivering sob racks Glass's body. His chest heaves. He's not lying. He'd seen nothing. But he'd smelled it. Smelled gunpowder and bleach.

'You must have a lot of self-control, John. Must be a strong character to have suspicions like the one you've been holding on to for five decades and never follow up on them. You're either somebody who knows what's best for them, or you're unnaturally free of curiosity.'

173

Glass does not reply. He seems to be struggling to breathe. His skin has taken on an unhealthy, greenish tone that reminds Mahon of the stone angel that had looked down upon him this morning as he revisited the site of the massacre. It had been a difficult journey to make. It had affected him more than he expected. Hadn't remembered it as such a pretty place, but then, he'd only seen it in darkness. It had brought back memories he had no desire to revisit. Memories of what he'd found. Memories of Flash Harry's handiwork. Recollections of driving with the window open so the stench of blood could dissipate into the snow and the wind. Those curses, under his breath. His promises, to Mr Nock. His guarantee to sort it out.

'You got pills, John? You need to take something?'

Mahon sits forward in his seat. He is growing concerned for John Glass. He hates to see people suffer if there is nothing to be gained by it.

'You want a cup of tea, John? I can open the freezer door. Take some deep breaths, you might feel better . . .'

Glass begins to claw at his throat. He can't breathe. It feels as though somebody is sitting on his chest and pushing him into the ground. And the ground is opening up. His mind is suddenly swimming with pictures. He sees himself at the door of the manor house. Sees himself pushing open the great double doors. Breathes in a waft of chemicals and cordite.

He'd known, then. Known that the scene he had stumbled upon was only a fraction of that night's story. But he had closed the door. He had run back to where Peter Coles was sitting with his hands tied, muttering to himself about liars and bones. He made up his mind to tell the detectives. Would point the CID boys in the direction of Clarence Winn's house. Len Duchess

174

had turned up. John had told him what he'd smelled. Told him where to look. And Len had smiled and told him not to worry. John Glass didn't open his mouth on the subject again. Didn't say or write a word until today. And he will never speak another.

Mahon watches as Glass's eyes roll back. He looks like a shark, for a moment. The pupils roll upwards into his skull and his mouth slides open. A set of dentures slip forward and protrude from his lower jaw.

Mahon gives a sigh. He reaches forward and pushes the dentures back into the old man's mouth. Feels it is the least he can do.

'Well, that was a turn-up,' he says, to himself. 'I hadn't made my mind up, to be honest. You might have got away with a slap.'

Mahon walks back to the kitchen. Has a look in the cupboards and the fridge for anything worth pocketing and decides there is nothing worth his time. For a moment, he wonders how many times he has done this. How many times he has stood in the homes of the dead. How many souls have passed through his skin and bones on their way to wherever the fuck they were going.

Wonders how many times he has cleaned up other people's messes.

He can't help but think of Flash Harry. Can't help but remember the scene he found when he went to check on the young lad's house guest. Can't help but remember how the gutted southerner had looked.

Mahon closes his eyes. He's a young man again. Handsome. Loyal. Fearless. He's a good soldier who has already proven himself in battle. He's a bit pissed off he hasn't been listened to. Pissed off Mr Nock has ignored his advice and given the job of

175

looking after the southerner to his new protégé. But Mahon's playing ball. He's keeping it on the inside. Doing his own thing and keeping a watchful eye.

In the theatre of his memory, Mahon is turning up at the house. Knocking on the door to the sound of silence. He's letting himself in and walking up dusty, dirty stairs. He's opening doors. Calling out. Trying to find the residents. And then he's in the bedroom. He's looking at the thing that used to be the southerner. Looking at her: the other one; draining out into the carpet and skin like marble.

Mahon takes a deep breath. Wishes somebody else had found what Flash Harry had done. Somebody else would have thought of themselves first. Mahon hadn't considered himself. He'd considered his employer. He'd known. Known what Mr Nock needed.

By his heart, Mahon's phone rings.

He looks at the phone. It's from a call-box number he recognises. There are still a few in Newcastle. Not everybody trusts mobile phones.

Mahon speaks to the caller for fewer than thirty seconds. Hangs up without saying goodbye.

Somebody has been asking questions. Some writer. An ex-cop. Has some links to Humberside and a detective with an exotic name. Mahon squints as he tries to recall where he knows the name 'Tom Spink' from. Clicks his fingers as he places him. Years back. Some shit happened in one of Mr Nock's snooker halls. Manager had called the cops before he'd called Mahon. And Mahon had helped him disappear.

Mahon considers the body of John Glass. Smiles, sadly.

Thinks: *It's a day for meeting old friends.*

He sniffs noisily. Tucks the handkerchief back in his pocket and lets himself noiselessly out of the flat. In a dozen brisk strides he has found the shadows and is crossing the broad green space without getting wet or leaving the pockets of blackness that puddle around the base of the trees.

Mahon is about to make a call on his own phone when the other mobile beeps at him. Mahon gives a tiny laugh, as if some other force is guiding him and giving him signs. He pulls the gangster's phone from his pocket and keys in the code he had pressed its owner into giving up:

*Let him go. You have no idea what you're up against. Contact us. We can be very accommodating to our friends.*

Mahon grins.

No idea what he's up against? He reckons he has a pretty good idea.

As he gets into his car and lights himself a cigarette, one simple thought swirls inside his skull.

*You poor bastards.*

# Chapter 12

Helen Tremberg and Suzie Devlin sit under the same umbrella, sharing the contents of Suzie's lunch. They are sitting on newspaper, on a wooden bench out the back of Wilberforce House. It's a pretty spot. Quiet. All neatly tended flower-beds and daintily labelled climbers; damp trestles and red courtyard walls. Water drips from a tall tree with attractive, sturdy branches. A small blue and yellow bird is fluttering, skittishly, between the ground and the far wall. To Helen, it almost seems to be asking why Suzie is not dining alone.

'I haven't had cheese spread since I was a kid,' says Helen, taking a bite of white bread and enjoying it. 'Brings back memories.'

'It's the best cheese there is. Well, I suppose there's melted cheese, but you can't really buy that, can you?'

Helen had forgotten the delightful oddness of Suzie's character. She's a sweet girl. She's fun to look at. She makes people happy, when they're not trying to kill her.

'How's life, anyway?' asks Helen, sipping from a carton of Ribena. 'You all sorted?'

Suzie grins and shrugs, as if suggesting that nobody can ask for much more than 'getting by'.

'Was hard what happened to Mel,' says Suzie, biting into a chocolate biscuit. 'We were just becoming friends. Don't know what I would have done if I'd lost Roisin as well. Though I suppose I kind of have . . .'

Helen doesn't know what to say. She's heard the rumours about why Adam Downey was in the McAvoys' home. She knows how much bullshit is being thrown around.

'I think she's spending some time with her family,' says Helen tactfully. 'She's been through a lot.'

'She's been through a lot her whole life,' protests Suzie. 'Nothing on earth could make her leave Aector. You know how they feel about each other. And to leave Fin . . .'

'You've tried to get in touch, have you?'

'Her phone's disconnected. She's not been on Facebook. I tried to call Aector at work but they say he's still off sick so I'm a bit stumped. Bit lonely too.'

'You're not seeing anybody?'

Suzie looks suddenly coy. 'We're taking it slow. He's a nice guy. Bit too nice for me, I suppose, but he's being very good to me. We met in the bank, actually. Paid off a bill for me and didn't object when I thought he was a psychopath or a stalker or something. Not a bad start to a relationship. Even helped me scatter Simon's ashes . . .'

Helen lets her talk. Enjoys the animation and enthusiasm in her face. She's the kind of person Helen would like to be friends with.

'Are you going to get your notepad out now?' asks Suzie, when she realises Helen has stopped paying attention. 'I don't mind.

It can't be easy, knowing when it's the right time to get down to business.'

Helen gives her an apologetic smile. 'You won't get into trouble?'

Suzie shrugs. 'Not illegal, is it? Having a chat?'

'Depends what we're chatting about.'

'Well, I reckon we're chatting about Piers Fordham. Do you know that name?'

Helen shakes her head.

'He's who I was with getting the coffees yesterday morning. Well, him and Mr Wilde. But he's Scottish and smokes a gazillion cigarettes a day and couldn't do a refined English accent if his life depended on it. So I'm thinking it's Piers you're after. Wouldn't be the first time.'

Helen can feel her heart racing. She suddenly has a name. A real identity to tie to the faceless manipulator at the end of the phone who revelled in her discomfort and thought he was putting it right when he sent her to a house that was about to explode.

'He's a solicitor, then?' she asks, keeping her voice even.

'Not as such,' says Suzie, blowing up the empty carton of Ribena and then squeezing it so that the air makes her fringe ripple. 'He was a solicitor. Had a private practice in Grimsby. Did a lot of duty solicitor work. You know the stuff. People smashing up kebab shops or hitting their ex in the face with a beer bottle. That was his niche. Came over here once in a while, or at least, that's what it says in his file. I handle personnel records, you see. Or "filing", as they call it at my place. He seems to have been very good at what he was doing, whatever it was. Had some high-profile clients and cases.'

180

'But you say he's disbarred, yes?'

'We don't exactly go on about it around the water-cooler but you can't help but google somebody when you do a boring job like I do, can you? And yeah, he was struck off about five years ago. He'd been ripping off the Legal Aid people. Claiming for cases that had never gone beyond a caution. Making up bogus clients. He was getting druggies to sign forms for him, claiming Legal Aid for cases that were totally made up. He made half a million, according to the report I read.'

Helen purses her lips and blows out. She's chewing her lip. Picking at the skin around her nails. She senses something taking shape.

'He went to prison?'

'Eighteen months, he got. Served less than seven.'

'Which prison?'

'Hull.'

Helen makes a fist. 'Your firm employs him, though, yeah?'

'Not on staff, no. He does investigative work. Sorts out things that need a bit of finesse and legwork. He's got his own firm but he does at least a day a week on jobs for us. A lot of probate. Conveyancing. Things that don't need a licence.'

'He makes a lot of money?'

'Not bad,' says Suzie. 'More than me. More than you, I should think.'

Helen scratches at the back of her neck, thinking. A crooked solicitor. A man with the balls to try to scam the big boys. A man who spent time in prison and got to see how hopeless and ill-disciplined the majority of criminals really are.

'What's he like?' asks Helen, bouncing her legs on the balls of her feet. 'Single? Kids? Gay? Straight?'

Suzie laughs. 'He's straight, I know that much. Tried it on with me a few times. I'm not keen, to be honest. He was married until he went to prison, I think. Don't know about kids. He's a bit too big for his boots, you could say. Always likes to let it be known he's got the goods on you. He was the only one who gave me a sly wink when I came back to work after the court case. Everybody else had the good grace to pretend they didn't know what I had been getting up to. He made it clear he knew, and that if I wanted, he could help me.'

'Help you with what?'

Suzie shrugs. 'Make it go away. Get a new job. A fresh start. Maybe have the bitch bumped off. I don't know. But he's that sort. Got a lot of, I dunno . . . swagger?'

Helen flops back against the bench. She doesn't know why she is so surprised. Every criminal case of note has been made on a stroke of luck. Serial killers have been stopped by routine vehicle checks; rapists sent to prison because one of their victims recognised their shoes or an identikit struck a chord with a copper. One phone call, made at the wrong time, made to gloat over the fate of Colin Ray, and suddenly Piers Fordham is in the frame for so many crimes Helen doesn't know where to start listing them.

'How do you contact him?' asks Helen. 'He's not an office person, I gather?'

'No, we tend to see him only a couple of times a month. He sends his case papers and invoices in from home. He's rarely in the office. Was only in yesterday to have some papers signed. It was a surprise when he asked to borrow the meeting room.'

Helen scratches her shin with the toe of her shoe and thinks hard. She can picture it clearly. Can see Piers Fordham slipping into a side room so he could phone Colin Ray and goad him. He was out of the way. He was invisible. None of the CCTV cameras could pick him up and the unregistered mobile phone would doubtless be going in the bin once he got outside. He'd made a call, and it was going to come back to haunt him.

'What is it you think he's done?' asks Suzie, brushing her hands clean on her trousers. 'Has he been ripping us off? I mean, I have a bit of responsibility for the accounts so I hope there's nothing going to cause me problems.'

Helen shakes her head. 'It's just routine,' she says, without thinking about it.

'No it's not,' says Suzie, with a grin. 'He's a bad one, isn't he? What's he done? What does Aector think? And the other one. Nice, but a bit scary.'

'Detective Superintendent Pharaoh,' says Helen automatically. 'She'll be pleased, I think. I can't really tell you much. I just wanted to get to know a bit about him.'

'Well I can give you his home address,' she says. 'And he's got a works mobile on him, in case we need him. You can track him down from that, can't you?'

Helen gives a smile, then turns away as the blue bird flutters down to the grass at Suzie's feet. Suzie puts a crumb of bread between her bare toes and lets the bird peck at it. She looks up at Helen, absurdly pleased.

'He's lovely, isn't he? I think he's going to be migrating soon. I'll miss him.'

'Piers?'

'No, the bird. Although Piers is always going on about the weather in Britain and hating it. He was playing about on his computer yesterday morning, looking at apartments somewhere hot.'

'A laptop?'

'No, one of the PCs in the back office. He had to see Mr Wilde and the boss was late in, so was killing some time having a coffee and fiddling on his computer. Nice place he's got his eye on . . .'

Helen feels like hugging the small, squishy and delightfully odd girl. 'I don't suppose your computers store things like what websites he may have visited, do they? Or do they wipe at the end of each day?'

Suzie laughs. 'No chance of them being wiped unless you do it yourself. I used to look at a few sites I shouldn't and it was a nightmare remembering to delete my browsing history. Why?'

Helen bites down on the tremble that is affecting her lower lip. In her coat pocket she can feel her mobile vibrating. Colin Ray, eager for an update. She's going to make him pretty damn happy. She can already picture them, walking back into the station and giving Pharaoh the bloody lot. Can imagine the warm handshakes and the hugs and the drams of celebratory whisky. Can see McAvoy's look of eternal thanks. Hopes that the image will rub out the one she carries with her – frightened eyes and falling masonry.

She turns to her new friend, wincing for effect as if to remind the girl of the injuries she suffered saving Roisin from death.

'Suzie,' she says. 'I think I might need another favour.'

McAvoy is looking at a satellite image of the Winestead area. It's a surreal sensation. He feels he should be able to see the roof of his own car. Should be able to put his hand out of the window, wave at the sky and see himself, tiny and pixelated, on the laptop screen in front of him.

The screen is almost entirely green. It's an area of woodland and fields, broken up by ancient hedgerows and boundary walls. St Germain's Church is a square of brown and grey in an oval of trees and grass. It is surrounded by darker grassland that comes to an end at the treeline. On three sides, the grassland borders arable land, though in this satellite image none of it seems to have been given over to crops. The trees begin to the right of the church and stretch in an impenetrable mass for hundreds of metres. There is only one significant gap in the canopy of trees and branches. It's the spot where the manor house and its outbuildings used to sit. The dirt track that leads to it is a tiny knife-slash in the greenery.

McAvoy expands the image as much as he can and stares at the red roof of the property. It's changed a lot since the Winn family called it home. The outbuildings have been pulled down. Audrey's old cottage is a pile of rubble and earth. Like the mansion owned by the Hildyard family centuries before, the structure has been demolished to try to bury the blood it has seen.

McAvoy endeavours to make sense of it. He puts his finger on the screen, touching the house. Fiddles with the cursor and the image jumps to include more of the local landscape. He places another finger on the church. According to the timeline, the Winn family left their home in the early evening for an after-dinner stroll. This was not unusual. At some point on that stroll they encountered Peter Coles. For reasons unknown, he shot all four family members with a double-barrelled shotgun. He then exposed the breasts of Anastasia Winn and sat looking at her and muttering to himself until John Glass turned up.

Something about the picture feels unsettling. McAvoy tries to imagine the route they would have taken. Through the trees.

Over the boundary wall. Across the grass and through the old moat, into the churchyard. If Peter Coles were playing with his gun in the grounds of the church, surely the Winn family would have heard and altered their route?

McAvoy flicks through the printouts and curses the lack of information. Every question he comes up with lacks a suitable answer. He wants to know what the family ate for dinner. Were they struggling to digest a large meal? Had they perhaps taken a drink and set out for a walk in the snow in high spirits. A post-mortem examination would give him such answers, but the report has yet to be located.

McAvoy removes his fingers from the screen and splays his hand. Expands the image of the churchyard and looks down at the drawing in his notebook. Places a finger on the location of each corpse. Clarence Winn, nearest to the church. His daughter a few feet away. Then further away, back towards the moat, his wife and youngest son.

John Glass's original statement is one of the few pieces of evidence McAvoy feels he can trust. He reads it through again and digests its contents. Cross-references with the document stapled to the back of the crime scene photos, outlining the injuries suffered by each family member.

The wounds Clarence Winn suffered were to the torso. His daughter's to the face. His wife was shot in the chest. His son had wounds to the abdomen and head.

McAvoy looks out of the window. Looks up at the church. It has a sinister air in this fading light. The soft rain and pewter sky seem to reinforce its air of timelessness and isolation. Were it not for the occasional sound of passing cars on the road to his rear, McAvoy could have stumbled into a different time and not realised it. He would not be surprised to see a Spitfire fly overhead or to hear a horse and cart clip-clop to a halt behind him.

'Abdomen and head, abdomen and head . . .'

McAvoy mutters to himself as he examines the documents afresh. Could one shot cause such damage? Or would it take an extra cartridge? Two shots to the boy, one for each of the others . . . five cartridges?

How did nobody get away? If Clarence were killed first and his daughter immediately afterwards, his wife and son would have had time to turn. Would they not have covered more ground? Or were they walking in two groups? Perhaps father and daughter were walking ahead and mother and son behind.

McAvoy slaps the steering wheel and lets out a grunt. He realises that his answer to every question he poses is 'I don't know'.

He steps from the vehicle and checks his watch. It's not quite 4 p.m. Fin will be at his after-school club for a little longer. He has time. Time to get himself damp and mucky, should he so desire.

McAvoy's boots sink into the mud as he closes the car door. He notices a fresh set of tyre tracks scored into the damp ground. Recognises his own from the last visit he made here and wonders whether the tread is that of the vicar. He knows that she still preaches here, once in a while. Wonders if perhaps somebody has visited a grave. Makes a note to look for fresh flowers or a scrubbed headstone.

The gate creaks as he pushes it open; loud and eerie in the absolute silence of the churchyard. He crunches over gravel and then onto the soaking, spongy grass. Walks straight to the place

187

where Clarence Winn fell. Turns his head and tries to work out where Peter Coles would have been standing. The church itself sits at the top of a slight slope. Clarence would have approached from out of the trees. He would have been lower than Peter Coles. The shot took him in the stomach, so Coles would have had to be aiming down. And yet his next shot took Anastasia in the face. Did he come stalking down the slope, raising his gun like a hunter? Or did Anastasia die first? Was she the first to reach the church? If Peter Coles killed her and bent to strip her corpse, he might have been disturbed by the unexpected approach of her father. He could have turned and fired. It would make sense. He would then be at a lower angle and more likely to aim for the torso than the head.

McAvoy raises an imaginary gun and goes through the various permutations in his head. He has fired a shotgun himself. Knows how it kicks. His dad has always owned a shotgun. Taught McAvoy how to hold it. How to tuck it into the shoulder and absorb the power. How to shoot while breathing out and to squeeze the trigger, not pull. McAvoy had been eight years old when he mastered it. Doubts he would be able to hit a barn door from ten feet if asked to do so now.

McAvoy tramps down the slope and pushes branches aside to wrestle his way into the copse of trees. He shivers as raindrops splash down the collar of his shirt. Feels himself sinking into a mulch of mud and foliage and quickens his pace as he steps into the dip at the far end of the churchyard. This was the moat that surrounded the Hildyard mansion. This is where the Lord of the Manor lost his son. McAvoy takes larger steps and comes up the other side of the moat. A low wall bars his way into the neighbouring field. He climbs over it and feels

188

his trousers growing cold and damp as he comes into contact with the old stone.

He crosses the neighbouring field. Rotten turnips sit in rutted grooves, the grass half folded into a bed of mud and stone. He is across the field in moments. Makes for the woods. Feels his hands slip on the greasy wood as he climbs over the mouldering, flaking fence, and climbs down into the deep embrace of the forest.

McAvoy finds it hard to imagine that this would be a popular place for an after-dinner stroll. Even if the woods were better tended half a century ago, the ground in March would have been muddy and slimy underfoot. Were the Winns dressed for the conditions? He wishes the evidence log contained anything to help him, but all he has is John Glass's vague description of what Anastasia was wearing, and that did not include any mention of what she had on her feet.

He pushes further into the woods. There are no paths, or any suggestion of which way to go. It is simply a thick, wet forest at the beginning of autumn. Dead leaves hang and fall from saturated branches. Rotten timber is mashed under his feet as he fights his way through a spider-web of spindly, clinging tree limbs. He feels his clothes snag and his feet sink and wonders what on earth he is doing. For an instant he feels like a story-book prince, hacking his way through a wall of thorns to rescue a sleeping maiden. Then he winces as a branch digs into one of the wounds on his back and the pleasant sensation of doing something noble disappears to be replaced by frustration and pain.

He pushes on, hoping the woods will thin out. He tries to remember the names of the trees but cannot quite get his thoughts together. He sniffs, loudly and unpleasantly, swallowing scents of dead vegetation and turned earth. He looks back the way he has come.

Breathless, sore, soaked to the skin, McAvoy pushes a thick branch aside and stumbles into a small clearing. He bends forward, hands on hips, and sucks in a breath of air. He has only walked through a hundred metres of woodland but he feels as though he has had to push his way through the crowd at a rock concert. His limbs ache and he can feel scratches and bruises upon his skin. He hopes to God there is another way back to his car. Isn't sure he can face battling back the way he has come.

McAvoy leans against the trunk of the nearest tree. It's reassuringly solid and cold. He wipes his forehead and looks around him. He needs to know what this woodland was like in 1966. Surely the Winn family would find a better route for an evening stroll than through this maze of thorns and branches.

He looks up, through the tops of the trees, and sees a vast, black cloud slide elegantly overhead. It seems to be bringing the night with it. It's getting dark. Rain still tumbles from a sky that seems to be sinking towards the earth.

McAvoy squints, as something catches his eye.

Across the clearing, behind a low, tumbledown wall, sits something solid and man-made. He squints through the gathering gloom. The shape seems familiar. He moves closer. Realises it's an old horse-trailer, abandoned long before. He walks towards it. Sniffs again and feels a pain in his chest. Christ he feels cold and lonely . . .

There is a camouflage net draped across the horsebox. Its sides have been painted a mottled green and brown. There are deep grooves in the forest floor where its thick black wheels scored their progress into the damp earth.

McAvoy wonders how long it has been here. The registration plate at the back of the large, oblong vehicle has been ripped off and the paint-job obscures both its origins and age.

He makes his way to the far end of the container. The door is padlocked shut. There is no doubting the age of the padlock. It is shiny, new and very solid.

McAvoy holds the lock in his hand and presses his other to the metal door. If he pulled the door he would perhaps be able to see through a gap in the hinges. But should he? Has a crime been committed? Is he being a policeman or just a nosy bastard? He stands, sodden and conflicted, and pulls on his lower lip as he tries to decide what to do . . .

'Worst mistake of your fucking life, mate.'

McAvoy spins. Loses his footing and grabs for the nearest branch.

A middle-aged man is standing in the clearing. He's wearing a waxed jacket, and wellington boots over an expensive shirt and trousers. He's wearing rain-dotted spectacles and is shaking his head. He looks distinctly pissed off.

'I'm sorry, I was just—' begins McAvoy.

'Don't bother,' comes a voice to McAvoy's left.

He turns his head. A hefty young man in a flat cap and camouflage coat is standing three feet away. He's holding a length of branch. A twig snaps and McAvoy turns to see another young man step out from the bigger man's shadow. He is Asian. Skinny and well-groomed, save the leaves in his hair and the mud up his calves.

191

McAvoy feels a tightening in his chest. Reaches for his warrant card then stops as he sees the middle-aged man produce a shotgun.

'We told you,' says the man. 'We're doing fine on our own. We don't need you or your protection. We won't pay. And you're a silly bastard for coming on your own, no matter how big you are.'

'Protection?' says McAvoy, confused. 'No, you don't understand. I'm a—'

'You're a dead man. That's what you fucking are.'

'Please, give me a moment . . .'

McAvoy turns his head just in time to see the nearest of the two men dart forward, arm raised. He flicks his eyes upwards.

And sees the branch come crashing down upon his head.

'Honestly, I promise you. A double espresso with a Red Bull in it. He necked it, right in front of me. You should have seen his eyes! Looked like somebody had put a piece of raw ginger up—'

Tom Spink breaks off before the end of the sentence, switching the mobile phone to his right hand so he can indicate and overtake the Land Rover in the middle lane.

'No, he sort of jiggled off after that,' he says, steering his old Vauxhall back to the inside lane and wincing as his windscreen wipers squeal another veneer of raindrops from the glass. 'Jittery? I'll say. Looked like a lorry with its engine running. I don't know where he was going but he won't have needed a car. Could sprint there in ten seconds flat.'

Tom is returning to the east coast after a quick trip north. He's spent a pleasant hour with a detective sergeant from Tyneside who had been a raw PC when Tom Spink had shown him the ropes three decades before. That young lad is close to retirement now. Got a gut and a bald patch. Got a red sheen to his skin and hair sprouting thickly in his ears. The meeting had done little to ease Tom's sense of his own mortality, but it had proved useful in terms of pleasing Trish.

'I'll send it all over as soon as I pull in. The bladder will be demanding attention soon, Nefertiti. You don't know you're born, you young 'uns . . .'

Tom grins at the enthusiasm in Pharaoh's voice. She sounds relieved. He likes being the source of that. Likes the fact she sends him a jokey card every Father's Day. He reckons he's done a better job raising her than her real dad ever did. Useless bastard. Sodded off when she was ten and left her to cope with a drunken mum, two younger brothers and a senile granddad all by herself. They said it was too much for her, and it probably was. Didn't stop her though. She was a copper in her head and heart long before she put the uniform on. Her childhood experiences were perfect training for the job she would eventually do. She learned how to care, while not taking any shit. Turned her into the person that has enriched Tom Spink's life for twenty years.

He's feeling pretty good about himself today. He'd expected his little mission to be trickier. Thought he would have to travel all the way to Newcastle and buy a few pies and pints before anybody remembered what they owed him and agreed to a favour. But the call from DS Benny Pryce had come through to his mobile only twenty minutes after Tom phoned the newsdesk at the *Newcastle Journal* and introduced himself as a writer putting together a book on the time Newcastle's crime bosses turned the twins away at the train station. He'd only had to mention a couple of names from the golden age of crime and the bloke at the end of the line was promising that one of his reporters would be back in touch within the hour. Tom had left his number and waited for the call. He'd been surprised to hear from Benny. Hadn't spoken to him since a funeral they both attended a few years back. He'd been friendly enough on the phone. Told him the reporters at the local paper were all kids and wouldn't know anything useful. Asked him what he wanted to know and said he was happy to help an old friend. Agreed to spare him the drive all the way up to Newcastle and met him in the car park of the service station at Scotch Corner; two hours from Hull and an hour from Newcastle. Benny had brought with him what Tom had asked for. Slipped him a single piece of paper containing all the properties with links to one Francis Nock. Filled him in on the latest developments on Tyneside.

'No movement on the severed arm, yet,' says Tom, squinting into the cloud that seems to darken and bruise as he heads further east. 'Not much more to say than you got at Breslin's briefing. They want to talk to Mr Nock and his big brute of a right-hand man. They knocked on the door at his mansion half a dozen times, but the only person there is a private security man and he says the old man is away convalescing. Doesn't have an address for Mahon, though Benny reckons he lives somewhere in the grounds. None of the usual grasses in the city centre have much to say and Lloyd's family are saying nothing. Proper old-school wall of silence, but there seems no doubt what's happened. Lloyd was considering his options. Mr Nock showed them what his options really were. He could stay loyal or he could die. And the Headhunters are missing one of their own. Questions are being asked. Word is, Mahon got to him. Wherever he is, he'll be having no fun.'

Tom looks at the sheet of paper on the passenger seat of the car. It's handwritten. A few addresses, some scribbles and a couple of asterisks, denoting that certain properties are owned by third parties and sham companies but have connections to Nock's empire.

'No, he'll keep quiet,' says Tom, in reply to Pharaoh's query. 'Benny wants the easy life. He didn't ask many questions, really. I think he knew there was more to it than just my literary leanings, but he's been a copper a long time and has seen Nock get away with murder time and again. Maybe he wants to see him exposed a little. Either way, it was good of him to help. Poor bugger looked knackered. Whole trip out only cost me a cappuccino in the end. Couldn't believe that bloke though. Red Bull and a double espresso? Seriously? How tired would you have to be? Oh shit, what's this . . . ?'

Tom sees the blue light flash in his rear-view mirror. He pulls a face and groans. He's got three points on his licence already and knows he's about to get three more.

'Bloody traffic police,' he says into the phone. 'Fuck, I'll have to pull over. Look, I'll edit the list and get it to you, then you can send it on to your slimy Headhunter friend. Take care. Bye.'

Tom terminates the call as the patrol car pulls level with him. A grim-faced young police constable in the passenger seat is pointing to the slip road that leads off the motorway and up and round into Goole. Spink frowns, knowing there is a stopping place half a mile ahead, but a sudden stern glare from the cop convinces him to do as he's asked. He checks his speedometer and realises he may have been going a tad fast. Curses, then indicates left and turns off the motorway. The patrol car follows him.

'Can't stop here, son. No hard shoulder, you prick . . .'

The road leads up to a roundabout with exits for Goole and the motorway. To his left is the country road, leading to the pretty little towns and villages that dot the scenic route to York. Tom sees the police vehicle's left indicator begin to wink so dutifully flicks his own on.

'You after a McDonald's?' he mutters under his breath as he turns left and cruises towards the little estate that offers a couple of fast-food outlets and a discount hotel.

Tom is about to pull into the estate when the patrol car draws level with him again, driving on the wrong side of the road. The policeman in the passenger seat gestures for him to keep driving.

'What's this, son? Where? Towards York? Why? There's a car park back there . . .'

Sighing, raising his hands, glancing in his mirror, Tom follows the car for another mile down the B-road. The landscape begins to look more rural. The potholes in the road become deeper, as though heavier, more agricultural vehicles have eaten away the track. Finally, Tom sees the police car indicate left and pull off into a lay-by. It's shielded from the main road by a mound of grass and earth. A red-painted wooden shack, offering bacon sandwiches and cups of tea, sits abandoned and graffiti-sprayed in front of a ploughed field.

'Really? This is the best place you could find for a telling-off?'

Tom kills the engine and puts his head back, looking at the roof of his car. He's going to have to smile sweetly. He'll apologise. Won't mention that he used to be a copper unless it comes up in conversation. He knows that, these days, telling young cops you used to be a policeman during the good old days is more likely to get you an extra fine than a new friend.

He sits forward in his seat. Listens to the rain hit the roof and the glass.

'Let's get it over with, eh, boys?'

He switches on the electrics so he can wipe the rain from the windscreen. Squints as the image clears.

The patrol car is gone.

'Where the bloody hell . . . ?'

Tom is in the act of taking his seat-belt off when his car gives a colossal lurch, with the sound of metal slamming into metal. He is thrown forward, smashing the bridge of his nose against something cold and biting his tongue as his chest slams into the steering wheel.

He tastes blood.

Sees in black and gold for a moment as his vision spins and swims.

The door is yanked open and strong, gloved hands pull him from the vehicle. He feels a sharp pain in his knee and realises he must have hurt himself in the initial impact. He tries to put his feet down on the pitted concrete but can't seem to find his balance.

He tells himself to concentrate. To think like a policeman. To stick his thumb in his attacker's eye and knee the bastard in the bollocks. But he feels weak and confused and his heart is racing so hard that he can't seem to hear his thoughts . . .

A fist slams into his stomach. It's a perfect blow. He doubles over, crippled with sickness and agony. Then a foot, clad in a simple black shoe, hoofs him beneath the jaw. His glasses fly off and his head snaps back, and he lands on his side on the wet road.

Tom is barely conscious as the hands go through his pockets.

197

Can manage only a groan as his phone and wallet are taken. Can't raise his head to see the man scooping up the piece of paper from the passenger seat and the notebook from the glovebox.

Tom passes out just as the man squats above him and stares deep into his eyes.

He is spared the terror of wondering just what his attacker is holding in his hand, or what he intends to do with it.

He is blessedly unconscious as the man begins his work.

But he wakes as the first nail splinters bone.

# Chapter 13

The lad in the flat cap doesn't expect the branch to break. He anticipates a jolting impact and a vibration up his arm. He is prepared for a grunt of pain and perhaps a spray of blood across his clothes and face. He has no other outcome in mind. Knows, just knows, that the big man in the damp clothes will fall to his knees, then onto his back. And then he can begin to really put the boot in . . .

McAvoy shakes rotten wood and dirt from his hair and his eyes. Looks down at the thug who is in turn staring at the stump of rotten timber he holds in his right hand.

'Will! Shift! Move!'

McAvoy turns in the direction of the voice. The older man is raising the shotgun.

'You're dead! I'm gonna—'

McAvoy reaches out and grabs the man called Will. Closes both hands around his shirt front and he lifts him clean off the ground. He plants his feet and swivels at the hips, then throws Will at the older man as if he is made of straw.

The impact knocks the other man backwards and he drops the gun to the forest floor.

McAvoy crosses the small space between them. Will is getting to his feet and swings a right hand, dazedly, towards McAvoy's head. McAvoy doesn't want to hit him. Knows how much paperwork will be involved. He ducks back and lets the punch whistle by, then slaps him, open-handed, on both sides of the head. Ears ringing, eyes wide, the attacker drops to the floor, clutching at his temple.

'Will?' shouts the older man. 'What have you done to him? You bastard! You're . . .'

McAvoy knows Will will be unable to get his bearings for a good few seconds so turns his back on him and kicks the shotgun out of reach. He closes his hand around the lower jaw of the older man and brings his face close to his own. Smells meat, gravy and red wine on his breath. Sees the flicker of the other youth behind him . . .

McAvoy turns and slams his hand, open-palmed, into the skinny lad's chest. The boy falls backwards as though he has run into a tree. He turns back to the older man and exerts enough pressure on his lower jaw to show that he could break it like a dried twig.

'I'm a policeman, you idiot,' says McAvoy, into the older man's face. 'I tried to say! I tried!'

Fear mixes with confusion in the older man's face. It morphs into an expression of relief, and then of fear once more as he replays the events of the last few seconds back in his head.

'Christ! Christ, I'm sorry, we didn't . . . I thought . . . I mean, fuck! Fuck!'

Breathing hard and pissed off to his bones, McAvoy lets go of the man then takes two steps to his right and picks up the shotgun.

'Seriously?' he asks. 'I mean, who behaves like this? Who thinks this is OK!'

He's shouting, louder than he has in a while. Blinks a few times and pinches the bridge of his nose until the spots stop dancing in his vision. He considers the gun. 'You have a licence for this?'

'Yes, yes,' mumbles the man. 'Shit, honest, we didn't mean . . .'

McAvoy turns away from him. Bends down and checks on the man called Will.

'Sit still for a minute. It'll pass. And you,' he says, turning to the Asian youngster who is coughing his lungs up into the leaves and dirt. 'Take deep breaths.'

He gives the older man his attention. Follows his own advice and slows his breathing. Rubs his hand over his face and tries to pick the bark and mud from his fringe.

'I'm Detective Sergeant McAvoy,' he says, and it feels suddenly wonderful to hear the words spoken aloud. 'I'm investigating the murders in the church in 1966. I don't know who the hell you thought I was but I know that whoever they are, they could well be dead by now. Who do you think you are? You don't attack somebody with a branch and a shotgun for trespassing. You just bloody don't!'

The older man seems to have recovered a little composure. He tries a nervous smile. 'My name's Jasper,' he says, with stuttered breath. 'That's all it was, Sergeant, we thought you were trespassing. We were just going to scare you, that's all. Heard you coming through the woods and wasn't sure you weren't a villain. Honest, I'd never have fired . . .'

McAvoy breaks open the shotgun. Looks at the cartridges.

'It's loaded,' he says. 'You'd have taken my face off.'

'Only cos you were beating up the lad,' says Jasper, with an air of petulance. 'We've had bother.'

McAvoy looks from Jasper to Will and then back again. There is some resemblance, but not much.

'Your son?'

'Nephew.'

'And this gentleman?' asks McAvoy, pulling the Asian lad to his feet and gesturing that he join the other two.

'Business associate,' says Jasper uncertainly. 'Liam, we call him. Can't say his real name. He's Will's friend.'

McAvoy frowns. Watches Will pull himself unsteadily to his feet.

'There's something going on here,' says McAvoy, uncertainly. 'This isn't somewhere you go for a little walk. Not dressed like that, anyways. Is there a path through these woods?'

'A path? Just a trail, you'd call it. Bugger to get the trailer though . . .'

Jasper bites his lip as the younger men turn fierce gazes on him.

McAvoy looks back at the camouflaged bulk of the horse-trailer; deliberately hidden and obscured in this remote, inaccessible spot.

'What's in that?' he asks. 'Is it yours?'

Jasper and his nephew exchange glances.

The Asian lad opens his mouth to speak. 'Are you arresting us?' His tone is non-confrontational. He is still wheezing and seems genuinely afraid.

'I don't bloody know,' says McAvoy, pushing a hand into his

hair and leaving it sticking up at mad angles. He wrinkles his face and thinks back to what has been said. 'You mentioned protection. Who did you think I was?'

Jasper examines the forest floor. Will and Liam look at one another, as if communicating with just their eyes.

'Somebody had better tell me what's going on,' says McAvoy.

For a moment the only noises are the sounds of the forest. Raindrops patter onto dead and dying leaves. The wind plays with spindly branches and crows scrap with magpies in the tangle of greenery.

'One phone call and I've got a dozen uniformed officers here,' says McAvoy, more confidently than he actually feels.

'It's a misunderstanding,' says Jasper, pleadingly. 'Look, we're not bad sorts, this is just a mix-up . . .'

'Seriously, I can barely hear a thing, mate,' says Will, arms wide. 'Can't we just shake and forget this happened?'

'The trailer's nothing to do with us.'

Will and Jasper turn fierce eyes on Liam at the mention of the trailer and McAvoy turns his attention back to it.

'Do you have the key for the lock?'

'It's not ours.'

'Of course it's bloody yours! And you tried to blow my head off for looking at it!'

'That thing's been there years,' says Jasper, soothingly. 'We were just out walking, honestly.'

'So this is your land, is it?' asks McAvoy. 'You're patrolling to make sure no trespassers come and steal your leaves?'

'No, no, but we know the owner and he doesn't mind . . .'

Liam is speaking now. He's rewarded with a hissed 'Shut up' from his friend.

McAvoy sighs. Breathes in a lungful of cold, damp air. Makes a show of reaching into his coat pocket for his phone.

'Easy, no need for that,' says Jasper hurriedly. 'Look, there's not much to tell.'

McAvoy realises he is still holding the shotgun. Tries not to let himself feel he is threatening these men. They are staying where they are out of civic duty and respect for the authority of the law.

'Who did you think I was?' he asks again.

Jasper is about to speak when Liam steps forward, his hand still on his chest. 'We've got some business interests,' he says. 'Here.' He nods at the trailer. Sighs. 'There.'

'We've had bother,' says Will, butting in. 'Couple of blokes came to see Uncle Jasper. Said they had heard we were making money. Wanted to help. Wanted to offer resources.'

'Bloody protection racket,' says Jasper bitterly. 'I told them I didn't need protecting. I've got a nephew who does boxing. Got my shotgun. Got the lad here. We don't need to pay anybody else. We're just a bunch of entrepreneurs. We don't want trouble.'

McAvoy stares at each of the men in turn. 'They said they would come back?' he asks.

'Made it clear,' says Jasper. 'We've been shitting our pants for days, haven't we, lads? I mean, they said it was a friendly offer but people like that don't like refusal, do they?'

'Like what?'

'They were young lads. Two of them. No older than the boys here. But they didn't do much talking. Just introduced themselves and passed me a phone. I spoke to this slick chap. Southerner, I reckon. Told me how much help he could give me.

204

Said it must be difficult, running a business in the middle of nowhere. Said he could take away those worries for a minor percentage.'

'And you said no?'

'My blood was up! Who did they think they were?'

'Where did this happen?'

'My bloody house!' he says, indignant. 'I just live down in Otringham. Jasper Blackwell. Didn't say, did I? Land here belongs to the next farm over. Never uses it, does he? And I hate to see it going to waste . . .'

McAvoy looks into the man's anxious, earnest face.

'Is it drugs?' he asks, nodding back at the trailer.

'Christ, no,' says Will, stepping in. 'Nowt like that.'

'Well?'

Liam gives a huge sigh and puts his head in his hands.

'I'm good with computers,' he says. 'Will and me met at university—'

'I didn't stay long . . .' butts in Will.

'My family do import and exports,' he says. 'I do a bit of buying and selling. Stuff you can get really easily here sells for a fortune back in Tunisia.'

'That's where you're from?'

'Me? No, I'm from India. I just have business connections there. Look, this is all a bit complicated . . .'

McAvoy tightens his grip on the stock of the gun. Picks his words carefully and chooses not to swear. 'What's in the trailer?'

'Bin-bags,' blurts out Jasper, suddenly. 'Charity bloody bin-bags! Easy money, no hassles,' he says, as if reciting it the way the idea was sold to him. 'Nobody gets hurt . . .'

205

'Somebody's going to get hurt in a minute,' says McAvoy, snapping. 'Now, pick a bloody spokesman and make some bloody sense.'

It takes ten minutes for the bedraggled trio to tell their story. Liam has family who sell second-hand designer clothes in countries where anything with a Western brand goes like gold dust. He used to make a bit of pocket money wandering around the charity shops and buying up anything that could be flogged for profit overseas. A year back he graduated from university with plans to go into computers, but couldn't find much in the way of work. Started doing jobs for the family firm instead. Those jobs became less and less legitimate over time. Somebody had realised how much easier it would be if people didn't bother donating to the charity shops at all and just gave the stuff straight to Liam's family instead. Liam knocked up a design on his computer and had the printing done back home. Had a job-lot sent over from India inside a shipment of fine tablecloths bound for a chain of restaurants in the East Midlands. And it turned out, as predicted, that there was good money to be made in fake charity bin-liners.

'People were chucking the stuff out anyway,' protests Will, in the face of McAvoy's disapproval. 'They didn't care where they ended up. Those bin-bags are a nuisance anyways. We were doing people a favour, taking them off their hands ...'

'They were giving them to good causes.'

'Well, so were we. They'd have made people happy overseas ...'

'I'm touched by your philanthropy.'

Liam had approached his friend Will and asked him if he would help with pick-ups and drop-offs. Together they left fake charity-collection sacks outside thousands of homes in the East Riding: all embossed with official logos and images of crying children. Will, in turn, had approached his uncle to ask if he knew of anywhere they could store the stuff they recouped until it could be shipped abroad.

'I live on an old farmhouse,' says Jasper, shrugging. 'Got a couple of outbuildings. Stuff was fine there until I got that call.'

McAvoy looks at the trailer. 'You couldn't fit more than two dozen bin-bags in there,' he says, frowning.

Jasper rolls his eyes. Holds up a hand as if in supplication. 'Underneath,' he says quietly.

'I don't understand,' says McAvoy.

'The trailer's just a marker, mate. You ain't seen nothing yet . . .'

The bogginess of the forest floor makes the going hard, but together the four men succeed in rolling the trailer forward a few metres.

'Brought it with a Land Rover,' says Jasper, wheezing. 'Years ago it was. Used to make a few drops of home-brew, I did. Was nice to have somewhere I could get away and have a think about the world. My granddad worked here, y'know. During the war. All this belonged to the manor house then, but it's all part of the next farm over now.'

McAvoy wipes the sweat from his head. He had been unsure about dropping the gun and letting the three men help him, but his curiosity dictated that he take the risk. He can feel his heart beating hard. Can feel moisture on his back and hopes it is perspiration rather than a torn wound.

'There,' says Will, nodding at the floor. 'This will all be taken into consideration, yeah? That we're helping you? You think it will be a community service order or something, mate? I mean, I know we did wrong but . . .'

McAvoy isn't listening. He's staring at a metal disc, a metre in diameter, set in a slight rise in the undulating forest floor.

'Dug them during the war, my granddad says. Had to sign the Official Secrets Act. Only told me when he was in his eighties and going a bit daft in the head. I didn't believe him, to be honest. Some underground bunker out in the middle of Winestead Woods? But I brought the metal detector. Still a million-to-one shot I found it.'

'You didn't tell the authorities?' asks McAvoy quietly.

'Didn't see it was any of my business.'

'You've made it your business, though, eh?'

Jasper looks a little upset at having his integrity questioned. 'It was a nice secret to have.'

'And you've dumped your knocked-off clothes down there, have you?'

Jasper nods. 'Almost burst a bollock getting the lid open. We were just thinking on our feet, weren't we, lads? These buggers were trying to muscle in. We needed somewhere safe to keep the stuff. Figured we could guard it if we needed to.'

'And shoot whoever turned up?' asks McAvoy, with a look of disgust on his face.

'Come on now, mate, we've helped, haven't we?'

'You've committed a crime.'

'Yeah, but . . .'

'No buts.'

McAvoy scratches at the back of his neck. He hasn't thought about the Winn family for half an hour. Wonders what the hell he is going to do next. He can't ask all three men to accompany him back to his car so he can drop them off at the police station. He's simply stumbled onto something. There has been no investigation. No proper search. He has no desire to start clawing through damp bin-bags in an underground bunker dug decades ago to house local resistance men in the event of invasion.

'I need your addresses,' he says, at last. 'Officers will be with you within twenty-four hours to discuss this properly. You are not to remove anything from either the trailer or the bunker. Your information may actually be very useful in connection with an investigation into organised crime. Would you be willing to cooperate with that?'

Jasper nods his head, childlike and grateful.

'Do you think we'll go to prison?' asks Liam, again, in a pitiful whine.

McAvoy is about to speak when his phone rings. He holds up a hand in apology and takes the call.

'Hello, guv. I may have something you'll be happy to hear all about . . .'

His face falls as he hears the sound of Trish Pharaoh dissolving into sobs.

The colour drains from his face.

Listens, without speaking, as she tells him about the horrors inflicted on the body of Tom Spink.

# Chapter 14

11.06 p.m. Hull city centre.

Pharaoh lights a cigarette from the tip of her last one and flicks the stub against the white-painted wall of the new police station. Slows her pace as she sees the figure outlined beneath the yellow street light on the corner of Myton Street.

A few metres ahead, a drunk man in a tracksuit and brogues is pissing on the tiled floor that leads through a clear glass door to the unmanned front desk of the gleaming new community policing centre. He's doing it quite artistically. Turning in slow circles for maximum coverage, while not letting the puddle reach the half-empty bottle of cider by the kerb.

'Bastards,' says the man when he catches Pharaoh's eye. Then, 'Fucking bastards,' for extra emphasis.

Pharaoh nods, acceptingly. 'You should poke your todger through the letterbox,' she says. 'Really show them who's boss.'

The man gives a grin. Wishes he'd had the idea before he emptied his bladder. Pharaoh gives him a nod. A look of approval. Sniffs hard and inhales a lungful of smoke. Walks behind him and shoves him hard in the back. Doesn't even turn around as he slips and slithers to the floor and starts shouting curses at her diminishing shape.

Pharaoh has bite marks on her index finger and wrist. She has chewed herself almost to the bone. The anger she feels has a heat and intensity; a dangerous potency that makes her feel as though her body is too small a container for it. She is having to walk just to burn some of it off. She's a mile from Hull Royal Infirmary now. Stamping her way down the quiet road at the back of the shopping centre. There are multi-storey car parks to her left and right and the presence of styrofoam takeaway cartons and smashed glass in the gutters betrays the hour. She can hear sirens somewhere. Can hear the symphony that accompanies a city grinding its way to a fitful sleep.

Pharaoh catches a glimpse of herself in the dark glass of a furniture store and turns her head before she has time to focus on the lines in her forehead, the bags beneath her eyes or the pouting lip of belly that her biker jacket fails to conceal. She hates herself tonight. Hates herself for what has happened to Tom Spink.

He'll be OK. That's what the young doctor had said. Going to need a lot of rest and painkillers but no injuries to anything vital for life. No, his attacker had instead made merry with his expendable parts. Fired half a dozen nails through the soles of his shoes and into his feet; two of which went all the way through and emerged, gleaming and gory, through the laces of his Hush Puppies. He'd snapped his arm backwards at the elbow. Hit him in the face so hard Tom had been choking on his own incisors when the paramedics arrived.

Pharaoh grinds her teeth. She'd sat by Tom's bed for a couple of hours, squeezing his hand and managing tight, thin-lipped smiles whenever his wife looked at her through red-seamed eyes. Managed to cough up a few promises that she would get whoever did this. Choked on her own spit as she kissed him on his wrinkled forehead and told him she was more sorry than he would ever know.

And she had begun walking. Didn't really know what else to do. She'd half entertained the idea of a drink in some unfamiliar pub but most of the city-centre boozers close the doors at 11 p.m. on a week night and she knows that should she pop the cork on a bottle tonight, she won't stop drinking until she can't see.

Her footsteps take her back in the direction of the dual carriageway. There are few cars on the roads. In the distance she can see a thin curve of moon bouncing off the inky black water of the marina. Can see the black mass of the *Spurn Lightship*, blotting out the masts of the pleasure craft that sit motionless to its rear.

She crunches across the gravel and broken glass of a car park that nobody would be fool enough to use. She remembers being here before; years ago. Was one of her first jobs in Hull. Her Chief Superintendent in Grimsby had offered to share her expertise with one of the high-flyers on the old CID team across the water. A prostitute had been left for dead in a skip. Every bone in her face had been broken. Pharaoh had been a detective inspector then. Had only just come back to work after having her third child. She'd been eager to get a result. Knew that whichever bastard had done it deserved what was coming to them and more. Had been only too willing to work day and night to put the bastard away. Turned out she wasn't needed. The Hull high-flyer had his own way of doing things. Ran a slick, efficient operation with a clear-up rate that was the envy of the service.

He was Humberside Police's blue-eyed boy and he was a smarmy, dangerous, egocentric wanker. His name was Doug Roper. He had been made a detective chief inspector just a couple of years before Pharaoh had first shaken his perfumed, moisturised hand. Already had the respect and admiration of colleagues who were double his tender years. Scared the shit out of villains and could charm grieving wives and mothers into peals of laughter with just a few words of inappropriate charm. He dressed like a movie star. Wore bespoke suits and Italian leather shoes. Groomed his facial hair into neat peaks and points and wore his hair longer than regulations allowed. He revelled in his image of a swashbuckling maverick and couldn't keep his face or his name out of the *Hull Daily Mail*. He was the symbol of Humberside Police. Pharaoh had formed the impression within about ten seconds of introducing herself that he was a prize prick. But she was in the minority. Women constables lined up to be bedded by him and he never had to buy a round with the lads. His coat-tails were a comfortable and fast-moving magic carpet and half the police force were trying to ride them. Pharaoh only worked a half-day on the case that had brought her to Hull. Was sent off on some fool's errand by Roper's right-hand man. He was a big, bullet-headed bully with capped front teeth and bad skin and he'd looked down her top like an artist considering a blank canvas when he had told her to go speak to the owner of the car park about CCTV footage that she already knew did not exist. Absolom, his name was. David or Daniel or something like that. He'd slithered away when Roper was brought low. She reckons he's probably still following the slimy prick around; cutting the crusts off his sandwiches and putting his condoms on for him before he banged his latest slag.

213

She remembers getting the call. Absolom, in his camp, greasy voice. Roper had arrested somebody. He'd confessed. Was a Bosnian guy, living in one of the nasty flats beneath Clive Sullivan Way. He'd liked the look of her and didn't want to pay for it. Couldn't get hard when she hitched her skirt up and lost his temper when she sighed. Roper got him sent down. It was a good result. A neat result. They had a witness who could place him there, and a DNA match. Her services were no longer required. She'd known just from the way he'd said the suspect's nationality that Roper was playing tricks. She'd run the name of the witness through the PNC database and found endless links between himself and Absolom. She'd smelled something rank about the whole affair, though she was still too career-savvy to take her suspicions to a top brass who worshipped the ground the pair walked on. The whole thing had left Pharaoh wishing a hundred varieties of death on Roper, Absolom and anybody else who thought of the pair with anything other than loathing. Making sense of her feelings about Roper is easier today. He's no longer a cop. McAvoy saw to that. Found out that Roper didn't care whether he put the right person away as long as he made headlines while doing so. Took his findings to the top brass and was rewarded with a place on Trish Pharaoh's new CID unit. Roper got his pension early. Left with a golden handshake and no stain on his record. Buggered off to work as an adviser for some posh firm of London corporate lawyers. Living the high life in a flat in Mayfair, last time she'd heard his name in the canteen. Left McAvoy with a reputation as a snake that he has had to half kill himself to remove.

Despite her fury, Pharaoh cannot help but smile as her thoughts turn to McAvoy. He and Fin had turned up at the hospital not long after 6 p.m. Pharaoh had heard his footsteps in the corridor and gone out to meet him. She hadn't meant to cry on the phone and certainly hadn't meant to dissolve into a puddle of snot and tears when she saw him. But it had happened anyway. She wept against him as he folded his arms around her and rested his chin upon the top of her head.

She grinds out the cigarette and comes to a stop against the wall of the boarded-up pub.

Roisin's contact details had been stored in Tom Spink's mobile phone. So had the address where she was staying in South Yorkshire. So had the notes from his breakfast meeting with Pharaoh; not to mention the list of properties belonging to Francis Nock that had been taken from the passenger seat. Pharaoh knows she has fucked up. Desperation made her incautious. She'd thought she could push the boundaries without them splintering. Thought she could manipulate the Headhunters without repercussions. They must have known she would edit the list. Must have known she would send her old boss and friend to make inquiries on her behalf. They'd simply made sure she understood how things worked. They were in charge. They took what they wanted. When persuasion didn't work they used force. And they had friends in patrol cars who were willing to help them beat a sixty-four-year-old man unrecognisable.

Pharaoh had wanted to tell McAvoy everything. Wanted to tell her where Roisin has been these past weeks. Wanted to jump in her car with him and Fin and race to Sheffield to reunite the great hopeless lump and his bloody perfect little wife. She might have done, too, had the call not come in.

Scowling, scrunching up her face, Pharaoh takes Bruno Pharmacy's phone from her handbag and listens to the message that was left on the voicemail service as she sat in the canteen with McAvoy and half-heartedly listened to what he had been doing out at the woods and some shit about an underground bunker and a charity bin-bag scam. She hadn't been paying attention. Had been too busy texting Dan in the Technical and Forensics unit, and warning what would happen if he didn't analyse the nails that had been removed from Tom's feet before the morning.

Pharaoh listens to the message again. Feels her heart squeeze.

'Detective Superintendent. I had rather hoped we could talk properly but I presume you are otherwise engaged, attending to your friend and confidant. Let me express my deep regret. I do not expect you to believe me, but it is important to me that I inform you we had given no instruction for the harming of Mr Spink. We are restructuring our organisation at present and some of the less reliable members of the workforce will soon be seeking new employment, or worse. I hope you appreciate that this is a sincere apology. As a demonstration of good faith I will continue to personally ensure that Mrs McAvoy is kept free from harm until such time as alternative arrangements can be found. I believe that the address in Sheffield has been compromised following today's unfortunate business. Truly, I hope you appreciate that the vision we had for our organisation does not correspond with some of our more recent indiscretions. . .'

Pharaoh had hung up so hard that she had snapped a nail. The bastards had known all along. Her well-spoken contact had kept Roisin's whereabouts private but there are others within the Headhunters who wish her harm. Pharaoh bites again at the fat of her thumb. Tastes her own sweat and sniffs the nicotine on her fingers. It's clear the Headhunters are splintering. The organisation may have started as a small collection of pragmatic individuals but they have had to recruit muscle that is not respecting the rules. And somebody is refusing to play nicely. For whatever reason, they want Roisin. And Pharaoh has no idea where to put her.

Pharaoh leans back against the damp brick of the pub. Used to be famous around the world, this place. The Earl de Grey. Known in every port on the planet as the seediest of dives and the place to go meet an accommodating lady. Had a cage in which varicose-veined grannies danced in basques and boas. Had quite the transvestite clientele, and on cold nights one cubicle in the male toilets needed a revolving door for the punters to take their turns with whichever hooker the landlady had allowed to conduct her business in a slightly warmer environment. Used to be a couple of parrots on a perch in the eighties. One of them got stabbed by a burglar who feared it would reveal his identity. The other died of a broken heart and was buried under Clive Sullivan Way. Pharaoh had simply shaken her head when she'd heard that story. Added another entry to her list of reasons to think of Hull as a seriously weird place.

As she stands and watches the clouds change shape in the black sky, Pharaoh suddenly feels bone-tired. She should be at home. But she's standing in the cold, resting her back against a boarded-up knocking shop, grinding her teeth over her failures and lashing herself for not knowing what to do next.

Pharaoh takes a breath. Holds it. Pushes it out slowly. Repeats the process until she feels a modicum of calm. She decides not to let go of the rage. Just folds it up and stores it with the rest. A picture is starting to form in her head. It reminds her of an old portable TV with the circular aerials that could only pick up

217

a picture when held at certain angles. The static in her mind is forming into something clear.

She pulls out her phone. Calls for a patrol car to take her back to her vehicle. Wonders if there is anywhere between here and home that might serve fried chicken and red wine.

Dials another number. Waits for the sound of a gruff Scottish accent to say a soft hello.

Hopes, above all things, that she was right to contact this man she doesn't know, and to ask him to take on a responsibility that could cost him his life.

'That relevant, you think?'

Colin Ray nods in the direction of the jeweller's across the street. Helen squints and makes out the name of the shop.

'McAvoy and Beardsmore? I doubt it. Just one of those things.'

'Fucker's everywhere,' says Ray, though there is no real malice in it. 'I keep expecting to find him in the mirror behind me, looking all sad and heroic.'

'Is that how you see him?' asks Helen, turning in her seat.

Ray shrugs. 'Don't think about him much. I know he hits hard, I'll tell you that. And chicks fucking love him.'

Helen turns away. She winds the window down another inch and feels the cold evening air turn the sweat on her brow into a chilly veneer.

They are sitting in Ray's Saab 95 on Oakbrook Road in Sheffield. It's a nice, cosmopolitan area with delicatessens that sell tubs of olives, anchovies and sun-dried tomatoes to people who spend their weeks browsing antiques fairs and helping to organise art exhibitions in churches and community centres. Helen likes it. They are little more than an hour from Hull and still very much in Yorkshire but the east coast seems half a world away. There was even some blue in the sky as they made the drive over, though the evening has drawn in quickly and the blue-black air beyond the glass contains a fine mist that soaks to the bone.

'This is her neck of the woods, isn't it?' asks Ray, spooning up the last of his lamb bhuna with the edge of a CD case. He licks greasy sauce off Bruce Springsteen's back then chucks the case onto the back seat. He pulls out his cigarettes and begins to puff, contentedly.

'Her, sir?'

'Pharaoh. She's South Yorkshire.'

'I think so. Mexborough.'

'Brian Blessed's from there.'

'Yeah?'

'Yeah. Always liked him.'

Helen doesn't know what to say. Gives a well-intentioned nod. 'Good.'

They have been here for over an hour. The car smells of curry, cigarettes and Colin Ray. Helen is used to the company of her male officers and is resisting the temptation to reach into her handbag and start spraying her surroundings with something floral. She contents herself with sticking her nose next to the gap between window and roof, inhaling fresh air like a dog.

'Somewhere nearby,' says Ray, nodding at the laptop on Helen's knees. 'Within a hundred yards. Fuck.'

Helen is keeping an eye on Piers Fordham's location. His car is parked a little way up the road. It's a black Audi; immaculately clean and with a state-of-the-art sound system. According to the data that Dan is feeding her laptop, Piers's office mobile phone is inside it. At some point he will have to return to the car and Colin Ray can get a proper look at the man he wants to hurt like no other. For now, all they can do is wait.

'Makes you wonder why we miss it,' says Helen, moodily. 'All the waiting. Sitting about.'

'Never got used to it myself, love. Always tried to find a quicker way, that's my problem.' Ray sounds oddly confessional. He must hear it in his own voice and quickly switches back to a more aggressive and sneery tone. 'Would be worse with the Flying Scotsman in the back though, eh? Bloody hell, we'd have his legs sticking out the front windows.'

Helen's phone beeps and she looks at the message she has received from Dan in the Tech Support unit.

'Dan's ready for home,' she says, sighing. 'He's going to leave the system on for us but wants me to know that if he gets into trouble he's blaming it all on you.'

'I signed the forms, didn't I?'

'You're suspended. Only a superintendent can request that a mobile phone be pinged for a location. And even then it's up to the phone company.'

'Yeah, but they played ball. And besides, I did sign it as a superintendent. Chief Superintendent Davey.'

Helen looks at him for signs he is joking. Watches as he burps and enjoys the taste of curried lamb.

'How are you still in a job?' she asks, aghast.

'I'm owed a lot of favours,' he says, grinning. 'And I know where the bodies are buried.'

'I bet you bloody do.'

They sit in silence for a time. The rain starts to come down more heavily and Ray switches on the windscreen wipers so as not to lose sight of the car up ahead. They are parked outside a nice old-fashioned property with a gable window and stone cladding. It's part of a terrace that runs far down the hill and stops by a row of shops. The Indian restaurant was a welcome discovery in amongst the jewellers, hairdressers, florists and delicatessens.

'Hold up,' says Ray, sitting forward in his seat. 'That's the fucker.'

The two detectives hold their breath and take in the short, plump man ahead of them. He has a big beard and long cashmere coat that reaches almost to his ankles. He's coming towards them, puffing on a cigarette.

'Where did he come from?'

'He must have got out of a car . . .'

'Which car?'

'I didn't see!'

'Fuck!'

Piers Fordham stops at his Audi. He presses the button on his car keys and the headlights flash with subtle German precision. He looks up for a moment. Stares at the apartment above the gardening shop a few car-lengths away. He gives a slow shake of his head. Climbs inside. A moment later he is cruising back up the road; his car making a soft, expensive purr.

'Do we follow, sir?'

Ray is chewing his lower lip. 'He must have come from a car.'

'Sir, do we follow?'

'We can find him again, yeah? On the tracker thing?'

'Yes, but . . .'

Ray opens his car door. 'Stay there.'

Helen's protests are lost as he steps out of the vehicle and into the rain. He inhales the South Yorkshire air. Expects steel and Brasso. Gets curry and wet grass.

221

'Right, ya fucker . . .'

Ray does a fine impression of a drunk. He begins to stagger. Giggles to himself. Totters and zigzags up the darkened road, bumping into parked cars and trying to free his hand from his pocket. In this manner it takes him a little under a minute to check the interiors of each vehicle parked in the street. He spots a Fiat 500 and barges into it, setting off the alarm. Suddenly the street is alive with noise and flashing lights.

'Come on, son . . .'

A little way ahead, a car door opens. It's a nondescript vehicle. A Renault or Vauxhall. Its driver is a thickset man. He's wearing white trainers, jeans and a puffer jacket. He looks angry. Crosses to the pavement and approaches Ray.

'What you fucking doing?' he asks as he comes closer.

In his pocket, Ray switches on the tape recorder. The man's accent is Eastern European. Russian, if he's any judge.

'You touch my car? You touch my car I fucking kill you.'

'Sorry, mate,' says Ray, slurring. 'You Russian? Beautiful country. I met a Russian girl once. Dirty fucker. Probably your sister . . .'

The man's face twists and he lunges at Ray. Ray suddenly becomes very sober. He turns and twists at the hip and kicks his attacker beneath the knee cap with enough force to send him sprawling to the ground.

'Back of the net,' says Ray, turning. 'Now, I think that deserves a penalty kick . . .'

He punts the fallen Russian in the ribs as he lays on the ground. A pocket knife tumbles from the man's pocket and Ray grins, evilly, as he picks it up.

'Carrying an offensive weapon? If I wasn't suspended you'd be fucked. As it is, I'll just do this . . .'

222

He unfolds the blade and crosses to the man's car. He plunges the blade into the rear tyre and smiles as air hisses out.

'Your mate,' he says, conversationally. 'Piers. Lawyer, of sorts. I'd love to know more about him. Can I maybe borrow your phone and ask around . . . ?'

'That'll do.'

Ray turns around. He has his hand inside the man's coat and his fingers around his mobile phone. He looks in the direction of the voice: clear and accented, despite the noise of the car alarms. A big man in a woolly jumper and flat cap is leaning against the bonnet of a big 4x4. He has a grey moustache and a broad, weather-beaten face. He's got a chest that convicts could crack rocks on. Behind him, a pretty, large-chested girl with dark hair and too many earrings is holding a baby to her chest.

'Police business,' says Ray, off-handedly. 'Go back inside.'

'The police dinnae do business like that. I'd make yourself scarce if I was you.'

Ray's face twists into a sneer. 'Jock, are you?'

'No, lad. I'm a Scotsman.'

'Good for you. Now fuck off back to Scotland.'

'I can't do that,' he says, walking forward. 'I'm just that way. Now, I hate to use foul language in front of a bairn but if I was you I'd piss off.'

Ray considers his options. Realises that doors are opening. Lights are going on. He's caused too much of a scene. He pockets the man's mobile phone. Holds the Scotsman's gaze and walks past him towards the waiting Saab. Helen is standing outside it, her phone in her hand; eyes wide and face pale.

'Fucking Jocks,' says Ray, slamming the door. 'Pikey bitches.'

Helen winds down the window as they pull away from the kerb in a squeal of rubber on wet road. They tear past the Russian's parked car and see him clambering painfully into the passenger seat. The large Scotsman is fiddling with a child-seat in the backseat of a large dark-coloured car.

Helen only locks eyes with the big man's passenger for an instant but it is long enough for her heart to all but stop beating. She recognises those blue eyes. That long, lustrous hair. The curve of the hips and the jewellery at her throat. Recognises the baby against her breast.

'Sir, I . . .'

'Don't say a word,' says Ray, spitting as he snaps at her. 'Did she ring? Your swinger? Your slag? Suzie?'

Helen can't catch her breath. Her thoughts are reeling as the car screeches through unfamiliar streets and she looks through a windscreen fragmented by a billion raindrops.

'She's on now,' she says, light-headed. 'Got the addresses of the sites he was looking at yesterday on the work computer. Some touristy stuff about Panama. The archives of the *Newcastle Journal*. A Google search on somebody called Mahon . . .'

Helen lifts the phone to her ear again.

'Suzie, yeah, that's great. What else? BBC homepage. News stuff. Science stories. A company in London. Some bigwigs in the City. And what? Personnel . . .'

Helen closes her eyes as she hears Suzie speak. Can barely bring herself to thank her and hang up.

'Well?' snaps Ray, eyes on the road and a fag between his teeth. 'Why's he even here? He's the big man, yeah? What's he doing sorting out surveillance and leg-work? And who was that bloody Jock?'

Helen says the name that Suzie has given her out loud. Tries not to let her mind do terrible things.

Ray says nothing for a while. Just smokes and stares and twists his hands around the steering wheel.

'We've got to tell her,' he says. 'Or him. Somebody.'

Helen nods. She doesn't want to make that call. Doesn't want to have to make sense of events that could not pass for coincidence.

'That was his wife,' says Helen, quietly. 'Roisin McAvoy. I don't know why she's here. Maybe she's hiding.'

'Not very well,' says Ray, without malice. 'Fuck, I don't know . . .'

Helen stares at the computer in her lap. The company mobile is beeping its way back towards Hull. The Russian that Ray left on the ground has no way of alerting his employer about what has just happened. They can talk to Piers tonight. They can get answers and maybe save a life. But they aren't police officers right now. She doesn't know what to do.

'Shaz,' says Ray, as if reading her mind. 'We'll let her put all this through the books. Get him in. Get a nice interview room and see how big he is then . . .'

Helen is barely listening. She is staring at a picture at the front of her mind. She is looking at the absolute fear in Roisin McAvoy's eyes. She is wondering how much horror it has taken to break such a powerful soul.

# Part Three

Part Three

# Chapter 15

The puddles reflect Mahon's hulking shape as he crosses the pitted, cracked tarmac of the car park.

He can't feel the rain as it pelts the deadened surface of the small rectangle of skin which is visible between his scarf and sunglasses, but he enjoys imagining the caress of the downpour upon his ruined features.

He steps between the lorries parked up in the truck-stop, eyes fixed on a vehicle at the rear of the compound.

Nobody sees him. The drivers are either stealing a nap in their wagons or holed up in the greasy spoon at the front of the service station, tucking into a variety of brown foods, dished up with toast and fried bread.

He passes a wagon with purple livery and slides into a shadow as the door opens. He slows his heart. Stops his lungs. The ligature eases down from his wrist and into his gloved hand.

A man, bulky, with a shaved head and a rash on his neck, turns up his T-shirt collar and half runs, half waddles away through the rain in the direction of the cafe.

Mahon steps out of the blackness and continues on to the dark green cab that stands at the back of the yard. It's hauling a nondescript blue container.

Without pausing, Mahon pulls open the driver's door. He climbs up the three steps and into the cab. Swishes back the curtain to the sleeping quarters.

The man asleep on the bunk is in his twenties. Wearing a black round-neck T-shirt and combat pants. He has a thin, pinched, Eastern European face, and a golden crucifix has snaked out of his top to lie, coiled, by his face as it rests upon the makeshift pillow of a luminous yellow coat.

The man wakes as Mahon takes hold of both his legs and pulls. He is wrenched forward, arms flying up to claw at the curtain, hauled through the gap in the seats. He looks up and for a fraction of a second, sees the colossal, deformed man in the black leather jacket and cloth cap who blocks out the dull autumn light of the rain-lashed car park.

Mahon leaps gently down to the tarmac, the man's ankles still held in his grip.

Groggy, spluttering, fuzzy with disrupted sleep, the man gives a half-strangled yell as he slithers into a seated position in the driver's seat.

Mahon's grip is immovable. He stands bolt upright, and without ceremony, as though pulling a soiled sheet from a mattress, he wrenches the man from the cab, taking two quick steps backwards.

The man's entire body leaves the vehicle, pulled far out over the hard, wet, glistening blackness of the concrete several feet below.

There is an instant in which the man feels he is flying; his

230

whole frame four feet from the ground – face, chest, groin, toes, all pointing skywards.

Then a sensation of movement.

A push in his chest.

The cessation of his trajectory and a sudden rush downwards.

And he slams into the ground.

His skull cracks like an egg.

Mahon stands over the man and waits for the gurgling sounds to stop. He pauses until the jam-like blood that seeps from the fissure in his cranium is running almost to the corpse's waist.

Then he turns and walks away.

It was not the man's fault. Not really. He'd been given the chance at easy money. All the reports Mahon had heard suggested that he had done his best to look out for the girls in his care. But Mr Nock controls the working girls around here. He runs a profitable service providing girls for the minimum-wage building crews and meat-packers that come over from the Balkans each year to earn themselves a wedge of illegitimate cash and then bugger off home before immigration officials catch up with them. He doesn't want any competition. Doesn't want anybody to spread their legs between Whitley Bay and Hadrian's Wall without him getting half the profits. The young lad bleeding to death on the ground hadn't known that. Had just done what some enterprising villain had asked of him. He was probably not even aware that Mr Nock wouldn't approve. Maybe didn't even know the name and what it meant.

Bloody Eastern Europeans.

Mahon is pleased to be back in the north-east. The couple of days away seem to have done him some good. He feels fit and well. Ready for what will come next. And Mr Nock is on fine

231

form. Had made his feelings clear on what should be done to the driver who deposited a dozen shivering and emaciated Slovenians at a house in Jarrow last night. An example needed to be made. It should look to the casual observer like an accident. But to those in the know, it should be a very clear statement of intent.

There's a gap in the chain-link fence at the rear of the truck-stop and Mahon slips through it without snagging his clothes. He crosses a patch of wasteground and emerges at the back of a housing estate. One of his favoured lads is waiting for him in the driver's seat of a nondescript Peugeot. Mahon grunts a hello as he climbs into the passenger seat. Lights himself a cigarette as the lad pulls away from the kerb.

'All grand, boss?'

'Champion,' says Mahon.

He settles down in the seat, wreathed in blue smoke. Watches the houses whizz by. Apparently it's a rough neighbourhood, this. Full of bad sorts, according to the papers. It's a warren of narrow streets and alleyways: back doors facing one another across strips of concrete where kitchen appliances sit abandoned and rotten mattresses lean against graffitied walls. The main streets are all steel shutters and speed bumps and the few patches of greenery have been churned to mud by the tyres of stolen cars.

'Howay then,' he says, at length, to his companion. 'What you got for me?'

Mahon's driver is called Hughie Lowes. He's in his late thirties and has been a friend of the Nock family since he was a boy. He's a safe pair of hands and a solid set of biceps. He also has an inquiring, tactical mind. Can punch his weight but can finish the *Sun* crossword in under ten minutes and knows how to work a computer and forge an MOT certificate with the same aplomb that he can snap a knee in ways that will never heal. He's a good-looking sort. Looks like a sports teacher on his day off. Trainers, cords, stripy T-shirt and a baggy cardigan. Frameless glasses and a wedding band. Hair shaved with a number-two guard and a day's growth on his chin and upper lip. He may run the firm some day. But that day won't come until Mahon says so.

'Benny Pryce,' says Hughie. 'That's whose piss you can smell, if you were wondering. We'll have to torch the Peugeot.'

Mahon nods. He hasn't got a great sense of smell. Hadn't noticed anything unpleasant but is willing to take his underling's word.

'I don't think he took their silver, Mr Mahon,' continues Hughie. 'I think he was trying to do us a good turn, to be honest. He says some ex-copper from Yorkshire got in touch with the lads at the *Journal*. Gave them some bullshit about a book he was writing. Benny had offered one of the young reporters there a favour if they alerted him to anybody asking questions like that. He got a call and said he'd look into it. Turned out the writer was an old colleague of Benny's. He'd told Benny the truth of it. Wanted to know any and all properties associated with Mr Nock. Benny did his old mate a favour and gave him the list but left half of the addresses off and stuck a few dead-ends and red herrings in there for good measure. Met the fella at Scotch Corner and gave him what he wanted. Then he said his goodbyes.'

Mahon sniffs loudly as the car turns right, past a small church erected from chunky, crudely cut bricks. There is no graffiti on

233

the church wall. The local kids know better. Some things are sacred, even to the damned.

'He got hurt, yeah? The bloke? The ex-copper?'

Hughie nods, keeping his eyes on the road. 'He's in hospital. Shit kicked out of him. You know that shit with the nail gun that happened in Hull and down south? He got a couple of nails in him down some side road near Goole.'

'Goole?'

'Shithole between Leeds and Hull.'

Mahon sniffs again. Lights another cigarette. 'Changing a tyre, was he?' he asks cynically.

'Some traffic cops pulled him over then buggered off. A car rammed him from behind. Dragged him out and went to work. Put nails in his feet.'

Mahon sits in silence for a moment. Wonders whether the attacker would have thought to wipe his prints from the nails.

'Where did we get all this?' he asks, with a jerk of his head.

'Fat fucker who used to be CID down in Hull. Don't know if you've met him. Linus. Back in uniform now but still has his ear to the ground.'

Mahon tries to put a face to the name but can't come up with anything. Wonders if he's ever met the bloke or if age is simply wiping his memory a little at a time.

'He's solid, is he? This Linus?'

'Knows how the land lies, that's all. Used to work for a bloke who liked to put a few quid in his personal pension fund. You remember Roper? Absolom? Crooked as a cat's cock.'

Mahon nods. 'All roads lead to Hull, eh? Fucking hell, we just got back.'

Hughie looks across at him apologetically. 'Don't know if we have to get involved any further, really,' he says, diplomatically. 'Benny says there's no way that list will lead anybody to Mr Nock. There's only you who knows where he's having himself a little rest. If these new villains want to beat up an ex-copper and piss off the law, that's their concern, not ours. As long as they stay out of Newcastle, why do we give a shit?

Mahon says nothing. Inhales cigarette smoke and holds it until his eyes water and his lungs hurt. Hughie's right, of course. They've got enough things to think about. Mr Nock's health, for a start. On the drive back from Yorkshire, the old man had been coughing up something that looks a little like shit. Mahon is no doctor but can't imagine that such a thing can be a positive sign.

'Got history, that house,' says Hughie conversationally, nodding at the glass. 'Remember my dad telling me about it.'

Mahon had barely registered which street they were travelling down. Hadn't noticed the shabby end-terrace property that somebody has covered in a shiny pebble-dash and hanging baskets. Mahon closes his eyes as soon as he realises where he is. Doesn't close them in time. The vision of the property sets off a flicker-book of memories. Sees himself, handsome and unscarred. Sees his old Ford Popular parked at the kerb. Mr Nock used to take the piss out of him for driving such a nondescript motor. Told him to splash out. To enjoy himself. To put his money into something with a bit of muscle and sex appeal. Mahon had shrugged it off. He'd liked the car. Liked blending in. Liked the fact it had enough room in the boot for a trio of bodies and a spade. Wonders what happened to the car. Whether they sold it or scrapped it after the southerners came for him. Whether he'd left anything sentimental in the glovebox . . .

*Christ, but the memories hurt . . .*

He remembers opening the front door and climbing those stairs and smelling the blood, the beer, the fag smoke, sweat and cum. Remembers the feeling in the pit of his stomach: the knowledge that everything had just turned to shit. Remembers their bodies. Him, heavy and slippy: a dead dolphin sliding around in his grip. Her, feather-light and perfumed: fragile and breakable, like a baby bird.

'Belonged to what's-his-name, didn't it? One-armed-bandit bloke. Got sent down, didn't he? Wouldn't stop banging on about being innocent . . .'

Mahon holds up a hand to stop his companion. He can't stand listening to any of it. Can't stand listening to the past being so misrepresented. He has lived through all the local legends. Has been at the heart of most of them.

'Sorry, boss,' says Hughie, shutting up. 'Like I say, that's where we're at. Benny's a team player. Got a bit of useful info out of him too. Shipment coming in, according to his snout. Thought we might divert it . . .'

Mahon nods, drinking it all in. He was killing somebody ten minutes ago. Is buggered if he can remember why that was . . .

'Linus said we should watch out for the bloke's mate,' says Hughie suddenly. 'She's a superintendent. Bit of a looker from the picture I found. Anyways, Linus didn't like to admit it but apparently she's good. And she's got this giant of a lapdog. Scottish bloke. Redhead. Jock name, he said. Told us not to even bother making an approach. Holier than thou, said Linus.'

Mahon turns his head.

'McAvoy,' he says, plucking the name from the air. He'd heard it spoken on John Glass's doorstep. Had watched the giant copper's back get smaller across Pearson Park.

236

'That's it,' says Hughie. 'You know him?'

Mahon closes his eyes and settles himself more comfortably in the seat. He gives a tired little chuckle and finds himself almost sad at the thought of what is coming.

He stares out of the window at the grey air and misery. Wonders, for an instant, what the big man's throat will feel like beneath his hands.

Closes his eyes.

'Don't know him yet,' he says, softly. 'But I will.'

# Chapter 16

McAvoy stares out of the window. It's set in a wall painted the colour of old newspaper and is bisected by rusting metal bars.

He jiggles his legs beneath the plastic table. Lines up his felt-tip pens next to his notepad. Sips at his plastic beaker of water.

Waits.

He has never been to this place before. Has heard of it, of course. It's got one of those names that kids throw out in the playground without really understanding. It's a place for crazies. For nutters. For the dangerous criminals who climb in through your bedroom window and cut your face off for the fun of it. It's home to some of the most dangerous people in Britain. It's marketed as a place for healing but everybody knows its true role. It's a prison ship, moored forever in the midst of open fields and winding back roads. It's a mental hospital for the criminally insane. It smells of chemicals and school dinners. Feels like a cross between a hospital and an army barracks. It's joyless, clinical, sterile and cold.

For Peter Coles, it has been home for eighteen years.

McAvoy rubs his head. Pushes his hair back from his face. Smooths it down again with the palm of his hand. Checks his clothes for crumbs. He's chosen to wear something less daunting than a suit, shirt and tie. Made the decision to put Peter at his ease. Feels a little odd in his dark trousers and a purple V-necked jumper. Doesn't like the picture on the visitor pass he is wearing around his neck. He'd blinked as the flash went off at the reception desk. He looks half blind in the image. Puzzled and unsure of himself. Half pissed.

He hears footsteps. Takes a breath. Turns his head and stands as the door to the visiting room swings open.

A man in a blue uniform enters first, Peter Coles behind him. A young West African man enters last, closing the door behind him. He gives Peter a little pat on the back as he takes three strides forward and reaches McAvoy first. Sticks out a warm hand.

'Dr Onatande,' he says, smiling wide. 'Gregory, if it's easier. And can I introduce you to my patient, Peter Coles?'

McAvoy turns his attention to the man he has come to see. He's small. A little stooped. He's looking at the floor and exposing a crown of grey hair that has receded a good three inches from where it was in the mugshots taken in the sixties. He's dressed in cheap blue jeans and a sweatshirt. Has pale, waxy skin, as if he hasn't seen enough sun.

'Hello, Peter,' says McAvoy, extending his hand. 'Pleased to meet you.'

Peter Coles looks up. His eyes widen as he takes in McAvoy's size. Gives a little nod and mumbled hello, then turns to Dr Onatande.

'Is he the one?'

His voice is quiet and his words indistinct, as though he is talking through burst lips and broken teeth.

'This is Aector McAvoy, Peter. Remember, we talked about this. He wants to speak to you about some things you might remember from when you were a youngster. Are you going to be able to do that?'

Behind McAvoy the prison warder rolls his eyes. McAvoy can almost hear his thoughts. Can sense him mentally scoffing at the do-gooders and touchy-feely *Guardian* readers who treat mass murderers like little boys in need of another teddy bear.

'Very good, Peter,' says Dr Onatande as his patient takes a seat on the cushioned, plastic-backed chair. 'I'll just make myself comfortable here, shall I? Or would you rather I left?'

Peter gives a shake of the head and Dr Onatande positions himself on a chair in the corner of the room. The warder stands next to him, his back straight and arms gripped at the wrist behind him. He looks like he's been a military man. Looks like he doesn't need much of an excuse to pull an inmate's arm out of its socket.

'I'm Aector,' says McAvoy, in the voice he uses to soothe skittish horses. 'It's hard to say, I know. Hector's OK, if you prefer that. My friend calls me Hector. What do your friends call you?'

Peter looks up. He has wiry black-and-grey eyebrows and stray black hairs curling out from his nostrils. He shaved a few hours ago and took a half dozen tiny scabs off his upper lip. They are scabbing over afresh; tiny pinpricks of crimson solidifying under the glare of the yellow striplights overhead.

'People just call me Peter,' he says, with a shrug. 'I got Colesy, for a bit. In a different place. There was another Peter so I was Colesy.'

'Do you like Colesy?'

Peter nods.

'Would you like me to call you Colesy?'

Another nod.

'Not Daft Pete?'

McAvoy feels bad for saying it. But he wants to see what reaction it causes in the other man's eyes. If he had expected temper, he is disappointed. Peter just looks a little sad. Shakes his head and shrugs again.

'That's what people called you at Winestead, isn't it? You were known as Daft Pete.'

'I didn't mind,' he mumbles. 'Was just nicknames. There was Big Davey, wasn't there. And Alf the Hat. Mick Chicken, cos he had poultry.'

'You seem to remember those days very well, Colesy. You haven't been there for the best part of fifty years. It's surprising you can recall names like that.'

'I'm good with names,' he says, with a glint of a smile. As he twitches his lips he reveals crooked white teeth. 'I can pronounce yours right, I'm sure. Listen: Aector.' He grins, broadly. 'That was right, wasn't it?'

McAvoy considers the man before him. Forty-eight years ago he took a shotgun and blasted a family to death because they caught him taking potshots at aeroplanes. That's the story the Home Office believes. That's the story that the papers will want to print. He violated Anastasia Winn. Exposed her breasts so he had something to look at until the police arrived. He's a psychopath who deserves every day of the five decades he has spent deprived of liberty.

But McAvoy wants to reach out and squeeze his hand; to tell him it's OK. He feels nothing but pity for the specimen before him. He wonders how other police officers would feel. Whether Trish Pharaoh would have charmed a full confession from him by now. Whether Colin Ray would be sitting on his chest and spitting in his eye.

'That was perfect, Colesy. Now, you do understand why I'm here, yes? It wasn't easy getting in to see you. I hear you don't get many visitors.'

'Nana used to come,' he says, looking away. 'She didn't like it very much but she came whenever she could get away. She was always a bit cross with me though. Sometimes it seemed she came to visit just so she could tell me off again.'

'Tell you off for what, Peter?'

He gives a tiny laugh. 'For making her life difficult, I suppose. People were mean to her. It was all right for me – that's what she used to say. I had a roof over my head and a bed each night and three square meals a day. She was right. I never argued with her.'

'She may have struggled to express her real feelings,' says McAvoy sympathetically. 'She was working very hard to help you, Colesy. She kept writing to the authorities and bothering her MP. It was her efforts that are going to maybe get you a trial at long last.'

Peter flicks his head towards Dr Onatande. 'He told me about that. Said they wanted to dig it all up. To make me think about it. I don't have to, do I? I don't mind staying here. It's OK. It's nice enough. I don't think I really want people looking at me and asking questions. We have a big telly here and watch programmes about crimes, if we're good. I don't think I'd like to be in something like that.'

McAvoy doesn't really know how to respond. He picks up one of the felt-tip pens and writes some shorthand scribbles down in the centre of the page.

'What's that?' asks Peter, suddenly interested. 'Is that Egyptian? Can you write Egyptian?'

McAvoy smiles across the table. 'It's called shorthand,' he says. 'It's a way of keeping up with what people say.' He turns to a fresh page and draws a two lines – one horizontal and one vertical. 'That says "Peter",' he says. 'And here' – he draws a shape a little like an unfinished cartoon of a mouse – 'that says "Coles".'

McAvoy rips the page from the notebook and passes it across the table. Peter takes it like an excited child and aims a grin at Dr Onatande. 'Can I?' he asks, and looks positively gleeful as his psychiatrist nods his assent.

McAvoy rubs his eyelids. Wonders what the hell he is doing here. Peter Coles almost certainly killed the Winn family half a century ago. He has no real reason to doubt it, save a sense of disquiet and some questionable paperwork. But to try the man before him for multiple murder seems positively obscene. He has spent most of his life locked up. He has had no liberty since he was nineteen years old. What would be the point of putting him in the dock and making him answer for the crimes of a man he stopped being before McAvoy was even born?

'If there was a court case, would you plead guilty, do you think?'

McAvoy asks the question quickly, while Peter is still excited by seeing his name on the scrap of paper and before Dr Onatande can clear his throat and suggest that the line of inquiry goes against what the two agreed when McAvoy called this morning and explained the urgent need to see his patient.

Peter's face falls. 'Would I have to say? I don't want to say anything about that. Why do people keep making me think about it? I don't like thinking about it.'

'It was a terrible night, Colesy. Snow was coming down, wasn't it? And the ground was frozen . . .'

Peter shakes his head. 'Wasn't frozen. Was boggy. I nearly lost a welly coming up the path. Made me laugh. Made a rude noise as I pulled it out.'

'You were at the church, yes? That's where you liked to go?'

Coles shrugs. 'Was peaceful. There was an angel in the grounds. Pretty face. I liked talking to her.'

'I understand you had been in trouble for causing mischief at the church though, Colesy. Something about shooting at the planes . . .'

Colesy shakes his head aggressively, like a toddler refusing to apologise. 'It wasn't me. I've shot rabbits, though I always felt a bit bad about it. But I told Glass, I would never shoot the church. And shooting at the planes was just silly. We'd had a few cans, that was all. Just being silly. I said sorry . . .'

'And Clarence Winn saw you, did he? And you thought you would get in trouble?'

Another fierce shake of the head. 'It's not like that. I didn't. I mean, erm, yeah, that's right. He caught me. So I did the thing. Y'know. The bad thing.'

McAvoy turns to Dr Onatande. The psychiatrist's face is expressionless.

'So you did kill them?' he asks quietly. 'You killed all five of them?'

Colesy looks away. Nods.

'All five?'

He turns his eyes back to McAvoy. Gives a cheeky grin. 'You're trying to trick me,' he says, wagging his finger. 'There wasn't five.'

'I'm sorry,' says McAvoy, making a great show of writing on his pad. 'It was just something John Glass said to me. Said to count the bodies.'

Peter scoffs and rolls his eyes. 'I wouldn't believe anything he tells you,' he says dismissively. 'He was in a right state that night. Doubt he could remember very much without getting his wires crossed. He didn't even have handcuffs, did you know that? I quite wanted to know how handcuffs felt. Had to use his tie! Left me tied up, all by myself, while he went running off in a fit. I was cross at him for that. And he didn't stick up for me when the spitty man started shouting at me.'

'The spitty man?'

'The detective. Duchess, he said he was called. Kept spitting when he shouted at me. I told him I didn't like it and he spat right in my face. It went in my mouth. He knew I hated that. So I kept my mouth shut. Didn't speak again.'

McAvoy stops writing. Looks at the shrunken, fragile spree-killer across the desk.

'Which one did you kill first?' he asks. 'Clarence?'

'Mr Winn,' corrects Peter. 'We didn't call him Clarence. The lads, I mean. He was the boss, wasn't he? Gave me a job because he said he knew I worked hard. He was a nice man. Stern but fair, my nana used to say.'

'But you killed him, Colesy. You took a shotgun and blasted him in the stomach with it. And you killed the rest of his family too.'

Peter looks down. 'Not all of them. Not the way you think. I mean . . .'

245

He stops talking. Folds himself up and shrinks in his seat.

'What is it you want to tell me, Colesy? Please, give me something. Just tell me why you did it. Why you thought it was OK. Was it Anastasia? Everybody has told me she was a pretty girl. And we know about the drawings you used to do of her. The thoughts that went through your head. It's OK, we all have thoughts we're ashamed of . . .'

Peter starts tipping his chair back on its rear legs. Starts bucking back and forth, as though riding a horse. 'I'd known her since she was little. She was my friend. It was just stuff in my head. I would never hurt her . . .'

'But you did hurt her. You took a shotgun and blasted her pretty face right off . . .'

Peter Coles gulps in a stuttering breath. His eyes fill up. He lets out a squawk; a squeak of dismay. Bunches his fist and digs it into his temple until the knuckle goes white and his forehead turns red.

'Easy, lad,' says the warder from by the wall. 'None of that.'

'Colesy, people need to know what happened. You remember Vaughn, don't you? He's in Australia now. He's got a good life and he's happy. But there's this hole in his life. He deserves answers. And you deserve to sleep without the weight of all this crushing down on you.'

Coles clatters backwards as the chair slips out from under him. He lands with a thud and both hands slap the cord carpet as his head comes down hard. McAvoy is out of his seat in a moment, crossing to where he lies, sprawled and confused.

'It's OK, Peter. You can talk to me. Get it off your chest. For Anastasia. For Vaughn . . .'

Peter Coles reaches up and takes McAvoy's hand in his. He

stares up into his eyes, his face a mask of conflicting emotions. He wants to talk. Wants to spill his guts. Wants to cough up the ball of lies that he has held like a hairball for half a century.

'No touching, Sergeant,' says the warder, placing an arm on McAvoy's and giving him a none too gentle shove. McAvoy stands his ground. Turns fierce eyes on the warder and plants his feet.

'You said "we",' stutters McAvoy, suddenly remembering. 'You said "we" had had a few drinks. You and who, Colesy? Your friend maybe? Vaughn?'

'Knew Vaughn,' he splutters, trying to get to his feet. 'Knew Vaughn, in Australia ...'

McAvoy turns to Dr Onatande and sees that the psychiatrist is shaking his head. He has broken his promise not to upset or overexcite his patient. The interview is being terminated. An angry email will no doubt be sent to Humberside Police and the Home Office. The prick of a warder will no doubt tell a few mates down the pub what happened today and the whole fucking thing will be in the papers by Sunday. McAvoy senses it all slipping away.

He steps back, hands up. Turns away as the warder hauls Peter Coles to his feet.

Distracted, jittery, McAvoy pulls out his mobile phone. Sees he has a message from Pharaoh. A few words, followed by the instruction not to be downhearted, and a little kiss on the end.

'John Glass,' says McAvoy, quietly relaying the information he has just absorbed. He locks eyes with Peter Coles. 'A neighbour found him dead in his armchair this morning, Peter. I just saw him yesterday. Seemed a nice man. A good man. Carried his secrets with him to the grave ...'

Peter's face falls open in a noiseless twist of agony and terror. 'He's still alive,' he splutters, backing against the wall.

'No, Peter. John's gone . . .'

'Not John. The big man. The one who said those things to Vaughn. The one with the blood on his lips . . .'

McAvoy steps forward, face creased in confusion. 'Which man?' he demands. 'That night? 1966? Which man?'

'Knew Vaughn. Knew Vaughn. Knew about me . . .'

'That'll do,' says Dr Onatande, opening the door and motioning for McAvoy to leave. 'Truly, you can't think you've done any good here.'

McAvoy opens his mouth to speak. Closes it again. Stares into Peter Coles's frightened eyes.

'He's come back?' asks McAvoy, trying to understand. 'The man, from that night. You think he's come back?'

'He never left,' sobs Coles, as the warder leads him from the room; piss trickling from his left trouser leg and snot bubbles bursting in his nose.

'I'm wearing the coat, Dan. I'm not smoking or brushing my hair or scratching my buttocks with your best pencil. I'm behaving. And if you look at me like that again I'm going to step on your face.'

The young Technical Support officer grins, a little sheepishly. Trish Pharaoh shouldn't be in here. She shouldn't be putting pressure on him to fast-track the fingerprint analysis. She shouldn't be glaring at him and looking at her watch. She shouldn't look so bloody sexy in an off-white lab coat and biker boots.

'It's contamination, you see,' he says, stammering. 'The

defence solicitor can have a field day. This stuff should all go to an outside agency. You know that. This is a favour and I'd get in such trouble . . .'

Pharaoh cocks her head and examines the geeky twenty-something. He's skinny, scrawny, bespectacled and quarrelsome. He has also never made any secret of the fact that if he were granted three wishes, he would use them all up on fulfilling his fantasies with Trish.

'This business works on favours and goodwill, Dan. I'm happy to be in your debt.'

Dan makes a noise somewhere between a gulp and a cough and turns back to his computer screen. He mutters to himself. Grumbles, under his breath, about detectives thinking they can just demand things from him. Whispers something sexist and accusatory about Shaz Archer and her constant demands that he help her bend the rules in exchange for her breath on the back of his neck. Grizzles like a stroppy toddler as he gives Colin Ray's name a good roasting. He should have been home hours ago. Instead he's having to ping mobile phones and teach Cretaceous-era detective chief inspectors how the internet works . . .

Behind him, Trish continues to perch on the end of one of the white wipe-clean desks, drumming her fingers on her thighs. She's bored and impatient. Late home. Got important things to do and no end in sight to her day. Her youngest daughter has to go to a birthday party at the village hall. Needs to buy a present for some ghastly nine-year-old with freckles and a slimy upper lip. Her second-oldest daughter, Jasmine, has a parents' evening that Trish will not be able to make. Her own mum will go in her stead. Nod wisely at the infallible teachers and make promises she doesn't know how to keep. Tell Jasmine off and then buy her sweets on the walk home. More than anything else, Pharaoh needs to know that Roisin and Lilah have arrived safe. She had no right to ask such a favour of the pair's new protector; a man she has never met. But he had said yes because it mattered, and because doing the right thing runs in the family.

'Here we go,' says Dan, turning back from the computer screen. He looks excited, and a little surprised. 'Does that make sense?'

Pharaoh crosses to the monitor. Bends forward and looks at the profile on the fancy monitor. Looks into a face she knows. Swallows as if her mouth is full of somebody else's sick.

'Makes sense, Dan. Wish it didn't, but it does.'

'Is this what you wanted? Is it, y'know . . . good work?' He looks earnest and sweet as he asks it, like a little boy wanting a kiss for drawing a picture. Pharaoh manages a smile and squeezes him on the shoulder. Her thumb rests for a moment on the little knuckle of vertebrae at the top of his spine and she is gratified to feel him shiver slightly.

'Great work, Dan. And for now, you'll keep this between us, yes? This is crucial. Got a lot to digest. And you'll hang around, yeah? For when the phone rings?'

Pharaoh doesn't judge herself for using Dan's attraction to her in this way. She'll do whatever it takes. She can't abide the female officers who totter around in miniskirts and high heels then pull a face when somebody wolf-whistles. Would never go to the lengths that people like DI Shaz Archer are rumoured to have gone in order to get people to talk. But she sees nothing wrong with a wink and a smile.

250

'Do you want me to wipe it?' asks Dan. 'The search?'

Pharaoh nods. 'Print me it off. And you're sure, yeah? No room for doubt?'

'There's always room for doubt. Like I said, the fingerprints were only a partial match. But when I cross-referenced all the possibles with that list of names you gave me, I would say that's your man. You didn't tell me – what did he do?'

Pharaoh is heading for the door of the Tech suite, pulling off the white coat and clutching the warm sheet of paper in her hand.

'He signed his own death warrant, Dan. He hurt my friend.'

Pharaoh is dragging her phone from her pocket as she emerges back into the corridor. It's chilly after the temperature-controlled perfection of the Tech unit. Pharaoh shivers. Heads back down the corridor to the canteen and retrieves her biker jacket from the back of the chair. The half-eaten baked potato she had left on the table is still there, congealing and solidifying and making her stomach turn.

She looks at her mobile. Counts down to zero and watches the screen light up. Hears a voice say her name after the third ring.

'My turn,' she says, quietly, before the wordy bastard can start to speak. 'I've got a name. It's the name of a man who is in an awful lot of trouble. And I don't know if I should keep it, or give it to you.'

There is a pause. The tiniest suggestion of a throat being cleared.

'I think you can rest assured that the name is already known to us. The man is, after all, in our employ.'

'Are you sure about that? You're sure he still works for you? I get the impression he and his pals are branching out.'

'You are a very astute woman, Superintendent. It's such a shame you have risen so high. You could have been quite the opponent if you were free from the demands of high office. I could arrange that for you, if you wish. I could see that you were a WPC once more, struggling to fit into that delightful blue uniform . . .'

'Leave off,' says Pharaoh, uncaring. 'You don't frighten me, mate. Even if I slapped the cuffs on you right now I don't know what I'd charge you with. You're a mouthpiece. You're the talker. You might have some people who can put the frighteners on but I reckon that when you put a group of ambitious young criminals together, it's hard to persuade them to play nicely. Your team isn't your team any more. And I'm getting a good idea whose they are.'

Pharaoh listens to nothing but breathing. Sniffs and smiles a little. Wonders if he's sweating. Whether he will call her bluff. Pictures Dan, sitting in the Tech unit, listening in and recording every word of the call that has been forwarded to her own mobile from Bruno Pharmacy's. Right now he'll be pinging the mobile phone for a location on the caller. Will be looking at a satellite image and finding wherever in the world this cold-hearted shite is calling from. She's one of the few officers with the authority to request the pinging procedure. She needs to make the request in writing and have it countersigned by another senior officer and has promised to do all that if it turns anything up. For now, she's simply calling in a favour. Her ledger of favours owed is filling up.

'You don't know where she is any more, do you? Mrs McAvoy, I mean. You lost her, I know you did. We watched the car for miles and there was nobody behind her.'

Again, there is silence, and Pharaoh pushes her luck.

'I don't think you want to find Mr Nock to kill him any more. I think you want to find his monster because you need his help. You've shown your protégés what to do and now they're branching out. But they've branched out in the wrong direction, mate. They've hurt somebody they shouldn't have hurt. And they've pissed me off.'

After a pause of a few heartbeats, Pharaoh hears the man clearing his throat.

'My apology last night was genuine,' he says at last. 'I am sorry this situation has arisen. Perhaps you are right. Perhaps we have expanded too soon. But we do hope to trim the fat. And the gentleman whose name you are guarding so jealously could be a place to start.'

Pharaoh says his name. Takes the man's silence as confirmation.

'I want to speak to Mr Nock,' he says at last. 'Or the large gentleman who has proven so—'

'Stop talking like a lawyer,' she says coldly. 'You give me a fucking headache. Now, listen to what I'm about to say and maybe, only the right people will get hurt ...'

# Chapter 17

The email pinged through while McAvoy was driving back from the Midlands. His phone gave a little vibration next to his heart and he knew, with cold inevitability, that he was in trouble.

He allowed himself ten whole minutes without pulling over and reading it. Ten minutes in which he listened to a programme on Radio 4 and refused to give in to his thoughts and fears.

Then he swerved into a lay-by and opened the message. He read it twice. Found himself wishing it contained more words. Instead, it was short and to the point. He had overstepped his boundaries. He had done more than the Home Office had wanted him to. He had alerted Peter Coles to the possibility of both trial and freedom and explanations were wanted. He was hereby requested to cease his digging into the events of 1966 and to file his report before close of play on Friday.

McAvoy had felt sweat prickling at his back. Had felt his skin turn crimson and hot. Had grown clammy at the temples and his hands were shaking as he buried his face in them. The message had been sent to Trish Pharaoh as well. Would she be in trouble because of him? He should have told her. Should have said what he was going to do. But she'd had so much to think about. So many other worries with Tom Spink and Bruno Pharmacy's death. Christ he'd fucked it all up again . . .

He didn't speak very much when he picked up Fin from after-school club, and the boy had seemed to know that his father needed some quiet time. He'd sat quietly in the passenger seat, doing his spelling homework and moving his lips as he read. McAvoy had seen him out of the corner of his eye. Had a sudden memory of Roisin doing the same – concentrating with furrowed brow on a word she didn't recognise and gently mouthing the letters as she spoke. He had felt as though he were folding inwards. Had felt her absence in every pore. Saw himself, momentarily, as a hollow thing; a husk or cocoon around absolute nothingness.

McAvoy had felt guilty about his silences with the boy. Tried to make amends with a takeaway pizza and chips which they ate in one of the parking spaces on Hessle Foreshore, watching the sky darken and the waters turn from vinegar-brown to metallic black.

'Is it Mammy?' asked Fin, through a mouthful of ham and cheese. 'Are you missing her?'

McAvoy had softened his gaze and pressed his damp forehead against the boy's own. 'It's a bit of everything, son. I think I've done things the wrong way again. Got carried away. Lost sight of myself.'

Fin looked at him, all brown eyes and innocence. 'I don't understand,' he'd said. 'Is it Mammy?'

McAvoy had smiled then; a tired, accepting kind of smile. 'Yes,' he'd said. 'I just miss her. Miss her like you do.'

'Bet she misses us too,' said Fin, poking a chip into the top of his triangle of pizza. 'At least she's coming back. Emily at school has a mummy in Africa. And there are lots of people with mummies and daddies who live in different houses. This is like a long holiday. That's what you said, remember. Do you think she'll say I've got big?'

'You'll be bigger than me one day,' said McAvoy, wiping a greasy knuckle across his nose. 'Bigger and better.'

Fin grinned, delighted. 'Will you still be a policeman then? We could be a team? We'd scare the baddies.'

McAvoy had smiled then. Both at the boy's sheer joyfulness and the sudden realisation that he had made up his mind. He was already in trouble. He may as well be truly damned as slightly damned. Hears his dad's voice, bleating on about it being as well to hang for a sheep as a lamb.

Here, now, McAvoy is feeling energised. He doesn't know what cause he is fighting for but knows he cannot walk away without knowing what happened that night and the nature of the big man with the blood on his lips.

His first call should have been to Pharaoh. But instead he called Vaughn Winn.

The entrepreneur had sounded less enthusiastic to hear from him.

*Haven't we already been through this, mate? I'm a busy man. I don't need reminding of the past every five minutes . . .*

McAvoy had been professional and businesslike. Kept himself on a tight leash. Had told him that he had visited Peter Coles in prison. He had made mention of another man at the scene of the crime. Somebody who knew Vaughn . . .

Vaughn had tried to laugh it off. Told him that Daft Pete was

256

still making things up. Why was he talking to the man who killed his family as if he were no more than a witness? What was he implying . . . ?

McAvoy had not even had time to apologise or explain. Vaughn had terminated the call brusquely and informed him that he did not wish to be contacted again.

McAvoy had sat looking at his phone for a while, and trying to make sense of it. In the passenger seat, Fin had looked at him expectantly, awaiting a progress report and an explanation.

Outside, the lights of the distant shore become a line of fool's gold, sandwiched between the twin darknesses of sky and land . . .

The phone rings. McAvoy and his son both jump and the phone clatters into the footwell. Fin picks it up, pressing the answer button with his tomato-stained fingers. 'Here, Daddy . . .'

'You got a receptionist, Hector?' asks Trish, her voice light. 'Hope he's getting a decent wage.'

'Hello, guv,' says McAvoy, smiling. 'Did you see . . . ?'

Pharaoh cuts him off with a sigh. 'I did. Do I want to know?'

'I needed to speak to him. You can't conduct a murder investigation without speaking to witnesses.'

'It wasn't a murder investigation, Hector. You were just meant to see if it would stand up in court.'

'Well it won't. The investigation was a shambles. All the evidence is missing and the statements are the words of dead people. I needed to know.'

Pharaoh gives a soft laugh at the other end of the phone. 'You really know how to make powerful enemies, Hector. You could probably use some friends.'

'I've got Fin,' he says, winking at his son. 'My new partner.'

'He looking after you, is he? He's a good boy.'

257

'How's Tom?' asks McAvoy, suddenly. 'How's it all going?'

Pharaoh makes a noise that sounds like a shrug. 'I'm making progress. I've got some things to talk to you about but we'll have a proper chat when I see you, yeah? It's all good. Everything's happening for a reason.'

McAvoy senses something in her voice that he hasn't heard before. It's a note of doubt. A timbre that is almost apologetic in tone.

'I'm sure you're doing what's right, guv.'

'That's what I love about you, Hector. You're good for my soul.'

McAvoy feels better for the chat. He had expected a bollocking and instead been rewarded with faint praise. He finds himself nodding. Warming to the ideas that his mind is presenting him with.

An hour later, McAvoy and Fin are parking the people-carrier on a muddy grass verge on Station Road in Patrington. To their left, a row of trees blank out the wide, open fields. The property they are visiting is a sturdy, two-storey construction from the 1950s with outbuildings off to one side and a large, comfortable saloon vehicle in the driveway. McAvoy wonders if the owner still drives it. Hopes, given his age, that he doesn't.

'You want the radio on?' asks McAvoy, stepping from the car and switching on the reading light above Fin's head.

'No, I can't concentrate. I'll write up our progress in my incident book.'

McAvoy wants to hug the boy so tightly that the nearness plugs all the gaps within himself. Instead he ruffles the boy's hair and closes the door. Crunches over shiny white pebbles past well-tended flower-beds and a front lawn mowed in perfect ver-

258

tical stripes. Raps on the wooden door. Waits for the light in the hallway to switch on.

Algernon Munroe is in his nineties now but could pass for somebody much more recently retired. He's a short, stocky man with a perfectly bald head and soft brown eyes. He's wearing a quilted robe over smart trousers, shirt, tie and jumper, and the monogrammed slippers on his feet look as though they were hand-crafted at considerable expense. He greets McAvoy with a smile.

'Will you come in?' he asks.

McAvoy points back to the car. 'Flying visit. Don't want to leave my son if I can help it.'

'You sound even more Scottish in person,' says Munroe. 'Western Highlands, is it? Maybe a touch of Inverness?'

McAvoy doesn't want to be distracted by small talk. But the progress he has made in his career has been made through bloody-mindedness and an ability to make people warm to him. So he smiles and nods.

'I'm a bit of a mongrel,' he says. 'Family croft's a couple of miles inland of Aultbea. And the accent got the edges shaved off at boarding school.'

Munroe winces theatrically. 'Boarding-school boy, eh? All cold showers and buggery, was it?'

The words sound strange coming in the refined English accent of this characterful old man. McAvoy gives a shake of the head.

'Soft sheets and three-course meals, as a matter of fact. Not sure on the buggery. I don't think I was anybody's type.'

'Count your blessings, eh? I haven't been anybody's type for years. Anyways, this won't get you back to your boy. I dug out what you asked for. Well, a friend did. I won't be climbing about in the loft again, I don't think. Could well be a family of asylum-seekers up there and I wouldn't know about it.'

He reaches behind the door and pulls out a brown file. The words 'Clarence Winn' are written in blue ink on the label at the top. Algernon Munroe was his solicitor from 1953 until his death. Had attended his funeral. Wasn't in the country when the family lost their lives but had grieved the loss of both client and friend.

'It all went to Vaughn,' he says, handing the file over. 'He'd rather have had his family, of course, but he did well out of Clarence's death. I handled the sale of the house. Transferred all monies over to his new pad in Queensland. He's done well on the back of it. He was always ambitious but I never had him down as a philanthropist. Wasn't exactly a black sheep but there was an edge to him that his brother and sister didn't have. He must have grown up quickly after what happened. Got his name on a few plaques around here, I'll tell you that.'

McAvoy opens the file and leafs through. Reads legalese and numbers; letters written on typewriters and dates decades back.

'And this?' asks McAvoy, nodding at a photocopied letter sent to Clarence Winn in 1964.

'Giving him a telling off, I was,' says Munroe with a soft smile. 'We'd done a bit of work on a Land Registry issue for him and needed to show he had the funds to seal the deal, as it were. We needed to see bank records. Clarence was old-school in that regard. He was the sort who kept his money under the mattress. A lot of them did round here. We found him some high-interest accounts and explained that certain policies would be rendered null and void if he was found to have a large sum of money in the house.'

'What sort of policies?'

'Life insurance, of course. They paid out to Vaughn as well. He'd put his money where we advised by then so there was no battle with the blood-sucking insurance companies.'

McAvoy presses his hands together, folder under his arm. 'You knew Peter Coles?' he asks, tactfully.

'Daft Pete,' says Munroe, nodding. 'Everybody knew him. Not such a bad lad before that night. Just a bit light-headed, if you understand me. His grandmother was a good soul. Hurt her, what happened. I was surprised she stayed here as long as she did. Still, by the time she moved away she could afford something worth getting excited about.'

McAvoy looks at the old lawyer and looks puzzled. 'She came into money?'

'Just what she'd been putting by. But Vaughn's a generous man.'

McAvoy's expression changes. 'She received money from Vaughn?'

'A monthly sum, administered by myself. Not insignificant. And it went up as he did better for himself. She was grateful, I know that, and kept quiet about it. Would have been a bit strange, wouldn't it? And she deserved a bit of good fortune. Bit of a spinster, despite the "Mrs". Her husband was a soldier who went off with a bit of stuff. Moved a couple of villages over. Tried to stay in contact with the family but never got much of a warm welcome from his ex or her family. Shame, really. Seemed good for Peter, the few times old Jasp was around . . .'

'Jasper?' asks McAvoy, closing his eyes. 'Does he have a grandson of the same name?'

'Bit of a wide boy, so I'm told. Causes a bit of mischief here and there. Doesn't tell anybody he's got some of Peter Coles's blood in him, though I bet he would if he knew that Vaughn's money still gets paid to Daft Pete every month. Must be a tidy sum, eh?'

McAvoy isn't sure what to say. Just looks at the old man and lets his expression of puzzlement say it all.

'Not the most normal thing, is it?' says Munroe, softly. 'But it wasn't Mrs Coles's fault, was it? And she suffered for what Peter did.'

McAvoy leans against the doorframe. 'If he did it,' he says, half to himself.

Munroe raises his eyebrows, gleeful and intrigued. 'They're not going to give him a trial, are they? Not after all this time? Christ, I never thought Mrs Coles would persuade them. Home Secretary must be wanting to hide some bad news.'

It suddenly feels cold on the doorstep. The warmth and light of the interior of Munroe's home looks inviting. McAvoy shivers in his jumper and pushes his hair from his face with a clammy hand.

'There are some peculiarities to be looked at first. Can I ask you, in all honesty, did you ever have any doubts about Peter's guilt?'

'He admitted it, didn't he?'

'He admitted being sorry for what had happened. And the detective who took that statement was perhaps not the most softly-softly of officers.'

'Duchess, wasn't it? Disappeared in the seventies after feathering his nest once too often. Weren't many tears shed for him here.'

'You knew him?' asks McAvoy, impressed at the old man's memory.

'Vaguely. Spent some time with a criminal practice when I was a younger man. Len Duchess had a knack of making evidence appear and disappear almost at will. And rumour has it he had enemies and friends in low places.'

McAvoy soaks it all up. Wonders what to do next.

'John Glass told me to count the bodies,' he says, at last. 'Do you know what that might mean?'

Munroe wrinkles his face. 'John's no spring chicken any more, Sergeant, so don't be taking anything he says too seriously. But maybe that's what Peter had planned. Maybe he was going to stick them underground. Who'd notice another corpse in a place built on them, eh?'

McAvoy doesn't move. Doesn't speak. Just holds the old man's gaze. Then he gives a brisk nod and a word of thanks then half walks, half jogs back to the car. He pulls open the door and Fin turns to him.

'How do you spell the name of the church?' asks the boy, his pencil poised above a page of neat joined-up words.

'You can see for yourself,' says McAvoy, starting the engine. 'We're going for a walk in the dark. A bear-hunt in the woods, just you and me. Would you like that?'

Fin looks out at the darkness. Back, at his father's shining, energised eyes and sweat-soaked forehead.

'Will there be anybody else there?' he asks, nervous and excited.

'None that can do us any harm,' says McAvoy, shoving the car into second gear.

They drive in silence for a few minutes. Squint through the dirty windows and the darkness and rain. McAvoy almost loses control as he spots the gap in the hedgerows. Feels the tyres slip and slide in thick mud as he yanks the vehicle left and pulls up in the shadow of the low, brooding building. Switches off the headlights and looks at the outline of black on black.

'You going to be brave?'

Fin nods and they step from the car into thick mud.

'A graveyard?' asks Fin, wide-eyed.

'We're going into the woods,' says McAvoy. 'Do you trust me? Will you be brave?'

Fin looks up at his dad and reaches out to take his hand. 'What are we going to find?' he asks.

'Answers,' says McAvoy, striding towards the treeline. 'And an unopened tomb.'

'I don't understand. Can you slow down . . . ?'

McAvoy reaches down and picks up his son, walking faster. He turns his eyes on his son. 'Have you started doing war yet or are you too little? Second World War? We won, yeah? Well, this man called Winston Churchill. He was our leader. A good man, for a Conservative. He wanted to make sure that if we did lose, there would be people who could make life difficult for the Germans. So they dug these bunkers . . .'

His voice is lost in the darkness as the trees swallow father and son.

Mahon stands silently in the hallway, and considers the man he has come here to take. There is little about him that he considers worthy of affection. He only knows a little about his character, but from his appearance Mahon struggles to see the benefits in letting him exist in perpetuity. He's a shaved pitbull; a sculpture of sinew and chiselled fat, topped by a shaved skull and eyes like an angry rat. He will have enjoyed what he did to Tom Spink yesterday. Enjoyed it more than the other vices he seems unable to go without.

Mahon dabs the spittle and rainwater from his face. Blinks a pink tear that drips onto his tongue. Tastes ointment and blood.

Mahon leans against the doorframe and watches the two men writhing in the bed. He can hear the slap of skin on skin, like wet fish being struck against one another.

The younger man, slim, pale, with muscles like a child, is on his back, mewing: a grizzled high-pitched whine that rattles with spit.

The other man's back is streaked with perspiration. The tattoo across his shoulders seems to move in the half-light; the illegible Latin letters morphing into new shapes and patterns. Mahon squints, trying to make them out. Gives up. Looks instead at the discarded clothes on the floor. Sees a wallet poking out of crumpled jeans; thick with folded notes. Sees black boots that still show splashes of the mud and blood of a lay-by in East Yorkshire. Sees the ID badge, spilling from a shirt pocket. The slick company logo and an office address near St Paul's in London. Mahon is in the right place. Is about to hurt the right man.

The bedroom is lit by a gaudy, brass-bottomed lamp which stands on the table by the bed. It is rocking, as the headboard slams back and forth, and the room's sparse furnishings swing in and out of focus. It's an expensive room, like a tart's boudoir. Red walls, gilt-edged frames to Moulin Rouge prints, black and gold, fleece throws. A row of bulbs surrounds the giant mirror on the wall behind the bed, but they are not turned on.

265

Mahon breathes in. Tastes the air.

Despite his appearance, his size, Mahon can make himself all but invisible. Beige trousers, today. Army boots. Black jumper, leather jacket, scarf, sunglasses and cord cap. Had himself a pleasant evening with a copy of the *Racing Post* and a bottle of brown ale. Took a pew in the corner of the sophisticated wine bar and watched the man the Headhunters want to die. He'd watched him play with his phone and drink his wine and pick at his olives and crisps. Saw him smile and snarl and pick at his teeth as he talked animatedly with his boss. Then Mahon followed him down to the waterfront. Saw him exchange words and notes with a pretty young lad in a tracksuit. Watched them walk together to the posh hotel.

Mahon followed them here, to the big property near the university: shiny silver cars on the driveway, wooden blinds and red chandeliers, mahogany floors and designer wallpaper. Soundlessly followed them in. Watched them kissing and undressing on the stairs, exploring one another, tonguing each other, tenderness giving way to aggression, to want.

Mahon stands now, and watches.

Waits.

Slows his heartbeat and diminishes himself to a pulse, a steady drum-beat. Becomes an automaton. A thing created with a single purpose, incapable of distraction or doubt.

Mahon crosses the room in three strides.

The teenager looks up and sees a giant; face grotesque and scarred beneath the mirrored lenses of his dark glasses.

The weight on his chest prevents him crying out.

The other man feels a presence behind him. A darkness. As though there are fingers on his neck. He looks up, stiff-limbed, not breathing, struggling to function through the glut of wine, cigarettes, release. He slides an eye upwards.

The thing he sees burns an imprint on his retina. It's a shadow puppet. A paper doll sliced from black card.

A darkness that doesn't just block the light, but denies its very existence.

Mahon brings down his fist into the man's twisted neck. Hears the click. The crunch. Sees the tension leave his body as unconsciousness swallows him whole.

The boy doesn't have time to register what is happening. His eyes are dry when the needle plunges into his neck.

An hour later, Mahon is sitting on the sofa in his cottage. The greasy prick who tried to turn Lloyd's head is a tangle of bruised limbs and mottled skin. His eyes are dull and his breath is a slow, weak thing.

Mahon's new prisoner is lying on the floor, his shirt open at the waist. There is a flat stone at the base of his spine, pushing between two vertebrae, and there are floorboards across his chest. Mahon is tossing a fist-sized rock in one hand and holding a mobile phone in the other.

He smiles as it rings.

'You were right,' he says, to Piers Fordham, down the line. 'Exactly where you said he would be. I do like it when relationships begin honestly, don't you, fella? It means that when things turn sour, the lies don't have to be punished.'

Mahon and his new associate talk for ten minutes. They come to an agreement. The Headhunters will allow Mr Nock to maintain control of his empire until he takes his last breath. They will stay out of Newcastle. In return, Mahon is going to solve their problems. The employees who have stopped taking orders from anonymous voices are going to have their wings clipped. And Mahon is the blade.

'You ready to talk to me, son?' asks Mahon, as the man on the floor begins to come to. 'Don't worry, your boyfriend's OK. Will wake up with a headache and a sore arse but only half of that is my fault. Now, turn your head slowly and have a look at the thing to your right. Recognise him?'

The man swivels his eyes and begins to groan.

'I believe you know him as a Headhunter. I'm not sure what that makes you. You're the mavericks, aren't you? You and your little crew. You're going your own way and upsetting people all over the bloody place. Well, this fella on the floor – he came up here to sideline my employer. I've set him right on that. And I've come to an arrangement with your old firm. I'm going to hurt you, you're going to talk to me, and then I'm going to tell that generous gobshite from Hull where to find your friends. Now, let's start, shall we? Why did you hurt the old copper? Tom Spink, I believe his name is. I met him once. Seemed a decent sort. Upright sort of chap. And you've put him in hospital. I'd love to know why.'

The man begins to writhe and grunt, then stops as the agony in his back courses through him.

'Lay still, there's a good lad. I know you must have a lot of questions. You might not even know who I am. But I know who you are, son. I've been doing this shit since before you were born. I pick up the phone, I ask a question, I get an answer. Mr Mouthpiece is an impressive man. Called an old contact of mine. Benny Pryce. Said he had an offer for me. We got on, if you can believe that. Told me your name. Told me you would be in the city. Told me you couldn't go more than a day or so without getting your tip wet with some pretty boy. You weren't hard to find. You're not a looker, are you? I mean, I can't talk but I've got an excuse. You're just an ugly fucker.'

The man bares his teeth. Tries to spit but it sprays across his own face and chest.

'You've fallen so far. You thought you were climbing the ladder when in fact you were sliding down a pole.'

Mahon leans forward and drops the stone softly on the nearest plank.

'You should have stayed a copper.'

# Chapter 18

Fin lives up to his word. His face is pale and his eyes seem to have been pinned open but he doesn't say a word as his dad hugs him to his chest and forces his way through the grabbing, soaking branches and stumbles into the clearing. They both have twigs in their hair and water seeping through their clothes and shoes. They are both cold. Both unnerved by the silence of the forest and the stench of rotting leaves and vegetation that rises from the disturbed leaves of the forest floor.

'There,' says McAvoy, pointing with the light from his mobile phone. 'Come on, nearly there . . .'

McAvoy's eyes shine with a zeal that verges on mania. He doesn't seem able to stop himself. Has lost all sense of who and what he is. It would only take a word of rebuke or a cry of unhappiness from his son and McAvoy would return to himself. He would run from this dark and eerie place and take his son to the kind of places that five-year-old boys are supposed to be at 10 p.m. on a school night. But McAvoy spent his childhood walking in the darkness of the moorland that surrounded his home. At Fin's age he felt comfortable walking through the seaweed and heather from the beach at Slaggan, all the way up to the water-lily lake where he and his mother used to picnic when she was still around. He had learned that the darkness is no more terrifying a thing than the light.

'Will you be OK if I put you down, son? Just lean against the tree and keep the light on me, yes?'

Dutifully, Fin leans against a moss-covered oak and turns the beam on his father. McAvoy has a wildness about him. In the glare of the torch beam and with the woods at his back, he seems a person out of time.

'There, Fin, there.'

Fin had been shining the light on the horsebox, trying to make out its edges amid the tangle of trees and leaves. At his father's voice he points the beam back at the floor and sees McAvoy crouching down, heaving a slab of stone from the forest floor and pushing it into a patch of mulched leaves.

McAvoy lets out a breath and rubs his cold hands. Waves distractedly, asking Fin for the phone. He closes his fingers around it and points the light into the darkness below him.

He turns to Fin. Gives him a smile. 'This must be how Santa Claus feels,' he says, staring into the absolute blackness of the hole in the earth.

'Or the Big Bad Wolf,' says Fin, his voice unsteady. 'You're not going in, are you?'

McAvoy considers the hole. Reaches down and feels a piece of decayed timber nailed to the brickwork. Reaches down. Feels another. Could he fit? It was built for men who travelled light. Built for people who had been taught to move fast and loose and to kill without thinking.

'Would you be OK? Fin? For a moment?'

Fin looks around him. The woods seem to be closing in from every side. He can barely see the sky. His dad wants to leave him alone as he slithers into this hole in the earth. Fin keeps his mouth closed, but manages a nod.

McAvoy knows that if he waits he will talk himself out of it. He takes a breath and swings a leg into the darkness. Presses his stomach and face to the carpet of leaves and feels around with his feet for the next step down. His boot catches on it, and he begins to inch his way lower; repeating the process until just his face is poking over the side. He takes hold of the brickwork with one hand and reaches up to Fin for the light with the other. He points it through his feet and sees a white, shimmering mass. It looks liquid in this light and McAvoy fears for a moment that the chamber has flooded. Then he glimpses the words, flickering beneath the beam.

The rotten beam beneath his foot gives way.

McAvoy grabs for the stone. Scrapes his knuckles on the bare brick. Hangs, for a moment, over nothing.

He looks into Fin's eyes. Sees the fear in his gaze. Feels a sudden, thudding, wave of guilt and shame as he realises what he is doing . . .

Then drops into the darkness like a stone.

A mountain of bin-bags filled with designer labels breaks his fall. He bounces and slides, tumbling like a thing made of straw, before his knees hit solid earth and he comes to a halt with a crash.

'Daddy! Daddy, are you there?'

McAvoy takes a second to get his breath. Looks around for the fallen phone and sees that it has landed face-up, its light staring straight up the shaft down which he has fallen.

'It's OK, Fin,' he shouts, short of breath. 'It's OK.'

He's not sure it is. He's fifteen feet underground in a damp, chilly chamber with a curved brick roof. He shines the light around him. The walls are bare brick, the floor compacted earth. To his right are the remains of what looks like an old cot-bed.

He swings the torch. Throws aside some of the bin-bags so he can see the far side of the chamber. There is a patch of greater darkness towards the far wall. He can feel air coming from it. Knows, in his bones, that this is the entrance to the tunnel system dug seventy-five years ago on the orders of Churchill. Knows that he is not the first man to have stood in its embrace and felt the chill of fear.

'Won't be a moment, Fin,' he shouts, wondering how the hell he is going to climb out. 'Just stay brave, yeah? I think the bear has been here but he's long since gone . . .'

McAvoy kicks aside some more bin-bags and squats down in front of the circular hole in the wall. From the little he knows about these bunkers, they can go back for hundreds of metres, with areas for weapons storage, bomb-manufacture and combat training. Their construction was a massive undertaking and preserving their secrecy an even harder challenge. Few people ever broke the word. Perhaps only a handful of people alive know of the bunker's existence. But that knowledge may have helped a man commit murder and pin it on a trusting, simple man.

McAvoy turns from the hole. His boots are still greasy with mud and he slips on the damp floor. He puts his hand out to stop himself and staggers against the wall. He hears tearing. Fears he has snagged his clothes on a jagged piece of stone.

He shines the torch up at the wall.

273

A strip of magazine is hanging from the brickwork. It shows the upper half of a buxom, dark-haired woman, soaping herself in a bathtub. McAvoy peers closer. Moves the torch. Up. Down. Sees the pictures and cuttings that have fallen over the years like so many dead leaves.

This was somebody's special place. A chamber, hidden from the world, in which they could hide their secrets and desires. McAvoy squats down and examines the individual pictures. They are titillating more than anything else. Soft-porn. Postcards of women in negligees. Pages torn from mail-order catalogues of matronly types in scaffolded bras and sexless knickers. There are cars too. Pictures of sleek vehicles throwing up spray around hairpin bends. A picture of F1 driver Stirling Moss, all sideburns and cigarettes. And drawings. Drawings of rifles. Handguns. A sketch of an underground chamber. A crude drawing of a girl in school uniform; her shirt ripped open and breasts exposed . . .

McAvoy sits back. Raises a hand to his face and wipes the dirt and sweat from his face.

The image is signed. Signed 'PC'. Dated, too. Not more than a month before the fantasy became a reality.

He wants to put his fist through the wall. Wants to hurt himself for his own stupidity. For being taken in by the sad eyes and the echoes across five decades of corruption and deceit.

He waves the light at the wall again. Knows that, if nothing else, he has something new to show the Home Office.

McAvoy catches sight of the piece of newspaper as he arcs the light back and forth. It's damp and tattered and hangs from a nail like a limp flag. But there is something about it that catches his attention and forces him forward in the darkness.

Four men. One tall and dark-haired. Another hiding his face with a beefy forearm. A smaller man, turning his face away from the glare of the flashbulb.

Vaughn Winn stands in the rear of the shot. He's wearing a silk scarf tucked into a Crombie overcoat. His hair is gelled back and he is staring into the camera with eyes of absolute blackness. They bore into McAvoy as he stares. He has to turn away. Blinks a few a times and returns his gaze to the image and holds it to the light. Somebody has drawn a pencil line around Vaughn's face. An arrow comes from the circle and leads to an exclamation mark. The words next to it are almost completely invisible but if he squints, McAvoy can just make them out.

*On my way, Colesy. On my way.*

McAvoy stands up, holding the piece of paper. From his pocket he takes an evidence bag and slips it inside. He leaves everything else. Will come back and do this properly with a forensics team and men in white coats. For now he has to find a way out. Find answers. Get back to his son.

He reaches up, tentatively pushing at the low roof as if expecting it to yield a sudden trapdoor or a rope ladder. Spins around, suddenly overcome with a need to leave this place. To sit, quietly, with a computer, and put his thoughts into order.

He would have missed the gap in the brickwork were it not for Fin yelling his dad's name. The sudden noise makes him turn his head back towards the hole he fell through. His eyes flick over something metallic. Pipes, protruding from a ventilation shaft above his head. A tiny, enclosed space above the main body of the chamber.

McAvoy stands on tiptoe. Reaches inside.

Later, he would say that he half expected to find the shotgun.

275

Perhaps he imagined a length of rope or the rotting remains of a stepladder.

But he is not wholly surprised when his fingers close around bone.

McAvoy opens his hand carefully. Retrieves it from the gap. Takes a breath.

His thoughts are spinning. He needs light. Needs more police officers. Needs a camera and a thousand evidence bags. Needs Trish Pharaoh.

Carefully, he extends his hand back into the gap. Angles the camera in his outstretched hand. Takes a dozen pictures of the body above his head; decomposing and dissolving in this place below the ground.

He puts the camera away. Concentrates on breathing. Returns to the middle of the bunker and looks up. Shouts up to Fin and is rewarded with a relieved shout.

McAvoy looks around him. Bin-bags, full of clothes. Tunnels, leading into the damp earth. A crumbling bunk-bed. A high, tight shaft of old bricks and greasy stone.

He starts tearing open the bin-bags. Starts tying trouser-legs to jumper-sleeves and scarves to designer shirts.

'Fin! Can you catch?'

Twenty minutes later he is slithering back onto the forest floor. He is feeling Fin's tough little arms around him and unfastening his makeshift rope from the trunk of the big oak. He is kicking it back into the darkness and pulling the stone back across the hole. He's covering the whole thing with leaves and sinking back to his knees.

'Dad?'

And then they are back through the branches; pushing

themselves back through a thousand grabbing wooden hands – stumbling over the low stone wall onto the soft wet grass at the back of the churchyard.

Only then does McAvoy look at his son.

'What did you find?' asks Fin.

McAvoy screws up his face and feels like giving in to a sob as his son reaches up and pulls a leaf from his hair.

'This man,' says McAvoy, pulling the battered piece of newspaper from his pocket and showing it to his boy. He points at the short man in the front of the picture. 'This is Francis Nock,' he says, as if the name should mean something. 'And this man, here, with his face covered – he and his brother did some very bad things in London. They were famous.'

'So who are the other two?' asks Fin, eager to please.

'This is Vaughn Winn,' says McAvoy, softly. 'The philanthropist. The do-gooder. He's with them!'

Fin looks confused but presses on. 'And him?'

'That's the monster,' says McAvoy, suddenly exhausted to his bones. 'I think that's the one who did all this.'

'And you're going to catch him?'

McAvoy closes his eyes. Hopes that when he opens them he'll be in bed with the woman he loves; listening to his children playing happily in the neat, tidy little room next door.

He opens his eyes to soft rain and black skies; to clouds like falling masonry.

'I'm going to try.'

# Chapter 19

11.06 p.m. Raywell, East Yorkshire.

Helen finds it hard not to let her jealousy show on her face as Ray turns the car down the long gravel track that leads to DI Shaz Archer's home. It's a luxurious ground-floor apartment set in converted outbuildings at the back of an imposing mansion house, sitting on a hill and overlooking a sloping woodland carpeted with bluebells and wild garlic. It feels like something out of a Brontë novel and makes Helen's own little bungalow in humble Caistor seem like the sort of place that Archer's chimney-sweep should live in. Helen has never been a fan of her senior officer. Archer is extraordinarily attractive, but Helen has come to the conclusion she is a cold, manipulative and arrogant bitch who was not smacked enough as a child. She makes Helen feel clumsy and undesirable. As they approach her home, Helen feels an overwhelming desire to change into something with a few more designer labels and, if possible, marry a doctor and win the Lottery.

'Nice,' says Helen sourly as the car bounces up the pitch-dark track. 'She must have saved up her pennies . . .'

Ray scoffs, nastily. 'Daddy bought her it,' he says. 'Bought her another one in Turkey and the two cars in the double garage at the back.'

'Lucky lady,' says Helen, trying to keep her voice neutral. 'My dad got me my first car. Citroen Saxo. Couldn't do much over 50 m.p.h. without bits starting to fall off but I still felt like Ayrton Senna.'

'Shaz wouldn't know what to do with anything that cost less than 30K. Used to the finer things in life.'

Helen turns her head and looks at the stone pallor of Ray's ratty face. She and Ray have shared something tonight. They're in this together now. They're a team she never expected to be a part of. She'll never get a better time to ask.

'You make an unlikely double act,' she says diplomatically. 'You and DI Archer.'

Ray parks the car in a courtyard covered with smooth pebbles and built around a pretty water feature. Tall trees cast moon-shadows onto its oily surface. Ray kills the engine and turns to Helen. He doesn't speak at first. Just sees off his cigarette and scratches his balls. He seems troubled. Unsure of himself. They have argued all the way back from Sheffield. Helen wants to ring Pharaoh. Ray has urged caution. Tried to explain the problems they will cause themselves if they go straight to the top dog. Shaz is the obvious person to take their findings forward. It's suddenly become too big for just the two of them. They need Piers Fordham properly investigated. They need to come up with a decent cover story as to how they came to suspect him. They need to make it official. Ray has vouched for his protégée and Helen has acquiesced.

'She's OK, y'know,' he says at last, with a shrug of one shoulder. 'I know she can be a stroppy cow and she needs to learn to keep her legs together but she's got a good brain and she's tougher than any lass I've ever known.'

Helen can't hide her surprise. She has never thought of Archer in those terms.

'She was a detective constable when I was a DI. Couldn't help but show us she was from money. Designer handbags and high-heels and stories about polo club – that should have been enough to fast-track her on its own. But she wanted to learn. She liked catching villains. I've never seen anybody who would be willing to do so much to succeed.'

Helen raises an eyebrow at that. She has heard the stories.

Ray shrugs again. 'So she unbuttons her blouse to get a confession? So what? You think the victims of crime feel cheapened by that? They get justice. They get somebody locked up. How is it worse than slapping the shit out of somebody until they sign what you put in front of them? Shaz cares, y'know. She's just got this streak. She's been a bit spoiled. When people upset her she takes it to heart. She doesn't forget.'

'I've never upset her,' says Helen, quietly. 'And she's always been a bitch to me.'

Ray smiles at that, his face filling with real warmth.

'You picked Pharaoh as a role model, love. You hurt Shaz's feelings.'

Helen flicks her hair behind her ear. Looks through her own reflection at the tasteful, U-shaped building with its sliding doors and expensive blinds and gorgeous designer furniture. She sees the door open and looks at her detective inspector. She's wearing a silk nightdress and has a cashmere blanket wrapped around herself. Her hair looks perfect at the front but artfully messed up at the back. She has bare feet, and though she is too far away to tell, Helen knows in her heart that each nail will be perfectly painted and manicured.

'She's hard to like,' says Helen, pointing at her. 'Too perfect by half.'

'By morning she's going to think bloody highly of you too,' says Ray. 'Look, I'll go give her the low-down. You best stay here. Have a kip or something. I'll try not to be too long, though she does tend to open a bottle of something posh when I call around . . .'

He starts to groom himself. Rubs his cuffs across his teeth and pushes his hair back. He looks nervous and excited, as though about to see somebody whose company he enjoys and whose opinion matters.

Helen watches as he steps from the car and crosses the courtyard. Archer leans forward and gives him a perfunctory kiss on the cheek. Ray starts forward, as though expecting to be invited in. Archer continues to bar his way. They talk for a few minutes. Archer disappears on one occasion and comes back with paper and pen. She scrawls down Ray's words and the pair talk as if Ray is a door-to-door salesman and Archer some dowager countess.

Helen takes in the rest of her surroundings. Admires the sleek silver Mercedes parked a little off to her left. Wonders if Archer has neighbours or whether Daddy bought the whole fucking place.

The sound of raised voices comes to her. Ray is speaking more animatedly now – shaking his head and gesturing wildly. Then he kicks at the gravel and stomps back across the courtyard. He climbs into the vehicle in a fury and slams the door; his chest panting and hair sticking up.

281

'Spoilt cow,' he says, ripping open a new packet of cigarettes. 'Biggest case of her fucking career, handed to her on a plate, and she's more concerned with getting her jollies . . .'

He turns the key and reverses across the stones with a sound like the deaths of a billion beetles.

'Got a man, hasn't she? Some perfumed ponce. Stinks like a bloody sales rep if you ask me. Not ready to introduce him yet, she says. Wants it to be the right time. He's sleeping. Best not wake him up . . . couldn't it wait until the morning . . . Fucking bitch!'

Helen says nothing. Ray looks hurt. She suddenly realises how lonely he is. How much he needs somebody to care about and to perhaps give a little shit about him in return. He had expected gratitude and enthusiasm. Had expected his protégée to squeal and hug him as if he had just bought her an expensive new car. Instead she had kept him on the doorstep. Kept him at arm's length. Taken his hard work and given him nothing more than a kiss on the cheek.

'We'll make up,' he says, to himself. 'Always do. I'm just . . .'

Helen doesn't know whether she should put an arm on his shoulder – make a gesture of kindness. 'Hurt?' she says, quietly.

Ray turns and snarls at her as the car emerges from the driveway and back onto the main road.

'Fuck off.'

The text message comes through at just after 2 a.m.

Pharaoh has been asleep for around forty minutes. She's in bed with her daughter Sophia, still wearing her dress and boots. She's curled up behind her with an arm around the teenager's cool, bare shoulders. Has her nose against the back of her neck.

Trish wakes up, confused and plastered with sweat. Her jolt waking Sophia, who grunts with the instant grumpiness of disturbed sleep.

'Mum?'

'Shh, it's OK. I'm going to my own bed . . .'

Pharaoh slides out from under the quilt and rubs her eyes. She feels her mascara, dry and brittle, turn to powder against her skin. Pushes her hair behind her ears and winces at the stickiness on her flesh as her thighs rub and squeak. She steps, off balance and half pissed, between little islands of clothes, books and shoes. Finds her way to the corridor in the darkness. Pulls out her phone.

'Well, well, well . . .'

Pharaoh slaps her face a couple of times and shakes some life into herself. Slowly she lets the smile move from her eyes to her mouth. Grins in the half-light and leans back against the wall of the hallway.

The message doesn't contain any words. Just a registration plate and the letters *PoR*. It's more than enough. She makes her way downstairs and finds her laptop. Fires it up at the kitchen table and switches the kettle on. Roots around in the fridge while it boils and shushes at her computer when it announces its readiness with a fanfare. She eats cooked ham from the packet and drinks milk from the carton. Drops a teabag in a mug then forgets about it.

Pharaoh sits down at the table and opens up a new email. Addresses it to the head of CID and copies in Assistant Chief Constable Everett. Deliberately excludes the head of the Drugs Squad, Aidy Russell, and praises, in particular, the actions of DC Ben Neilsen and Detective Sergeant Aector McAvoy in securing the information. She'll work out later what they are supposed to have actually done.

She begins to type . . .

After half an hour, Pharaoh pours herself a glass of wine. She sends the message, picks up her phone, and waits for her contact at Border Force to ring her back.

'You're sure?' he asks, sleepily.

'I promise,' she says.

They chat for a few minutes. He knows better than to ask where the information came from. She knows better than to ask what he will do with it. But in the morning, if she has played this right, the local papers will be boasting of a major drugs seizure at Hull Docks and the government's anti-smuggling agency will be getting pats on the back. So will she, her boss and the top brass. Trish has been a copper a long time. She knows how to play this game.

By 3 a.m. Pharaoh has done a day's work. She should go back to bed, really. Should get some rest before a busy day of bollockings and praise. She's tired enough to sleep but can't bear the thought of only getting three hours of unconsciousness before her alarm goes off. Decides to just wait until the sun comes up. She watches some TV and plays a game on her phone. Eats a chocolate bar and puts some school dresses in the washing machine. Makes the girls their packed lunches alongside an extra peanut butter sandwich for herself.

It is not quite dawn when the phone rings. She recognises the number.

'She's sorted,' says a gruff Scottish voice. 'Asleep. Little one too. Nobody followed us. Nobody saw. She's not speaking much but we're like that. It's OK.'

284

Pharaoh gives a warm, soft smile.

'It's so good of you to do this . . .' she begins.

He cuts her off, brusque and baritone. 'He's OK, yeah? Aector?'

Pharaoh sighs. 'He's doing good work. And we're getting there. He just needs them home.'

'He doesn't. He needs them gone.'

'You can't say that,' she says, bristling. 'They make him whole. They make him what he is . . .'

'They make him vulnerable,' he says. 'Too much heart, that one. He doesn't know what to do with it. She's a good enough girl and I'll keep her safe. But don't you go thinking she's a sweetheart. She's trouble, Superintendent. You don't know the half of it.'

Pharaoh looks at the phone for a moment after he hangs up. Wonders whether she should give his words some attention or whether they will just give her another headache. She decides not to think about it. To finish her wine and her sandwich and make the girls some breakfast like a proper mum.

She wonders if she should call Aector. Reassure him. Explain why she has done what she has done.

Decides to leave it for now. There will be time enough soon. Time enough for apologies and reasoning.

She stops her imagination before it can hand her the picture it is painting. A picture of Aector McAvoy, white-faced and accusing; furious and crushed. She knows how he will react. Knows that he will drive through the night to his wife and child and bring them home were he to learn that Roisin and Lilah are staying on the family croft with the father he has not spoken to in years.

The view is magnificent. The water is crushed diamonds and sapphires; the sun a burnished pocket-watch against an unruffled blue silk. The sand is untouched. Unsullied. As pristine as the white walls and the glass chandeliers and the night-light that offers a view of stars that shine like sugar crystals on a canvas of black velvet.

Piers Fordham purses his lips, as though admiring the curves of a pretty girl. Looks at the little red stripe on the corner of the image that fills the computer screen: **SOLD**.

In a little under a year it will be home. Islas las Perlas. He will have a home in paradise, overlooking the Pacific Ocean. His days will be about rum, grilled fish and shoulder massages from brown-skinned girls in too few clothes. Hull will be a memory. A cold cloud of drizzle and piss that he will be happy to push into the deepest recesses of his memory. He hates this city. Hates the weather and the accent and the washed-out nobodies who roll cigarettes with one hand while mopping up bean-juice and fried bread with the other. This country, this county, this city – they have all cost him. Cost him women. A business. Liberty, for a time.

But this year has brought Piers Fordham ample compensation. He has come to view his time in prison as a networking opportunity unlike any he has enjoyed in his legal career. He has seen how criminals work. Spotted the flaws in their reasoning and exploited their fears. He has done as he has been asked and demanded far more of others. He has made the boss of the Headhunters very rich indeed and he has pocketed enough to keep himself comfortable for the rest of his life. There is no reason for anybody to kill him. Precious few know who he is, and those who do are glad to have him on the payroll.

Tonight, he extinguished a minor blaze. A man like him shouldn't have had to deal with such little details but he'd taken a personal interest in Roisin McAvoy and felt some degree of compulsion to see it through. He'd done the job as well as he could be expected to. Cut off the oxygen to the one problem that has been causing him disquiet. He'd enjoyed sending the text to Pharaoh. Enjoyed the clean precision of keeping his word and chopping the head off the snake that had been threatening to drag the Headhunters down. It's all coming together. And he can't help but feel pleased with himself.

Piers looks at the clock in the corner of the monitor. It's gone 2 a.m. He should be in bed. Should be wearing his fine silk pyjamas and sleeping in sheets of Egyptian cotton. Instead he is sitting in the dining room of his sprawling home on Hull's palatial Newland Park; drinking fifty-year-old Macallan and trying to develop a taste for Cuban cigars. He isn't sure he will have much success with the latter. His mouth feels numb and tingly and his fingers smell like a damp ashtray. He fancies that he will stick to the vices he already knows. Will finish his drink, take a sleeping pill and fall asleep looking at the little movie in his phone. It shows a tall, plain-faced detective constable, pushing backwards, naked and soaked with sweat, grinding against the toned body of a young man with an impassive face and immaculate tattoos. It is a film that represents victory. Ownership and power. He would have liked to keep his word to Helen Tremberg and delete the video when she did him a little favour a few months back. But the man in the video has gone from being an asset to a headache, and Piers enjoys watching him nude and vulnerable. It represents the situation the greedy bastard is about to find himself in. He wonders if Mahon would be willing to video his annihilation. It would be nice to watch the two clips side by side . . .

This is Piers's little celebration. His toast to his own success. The house in Panama is bought and almost paid for. He needs to transfer another couple of million from his bank in Liechtenstein to the deeply private Panamanian account of the estate agency, but that is a mere formality. He has more money than he knows what to do with. It has been a good year. He had his doubts at first, of course. Didn't know if he could pull it off. But the criminal anatomy is made up of brains, brawn and balls, and Piers has two of those qualities in abundance. What he lacks in muscle, he compensates for with an uncanny ability to persuade people to do what he wants. He is not a strong man. He's short, overweight and has only managed to disguise the burst capillaries and pockmarks in his face by growing a beard that seems to reach almost to his eyes. He is not an attractive man, but that will stop being a problem soon. He has enough money to buy whatever face he wants. He, and his partners, can stop this soon. Can stop pretending. Can stop putting on a show. His new associate has done what he was asked to. The rotten apples who have been threatening his security have been pinpointed and will have been brought to heel before the day is over. Mahon has been a godsend. The Russians are good at what they do, of course. They're blunt, brutal and respect the chain of command. His employer had promised him as much when he first allayed his fears about his personal safety.

*That's the beauty*, he'd said, soft and smooth and flawless. *Nobody knows who anybody is. They have their own teams but under us. Under me. And they don't know who I am. They respect the voice. The money. The results. It will work, Piers. It's worked before. Back home. Back before ...*

The boss has never been proven wrong. The only slip-ups have been when the Headhunters have accidentally recruited somebody incompetent or psychopathic. Piers's own crew are blessedly free of such idiosyncrasies. They do what they're told. Pharaoh was no doubt trying it on when she said that Nikolai had lost Roisin. The lad is focused and resolute and will be calling Piers before the morning to get a new fix on her location. He'll watch over her. Keep her safe. After all, a baited hook is no good if the worm wriggles free ...

A shape flickers in the computer screen. For a moment the blue ocean and perfect sky turns black.

Piers spins in his chair, sloshing whisky on silk.

'I hear you've been trying to find me.'

Piers closes his eyes. Feels his chest contract and the hairs rise on his skin.

'You're in Hull, then' says Piers, trying to keep his voice calm. 'Excellent.'

He sniffs, hoping his nose won't run. Gets a smell of rich aftershave. Of foreign cigarettes. Of sweat and bodyspray.

'Capital, yes. And can I say that it gratifies my heart to observe that you are in such prime physical condition ...'

The man with the gun laughs. Shakes his head.

'Your fucking voice,' he says. 'I hear it in my sleep. Sounds like there's a dictionary half open in your head. Just stop talking. You can beg, of course. That's always nice to hear. I thought you'd have a bit more about you, to be honest. Be a bit more of a looker. You're a bit normal, aren't you?'

Piers raises the crystal tumbler to his lips with a shaking hand. It had been so close to perfection. If he had just asked for a guard tonight. If he could just have kept himself safe and anonymous for another few hours, the man in front of him would be dead and Piers's future would be rum and sunshine.

'You don't have to do this. We're doing so well. Everybody's making money ...'

The man scoffs. Scratches his head with the gun he holds in his right hand.

Piers drains his drink. Hopes the man doesn't hear the glass rattling against his teeth.

'It was working,' snaps Piers. 'Small teams. Big rewards. Nobody knowing who they represented save their own team leader. It was perfect. You had to risk it. You had to try and take more than your share. Did we not treat you right? We paid you for every job you did. Look, I can help you. Your friend ... up in Newcastle ... he's in danger ...'

The man with the gun clamps his teeth together with a noise like snapping wood. Gives a terse shake of the head.

'You're talking shit, Piers. You do it better than anybody else but right now it's staining your teeth. You promised me the earth and you gave me pennies. You made me charm the pants off that lass. You promised I'd get my moment in the sun. I'm not rich enough. I'm here for the same reasons you are. I want money and I want respect. It's time for you to go, mate. I don't care who your boss is, though I have a bloody good idea. He can come after me if he wants, though I think it's more likely he'll see the benefits of putting things in my hands. You have to go. This is mine now. You can't run a protection racket for criminals, Piers. You can't run a recruitment firm for villains. It was never going to work.'

'But it has worked,' he says, turning desperately to the computer screen. 'I'm just a bloke! A man at the end of the phone. And I have lifelong bloody criminals coughing up a fortune and trembling when they speak to me. Look at this house. How much do you think the boss is pocketing if I can buy a place like this? A year. Two years tops. That was how long he said we had before people got wise. We're making a fortune. Why do you have to spoil it all?'

The man says nothing. Blows out air through his nose.

'They'll come for you,' says Piers, his voice growing high-pitched and excited. 'You might have your own little team but we've been doing this a while. The boss's boys will hunt you down. There's a beast coming for you. A monster. He's hurting your friend right now. Carving him up . . .'

'A monster? Do you mean the old bloke with the wrecked face? The one who works for the breathing corpse? Don't you worry, Piers. We have plans for him. The copper too. All of them. You've had a good run, Piers. But you can consider this the most hostile of takeovers.'

The man steps forward and hits Piers across the face with the barrel of the gun. Blood sprays across the computer screen; crimson droplets splattering over perfect blue waters and high, vaulted roofs.

'We've got a lot to talk about before the morning, Mr Mouth-piece,' says the man. 'And you know how you love to talk.'

Piers Fordham dies within the hour.

It's the longest hour of his life.

# Part Four

Part Four

# Chapter 20

*Pretty*, thinks Ray, as he sits in his dark car and stares at the impressive detached property across the quiet, curving street. *Pays well, being a cunt.*

He shouldn't be here. Should be back in his minging bed, having a tug beneath yellow-stained sheets in a room that smells of socks and spilled wine. Places like Newland Park make him feel like some vile and contagious specimen. Make him feel like shit on a shoe. He could never afford a house like this. Could never get a woman who could afford it either.

Hull doesn't have many luxurious neighbourhoods. Newland Park is part of a truly exclusive club. Most of the people with money in East Yorkshire move out to the towns and villages. Hull itself is a virtual sink estate for a much larger region. Those who find themselves longing for an HU postcode fight long and hard to get a place on this quiet, tree-lined road, where Porsches and Range Rovers sleep behind wrought-iron gates and workmen give well-tanned women the kind of gardens they can show off in one of the local glossy mags.

Piers Fordham's house is an old-fashioned, three-storey construction with big bay windows and a modern conservatory, facing a neat front garden that has been given over to tarmac and a few pot plants. The property is in darkness, save for a faint glow from a downstairs window.

*Sleeping*, thinks Ray, grinding his back teeth. *Dozing on goose feathers, under cotton that feels like a virgin's thighs*. He sniffs deeply and spits out of the open window.

It is a little before 3 a.m. He parted company with Helen Tremberg a couple of hours ago. Dropped her back at the train station without a goodbye and went for a couple of shorts in one of the pubs he can rely on for a lock-in of an evening. He's pissed now. Soaked through with alcohol and sodden from the tumble he took as he staggered from the watering hole and toppled into one of the larger puddles in the kerb off Spring Bank.

'Smarmy fucker,' he says, under his breath, as he opens the car door and feels the light rain on his red face. 'Tolerate me, will you? Fucking tolerate me?'

Ray lays his face on the cold, damp metal of the car roof. His argument with Archer has hurt him in a way he cannot really explain. He supposes he just wanted more from her. Some thanks. Some praise. Some words of wonder at his abilities as a detective. He doesn't give a shit about what most people think of him but Archer's opinion matters and as he stood on her doorstep and kept her from her new man, he had felt like he was an embarrassment to her. He doesn't know how to deal with his feelings. He wants to lash out. Wants to hurt. And the only person he can picture on the receiving end of his fists is Piers Fordham.

'Dead man. Fucking dead . . .'

He staggers across the street. Leans against the green-painted lamp post until the world stops spinning and breathes in the damp air; scented with wet grass, turned earth and fresh herbs in a myriad of window-boxes.

Ray doesn't know what he intends to do. He fancies it will involve violence of some sort but he is more likely simply to stick his dick through the bastard's letterbox and piss all over his hallway carpet.

He staggers up the driveway. Thuds against the front door and slides down the wood. He rests his head against the glass of the bay window. Wonders if it would be a bad idea to fall asleep.

A moment later, Ray opens his eyes with a start. He feels dull-headed and fuzzy. Feels dry-mouthed and bruised, as though he has been put in a sack and hit with a rubber hose. He blinks, hard, and focuses on the warm, low light that shines from the downstairs window. He presses his face against the glass. Focuses a little. Lets the light and the dark swim and mesh together until he can make sense of what he sees.

Piers Fordham is lying on his back on the tiled floor of an L-shaped kitchen. In this light, it's hard to tell how much of his face is beard and how much is thick black blood.

Rays sobers up instantly. Opens his mouth wide and feels his jawbone crack as he takes a deep breath of cold air.

The front door doesn't give as he puts his boot to it. He has to pick up a brick from the loose slabs of the doorway. He smashes it against the brass handle of the front door then hoofs it again, putting his weight behind it. The door bursts open and Ray stumbles into the hallway. In half a dozen steps he is into the kitchen.

Piers is still breathing. His chest is rising and falling like that of a sleeping dog. But each breath produces a fresh spray of warm, crimson blood, which settles on his face in a mist.

'Fordham,' says Ray, crossing to his side and squatting down beside him. 'Fordham, can you hear me? Fordham? Who did this, mate? Who did this?'

For months, Colin Ray has wanted to stand over the fallen, bleeding body of this man. For months he has fantasised about finding him and taking his revenge. Here, now, he cannot think of the dying man on the floor as anything other than a victim needing help. There will be time for questions and justice later. For now, he simply needs this man to live.

'Piers. Piers, mate, can you hear me? Can you hear me, son?'

Ray turns away from the broken face of the man who has taunted and tantalised the police for a year. He pulls his phone from his pocket and dials the first 9 of the three digits that could save Fordham's life.

He feels a sudden pressure at his sleeve.

'Please,' says Fordham, through broken teeth and fading eyes. 'Please . . .'

Ray closes the phone. Closes his eyes and sits down next to Fordham. He leans forward to hear what the man is saying. Smells blood and filth and floor polish. Something else, too. Around his throat. Where a forearm has been pushed up into his beard. That familiar, pungent perfume. That stench . . .

'Clever fucker,' says Ray, and puts his face in Fordham's gaze.

The man is moments from death. Whoever did this to him left him to choke on his own blood. Beat him within an inch of his life then asked him to crawl the rest of the way.

'Shaz,' says Ray quietly. 'You silly bitch.'

Fordham's eyes lose focus. He coughs and a stream of blood and mucus splatters the front of Ray's shirt. 'Shouldn't ... Should never ... wouldn't listen ...'

Ray nods. Takes Fordham's hand and holds it as his breathing slows and the light in his eyes begins to wink out.

'Panama,' he says; his voice a hiss. 'Just ... jus' tryin to make a living ...'

'What did he get from you?' asks Ray, holding the man's hand as the warmth leeches from it. 'Why does he want McAvoy's wife? Why were you there, in Sheffield?'

Fordham seems to shrink. He becomes smaller, as if squeezed in a fist. 'The Scotsman. Wants to hurt him ... for what he did ...'

'And the Russian?'

'Protection ...'

'And where's yours, Piers? Where's your protection?'

Fordham seems to be trying to speak. Seems to be trying to move. His head lolls and one hand weakly flails to his left, as though swatting at a fly.

Piers Fordham takes a last breath.

Dies.

For a minute, Ray does nothing but sit and think. He keeps his eyes closed and rubs a thumb at the blood on his shirt. He follows the line of Fordham's dead eyes. Follows the line of his outstretched hand.

The sirens are drawing closer by the time Ray has prised up the floorboard. He shines his own phone into the darkness. Gives a humourless laugh as he spots the dozens of mobile phones; all without batteries and memory cards, sitting on a pile of ledgers and polythene bags full of memory sticks.

He reaches in. Presses the floorboard down again. Hammers in a nail with the flat of his hand.

Slips out the front door and is back in his car before the blue light of the police car rounds the corner and causes curtains to twitch in this most palatial of neighbourhoods.

Two lads jump from the car as it screeches to a halt. A neighbour, illuminated by yellow light and framed in his doorway, points to the property where he heard the bang.

In the darkness of the car, Ray clumsily slots in the battery and memory card from the phone he had managed to grab. After a few seconds, the screen is illuminated. He starts to scroll through messages. Names. Contacts . . .

Mutters to himself through a grimace and smile.

'Oh, Colin, they're gonna welcome you back with open arms. You could have had all the glory, Shaz. Could have shared . . .'

He freezes where he sits. Lets his thoughts dwell, for a fraction of a second, on his only friend.

He knows he won't sleep until he answers. Knows, too, that the slick, perfumed bastard will be long gone.

Ray stays in his car until the first of the CID men start to arrive. He could step out and join them. Could come clean. Say he had been following a lead and found the bugger dead. Instead, he eases the car from its parking space and moves away before any of the uniforms can take down the plate.

Two words, beating in his head.

Shaz.

Bitch.

# Chapter 21

6.14 a.m. Flamborough Head, East Yorkshire.

Mahon pours hot water onto the packet soup. Stirs it absent-mindedly; the spoon not touching the cup. Raises the scalding liquid to his lips and takes a sip. Puts the cup back down on the work surface and looks at his reflection in the darkened glass. Holds his own gaze for a good few seconds before he has to turn away.

Mahon has never really mourned the loss of his good looks. The circumstances of their ruination still cause him a feeling a little like distress, but he was never much of a seducer or interested in romance. If anything, the face he has worn these past five decades suits him more than the pretty-boy looks he had worn when he first made Mr Nock's acquaintance. People didn't take him as seriously as they should. They just saw the movie-star smile and the dreamy eyes and didn't know until their throat was being crushed beneath his boot-heels that he deserved to be thought of as formidable. That was Flash Harry's problem. Thought Mahon was just some sort of mascot. Thought he was a bit of window-dressing for the boss. He didn't know what

Mahon really did for the top dog. Didn't know he was more than a driver and occasional collector of debts. If he had, he'd have listened. If he had, he'd never have stuck the blade into the southerner or that poor bloody girl . . .

'What was that fella's name, Raymond? The poofter. Big bloke. Wouldn't buckle?'

Mahon turns. His employer is standing in the doorway of the little chalet. He's dressed in burgundy cord trousers and a blue golfing jumper beneath a tweedy jacket. His clippered white hair clings to his craggy head like moss to a cliff and the designer spectacles on his nose have turned dark in the light of the kitchen strip-light. He looks at least ten years younger than his age. Could be a movie icon on a TV chat show; giving a little twinkle and showing he's still got the moves.

'Which poofter, Mr Nock?'

'Ran that bar. Stuck a coin to the floor so he could check out people's arses. You remember.'

Mahon nods. 'Began with an S. You gave him a pass when he put Alan through that window. Said you couldn't offer him better protection that he could provide for himself.'

Mr Nock smiles. His teeth are whiter than his hair. 'Why did I do that, d'you think?'

Mahon smiles back. 'Good marketing. Good for the image. You made it clear that if anybody thought they were better off without your help, they were welcome to try and demonstrate it.'

'Nobody did, did they?' asks Nock, with a slight shake of the head. 'Nobody tried to go their own way. And the poofter bent the knee in the end, didn't he? Soon as people heard he wasn't under my protection his life got very difficult. So he paid. They all pay in the end, don't they, Raymond? Even now.'

302

Mahon takes another sip of his drink. Begins to make Mr Nock a cup of tea. He enjoys these moments, when Nock confides in him or asks him to fill a gap in his memory. They have been more common, of late. Mr Nock's memory is beginning to leak. He cried out in the early hours, this morning. Seemed lost and confused. Mahon had sat with him for a while. Hadn't known if he should talk or sing or hold his bloody hand. Just sat and watched the man who has guided his life. Watched him wriggle and kick like a toddler with flu.

'They all still respect you, Mr Nock. They all still pay what they should.'

'Changing world,' says Nock, with a sigh. 'Don't reckon we'd have done so well if we were starting out now, eh, Raymond? How do you get a McDonald's to pay protection money? How do you nail somebody to the Tyne Bridge when there's video cameras everywhere? How do you launder money when everything's kept on a computer? It makes my head hurt. I think the young ones are welcome to it, to be honest. Let them find a way to make money as a criminal when the whole fucking system's run by crooks.'

Mahon presses the teabag against the side of the cup with fingers that don't feel the scald.

'You'd still find a way, Mr Nock. You've got that kind of mind.'

Nock takes the tea from Mahon's outstretched hand. Looks around him. 'It's nice being back here. Haven't seen it in years, have we? Lovely view when the sun shines.'

Mahon busies himself tidying the kitchen. He doesn't want to tell him that they were here just a couple of days ago. That they sat in a cafe up the road and ate egg and chips and talked about Mr Nock's daughter and the time the three of them came here when she was a teenager and had played crazy golf and eaten candyfloss and sheltered in a little cave on the beach as great frothy waves rushed up the shingle and sand.

'Good cup of tea, Raymond. Just the way I like it.'

Mahon has been making cups of tea for his employer for half a century but still enjoys the compliment. He turns to say thank you but Mr Nock has already returned to the living room. He'll be sitting in his high-backed chair, watching the waves. Might be listening to something only he can hear. Might be on the phone to his daughter, sighing as she explains how she has managed to ruin her latest relationship and write off the new Maserati.

Mahon's thoughts drift. He finds himself remembering the night they came for him. It was late springtime, early summer, only a few weeks since the deaths at the church. He hadn't really expected to get away with it. Was still looking over his shoulder and telling lies. But he had allowed himself to hope. Had begun to imagine that perhaps his relationship with Mr Nock would be enough to spare him the southerners' retribution. It hadn't. Not that time, anyway. Not the night they came for him. It was his bloody soppiness that got him in trouble. Should have been paying attention. Should have had his hand on his gun and the other on the bag of money in the passenger seat. Should have seen the van as it pulled up. Should have seen the bloke in the donkey jacket standing by his window, blocking his only other escape from the idling, old-man car. He'd been watching blossom fall. Had been enjoying the sight of the pink confetti tumbling from the tree. He can't quite recall where the tree was, now. Can't remember what he was doing there. Collecting, probably. Maybe keeping an eye out for Mr Nock while he saw one or two of his girls. But he knows it was cherry blossom. Knows it seemed incongruous against the landscape of greys and browns.

And then they smashed the glass. He'd had no time to react. Before he could even gather his thoughts he was being dragged through the broken window, glass cutting deep into his skin. Boots were thumping into the side of his head. He felt metal at his wrists. Felt coarse material over his face. Banged his knee and fractured his thumb as he landed on the wooden floor of the van. Kept fighting until they hit him in the back of the head with something hard and metallic.

He'd woken up in a large, stinking room with sawdust and shit on the floor and a high roof of curved corrugated iron. He was naked and tied to a chair. Blood had run down his neck to pool in his lap and he could feel more blood at the base of his back.

There were three of them. Smart suits and bad teeth. Broken knuckles and broad shoulders. They wanted to know what had happened to the man Mr Nock had vowed to look after. Wanted to know more about what he had said the day he disappeared. Asked him about Flash Harry. Asked why he had taken a trip to a little place in the arse-end of nowhere a few months back.

Mahon had kept silent. Kept his mouth shut as they beat him with a length of chain. Bit back his screams as they broke his fingers. Sent his mind somewhere else as they took the blade to his face and slashed the corners of his mouth as far back as his ears. He only lost consciousness when they put the bullet in him. They'd been almost respectful of him by that point. They knew he wasn't going to speak. Had stopped even trying to persuade him to save his own life. The kill-shot was delivered almost grudgingly. It entered his chest from a little over three feet away and opened a hole in him that seemed to suck the rest of him inside it. He disappeared in a tunnel of blackness and air. Woke up only as they lifted the gate and let the pigs come for his corpse. Woke up as a great stinking mouth closed upon his blood-soaked face and tore away half his cheek. Lashed out with a bare foot as another bristled snout closed upon his calf muscle in an orgy of squealing, ravenous madness.

They came back for him, then. Heard his shouts above the noise of the beasts. Took another shot at him as he rose up from amid the mass of thrashing bodies. The shot missed. Hit one of the animals in their shit-streaked sides. The other beasts fell upon it. Tore flesh from bone. And Mahon had leapt from the pig-pen like a demon. The man with the gun had been the first to die; his neck snapping cleanly in Mahon's huge, bleeding hands. Then he picked up the gun and took the other two men in the back as they ran for the sliding door and the safety of the darkness beyond.

The doctors didn't expect him to live. When he arrived at the hospital, three hundred miles from home, the nurses had screamed. The doctors thought he was already dead. But word reached Mr Nock. And Mr Nock said that Mahon's death would be unacceptable. No time or expense were wasted. They put him back together. Saved what they could of his face. Wouldn't let him see a mirror for months. Mahon hadn't cared. Something had changed within him. He felt reborn. Transformed. And when Mr Nock walked into his hospital room and held him like a father, tears had spilled from both their eyes and soaked the bandages and bedsheets. Then Mr Nock had examined his face. He had kissed his head and told him he was beautiful. And he had told him that the southerners were not going to be a problem any more.

Mahon brings himself back to the present. Thinks of all that the coming days will bring. He has enjoyed his communications with the man who had introduced himself as Mr Mouthpiece. Liked his style. He's seen his type before, of course. Seen them all come and go. Ambition is an ugly thing, and not something he has ever been troubled by. The Headhunters could have made a fortune if they hadn't brought in the wrong man to run one of their teams. Now that man is destroying what they had carefully cultivated, and Mahon is going to have to put it right – provided the man at the end of the phone stays alive long enough to make good on his side of the bargain. Mahon knows his time is running out. Times are changing. The events of half a century ago are coming back into the light. Bodies are rising from that cold, damp ground.

As if his thoughts have willed it to life, Mahon's phone beeps. He reads the message from a man who understands what loyalty really costs.

*Do you know a Sergeant McAvoy? Been asking. What do we say?*

Mahon takes a breath. Dabs at his mouth. He pulls his wallet from his trousers and retrieves the two business cards. He knows intuitively what has to happen now. He just needs a little more time. He needs to give the copper just enough. Needs to put his face in the light and let the big ginger bastard decide what he sees in his gaze.

The call is answered on the eighth ring. A Scottish voice, whispering, as if trying not to wake a sleeping child.

'Sergeant,' says Mahon. 'I have a nagging suspicion you've found some old friends of mine. We really should talk. Can we meet?'

McAvoy can't get the sensation of bone off his hands. It feels as though his palm is still holding the cold, rigid femur, with its strands of flesh and fabric. He imagines it as something yellow and unyielding, like pig's teeth. Can see the tiny, porous holes along the side of the limb. Can imagine the joints moving against each other; grinding, as stone against stone, twisting in the sockets, coming apart like pieces of chicken. Can see the knuckled ridges of a kneecap, sitting above joints that gnaw and mash; flesh decaying, cartilage crumbling, deep in the fetid blackness, in an underground place that was never intended as a tomb.

He wants to spoon up behind Roisin. Wants to hide his face from the horrors by pressing his nose and mouth into her hair. But Roisin is gone.

He looks again at the pictures in his phone. They were snatched, in the darkness, with a flash that bounced off the walls and made his pupils shrink in pain. They are vague and blurred. But they are unquestionably corpses. There are bodies in that hole in the ground. Bodies, shoved into a ventilation panel in the ceiling of a subterranean bunker. Bodies that were put there years before by somebody who knew just where to find it and how to keep it hidden.

McAvoy sits in the darkness, his arm around his sleeping son, and listens to the soft slap of shifting water against sand and rotting timber. He cannot even find the mental space to file away his thoughts on John Glass's death. He'd received the news via email, on the nightly CID round-up. An old man, found dead in his flat, by a neighbour who had popped by to borrow some gravy granules. Heart attack, it seemed. Poor old boy. Used to be a copper . . .

He feels the sensation of bone once more. Wonders if it would suggest he was losing his mind if he were to go wash his hands one more time. He has felt blood and bone before. But before, he has been able to cocoon himself inside Roisin. He has found strength in her kisses and grown braver for her love. Alone, he feels weak and sick. Wants to phone somebody stronger so they can tell him what to do next. He knows he needs to tell Pharaoh what he has found. There are at least two bodies down there and it is inconceivable to him they are not linked to the events at Winestead. What troubles him most are the pictures by Peter Coles. The lad seems to have used the place as his personal treasure trove. It's his special place, his refuge. It's a cosy, dark, private cave where he could write down his fantasies and keep his dirty little secrets. McAvoy knows how its discovery will be received. It will condemn Peter Coles to a life inside. He doesn't know how he feels about that. He wants to ask him. Wants to know where Peter Coles wants to be, even though he hates himself that such a thing matters.

He holds up the pieces of old, dirty paper. Reads again the young boy's fantasy about the girl next door. Reads again about how he wanted to cut her bra off with a Stanley knife, the way he had read in one of his mucky magazines. McAvoy purses his lips. He's trying not to be a hypocrite. He knows that what exists in the imagination does not have to damn the rest of the soul. There are things that he and Roisin have talked about while exploring their darker sides that would horrify those not used to letting their physical and mental desires intermingle. But he cannot escape the conclusion that there was a dark side to Peter Coles and that the boy's secret and special place is littered with the dead.

By the light of his phone, McAvoy looks afresh at the newspaper clipping. Looks again at Vaughn Winn; done up to the nines and with his hair slicked up in a pompadour. He's handsome. Confident. Standing shoulder-to-shoulder with a well-groomed thirty-something and two very familiar faces.

Neither of the calls McAvoy is waiting for have come through. Vaughn Winn has yet to call him back and explain the significance of the photograph. The CID team at Newcastle have not replied to his three phone calls, requesting information on a local man by the name of Francis Nock. He's not sure he needs the second call. A Google search has filled in some of the background. And a picture is starting to form in McAvoy's mind.

He sits in the dark, stroking his son's head with a hand that still remembers the touch of bone. He shouldn't have taken the boy. Shouldn't have made a murder investigation into a game. But Fin's sleep remains untroubled by nightmares. The boy's eyes had been filled with excitement, not fear, as they made the drive back to the crappy little hotel. And Mammy is not here to tell either of them off for being so reckless.

McAvoy feels his eyes closing. Feels the weight of the day pressing down on him. Feels his limbs grow warm as sleep takes him. Turns the sound of his ringing phone into a part of his dream.

Only wakes as Fin holds the call to his face and a killer says hello.

*She couldn't*, thinks Ray, wiping his nose on his hand. *Couldn't have known.*

For a decade, Shaz Archer has been his pet project. She's been his understudy, confidante and friend. She's been somewhere between a daughter and a wife. He's tucked her into bed after one too many vodkas. He's draped a blanket around her shoulders and held her when she has cried. He's told her about himself. About his wives and children. About the bad things he has done. He's kissed her cheek, her forehead, the tip of her nose. He's barely even had a wank over the silly cow. She matters to him . . .

Her new man has just killed Piers Fordham. Beaten him to death. He's removing the top tier of the Headhunters and he has just completed the most hostile of takeovers.

Ray has been a policeman long enough to spot the obvious. Somebody has found a way to get inside the investigation. They've done so by getting inside Shaz.

He crunches over the gravel. Breathes in deep and smells the ale, cigarettes and vomit that he associates with this hour. Wonders what the hell he is going to say. He'll help her, of course. He'll take the blame, if necessary. Shaz is his friend. She has a bright future. She's made a mistake. That's all. Spilled her guts to the man in her bed and betrayed the identity of Mr Mouthpiece. But who hasn't made the odd mistake? She's a good person. A good cop. A friend . . .

Later, Ray will wish he had looked in through the windows before he rang the bell. Later, he will have a brief period in which to chastise himself for his foolishness in knocking on Shaz's door.

Here, now, he has little time for such regret.

The door is answered by a tall, good-looking man in his mid-thirties. He's naked, save for a sheen of sweat and some tasteful tattoos. Shaz Archer's perspiration anoints his skin. He's smiling, and he's holding a gun.

'You fucking . . .'

Colin Ray's temper takes over and he lunges forward.

He is hit in the head so hard that he is unconscious before he hits the floor.

The man who stands above him and scratches his balls is called Mark Oliver. He used to make a living conning vulnerable women into bed and then taking everything he could. Then the Headhunters took him under their wing. Used his skills to find the weak spots of their enemies. They gave him a glimpse of a life he wanted more of. He got greedy. Saw an opportunity and took it. Charmed a posh copper and recruited a few old friends.

Mark has got very good, very quickly.

He's not killed a copper before.

But he reckons he'll pick it up as he goes along.

# Chapter 22

Next day, 3.18 p.m.

The lighthouse on Flamborough Head. An exclamation mark of whitewashed stone, jutting from a sodden spit of green headland into a sky of rotten timber.

Francis Nock is pissing against the lighthouse wall. He's wearing pyjama trousers and a fleecy shirt. His feet are bare. His hair is plastered against his wind-slapped features by the rain that blows in off the sea. Above, gulls swirl and scream, spun by a wind that has not paused in its rush across hundreds of miles of ocean.

Nock looks up. Sees dragons in the sky.

He hunches down into his shirt and tucks himself away, still pissing. He puts an arm above his head, as if expecting to be carried off and dashed on the rocks below.

Nock feels somewhere between sleep and death. He doesn't know where he is. Has a vague understanding that he is far from home and that people tend to do what he says, but right now he would not recognise either his name or reflection. He is a frightened child, lost and bewildered, shivering in the rain and searching for something that he cannot name and only feels in the memory of his bones. Nothing here is familiar. He feels as though he has awoken into a half-formed world. He expects the green of the new-painted grass to smudge against his feet. He feels that should he wipe his hand against the lighthouse then it will pass straight through. His thoughts feel insubstantial. He has to approach his memories carefully. Needs to sidle up to the flashes of familiarity that his dementia-seamed mind vomits up. He knows only that he is lost. Knows that he is seeking somebody out. Knows that when he woke, the man who looks after him had gone and that it suddenly felt unacceptable to be alone. He feels, too, the absence of something fundamental; something central to his being. He remembers things like snatches of nightmare. Remembers splashing petrol onto bare legs. Recalls how it feels to stick a blade between two ribs. He feels snatches of guilt and pride. Bristles at the thought of disrespect. Fears discovery. Fears anonymity. Fears bullets and solitude.

There was a time when Mr Nock would have recognised this little street with its stone bungalows and its simple, old-fashioned tea shop. He used to like it here. Knew a lass in the village whom he used to enjoy fucking a couple of times a year. He owns the freehold of the chalet park on the next rise. Owns half a dozen caravans and a farm within a five-minute drive. There was a time when he and Mahon would stroll along this clifftop talking about who was earning their keep and who needed to be cut loose; which revenue streams were paying out and who was taking the piss. It is a place of happy memories for him. But here, now, his memories are a swirl of wet paint; a dance of gulls and black cloud.

When the police car pulls up, he will run from it and not towards it. The older, more experienced uniformed officer will wonder for a moment what that says about the old, rain-soaked man. Then he will shrug the thoughts away and place a blanket around his shoulders and try to elicit a name.

The younger constable will check Mr Nock's pockets. He will find the squares of card that Mr Nock picked up from the kitchen counter when he woke this morning into a world that spun and dipped and shrank away from his grasp. He will find business cards for two members of the Serious and Organised squad. He will call the first number and leave a voicemail. And then will he will ring the curvy, motherly, sexy detective superintendent that half a dozen cops he knows would leave their wives for. He will tell her that a man with her business card has been found wandering on the clifftop. He's an old man. Got a debit card belonging to a Raymond Mahon. And he will tell her, in response to her questions, that he is quite certain the man does not have half his face missing.

The constable will hang up, satisfied he has done his job.

And then he will make another call. A call far more profitable.

He will call his paymasters. He'll call Mark Oliver. And he'll tell him that Trish Pharaoh and Francis Nock will soon be together, in the darkness of this remote clifftop village.

Alone, and ripe for the taking.

1.49 p.m. Raywell Old Hall.

Mark Oliver sits on a burgundy Chesterfield sofa, watching a wall-mounted flatscreen TV. He is hunched forward; his bare feet resting on stripped floorboards and his hands pulling at the material of his dark jeans. Two mobile phones sit on the glass coffee table in front of him, alongside a crystal tumbler of Scotch and a small, sleek laptop.

The TV is tuned to the local news. A dark-haired reporter is interviewing an ugly, round-faced policeman against the backdrop of the city docks. He's looking smug. Smiling, despite the rain that blows in sideways against his face. The estimated street value of the shipment will run to several million, according to the graphic that runs along the bottom of the screen. The cop keeps mentioning Humberside Police's Serious and Organised squad and the hard work of one officer in particular, Detective Superintendent Patricia Pharaoh . . .

The man leans forward. Empties his glass in one swallow. Reaches down and picks up the bottle. Refills the tumbler and takes another swig.

A few hours ago he was standing over Piers Fordham's body, watching the life bleed from him like red wine from a dropped glass. He'd won. The Headhunters were done. He'd slipped inside and taken over. He'd taken command.

Here, now, it feels like things are slipping from his grasp. This shipment was the one that was going to make him. He'd needed capital to fuel his ambitions. He'd joined the Headhunters in order to secure the funds to launch his own enterprise. It had taken him a long time to build up the contacts and clout to make a deal with his Albanian suppliers. He'd seduced a lot of women and let himself be used by men in ways he never imagined. He'd made people like him. Had played endless parts and been a lot of different people as he made the right network of influential friends. Learned which palms to grease and whom he should never, ever upset. All he needed was funds to get things started. Those funds have just disappeared; seized at

Alexandra Dock. He's fucked up. He's a dead man. And he has nobody to blame but himself. It's the second time he has under-estimated his opposition, and this time he has even further to fall.

There was a time when Mark considered himself untouchable. He has always been very good at the things he has tried. He got two years through a law degree before he found he could make more money playing cards. Spent a couple of years on the gam-bling circuit before he upset some people and took a beating for his trouble. Took a job teaching casinos how to spot the con-men. Then he conned them too. By thirty, he had been inside only once and had learned how to get whatever he wanted out of people. His time in prison was a networking opportunity. When he came out he started getting commissions. Private investigators would pay him to see whether distrusted wives were ready to jump into bed with somebody charming. Then the clients became richer. Scarier. He had to get women to share their security passwords. Had to keep them busy while other people stole the keys and pass-cards for the companies where they worked. Soon he was bedding women so they could be filmed. Blackmailed. Used for leverage. He became important to important people. But Mark wanted more. He saw himself as more than just some pretty gigolo. He had ambition. Had ideas. He wanted a chance to prove himself and the Headhunters promised that and then failed to deliver. He had no choice but to use his skills. Chatted up one of their best earners. Let the ugly fucker do what he wanted to him but got information in return. Found out where they were weakest. Poured honey in a few ears and persuaded a few bottom-feeding lads to join him. Put together a little crew and began to earn. The Headhunters didn't stop him. After all, he was handing over a large chunk of his earnings to their organisation. He debased himself with the poof as many times as he could endure. Turned his head a little. Became more important to him than loyalty. Mark suffered, but learned all about the Headhunters' plans to remove Mr Nock from the throne. Soon, Mark felt comfortable to share his plans with the nasty bastard who liked to hold him and stroke his hair after fucking him so violently it made his teeth rattle. His name was Dave Absolom, and he used to be a copper. It was Dave who told him about the problems Nock was giving them. One of the Headhunters' best men went to speak to an old Geordie villain called Lloyd. Lloyd ended up in bits on the beach and the Headhunter disappeared.

That was when Mark decided to make his move. He approached the organisations that had shown displeasure with the way the Headhunters had steamrolled into their operation. Mark had offered to put things back to how they used to be. All he wanted in return was the right to supply their gear and guns for twelve months. They bankrolled him. He used his connections to set up a shipment. Guns and gear. Only one other person knew when the drugs were coming in. Mark felt invulnerable. Felt emboldened. He sent Absolom to demonstrate the Headhunters' frailty. Absolom was only too happy to please the object of his affections. He headed north to find Francis Nock and kill the old fucker. Had him beat Tom Spink half to death on the way. Had him spread rumours and lies about Francis Nock in a bid to draw the old man out. He had done more than that. He'd drawn out Raymond Mahon. And Mahon had tortured him until he gave up everything that Mark had worked for.

Mark drains his drink. Pulls at his dark hair. He stands and looks at himself in the reflection of the TV screen. He's still good-looking. Tall. Sunbed-tan. Neat line of designer stubble along his jaw and upper lip. Slim, toned body and ink to die for. He's unblemished. Mark knows how to fight but none of his scraps have left their mark on his skin. He's too greasy for that.

Mark should be feeling fabulous. He has played it all perfectly. Even found himself a tasty piece of skirt on Pharaoh's team. Shaz Archer has been a godsend. She's hungry, ambitious and as filthy in the sack as any of the whores that Mark has used for his own pleasures. She'd been easy to seduce. Vanity, that was what it took. Wanted to be told she was good and that all those around her were nothing. Mark had obliged. Had liked the way he had backed up her opinions on the bitches at work. Tremberg. Ha! He remembered fucking that fat backside. Remembers her pathetic neediness. The way she'd clung to him. He hadn't had the pleasure of Trish Pharaoh yet, but she's caused him headaches this week and he hopes he gets the chance to meet her very soon. Archer had lapped it up. Sneaked him into the station and let him fuck her on Pharaoh's desk. She's given him everything she knows on the Headhunters. When that scruffy old fucker Colin Ray turned up at her door and told her that Piers Fordham was the mouthpiece of the organisation, all the pieces came together. Mark killed him with pleasure. Had gone to sleep with Shaz's sweat and Fordham's blood on his skin and woken up expecting a phone call to say the shipment had arrived safely and he was about to become a very rich and important man. Instead, he had switched on the news and seen his world collapse.

On the table in front of him, one of the phones begins to ring. It's Shaz again. She's just checking in. Seeing if he's OK. He'd

319

been quiet this morning. Is everything OK? Has she done something wrong . . . ?

Mark ignores the call like he's ignored the others. He doesn't know what to say to any of the people who have been ringing and demanding answers. He can't think straight. Rage is clouding his vision and his thoughts. He wants to hurt Pharaoh. She's the one taking credit for his downfall. He wants to tear Francis Nock apart. If Mark hadn't tried to get to the old man he would never have put Absolom in the hands of Mahon. He wants to hurt somebody. Anybody. Everybody.

Mark stands and crosses to the hallway. The man tied to the radiator is bleeding from a wound to the head and is holding himself in a way that protects his broken ribs. Mark kicks him in the guts anyway. Presses his bare foot against his bleeding face and punches him twice in the top of the head.

Colin Ray is gagged with a pair of Shaz Archer's worn knickers and a length of gaffer tape. He doesn't make a sound as the blows come. Waits until Mark has finished then tries to say the word 'cunt'. It makes him choke. His eyes start to stream and blood runs from his nose. Mark pulls the gaffer tape from his mouth. Watches as he pukes up the red lace thong and a length of bloody spit and bile.

'Shouldn't have knocked, old man,' says Mark, through his teeth. 'Should have sneaked in. Should have waited for her to come back from work.'

Ray growls. Coughs crimson phlegm onto his clothes and raises his eyes to Oliver's. 'You should mute the telly, son. I can hear every word they're saying about your fuck-up down the docks. You're a dead man. I'd go now, while I still had the chance.'

Mark shoves the knickers back into his mouth and bangs his head off the radiator.

'You're not me. There's nobody like me.'

Mark returns to the living room. Lies on the sofa and closes his eyes. Broods on pain and revenge and all the ways he's going to fuck Trish Pharaoh when he gets his hands on her fat little frame. He falls asleep and dreams of blood and bones. Wakes, sticky and confused, to the sound of a ringing phone.

Oliver doesn't recognise the number. Isn't sure if it's another of his creditors demanding delivery. But he takes the call.

A minute later, Mark Oliver is smiling again. Knows where to find them all and how to get them all together for one blessed extermination. Gives himself a little pat on the back. He'd known from the start that he would get nowhere without tame policemen. It had cost him a few inches from his stack of notes, but the coppers he had in his pocket were proving to be worth their weight in gold. Finding the right men for the job – that was the problem. How to find those with the capacity for a little gentle corruption. That was the skill that Oliver possessed. He saw what people wanted and he helped them get it.

He picks up the other phone and calls the last number that Piers Fordham rang before he died.

Baits a trap.

He can barely keep the grin off his face as he rings his driver and tells him to bring three good men. They're taking a trip to the seaside. They're going to put everything right. An old man is going to die and they're going to take his enforcer apart piece by piece. And if he plays this right, he's going to get his drugs back and take out his frustrations on an interfering bitch.

Mark wipes himself down with a tissue and slips into a silk shirt. Makes himself look good. Preens and poses and pampers himself to perfection. By the time he's done he doesn't want to soil himself with Colin Ray's blood. Decides to leave the fucker where he is. He'll be a treat for Shaz when she gets home.

Silly cow didn't know what she was letting herself in for. She will soon.

Before Trish Pharaoh and Deputy Chief Constable Bruce Mallett entered the squat pea-green pub off Hedon Road, it had six customers. Six customers, and perhaps twenty-three teeth. It is not a sophisticated establishment. It sits fewer than two hundred yards from HMP Hull and is the first stop for many of the inmates spewed out of the big wooden double doors and onto the busy road that leads east to the docks and west into Hull. A previous landlord used to provide a free pint for anybody who could prove they had been inside for doing harm to a copper. Those days are gone now. The bar does well out of the prison's guards, who stop in for a drink after their shifts and drain a few jars with people who, a few hours before, they were responsible for locking up.

Pharaoh wouldn't have picked the place for a celebratory drink but her senior officer is the kind of man who likes to get his feet wet in the gutters from time to time. He's new to Humberside Police's top tier of officers but knows Hull from way back. He started out here in the early eighties and learned the ropes from old-school coppers. His career has been an impressive one. He was a sergeant by twenty-five, an inspector by thirty and was running a CID team in Worcester by the time he was thirty-four. He's pushing fifty now and was a surprise appointment when the new Humberside Police Crime Commissioner appointed him Deputy Chief Constable a couple of months back. Mallett is popular with the troops. He's big, forthright and ugly. He has a perfectly round head, shaved clean as a watermelon, and his teeth look like he ordered them off the internet and hammered them in himself. He has already proved himself to be one of the lads by downing a pint of vodka at a leaving party and there are plenty of officers who would put money on him to last more than five seconds with McAvoy in an arm-wrestle. Pharaoh likes him, which is why she allowed him to pose for the photographs in full uniform at the docks this morning; smiling proudly in front of a table that groaned under the weight of seized cocaine, heroin and firearms. Pharaoh hadn't felt the need to get her mug in the photographs. She's tired after a sleepless night and has black bags under her eyes that would probably drive her to suicide if splashed on the front of the *Hull Daily Mail*, so is content just for those in the know to be aware of where the intelligence came from. Her friends at Border Force are busy toasting her name with expensive champagne. Her own treat is a double vodka in this shitty pub half a mile from the scene of her triumph.

Pharaoh looks around at the now deserted bar. Mallett's presence has been enough to persuade the usual drinkers to bugger off and get pissed somewhere else. The two of them are sitting at a circular table beneath a dirty rectangular window obscured by an even dirtier lace curtain. Mallett is drinking bitter from an old-fashioned tankard and tearing the beer mat into strips.

'Bloody good result,' he says, loudly, for what must be the twentieth time. 'Bloody good. I hate to think in headlines but this kind of thing always helps us look a bit less shit, don't you think? Somebody's going to be spitting blood, don't you think?'

Pharaoh smiles and sips her drink. She wants to make it last. Doesn't know her boss well enough yet to drain four doubles, then drive home.

'Got lucky with a tip, sir. Friend of a friend, favour owed – that kind of thing.'

Mallett examines her over his glass. Gives her a look that suggests he knows she is being evasive and that he doesn't mind in the slightest.

'You got somebody hidden away with their balls in a mincer, Patricia? I don't give a shit where it came from. Border Force are doing cartwheels, I've got a nice seizure to keep the suits happy and your unit has proven why it was set up. It's a good bloody day, love. If you tell me you had to put the thumbscrews on to get it I'm not going to stop enjoying my pint. Just a shame it's going to get bumped for that pissing lawyer, eh?'

Pharaoh nods and twists some life into her neck and shoulders. CID has spent a busy day trying to piece together why somebody would want to beat a disbarred lawyer to death in his own house on Newland Park. Pharaoh's not involved in the case but has at least used the investigation to rid herself of one annoyance. Shaz Archer had requested to be seconded to CID to lead the investigation into Piers Fordham's death and Pharaoh had been happy to agree. She reckons Archer was pissed off at not being invited along on the early-morning raid at the docks. Hopes the rich bitch will use the incident as an excuse to make the transfer permanent. Colin Ray will be back at work soon and the last thing she wants is the two of them plotting her downfall at a time when she has just given the unit its biggest success to date. She wishes McAvoy had been there to share some of the praise, but he's still officially on sick and wasn't even answering his phone when Pharaoh called him last night to update him on developments. She wonders if he's upset with her. God knows, the Peter Coles case is a thankless task. She can't help feeling that she may have stitched him up by accident, and even if she hasn't, she expects to break his heart when she tells him where his wife and child are. She has tried to do everything the right way and ended up wronging only one person. But that person is the one that matters most.

'Arrests would be nice,' says Mallett, thoughtfully. 'One driver isn't going to cut it.'

Pharaoh agrees. The driver of the lorry was Albanian and had taken his arrest with good grace. There had been no tantrums or protestations. He'd known what was coming as soon as the officers threw open the back of his wagon and the dogs climbed aboard. The stash was found inside the hour, hidden inside adapted metal bars and pipes that his manifest claimed were destined for a welding company in the East Midlands. Pharaoh doesn't reckon he'll talk. Not yet, anyways. The breakaway crew from the Headhunters are too dangerous to risk upsetting, though whether that will still be the case for long is hard to say. The new crew will be unable to keep their promises. The guns and drugs they have promised their associates will not materialise. The Headhunters have crushed the uprising. Whoever it was they employed to extract the information that led to the raid, they had carried out the job with aplomb. Pharaoh just wishes she could shake away the feeling of unease. She has received information from dangerous sources before, and she cannot argue with the feeling of a job well done. But she fears that blood has been spilled to provide her with that information. She feels again as though she has been steered from the start. She worries that perhaps her own idea of right and wrong is blurring. She wishes she could talk it through with McAvoy and knows that she never will. His own ideals are too painful to live by. She's just grateful that she is the one who has to make the decisions and that he is spared them. The man would screw himself into the ground like a puppy chasing its tail if asked to wrestle with such moral conundrums.

'I got a nice email from some prick in London,' says Mallett conversationally. 'Breslin. Slick chap. Very southern. All the words spelled correctly. Said to pass on his congratulations over the raid. Good result. Reckons you've got them on the ropes but wonders if perhaps, next time, you could share the information with the rest of the symposium before rushing in. I've subtly suggested he fuck off. What's a "symposium"?'

Pharaoh smiles. Drains her drink. Holds up her glass and waits for the barman to grudgingly bring her another.

'A meeting of minds, was how he described it,' she says, smiling. 'Talked about starbursts and popcorn.'

'He taking you to the pictures?'

'Popcorning, apparently, is when ideas bubble up and burst open, like popcorn . . .'

'Christ.'

'Yeah, well, was useful, I suppose. We got some handy information. Something about the Headhunters imitating some Eastern European MO from years back. And we found out about the problems they were having. Even so, I reckon we gave away as much as we discovered.'

'There was a security breach?'

'They know more about us than we do about them.'

'But they'll be hurting from today's raid, yes?'

'The Headhunters? No, they'll be laughing, sir. It's one of their teams that has been causing the bodies to pile up. They recruited the wrong man and he's brought a lot of ambition with him. He's stopped taking orders. I think today's raid has only served to help the Headhunters show who's really in charge. And I'm not sure it's us.'

Mallett broods for a moment. Shrugs.

'At least it's off the streets, eh? A drop in the ocean is better than no drop at all. And say what you will about these Headhunter bastards, they don't hurt civilians if they can help it. I was sorry to hear about Tom Spink, by the way. How's he doing?'

Pharaoh looks down. Clinks the ice in her glass. 'He's tough. Will be back on his feet eventually. I didn't know you knew him.'

'Tom? Showed me around when I first started out. Him and Mike Canard. Tall bloke. Into trains. Big brain on him, though his missus was a terror. They were my teachers when I was green as grass. Lost touch over the years but I saw his name on the incident report. Send him my best, will you? I know you're close. Was a real shame that had to happen. Somebody clearly went too far.'

Pharaoh looks away. Stares through the grimy glass at the stream of cars making their way up Hedon Road in the drizzle and gloom of a wet weekday afternoon in east Hull. She's unsure how she feels about her friendship with her old boss being common knowledge in the top tier. Wonders, for a moment, if Tom had tried to grease the wheels of her promotion. Called in a favour or two with other grateful protégés who have risen to the top. She knows he will have done it purely from his fondness for her and that thought seems to catch behind her eyes. She feigns a cough in case tears threaten to spill.

'He's one of the few ex-coppers who doesn't seem lost,' she says, turning back to Mallett. 'He's found something else to be. So many coppers just lose themselves when they hang up the warrant card. You've seen them. Drunks and security guards. Or both. Sends shivers right through me, the thought of what I'll be if I'm not this.'

Mallett seems to be thinking. He scrutinises her. Takes in the wavy black hair and blue eyes; the strong scent of perfume and fags, the irrefutable swell of cleavage and the half-hearted make-up around the wrinkles on her forehead and neck. When he speaks again his voice is lower than before.

'I'm nearer the knacker's yard than you, love. People don't get it, do they? What it means to do this job. What it does to you. It pays to think ahead. There's a company in London always needs good coppers when they're done locking up villains. They know how to compensate people for their expertise. Consultancy work – that's the future for old campaigners like you and me. You should give my mate a ring – he'd be glad to hear your voice.'

Pharaoh nods, looking down at the shredded beer mat in front of Mallett's big white hands.

'There are some coppers go to the dark side,' says Mallett, holding his gaze. 'Some bastards slide across and become the thing they used to chase. They see opportunity. They see how little difference they've made on the side of law and order and decide they may as well make some money.'

Pharaoh takes a breath. She examines Mallett for signs of duplicity.

'Any copper who doesn't think we're winning needs to catch more crooks, sir. No problem's going to be fixed by joining the enemy. It's hard, sure. But at least we do a job where we make a difference of some kind.' She stops herself and smiles. 'I sound like my sergeant.'

'The big lad?'

'McAvoy, sir. My best.'

'Still on sick, I'm told. Bad business at his house. His missus had been shagging one of the villains. Am I right?'

'It's complicated.'

Mallett's ready smile falls and his face becomes hard. 'I'm a bright man, Superintendent. I can handle complicated. Let's hope McAvoy can. That missus is of his is going to hold back his career, you know that, don't you? Poor lad. How did he get tangled up with a gypsy?'

'A gypsy, sir?'

'Come on, love, we all hear the rumours. Threesome, wasn't it? With that other fella who got splattered on Holderness Road. That McAvoy's a fucking Jonah, isn't he. He should watch his step. Get shot of that lass before she causes him any more bloodshed or harm. You've had a good result today, love. We're all happy. You should be able to relax and enjoy it and instead your mind is a million other places. Maybe you should unburden yourself a little. I can help, love. I can even make sure somebody has a word in the pikey's ear – make sure she doesn't come back. Would be best for him in the long run. She's away, isn't she? Give me a clue or two. Where would we find her . . . ?'

Pharaoh rubs a knuckle with a cold, dry palm. Keeps her eyes on Mallett's. She doesn't know where the conversation is going. She'd accepted the invitation of a drink without question. But she knows little about her new Deputy Chief. She feels suddenly vulnerable. Can't help but think of the piggy little eyes of Dave Absolom staring at her from the computer screen as she sat beside Dan in the Tech department. Wonders why her boss has chosen this tiny, deserted pub. Wonders whether she has been a fool . . .

A sudden trilling in Pharaoh's pocket curtails her trail of thought. She apologises and takes the call. It's from an unfamiliar number but Pharaoh answers it with her full name and title. She says it loudly, so the barman can hear. Looks around for her handbag and starts scrawling blue ink in her notebook as her heart begins to race. She half knocks the table as she stands, and Mallett is too busy cursing and wiping spilled beer from his uniform to stop her as she heads for the door.

Within moments, Pharaoh is running through the rain. She's half a mile from her car and a long way from knowing what the fuck she thinks about anything. All she knows is that Mr Nock has been found wandering on a clifftop at Flamborough Head. She knows he is in danger and that her decision to bend the rules may have placed him there.

Bodies are piling up. Castles are crumbling.

And she feels alone in a war where uniforms count for nothing.

# Chapter 23

McAvoy doesn't know why he has made an effort with his appearance. He's wearing his good grey suit with a thick checked shirt and double-knotted purple tie. He's trimmed the hair around his ears and shaved his stubble into a neat goatee. He's wearing the long cashmere overcoat that Roisin bought him and which he stitched up by hand after a killer stuck a blade through it and into his skin. He looks more than presentable. He looks good. It seems to matter, somehow. He doesn't know what today will bring. Doesn't know if he is about to solve a multiple murder or simply stick a rake in the swollen belly of corpses long since forgotten.

He leans against the bonnet of his car. Feels the light rain and cold wind keep the blush from his face. Feels his hair and coat-tails play with the breeze. He checks his watch. Breathes in through his nose and out through his mouth, trying to keep his heart steady and his hands from shaking or making fists. He wants to look relaxed. Confident. Wants to appear like a sea-soned detective who meets gangland enforcers and serial killers every day.

It's mid-afternoon. Already the day is giving itself over to the gloom of evening. The dark clouds have folded into the grey-brown stillness of the sea. McAvoy stares at a miserable horizon; a pulp of smoke and damp charcoal. He is standing at Alexandra Dock, just off Hedon Road. One of the monstrous super-ferries is a little way to his left: a toppled office block of whites and blues against the grey of dock and sky. There are four other vehicles in the little car park. It's a popular place on these dreary days. Old couples like to sit and watch the waves; to stare at the swirling, keening gulls and the distant towers and lights of the oil refinery on the far side of the estuary. Families are drawn to the idea of travel, of departure, of escape. McAvoy has watched mothers and fathers of young children stare wistfully at the departing ferries as their giggling, gleeful offspring wave at strangers and imagine they are saying goodbye to loved ones bound for adventure.

In the small sports car to McAvoy's right, a young man with a dark beard and too much hair dozes in the driver's seat. The light rain has made his windscreen opaque. Further away is a blue van with open back doors. A short, fat, unattractive man in a Hull City raincoat is keeping an eye on a fishing rod – its line stretched taut as it scythes into the waters beyond the little footpath that leads down to the housing estate on Victoria Dock. The other vehicle belongs to a reporter from the *Hull Mail*. She's sitting chatting on her mobile phone, and eating a fruit salad from a Tupperware box. She has no desire to go back to the office yet. Would rather sit and watch the waves and argue with her mam than go and write up the latest developments on the drugs raid that took place a few hundred yards away in the early hours of this morning.

McAvoy sniffs. Breathes in the cold air. Catches the whiff of diesel and creosote. Smells sawdust and grease. Fills himself up with the mixed aromas of this unwashed city by the sea. Wonders whether he should have worn his stab-vest beneath his coat.

At 2.07 p.m., a flat-bed pick-up truck pulls into the car park. The man at the wheel wears scarf, sunglasses and baseball cap. He has a leather jacket on with the collar pulled up and the hands that grip the steering wheel are clad in calfskin.

McAvoy purses his lips and blows out a stream of nervous breath. He has spent the morning learning all he can about this man. Has spent the past few hours acquainting himself with the record of Raymond Mahon. The rumours. The associations and legends. Mahon deserves more than respect. He deserves fear. McAvoy does not expect to be able to arrest him alone. Does not expect he will need to. Mahon knows the rules. Knows that any information he provides will be inadmissible in a court case. A second officer would need to be present to verify his words and Mahon had made it clear that McAvoy was to come alone. He had even allowed him to pick the location. McAvoy had chosen the docks purely because it offered privacy along with the safety net of CCTV and a handful of witnesses. He used to walk here with Roisin. Used to push Fin in his stroller as his mam and dad ambled along the water's edge and fantasised about one day owning one of the big four-bedroomed detached properties that overlooked the water. The home they finally bought is four miles further down the coast. The motel he now calls home a little further still. Both are marked by the distant shape of the Humber Bridge; a vertical slash of tarmac and metal that punctures the clouds and provides the horizon's only line.

McAvoy straightens his tie as the other man climbs from the vehicle. He tries not to show his nervousness. There is no doubt that those gloved hands have taken life. This man has served serious time. He has served a north-east crime kingpin for five decades. And he may well have committed the crime for which Peter Coles has been incarcerated for half a century.

Mahon walks forward, his steps light, his bulk imposing. As he nears, McAvoy glimpses the ruination between the rim of his spectacles and the collar of his coat. Sees the wet, pink, slimy mass of torn skin. The yellow teeth. He tries to keep his revulsion from his face. Tries and fails.

'I'm used to it,' says Mahon, waving his hand towards his face. 'Don't blame yourself. I'd make myself feel sick too.'

McAvoy doesn't know what to say. Stands motionless for a second. Then he reaches out a hand and takes Mahon's in his. Feels the strength in the grip. Wonders, for a moment, whether he could outmuscle this old man if it called for it. Fears he already knows the answer.

'Your boss has had a good day, eh? Tell her she's welcome.'

McAvoy narrows his eyes. He had heard about the raid on the news as he drove here an hour ago. Heard the plaudits thrown the way of the Serious and Organised Unit. Had felt like pulling over and punching the steering wheel when he realised what he had missed out on by not taking Pharaoh's call. He wants to be by her side. Wants to be part of something. Feels so alone: here, among the ghosts and the screaming gulls.

'Hell of a place to be, eh? Hull, I mean. Never been a fan. Can't say my own neck of the woods is much more palatial, like. Newcastle's a funny place, I've always said. Everywhere's uphill. How's that possible? Like Edinburgh, isn't it? Uphill whichever direction you're going. You get big thigh muscles if you live there, of course. That where you got yours? Your university was there, wasn't it? Rumour has it you were going to be something spectacular until you grew a conscience and became a cop.'

McAvoy still hasn't spoken. Doesn't quite know which way to play this. Wants to know if he is in danger of being hurt or just looking a fool. Decides to play Mahon's own game.

'I doubt you would have crossed paths with me then,' he says softly. 'You were inside again. Firearms offences. Should have been more, by all accounts, but a witness changed their statement and they could only do you for possession. Wasn't much of a stretch for somebody with your record. Soft time, I think it's called. Not compared to the seventeen years you did for killing Randall Mosedale. Shotgun, wasn't it? Bad sort, so I'm told. Bit of a villain. You didn't say a word in your own defence – not in interviews or during the trial. Impressive. No wonder Mr Nock has kept you around for so long.'

The two big men stand on the dock and examine one another. Absorb each other's muscles and scars. Mahon is the first to smile.

'Randall Mosedale? Randy, to his mates. Summed him up, too. Went too far with the wrong girl. I was just going to give him a bit of a slap but he pulled a gun. I didn't know the daft bastard was under surveillance. He had an undercover cop on his crew. Saw the whole bloody thing but never said a damn thing about it being self-defence. That's coppers for you, eh? The truth's what you make it. Shall we take a little stroll?'

McAvoy rubs his eye and pushes his hair back from his face. They fall into step, mooching along slowly with the sea to their

335

left. They both nod hellos to the fisherman. Duck under the taut fishing line and turn right to where the massive canal gates stand open, as if a monster has just been released from a prison of iron, wood and stone.

'Sea's supposed to be blue, isn't it?' asks Mahon, pointing at the brown water and the thick chocolate fondant of mud that sticks to the stones of the sea defences. 'Is this where they empty dirty radiators?'

'It's a pretty clean waterway, actually,' says McAvoy, because he can't help it. 'Dangerous though. One of the hardest to navigate in the world.'

'All the old river pilots got the boot a few years back, didn't they?' asks Mahon chattily. 'The port authority wanted to save a few quid and cut them adrift. Made life as difficult as possible for them. Was like the seventies all over again. Reckon I would have enjoyed the seventies if I'd been on the outside. Strike-breaking was a speciality of a crew I used to have some dealings with. Not sure I would have been able to bring myself to do that, personally speaking. I don't really understand politics but I've never been on the side of the rich.'

McAvoy casts a glance at his companion. Wonders if he is joking. 'Mr Nock's not short of a bob or two,' he says cautiously.

'He's worked hard for it,' says Mahon, without malice. 'Started with nothing. Had to get his hands dirty for years to get himself where he was. Where he is, I mean.'

'Dirty with what?' asks McAvoy. 'Honest toil or blood and tears?'

Mahon looks at him and smiles: a ghoulish, horrifying thing. 'Where did they find you, mate? Seriously?'

'What do you mean?'

Mahon shrugs. 'Wouldn't know how to buy you, mate. Wouldn't know what to offer. Of course, I haven't had very long to sniff around. Few rumours. Interesting CV. Lots to learn about the missus and the people you've upset. Don't know what we'd have made of you, back in the good old days. Mr Nock would have made that decision. I'd hate to have had to carry it out though.'

Their footsteps take them past a timber yard, shielded by steel bars. To their left there would be nothing to stop their fall should they slip over the edge of the footpath and down into the thick mud and standing water.

'You asked me here to talk about 1966,' says McAvoy, trying to keep his voice steady. 'You said you had information.'

Beside him, Mahon takes a deep breath. Behind his coloured lenses, he blinks, long and hard. He seems to be watching a snippet of film in his head. Eventually he stops. Leans back against the steel. Lights a cigarette and pushes a plume of smoke into the gloom.

'You've been down there, haven't you?' he says, at last. 'The hole.'

'The bunker?'

Mahon nods. Looks away. 'Saves a bit of time, then. Would hate to have to draw you a map. Figured when I heard you talking to Glass that you were going to be the bugger to dig it up.'

'You killed him?'

Mahon smiles, indulgently. 'Natural causes, mate. Pity, to be honest. I liked him.'

'You scared him to death, then.'

337

'Wasn't me that did any of this. I paid a fucking heavy price for what you found in that hole in the ground.'

'Not as heavy as the Winn family. Not as high as Peter Coles.'

Mahon slides his sunglasses down his nose. Looks at McAvoy with his pink, rat-like eyes. Gives the slightest shake of the head.

'You put any of this together, Sergeant McAvoy? You got any fucking idea what happened or why?'

McAvoy looks down at the mud and stones below. Watches crows and seagulls fight over the same tattered scrap of nothing. Screws up his eyes and lets himself talk.

'Vaughn was one of your boys, wasn't he?' he asks softly. 'One of Mr Nock's. He may be some slick businessman in Australia these days but all those investments he makes in the local community are just a way to salve his conscience. His family died because he upset somebody. His family died because he got in with the wrong crowd and ended up working as a bloody gangster's muscle at the time the big boys from London wanted some action. How am I doing?'

Mahon sucks half an inch off his cigarette. Flicks the ash off the end and watches it fall down like black snow.

'The bodies in the bunker,' says Mahon, at length. 'How're they looking? Well? Handsome? Identifiable?'

McAvoy doesn't answer. Finds his leg jiggling as he tries to keep up. Tries to make sense of what he thinks he knows. Replays the last few days in his head. The scene of the Winn family's murder. The conversations with Vaughn. The strange, bewildered figure of Peter Coles. The fear and paranoia of John Glass. He knows he is missing something. There are too many bodies. Too few answers. Peter Coles had said they knew Vaughn.

338

*Knew Vaughn. Knew Vaughn, new Vaughn, new Vaughn . . .*

'A new Vaughn,' he says, suddenly, turning his head to Mahon. 'He's not bloody Vaughn Winn, is he? The injuries to the faces . . . the smell of gunsmoke in the house . . . what Glass smelled and saw . . .'

Mahon turns to him. He suddenly looks as old as the man he serves.

'Mr Nock always said it would be taking pity that would cost me,' he says, turning back to the horizon. 'Always said I needed more steel in me. It was pity that cost me my face. Pity that nearly cost me my life. They nearly took all my pity from me that night. Nearly made me the monster people see. Maybe they managed it, I don't know. I still think I did right. I still think Flash Harry deserved everything he got.'

McAvoy says nothing. Just waits. Tries to keep his heart from racing and resists the urge to grab the old man by the throat and shake the truth out of him.

'Vaughn was a headcase,' says Mahon softly. 'His dad and Mr Nock had history. Made some money together during the war. Clarence met some lass in Hull and sold his Newcastle business interests to Mr Nock. Moved out to the middle of nowhere and tried to become Lord of the Manor. Tried to play a straight bat. Had himself a nice little family and sent Mr Nock a Christmas card every year. Problems began when young Vaughn was a teenager. He was a bad lad. Dangerous. Liked women's clothes. Liked to draw. Liked to hurt animals and watch his sister in the bath. Clarence kept it as quiet as he could. Even kept that bloody simpleton Peter Coles nearby so people would think it was him and not the squire's son who was causing problems in the village. Made no difference. The boy needed discipline. Needed an outlet. So Clarence called Mr Nock and the boy came to the north-east to learn how to behave himself.'

'He went to work for Mr Nock?'

'We found him a job in one of our clubs. Took to it like a duck to water. He had money, you see. And style. Liked to dress up. Big bloody pompadour and camel-hair coats. Done up like a peacock. But he was tough. Sorted out some trouble one night and Mr Nock took a shine to him. Let him into a few of the other business interests we had at that time. Gave him a little crew to work with. Gary and George. Thick as planks but good at taking orders. They made good money with Vaughn. Became Mr Nock's blue-eyed boys.'

As he says it, Mahon's voice betrays him for a second. There is a flash of something personal in the way he says it. A flicker of an old grudge; a long-held ember of having been over-looked.

'Vaughn never gave himself away to Mr Nock. Never showed what was going on behind the eyes. Was just a pretty boy with a big bright smile. But his eyes were dead. I knew what he was first time I saw him. But nobody listened to me.'

McAvoy huddles into his coat as the rain starts to come down harder. Wonders if the older man will do the same, then realises that Mahon is too lost in memory to give a damn what the present throws at him.

'We'd made friends with the southerners,' says Mahon softly. 'The twins. Come to an understanding. There was a spot of bother down in London. A shooting. Cost them dear in the end but it took a bit of time for Nipper Read to piece it all together. When it first happened, they needed their shooter to keep his head down. To stay out of trouble in a friendly place. So they

340

sent him to Mr Nock. And he gave Vaughn the job of keeping him safe, happy and out of the way.'

'It went wrong?'

'Vaughn had a girl. One of our girls.'

'A prostitute.'

'If you like. She was a nice girl. Sweet. Young. Probably too young, though nobody really made a song and dance about that. Vaughn liked her. Said she reminded him of his sister.'

'Jesus.'

'And Terry took a shine to her too.'

'Terry?'

'The shooter. Southerner. One of the twins' boys. Terry, his name was. Loudmouth bastard. Vaughn had him holed up in this flat we owned. Gary and George took it in turns to bring him what he wanted. They brought him too much. Too much drink and drugs, and in the end too much of the wrong woman.'

'Vaughn's girl?'

'Terry didn't just want to have her for an hour or so. Kept her at that flat like she was his personal slave. Made her stay naked. Treated her like a dog. Ate his dinner off her back. Made her do things she hated and made her say she loved them. Word got back to Vaughn. And Vaughn let the other side of himself out.'

'What happened?' asks McAvoy quietly.

'He killed Terry first. Cut him up like a side of bacon.'

'First?'

'Then he killed her. The lass. The tart he liked. Poor bitch.'

'Why?'

'Because he was a fucking evil bastard. Who knows what happened inside his head? Maybe he thought she enjoyed it. Maybe he didn't like caring about somebody. You ask me, he killed the southerner and enjoyed it so much he wanted to do another. She meant nowt to him. Not really. He liked her but preferred himself and in that moment, all he wanted was to feel his knife go in as many warm bodies as he could find. All I know is that by the time I got there the place was a bloodbath and they were both dead in the bedroom.'

'Why were you there?'

'It felt wrong. Mr Nock doesn't make many errors of judgement. He didn't know what Vaughn was. I did. And I knew what he was going to do. I may have called him Flash Harry and made a joke of him, but I should have made it clear. He was bad. Worse than any of us. A bloody liability.'

McAvoy's breath catches as he tries to speak. Mahon lights another cigarette. Tells him to be quiet. To just listen.

'Vaughn was from money. It was bloody obvious what he was going to do next. His dad kept cash at home. Mr Nock and me both knew it. Vaughn knew it too. He'd just killed an enforcer for the London firm. He couldn't stick around – even if Mr Nock offered protection. He needed cash. So did Gary and George.'

'You went after them?'

'I took a call while I was cleaning up the flat. It had all gone wrong.'

'He robbed his family? Killed them for the money?' McAvoy feels bile and temper rising.

Mahon shakes his head. 'They were all wired. Drugged up. They were supposed to wait until the family went out for their walk so they could go take the cash. But they didn't go out. Stayed in that night because of the snow that was due to fall. Late in the year for snow but that's fucking Yorkshire for you, eh? So Vaughn decided he couldn't wait. Went in with masks on and rounded up his mam and dad and brother and sister. Scared the shit out of them. Told Clarence to fill a bag with money. Then Peter Coles walked in the back door. And he saw straight through the balaclavas and said hello to Vaughn like they were two best friends and this was all just a game.'

'Jesus.'

'Clarence went for his son. Needed to know. Tried to pull the balaclava off him and the gun went off. Clarence was dead before he hit the floor. Peter was first to react. Threw himself at the girl. Anastasia. Wrapped his arms around her like a shield. The shot that Gary aimed at her jammed in the cartridge. Blew up and nearly took his hands with it. George's gun went off properly. Took Mrs Winn in the guts. Blew her half apart.'

McAvoy can't speak. Just closes his eyes and listens to the ocean and the words.

'Vaughn knew he was in too deep,' says Mahon.,'Knew whatever happened now he couldn't fix. Daft bastard thought Mr Nock would be able to take care of it. But it was me that answered the phone when it rang at the flat where the lad had left his two bodies. Me who said I would take care of it. Me who put the bodies in the boot and headed to Yorkshire.'

McAvoy's ears are filled with static. He can hear his own blood.

'You set up Peter Coles,' he says quietly. 'And you murdered Vaughn's brother and sister.'

Mahon coughs: a guttural, ugly, unhealthy sound. He spits blood and mucus into the sea.

'I had them clean the place up. Had them bandage Gary's hand. Gagged and tied the brother and sister. Was a mess in

343

there. I couldn't just disappear the bodies the way we could in Newcastle. People would know. There were too many loose ends. It was Vaughn who said we had to kill them. Vaughn who said his old mate Peter liked to play with guns and had been stealing his sister's knickers off the washing line. Vaughn who suggested we butcher his whole family so nobody could pin anything on him.'

McAvoy swallows, hard. His mouth is dry, his face wet with rain and sweat.

'You went along with it?'

'Tried to. But pity's a bitch. And I took pity on Anastasia and her brother. Took pity on that bloody simpleton. We spent a day in that house, with its blood and bleach and gunsmoke. I saw the grace in Anastasia. Saw the fear in her brother's eyes. It wasn't the kind of job I had signed up for. And the danger wasn't to Mr Nock – it was just to Vaughn. It was dark when I dragged the bodies out there. No snow yet. Not much time to do what I had to do. Vaughn was excited, like a child at Christmas. Had picked out the spot in the churchyard where he wanted his sister to die. Wanted to make it look authentic, too. Stripped her, there in the church. Slapped her about, cock like a rock in his pants. Gary started slapping the lad. And I was standing there with Clarence's blood all over me and Peter Coles looking at me like I was the devil.'

McAvoy looks at the old gangster. Imagines who he used to be, and what he became that night.

'. . . a new Vaughn . . .'

'I did what had to be done. I took Gary's gun from him and blew his fucking face off. Vaughn turned like he'd been slapped. My gun jammed, just like George's had. I broke it over George's

344

head. Then Vaughn raised his own shotgun. Turned those dead eyes on me. It was like staring into a shark's soul. And Peter just flew at him. His hands were tied, and he didn't know why his friend was doing these things, but he knew Anastasia was in danger. Vaughn dropped his gun. And I shot his fucking face off.'

Mahon leans back against the wall. He looks lighter, somehow. Insubstantial. The rain is thick on his glasses and droplets run into the hole in the side of his face.

For a full minute, neither man speaks. Then McAvoy clears his throat.

'It was Peter that showed you the bunker, yes? Where he and Vaughn used to hide their secrets. You put the bodies there and stuck the lid back on.'

'It was the only way,' says Mahon. 'The boy and girl would never have been safe. People had to think them dead. And whoever killed Terry was going to be the focus of all kinds of vengeance from the twins.'

McAvoy wipes rain from his face. 'The girl. The prostitute.'

'We dressed her in Anastasia's clothes,' he says flatly. 'And then I shot her in the face.'

'The boy?'

Mahon smiles, limply. 'A new Vaughn.'

McAvoy squashes his hands together. Tries to push the shaking from his bones into the sea wall.

'Stephen became Vaughn Winn?'

'Took his brother's identity. Took his sister with him to Australia. Lives a good life, so I'm told.'

'And Anastasia?'

Mahon shrugs, sucking at his ruined cheek. 'Lived a good life too. Died a couple of years back. Heart failure. She'd had kids and grandkids. Worked in the equestrian world. Married a good guy, from what I hear.'

'The real Vaughn is in the bunker,' says McAvoy, half to himself. 'Him, Gary, George, Terry. It's a tomb. It was Peter's secret place, wasn't it? Where he and Vaughn could read mucky magazines and hide away . . .'

'I thought the stone would have been rolled away years ago,' says Mahon. 'I never expected them to stay buried so long.'

McAvoy watches as the wind raises white caps on the pewter sea. 'And Peter Coles?'

Mahon closes his eyes. 'Somebody had to be blamed. He was already afraid of me. And when he knew Anastasia was in danger . . .'

'He took the blame.'

'He already thought he was to blame. He thought he'd killed Vaughn. Thought it was his fault Clarence was dead. Just kept saying he was sorry. I left him there, staring at the poor bitch's tits in the moonlight. Went and found John Glass. Put in a call to a tame CID man by the name of Len Duchess and tried to keep things from unravelling.'

McAvoy looks at Mahon's face. At the ruination and pain.

'They came for you? The twins.'

'They didn't get all of me. And Mr Nock wouldn't let them try again. He's my employer. My friend.'

'Jesus,' says McAvoy again. 'Where did he find somebody like you?'

Mahon turns his gaze towards McAvoy. Pulls down his collar and smiles with teeth that look like they should be grinning from a rotten skull.

'I was nothing before he put me to work,' he says. 'I've lived my life to keep him where he is. He deserves to see it through. Doesn't deserve what he's become.'

'Deserves?'

Mahon shrugs. Rubs his forehead with his gloved hand. He looks tired. Pained.

'I'm phoning the bodies in,' says McAvoy. 'Peter Coles doesn't deserve to have spent fifty years in mental hospitals. The truth is important. The truth matters.'

'The truth is whatever the cops say it is,' whispers Mahon. 'I just need a little time to keep Mr Nock on top. Just until he slips away. Then you can pin the lot on me. Do what you like. Let Peter out if you think it will help anybody . . .'

'That isn't how it works,' says McAvoy, shaking his head. 'You don't dictate. You may have had pity but you killed people. You're a murderer, whatever your intentions.'

'You've killed,' says Mahon softly. 'You've got blood on your hands.'

'That wasn't . . .'

'I've told you this so you'll understand. I've told you because I sense you're a decent man who appreciates that a few more days won't matter to bodies that have been in the ground that long. I can be helpful to you. Give you everything. Time's running out. Mr Nock's drifting away. I can give you the bloody Headhunters if you just wait . . .'

McAvoy is shaking his head: as much to stop temptation as to say no.

'Raymond Mahon,' he says, reaching into his pocket for his phone. 'I'm arresting you . . .'

Mahon's hands move with such speed that McAvoy doesn't even feel pain until he's already on the floor, clutching his throat. He looks up through watery eyes and sees Mahon retrieve McAvoy's phone from where it has fallen. He tries to move. Tries to stand or get control of his legs. He can do neither. The blow to the throat had been so precise it seemed to cripple him upon impact.

McAvoy tries to focus. Sees Mahon examine the picture on the cracked screen. Of the dark-haired Romany girl and the son and baby daughter in her arms. Mahon stops still. Chews his coat collar. He retrieves another phone from his pocket and watches the screen for a moment. Puts it to his ear and listens to the message left half an hour before. Doesn't recognise the voice. Doesn't care. Mr Nock has been found wandering on the clifftop. He has been released into the care of a CID woman by the name of Pharaoh. She's taking him back to the chalet he managed to give them as his address. Piers Fordham, the Mouthpiece, is dead. And both Nock and the copper are going to die . . .

McAvoy gulps down air. Finally manages to get some life in his legs. Falls against the sea wall and bumps his head, feeling as though there is a boot upon his throat.

Mahon looks at the big Scotsman. The grim determination. The scars and muscles and the fractured soul. He has no other allies. No help he can call upon. No heavies for a hundred miles. He hauls McAvoy to his feet. Takes his arm and drags him towards the car.

'Your wife. Your child. Your fucking boss. You can have them all,' says Mahon, as the rain begins to pummel the ground.

He turns to McAvoy and pulls a gun from his pocket. He thrusts it into McAvoy's ribs. Turns desperate eyes on him and rips the glasses and scarf away from his own face. Throws his hat into the sea. Stands on the path with his rotten skull and twisted features scowling into the face of the gale.

'Help save his life and I'll give you mine.'

# Chapter 24

Pharaoh looks at the man who has ruled the north-east for more than half a century. Finds herself shaking her head. He's in good nick. All designer labels and fancy aftershave. No rogue eyebrows or tufts of wiry hair in his earholes and nostrils. He's taken care of himself, this one. Just doesn't know who he is today. Woken up a stranger to himself. Looks frightened and cold. Only found his way here because some sweet old dear with a terrier had seen the police car and wondered if she could help. Told them about the newcomers in the white chalet and the big man she kept seeing on the clifftop. The keys in the old boy's pocket had fitted a treat.

She pushes the mug of hot chocolate towards him. Urges him to drink it.

'Poisoned,' says Nock, turning suddenly furious eyes upon her. 'Fucking cops. Fucking cops!'

Pharaoh rubs her face with her hands. Pushes herself out of the armchair and takes the mug back to the kitchen. It's dark beyond the glass. If she squinted she would just about be able to make out where the sky stops and the water begins, but

Pharaoh has no interest in such things. She's mildly intrigued by the size of the gulls. Hasn't seen any this big before. It's like the sky is full of dragons. Their black, twisted shapes pass in front of the yellow moon, casting shadows on the clifftop that stretches away to the rear of the little chalet. She suppresses the urge to shiver. Wonders what the fuck to do next.

Pharaoh came to get answers. Had driven up the coast on a whim. Entertained notions of giftwrapping a career criminal for her colleagues in the north-east and securing another high-profile conviction for her unit. Instead she had found a living corpse. Nock may have been a powerful man once but right now she is only staying with him because she is too afraid for his safety to leave him on his own. She has no doubt that the dementia is genuine. For a moment she had thought that perhaps he was acting senile as part of some elaborate con. But the look in his eyes is too real for that. He's lost himself. There's a wire come loose in his head and he can't find the people who care for him. His enforcer is nowhere to be found. Nock has reacted with silence and swear words when questioned on his whereabouts. Pharaoh has asked him if there was anybody else she could call. Told him that bad men might be trying to hurt him. Told him she was a policewoman and that she was concerned for his safety. He's made the noise of a police car then spat down her dress.

She searches the cupboards for something stronger to drink than tea. Finds an old bottle of brandy behind the bleach and furniture polish. Takes a swig from the bottle and feels the pleasing burn. Turns her attention back to the window and watches the rain batter against the glass. She can't get a signal on her phone here. Will have to pull on her coat and battle down to the end of the road if she wants to call the two uniforms who released Nock into her care. She doubts they will be pleased to hear from her. Doubts they will have the manpower to come and sit with Nock until she can think of what to do with him. Wonders whether she might be better calling McAvoy. He and Fin could drive up. They'd be here in an hour. Could keep her company and have a giggle. Make an adventure of it. Play happy families . . .

Pharaoh tuts at herself. Feels sick at the thoughts that creep up on her unbidden. Wonders what the fuck she is thinking. She'd be willing to put a child in the firing line, just to spend time with his daddy . . .

Over the noise of the gale and the rain, Pharaoh hears the low, throaty hum of a large vehicle. It's a 4x4 of some kind with a V8 engine. It sounds a little like one of the force's BMWs. Could the local bobbies be checking in? She'd love nothing more than to climb back into her sports car and get back to civilisation. She puts the brandy bottle back in the cupboard and walks through the living room to the wooden front door. Throws it open with a broad smile and tells the young policeman on the doorstep that she's delighted to see him and that he should get his arse inside and out of the rain.

The young constable moves to the side.

And Mark Oliver hits her in the head with a police baton.

'Pharaoh,' he says, smiling, as she hits the floor. 'You're thinner than you look on the telly. But I was watching in widescreen.'

Pharaoh is unconscious. The blow was so hard that that a back tooth was dislodged on impact and has wedged in her throat.

She begins to choke.

Oliver tuts and uses a polished shoe to roll her into the recovery position. Uses the point of the baton to lift her dress and poke around.

'Granny pants, Patricia? I'm disappointed.'

Three men step over her body as they make their way into the living room.

Oliver closes the door. Pulls down Pharaoh's dress and examines her exposed breasts. He shrugs, tucks them away, then reaches into her mouth to remove the blockage.

'We're going to have such fun.'

A mile away, McAvoy is sitting in the passenger seat of Mahon's pick-up. The heavy rain and deep black of the night sky make it almost impossible to see the curves in the road but Mahon seems to know when to turn the wheel. McAvoy, with his keen eyes, sees only the occasional flash of a living-room light or the white flick of a rabbit's tail as they career through potholes and rutted tarmac, mud, puddles and spray.

'Answer,' says Mahon, into the phone, as he tries to ring the chalet one more time. 'Please!'

McAvoy has never seen desperation like this. Mahon seems unhinged. The thought of not being there to protect Mr Nock seems to have caused something to come apart inside him. He no longer has the gun trained on McAvoy. No longer gives a damn what happens to him or when. He just wants to see Mr Nock through safely to an end that suits him. That is all he has ever wanted.

Were he so inclined, McAvoy could open the door and jump out into the damp grass at the roadside. But through the stuttered madness and unintelligible grunts, he has learned that

353

Pharaoh is in danger. Learned, too, that the Headhunters have been watching his wife and child. They know where she is. And only Pharaoh knows how to get in touch with her.

McAvoy has been afraid before. He is no stranger to terror. But this is something different. He cannot feel his body properly. Can hear his own blood in his ears. Doesn't seem to be able to get his words out or stop the trembling that threatens to shake his teeth loose.

'Please,' he says, through clenched teeth and shivering lips. 'Please.'

Neither man knows what they will find at the chalet on the clifftop. But both know that tonight, there will be blood.

'Are you fucking kidding me?' asks Oliver, arms wide.

He is grinning, arms outstretched, looking at his men for approval as they lounge against the walls of the tiny room.

'You're the great Mr Nock? You look like you've just been dug up! You're older than my fucking granddad, and he's dead! Jesus, no wonder you stay out of the limelight. Anybody who saw you would laugh their tits off.'

In the little armchair behind him, one of Oliver's men gives a high-pitched titter. He's a young lad. Big-boned and fleshy, with his blond hair cut short on top but with a straggly little ponytail down his neck. He's all jogging pants and white trainers, knock-off T-shirts and sporty cars that boom out drum-and-bass. He's doing well for himself, considering. Couldn't earn this kind of money legitimately. Couldn't get a job with an arrest record like his. He likes working for Oliver. Likes being allowed to hit and hurt and terrify. Knows that tonight he's going to get to fuck a copper. Can't keep the excitement out of his laugh.

'I hope your monster isn't going to be as much of a disappointment,' he says, lighting a cigarette with a gold lighter. 'I have to say, today is proving to be full of ups and downs.'

On the sofa, Mr Nock gives a little laugh. 'Monster,' he says. 'Funny.'

From the hallway comes the sound of Pharaoh coughing. She retches. Wheezes. Falls back to the floor.

'For fuck's sake,' says Oliver, turning his back on the old man. 'Stay still. It will be your turn soon enough . . .'

Oliver puts his fingers into Pharaoh's mouth again. Turns around to say something witty to his men.

Pharaoh bites down. Crunches through flesh and bone.

'They're here,' says Mahon desperately, as he stops the car and the headlights illuminate the two vehicles parked on the clifftop. 'Fucking cops too.'

He turns to McAvoy, as if seeking guidance. Feels wind and rain on his face as the door swings open. Watches, as McAvoy runs through the gale towards the tiny property, tearing off his coat as the gale whips at its tails.

Mahon's shout of warning is lost on the wind. Never reaches McAvoy's ears.

And McAvoy never reaches the house.

The door of the police car swings open.

And the first of the bullets starts to fly.

The scream awakes something inside Mr Nock. For a moment the fog of his thoughts is pierced by a bright white light of clarity. He's at Flamborough Head. Raymond is away, taking care of business. These men mean him harm. And some sexy cop has just bit the fingers off a slick cunt who reminds him of some dead-eyed greaser from the good old days.

The men in the room haven't even bothered to draw their guns. One has a shotgun inside his coat but none are paying him any attention. Mr Nock moves quickly. Slides his hand down the side of the sofa in the hope that there will be a gun or a blade. He finds a pen. It's not much, but in the right hands it can be lethal. Mr Nock possesses such hands.

He moves so fast that the nearest man doesn't even turn his head in his direction before the biro has been plunged into his throat and ripped upwards to his jawline. Blood sprays upon Mr Nock's face and he finds himself smiling.

Finds himself alive and energised, clear-headed and very, very pissed off.

'You bitch! You fucking bitch!'

Oliver is clutching his bleeding hands. His face has gone an unhealthy grey. He's trying to wrap a handkerchief around his hand but can't do that at the same time as fending off the venomous blows that Pharaoh is thumping into the side of his head.

'Shoot her!' he's screaming. 'Shoot her!'

Pharaoh takes a handful of the slick bastard's greasy hair and smashes his face against the wall. She can taste his blood. Still has a chunk of his skin stuck in her back teeth. She can feel him trying to push her backwards but knows that if she lets go of him the men in the other room will cut her in half with their shotguns. So she holds him tight. She bites and claws and hits punch after punch after punch . . .

356

The fat lad in the jogging pants fumbles with his gun as the spray from the other man's wound gushes across his hands and face. He recoils in shock and instinctively closes his eyes, finger jerking at the trigger as he jerks. The gun bucks and a bullet flies high and reckless. A tall man in a leather jacket ducks in the act of pulling out his shotgun. Only Mr Nock remains unfazed by either the blood or the firing pistol. He kicks out at the man with the shotgun and his old, bony knee mashes into his balls. Mr Nock takes the shotgun from his grasp. Lunges with the barrel into his open mouth; mangling teeth and lips and enjoying every second of it. He cocks the weapon and prepares to blow the bastard's head off. Feels a hot, searing pain as a bullet takes a chunk out of his hip. He staggers back, knocking pictures from the wall. Pulls the trigger and takes the whole of the left side of the fat lad's face. Slides himself along the wall and into the corridor. Watches as the tall, good-looking man tries to pull a pistol from his own pocket to use on the curvy, dark-haired woman with the bleeding mouth who is ramming her fist into his eye . . .

Mr Nock raises the shotgun. Doesn't give a fuck who he hits.

McAvoy turns at the sound of the gunshot. Sees a young man in police uniform standing by a police car, dripping with rain. He holds a shotgun in his hands. Wisps of smoke are rising from both barrels.

Both barrels . . .

McAvoy charges towards him. Hits him with all the combined rage and frustration and heartbreak of these last weeks and months and years . . .

Feels the satisfaction of a punch perfectly thrown and a jaw perfectly broken.

Turns back to the house. Spins at the sudden roar of an engine.

And watches as Mahon drives the car at 60 m.p.h. into the side of the chalet.

Mr Nock's shotgun blast tears a hole in the ceiling just as the pick-up truck demolishes the wall. Oliver and Pharaoh both throw themselves to the right. Oliver's hand finally closes on his gun. He drags the door open. Tumbles out into the wind and the rain and the darkness, shooting behind him as he flees.

Amid the rubble and the dust and the falling beams, Mahon sits in the driver's seat and looks through the shattered glass at the scene before him.

Sees the bullet go straight through Mr Nock's middle.

Watches the old man look down at the wound with some surprise, and then fold in on himself.

Inside Mahon, something dies. He stumbles out of the car. Collapses on his knees in front of Mr Nock and sees the spirit leave his body and the light leave his eyes.

He stands. Opens his jaw wide and feels the flesh tear.

Pulls open the door and sees the slick bastard running for his car.

Sees McAvoy standing there, motionless, his face a mask of confusion as he squints through the storm at a figure he seems to know.

Mahon is an old man but he channels all the strength he has into his sprint across the clifftop.

Oliver doesn't hear him approach. Thinks that the scream is that of gulls and gale.

Only turns at the last possible moment.

Mahon picks him up as if carrying a straw man.

They go over the cliff edge as one.


Pharaoh stands in the doorway of the ruined house. Spits and gags and falls to her knees.

And then McAvoy is holding her in his arms and stroking her hair from her face.

'You knew,' she says, through bleeding lips. 'You came.'

McAvoy holds her close, expecting sobs. None come. She just clings to him, and breathes him in.

There will be time for everything else later. Time to fix this and make it work.

For now, all that matters is the nearness of somebody who cares.

Somebody whose face swam in her mind in the moment she thought she was about to die.

# Chapter 25

11.14 a.m., Clough Road Police Station.

An upstairs office, furnished with thoroughly modern appliances and painted a shade of peach so sickly that its occupant worries it will affect her calorie count.

Pharaoh is at her desk. Her gum has stopped bleeding and she has an appointment to have an implant fitted into the hole. She thinks she may have swallowed the original tooth. Has no interest in its retrieval.

The fact she is at work at all is a cause of much appreciative comment in the canteen downstairs. Pharaoh is known to be tough. But last night she got caught up in a gunfight when some men tried to kill an old gangster at his hideaway on the east Yorkshire coast. According to her report, she'd tried her best to save him. If one of the local coppers hadn't turned up she might even have managed it. As it was, she'd had to go and help the young uniformed cop. He'd been knocked out cold by one of the intruders. Pharaoh had saved his life. Lost a tooth and got a kicking for her troubles but had hit back twice as hard. Had stayed and supervised the scene and the initial stages of the investigation. Called her sergeant up at home and got him there inside the hour. Would be looking after the investigation herself. Pharaoh has her pick of the jobs at the moment. Her star has never shone brighter. Should enjoy it, while it lasts . . .

Pharaoh stares out of the window at the busy road. The new offices face a retail park. It's all electrical stores and furniture warehouses offering zero per cent finance for the next three years. She'll maybe pop across in her lunch hour. Help McAvoy pick out a sofa for the new house. Take the piss at his expense and try to find cushions the same colour as his blush.

She reinstated McAvoy in her office at 9 a.m. Won't let him take the lead on the investigation into the events at Flamborough Head. She knows he'll find out what really happened, and that's the last thing anybody needs. She told him it was just some bad men. Perhaps a branch of the Headhunters, trying one last time to get a foothold in the north-east. He'd taken her at her word. Silly sod always fucking did.

There was no moment when Pharaoh considered telling him the truth. Neither Mahon nor Oliver has washed up yet and Pharaoh can't institute a search for them without giving away more than she wants to. She had expected him to be furious when she told him where Roisin had been. Had expected him to bellow in her face or break down and sob. But he'd simply nodded. Kept it all inside that great big head and heart and told her that he would go and get her as soon as it was convenient for the squad. And then he'd told her about the bodies in the underground bunker.

The Home Office had been far from pleased with McAvoy's discovery. It meant Peter Coles was innocent. Worse than that, he was some sort of fucking hero. If any of it came out, the headlines would be catastrophic. Pharaoh had enjoyed the moment. Had let her contact at SOCA vent a little spleen. And then she had told them what had happened the previous night. She'd told them how hard McAvoy had worked and about a few little problems he was having. Had suggested that, amongst friends, favours were commodities.

By this evening, the bodies will have been removed from the bunker and incinerated. Peter Coles will have been transferred to whatever kind of facility makes him happiest to live out the rest of his days. And Detective Sergeant McAvoy will receive a special discretionary payment for his brief secondment to SOCA. It will be enough to cover the repairs to the house and to fill it with things that will make him smile. He won't question it. He doesn't know what politicians earn. Presumes that it's all above board and will simply be quietly grateful that his work is appreciated.

Pharaoh crosses her legs and breathes out a lungful of cigarette smoke. She shouldn't be smoking in the office but nobody is about to tell her otherwise. She's hero of the fucking hour. The shipment at the docks was a terrific seizure on its own but she's wrapped up the murder of a city lawyer and given an eye-witness account to the clifftop murder in the space of the past twelve hours. Piers Fordham's murder is a long way from being tied up but Shaz Archer has heard from one of her sources that he had upset the wrong people in prison. Reckoned it would either be tied up with a quick confession, or never solved.

Pharaoh closes her eyes. Finally gives in to it. Finally lets the sobs come and her chest heave as she shakes and shudders behind the locked door of her office. Thinks of her kids. Of her

362

crippled bastard of a husband. Of Tom Spink. Of her mam. The people that matter to her. She nearly lost it all. They nearly lost her. She doesn't know why she does this job. Why it matters. Why any of it matters. She's due a good pension. Could quit tomorrow if she chose. But she won't so choose. This is who she is. It's what she does.

Pharaoh slides open her desk drawer and looks at the bottle of whisky. Indulges in a little smile.

She thinks of Dave Absolom, and knows. Knows beyond doubt who is coming for her friend.

Shaz Archer hasn't shed any tears for Mark Oliver. The bastard walked out on her without a goodbye. So what? Plenty more fish in the sea, though they may not be quite so good-looking or eager to indulge her kinky side. He knows where to find her if he wants her. Knows he'll have to work hard to win her favour . . .

That's the story she tells her friends, anyhow. In truth, Shaz doesn't expect to see Oliver again. Doubts anybody will. She's heard what Pharaoh has told everybody about what happened on the clifftop. Doesn't believe a word of it. She has her own contacts. Knows the sergeant at the local station and has it on good authority that the young copper whose life Pharaoh saved wasn't even on duty and is planning on handing his notice in as soon as he can eat solid food again. Has it as gospel that McAvoy turned up with him while the bullets were still flying.

Shaz isn't going to rock the boat. She's worked too hard and too long to spoil it by being heard to badmouth everybody's favourite boss. No, she'll keep her mouth shut. She'll stick with the squad. She'll use what she knows about a certain consultancy firm in London to secure some decent convictions for her big City friends. And she'll move when the time is right.

For now, Archer has only one problem to deal with.

She needs to stop thinking about Colin Ray.

Shaz is a pragmatist. She knows she has made the right decision. She doesn't trouble herself with old-fashioned crap about right and wrong, but she does know that she owes Colin a lot. He deserves better than this. Her head is still full of the moment they took him away. The moment when he managed to get the bag off his head for just long enough to lock eyes with her. His gaze had spoken of sorrow and betrayal. A hurt beyond understanding. She had done that to him. Sure, she can justify her actions. The boys would have slit his throat and cut off his face and hands if she had not asked them not to. She has a soft spot for her mentor. She hopes that the boys will persuade him to take the money. To go away and not come back. If not, they can be surprisingly resourceful. Colin has kids. Ex-wives. They'll find his weak spot, and press. And if all else fails, they'll shoot him so full of drugs he'll be lucky to remember his own species. All in all, she should probably have just agreed to his death. She must be getting soft.

Sitting at the mirror in her perfect bedroom, Archer sprays her naked body with an extra squirt of the perfume she wears when she's feeling pleased with herself, then looks at the figure in her bed. He's lying in the same sheets where she fucked Oliver for the last time. Lying where Oliver would have died, had he not run out on her.

She blows him a kiss and walks to the kitchen for a glass of wine.

Archer has no doubts the man in her bed will find a way to

make everything right again. He turned the Headhunters into a multi-million pound organisation. He became the poster boy of CID without anybody knowing who he really was. And he has a viciousness which eclipses that of any villain she has ever met.

He's handsome, for his age. Cyrillic tattoos adorn his body. His name is Doug Roper. He came here to kill Mark Oliver, but Oliver was already dead. Roper doesn't blame Archer for that. She did well, keeping him here. Was willing to do whatever it took. Put herself through some disgusting shit just to please Roper. She is looking forward to the rewards.

Of course, he still scares her. There is an emptiness in him that only power and violence seem to be able temporarily to fill. He has had a good week. Everything has happened as it was meant to. Mr Nock is dead and his enforcer gone. Mark Oliver has played his part and been removed. Dave Absolom and Piers Fordham have been removed. Their deaths were a shame but a necessity. They knew too much. And for what Roper has planned, he cannot leave himself vulnerable.

The only hiccup was McAvoy. Roper had wanted the bastard to suffer longer. Had wanted his wife and child to be absent from his home until the Scottish cunt was on the edge of madness. And then Roper was going to break his heart and his body all at the same time. The sanctimonious prick got lucky. And Roper doesn't like that. He has such pain planned for the man who cost him his career and his position that he gets breathless just thinking about it. The big man is going to suffer beyond enduring, however long it takes.

Archer drinks her wine and looks forward to the future. She'll miss her friend Colin Ray. But the silly bastard thought he was her father. How could he be? After all, Shaz was beautiful, and everything about Colin was ugly.

Archer raises her glass and toasts her man.

They smile at one another; two sharks sniffing blood.

*Let's get started.*

# EPILOGUE

It feels like the edge of the world, this place.

Feels timeless.

Forgotten.

The last villagers left Slaggan in the western Highlands in 1942. Gave their crofts over to the elements. Let the wind and the rain beat the stones to rubble and dust. Let the bog suck the foundations into the earth. Let it die beneath gunmetal skies.

McAvoy leans against the tumbledown wall and watches the sun throw silver highlights into the grey swell of the water. Sees two rocks appear from out of the surf. Smiles, as one barks to another, then disappears in a splash of fur and flipper. He points the seals out to his son. Ruffles the boy's hair and squeezes his hand. Tells him about the island in the centre of the loch. The old folk tales his dad used to tell him before he abandoned him for a life that offered more possessions, and fewer things worth treasuring.

He breathes in. Breathes in the smells of his childhood. The salt water. Seaweed. The distant tang of freshly dug peat

367

smouldering on flame. Catches the faintest whiff of heather and water-lilies.

And there, beneath it all, the stale taste of bones.

McAvoy feels the sun on his face. Feels the cold breeze roll in off the sea. He cannot call himself content. His insides twist at the unasked questions that grip and pull at him. He cannot help but keep replaying the events on the clifftop in his mind. Can't help but think of Mahon and the other man, tumbling over the rocks and into the water. Wants to know what will happen to the bodies in the bunker. Wants to know who did this to him and who was so desperate to keep him and his wife apart.

Eventually, he will ask the questions. He will sit Pharaoh down and look into her eyes and ask her to tell him the truth.

But for now, all that matters is the woman walking towards him across the heather and the thick green grass. She carries his child on her hip. She walks painfully, as though her legs trouble her. Black hair streams behind her, and her pretty, elfin features break into a smile as she locks eyes with him. She tickles their daughter Lilah, and points out the big man with the ginger hair who leans against the fallen wall of a crofter's forgotten home. Lilah recognises the man. Gives a huge smile and tries the word she has been practising.

Behind her, McAvoy's father sits in the driver's seat of an old blue Ford and watches as his big, strong, silly bastard of a son collapses in the arms of his wife and child. He wants to follow her across the grass. Wants to run to his son and tell him he is sorry for the stupid things he said and the ways that he has said them. But he won't. Not yet. There will be time for that later.

Here, now, there is just the light, and the mingled scents of a place untouched.

There is a family, reunited.

# ACKNOWLEDGEMENTS

There are many people who contribute to bringing a book to life. In my case, many of them are fictional and live only in my head and whisper things to me in my sleep, but I'll thank them separately. In the real world, I remain forever grateful to the team who make my books considerably better. Jon, Rich, Ron and Margot at Quercus are true friends for whom I have nothing but love and admiration. Gratitude, respect and several cigars go to my agent and friend Oli. In the crime-writing world there are too many people who inspire me to name them individually here, but a special hug must go to Mari Hannah – a great writer and true mate.

I have a lot to thank my grandfather-in-law Michael Duck for. This book came about as a consequence of the conversations we had while waiting for a variety of doctors, nurses and well-wishers to come and fix the things that were knackering his body. We sadly lost Mike before he could see this book on the shelves but wherever he may be, I'd love for him to know how much I admired him. He was a good copper, and a better man. Tall, clever, patient and loving, it pains me to not have noticed how very 'McAvoy' he was until so late.

George and Elora, you will always be my everything. Thank you for being weird.

And here's to you, dear reader. Thanks for taking an interest. I'd look a right prat without you.

D.M., April 2014.

# DEAD PRETTY

## DS MCAVOY: BOOK 5

### David Mark

Hannah Kelly has been missing for nine months.
Ava Delaney has been dead for five days.

One girl to find. One girl to avenge. And DS Aector
McAvoy won't let either go until justice is done.

But some people have their own ideas
of what justice means . . .

*Turn the page to read the exciting opening chapter.*

# I

*Monday, 2 May, this year*

The kiss is sticky. Inelegant. A sensation not unlike biting into a ripe peach.

He feels her hands on his back, her cold fingers applying gentle pressure on each of his vertebrae as if his spine were a clarinet.

Small, neat teeth clamp playfully on his lower lip.

She moves as shadow, insinuating herself into the gap between his broad left arm and the sleeping child he holds so protectively in the crook of his right.

'Let it go, Aector. Just for a moment. Please.'

Detective Sergeant Aector McAvoy pulls his wife close. Feels her settle in his grasp with the same spirit of contentment as the little girl who snoozes against his chest. He strokes the soft skin of her taut, tanned belly and feels her shudder and laugh as he finds her ticklish places.

Her giggling gives their embrace an oddly teenage air; turns this coming together of experienced and familiar mouths into something inarticulate and clumsy. Lips overspill. Take in chin and neck. He feels the blast of air from her nostrils as she exhales, hungrily, into his open face; snorts his breath in a grunt of wanting; tongue like a spoon scraping a yoghurt pot . . . and then she is pulling away, rising like smoke, leaving a fading ghost of scent in the warm air around his flushed cheeks. He breathes deep. Catches the scent of suncream and citrus, of outdoor food and wine. Her skin lotion and cigarettes. He wants her, as he always wants her. Wants to wash himself, lose himself, in her movements, her affection . . .

And then he feels *her*. Hannah. The missing girl. Reaching upwards, through the bones and the splinters and the deep dark earth. Her fingers grabbing at his trouser legs. He feels suddenly cold in his chest and hot in his belly. Makes fists around his wife's hair and ignores her gasp of pain and surprise. Pushes her head back and buries his face in her neck; making a cave for the thudding din of his thoughts.

*She's here. Here, beneath your feet. Here, waiting for you …*

'I'm sorry,' he says, and his refined Scottish accent is dry as ancient bone.

'I like it,' says Roisin, placing a kiss on her daughter's forehead, and then stretching to plant a similar smooch on McAvoy's nose. 'I can handle a bit of the rough stuff. But let her go for a little while, eh, my love? Just try.'

It is bank holiday Monday, just after 4 p.m. A bright spring day. Nap time for Lilah. Above them, the bluest of skies and a round, orange sun. Viewed as a photograph, the image would suggest darting swallows, fat bluebottles. In truth, this valley with its muddy, root-twisted footpath, its gorse bushes and cow parsley, its dandelions and wild garlic, channels a wind that cuts like steel. Even McAvoy, inured to the harshest of elements during a childhood battling hail and snow on his father's Highland croft, suppresses a shiver as the wind tugs at his sweat-dampened fringe. Shivering, they retreat into the shadow of the small, squat church that stands to their rear to find comfort among the headstones and the lichen-covered memorials. Enjoy the distant haze of bluebells, curling around the trunks of adolescent trees like tendrils of cerulean smoke.

The trio hold one another in silence as a chilly gust, unimpeded in its rush from the North Sea, tumbles down the valley. It shakes loose a maelstrom of apple blossom from the overhanging branches. Petals cascade like snow, landing in Roisin's jet-black hair and tickling her skin.

'It's pretty here,' says Roisin. 'I've always thought that if people are going to go missing or get murdered, they should do so in pretty places. It makes it much nicer for me and the bairns.'

'Don't,' says McAvoy, shutting his eyes tight, like a child turning his face away from a spoonful of something unpleasant. 'What if she's here, Roisin? Under our feet, right now. What if we've already stepped on her face?'

Roisin shakes her head and reaches down to pick a daisy. He loves her ability to do something so simple and innocent. Loves that she indulges him his obsession. Has made space in their relationship for the missing girl.

'There are worse places to be left alone,' she says, and starts plucking petals from the flower. 'He loves me, he loves the dead lass, he loves me, he loves the dead lass . . .'

McAvoy isn't sure whether to chide her for insensitivity or kiss her for being so adorable. It is a dilemma he faces most days. Were he not a policeman he doubts he would care much either way. But McAvoy was a policeman in his soul long before he put on the uniform and even today, as acting senior officer on call, he cannot forget that at any moment his phone could ring and inform him of another horrible thing done in the name of passion, revenge or desire. He carries his job with him at all times. Feels the burden within him, and without, like a rucksack full of bricks whose weight only diminishes when he takes his wife and child into his embrace.

Beneath his grey woollen coat, McAvoy has squeezed his considerable bulk into a dark blue suit, complete with yellow shirt and old school tie. His suits are specially made, bought off the internet from a supplier specialising in men of stature. McAvoy has stature to spare. He is a conservative 6 foot 5 inches. He has a rugby-player physique and a handsome, scarred face topped with unruly ginger hair. Grey hairs have begun to speckle his beard and the darkness beneath his eyes betrays the things he has seen. He would look like a nightclub bouncer were it not for the gentleness around his cow-eyes and the freckles that spray across his pink-and-white cheeks.

Roisin, ten years his junior and made all the more elfin by her proximity to her towering husband, wears tight black jeans and a designer sweatshirt beneath the burgundy leather jacket she opened with such excitement on Christmas morning two years ago and has barely taken off since. McAvoy knows that despite the cold, Roisin would be wearing something more revealing were it not for her self-consciousness over the scarring on her legs. She used to love showing off her skin every time the sun pushed its face through the clouds. But an accident two years ago ripped holes in her shins. Left her perfect legs looking like somebody had carved their initials to the bone.

McAvoy looks around him. Marvels at the absence of company. He had not really expected to find an army of Japanese tourists in the grounds of St Ethelburga's church but imagined there would be at least a couple of ramblers and a picnicker or two. Instead, he and his family have Great Givendale to themselves. It has a timeless quality, this place, in this moment. He fancies that he and Roisin could be plucked from their own time, transplanted to a different century and the view would remain unchanged. Reckons they would be unaware they had tumbled through the ages until the locals turned up and started jabbing him with pitchforks and suggesting that both the witch and the giant be burned without delay. In truth, the little church to McAvoy's rear was only built in 1849 and in times gone by, the geese that are busy having a noisy argument down by the tear-shaped pond would be surrounded by onions and sitting in a pot.

'I don't mind,' says Roisin, softly, as she settles back against the wooden bench and nods at his shirt pocket. 'You can tell me again. I won't snore. And if you argue, I'm hitting you.'

McAvoy considers protesting but his left bicep is already sore from the repeated punches she gave him while driving here, and he doesn't think he can take another of her 'love-taps' without making a girlish noise. Roisin does not know her own strength.

McAvoy unfolds the rectangle of paper and waves it at a butterfly that seems to have taken a liking to Lilah's brightly coloured summer dress. He looks again at the tangle of lines and smudges of forest that make up his satellite map of the area around Pocklington, on the road from Hull to York, where East Yorkshire becomes North Yorkshire and the house prices start to rise.

Lets himself think of her. *Hannah*. The missing girl. The young lassie who was just beginning to live . . .

The Serious and Organised Crime Unit of Humberside Police has been searching for Hannah Kelly since August of last year. Since that time, McAvoy has got to know this rural landscape pretty well. Has snagged his clothes on just about every briar and branch. He knows she's here somewhere. He just doesn't know where to dig. Doesn't know whether it's wrong to bring his family here for picnics. He shivers at the thought that he missed something while lost in a daydream about walking through these woods with his wife and children.

'Make a nest,' says Roisin, nodding at the damp grass.

McAvoy obliges, shrugging off his coat and laying it down. He folds Lilah into its soft, grey arms. He kisses her cheek; his nose touching the tiny plastic device that helps her hear her parents' words and which she has grown adept at blaming for her occasional acts of disobedience.

'Go on,' says Roisin, putting her legs across McAvoy's as he sits down on the bench. 'You'll feel better.'

McAvoy doesn't need his notes. Knows the whole sequence of events off by heart.

'At just after one p.m. on Sunday the twenty-ninth of August, Hannah phoned for a taxi. It picked her up from the back of the Bowman's Tavern in Howden twelve minutes later. Hannah shared a house around three hundred metres away, on Bridgegate, with three friends. She had been invited with them to see a movie at the leisure park at Castleford but had declined, saying she had a migraine. When she ordered the cab, she told the operator she was heading to a village on the road to York but couldn't remember the name. When he picked her up, she said it was Millington.'

'That's the place we had the ice cream, yes?' asks Roisin. 'Pretty little village. Top of the hill?'

McAvoy nods. 'She told him to take her to the Gait Inn. We had a drink and a meal there just before Christmas, remember? Lilah drew on the table with her fork and you called the landlord a fecking eejit?'

Roisin grins at the memory. Encourages him to continue.

'She talked a lot on the journey. Sat in the front and gabbled. Told the driver about her work.'

'What did she do?'

'Press Association in Howden. TV listings for the *Radio Times*. She did two years of an English degree at the University of Hull but didn't finish it and took a job there on a recommendation from a friend. She was pretty good, apparently, though I'm not sure what qualifies as "good". Anyhow, the driver asked her why she was heading out to the middle of nowhere. She said something about meeting an old school friend who was staying at the temple up the road.'

'That's the big place? Looks like Downton Abbey?'

'The Madhyamaka Kadampa Meditation Centre, yes,' says McAvoy, stroking his wife's leg and remembering the gales of laughter that his boss and friend, Trish Pharaoh, had thrown his way when he first read out the name – begging him to repeat it again and again. She makes him do the same with the word 'purple' when she's bored. Apparently the Scots can't say it, though that came as news to him.

'Sounds exotic,' says Roisin. 'A good place to hide who you are.'

McAvoy shakes his head. 'We've checked several times and none of the guests, staff or residents at the temple had any knowledge of her.'

McAvoy tails off. Scans the treeline. Spots his son, still happily beating a sycamore to death with a branch as he fights dragons and defends fair maidens in his mind's eye. He reminds himself to teach the boy the Latin name for the tree when he comes back, sweating and excited and demanding to know where the next sandwich is coming from.

McAvoy looks at his wife, and tries to keep it light as he proceeds.

'So we presume that it was a cover story. The driver said she had a sports bag with her and was wearing jeans, a sweatshirt and trainers. He dropped her at the pub. There were a dozen drinkers outside, enjoying the sunshine and hating the ladybirds.'

'A loveliness of ladybirds,' whispers Roisin to her sleeping child, and looks at her husband proudly. He grins back.

'Aye, the plague of last summer. Couldn't pick up a glass of lemonade without finding a hundred ladybirds using it as a bubble-bath. But the ramblers outside the Gait were willing to put up with it. They saw her get out of the cab and go inside. She gave them this little wave. And not long after she came out again, dressed in a little white tennis dress and Doc Marten boots.'

'Bit of a transformation,' says Roisin, sneering slightly at the very idea of such a combination.

'Not her usual sort of outfit either, according to her friends. Prudish. That was the word they used. Not much skin on show. They couldn't even imagine her wearing something like that.'

'Was her hair up or down?' asks Roisin, chewing on her lip.

McAvoy has to fight the urge to grin. Detective Superintendent Trish Pharaoh had asked the same question.

'Down,' he says. 'The drinkers outside said she looked a million dollars. At first they wouldn't have recognised her as the same girl. Heavy eye make-up too. She gave them a smile. Same little wave. Hoisted her bag. Set off up the road.'

McAvoy turns his head in the direction of the road in question, Grimthorpe Hill. Fastest way from the middle of nowhere to the back of beyond.

'Three different motorists have come forward to say they spotted her walking this way from Millington. The last of them was about a quarter of a mile from here. She was looking at her phone as she walked. Looked a little warm but not unhappy. Certainly not running from anything or anyone.'

'And then?'

McAvoy rubs his face with his large, rough palm. 'Her mobile phone disappeared from the network. There's quite a good service up here, surprisingly. They could pinpoint pretty damn close to where the signal went dead. And that doesn't mean switched off, Roisin. That means somebody taking the battery out. The tech wizards can still pinpoint a dead phone.'

Roisin nods. She knows.

'Her friends didn't report her missing until the next day, and even then it wasn't to the police. She didn't turn up for work and her boss asked one of her housemates where she was. She was as surprised as the boss that Hannah hadn't shown up. Started ringing her and got no response, then realised her bed hadn't been slept in. That night one of them spoke to their parents and they suggested calling the police. So they went to the local station. Got a PC who told them she was a grown woman and probably just with a bloke. It didn't come to CID for four days.'

'What was she like?' asks Roisin, as she nibbles on a piece of hawthorn leaf she picked in the woods and which she said reminded her of being a kid. Why she wants to remember that time is beyond McAvoy, but he doesn't like to make a fuss.

'CID got in to her Facebook account and her emails,' says McAvoy, looking away. 'She had a blog. Nothing much to get excited about for months – it was all favourite films and why she liked cats and whether *Toy Story* was an analogy for life. Just the thoughts of a young girl. She was a romantic. Like a child, really. Used to buy wedding magazines even though she was single. Saw life like a Disney princess.'

McAvoy nods his head in the direction of the cornfield that runs parallel to the woods.

'The screensaver on her computer was a photograph taken in those woods,' he says, looking down at his feet. 'And on her work computer she'd searched Google Maps for the route from Millington to Great Givendale. We haven't found her laptop. She hasn't taken any money from her bank account since she vanished but she made no major withdrawals before her disappearance.'

'Did she have much to withdraw?'

'Not a lot, but a few hundred quid comes in handy when you're planning a new life.'

'And there was no sign of a man?'

McAvoy pushes his hair back from his face. 'Yes and no. She had a boyfriend at university but it wasn't really serious. And the lads she'd been out for drinks with at work were all adamant that she was an innocent.'

'An innocent?' asks Roisin, and enjoys McAvoy's blush.

'She'd still wear white at her wedding, is what I mean,' says McAvoy. 'And not all young men think that's a virtue. I've spoken to a lot of her friends. They were pretty clear that for a long time she was a lot of hassle for not much reward. She was a good girl, Roisin, whatever that might mean. Then things changed.'

'Changed how?'

'I just get the sense that she found somebody. Little things. Her friends said she was acting a different kind of giddy. She was always giggly and happy but she had that little swagger in her step. And the entries on her blog seemed a bit more worldly.'

'You think she lost her virginity,' says Roisin, and this time, she doesn't make fun.

'I think she was preparing to. And she visited peculiar websites on the work computer. Nothing dirty, just interesting essays on different kinds of arousal. And spells, too.'

Roisin gives in to a grin. 'I like this bit. You always go red.'

McAvoy obliges. 'She visited a site about love potions. Ways to get a man to fall in love with you. How to trap them and keep them.'

'Did she never consider good cooking and lots of baby oil?' asks Roisin.

'This was dark stuff. All about scents and using your bodily fluids to create a potion. There was one that talked about getting somebody to drink a coffee laced with your, erm, monthlies . . .'

Roisin pulls a face. 'Not my idea of a Bloody Mary,' she says. 'There are definitely better ways to get a man's attention.'

'She had her eye on somebody. Her phone records don't show much in the way of unusual activity but she did receive a lengthy video message about a month before her disappearance from an unregistered mobile phone. We traced the phone from the distributor. It was sold through a market stall in Goole. The owner kept good records. Remembered the lad who bought it because he was always coming back to complain and whine. He contacted uniform the second the kid came back. It was David Hogg.'

'Who?' asks Roisin.

'The hit and run, a mile down the road from here,' says McAvoy. 'Teenage girl out with her horse on a country lane and a fool in a stolen sports car comes around the corner at ninety mph and takes out horse and rider. Leaves them to die. The girl won't walk again. The horse had to be destroyed at the scene. A nearby farmer heard it screaming. Said the sound will never leave him.'

'Oh yes. Bastard,' says Roisin, remembering the story. McAvoy knows her pity is shared equally between human and horse.

'CID have no doubt the driver was David Hogg. Lives in Market Weighton. His uncle's a hard case and tidied things up. By the time David was arrested the car had been scrapped and there was nothing to link him to the accident. He laughed his way through the interviews. Even answered a few of the questions with neighs and whinnies. Got away with it.'

'And Hannah knew him?'

'We don't know; he wouldn't talk to us. We've found no link between them. Just the video, and we've no way of viewing that. Hogg's phone can't be traced and he mumbles "no comment" no matter how hard you lean on him.'

Roisin smiles, remembering the first time McAvoy told her this story. 'Jaw wired shut?'

'He'll be having his food mashed for years to come. His ankles and wrists were smashed and his face pummelled. Looked like he'd been kicked by a horse, then run over. His uncle had the cheek to demand what we were going to do about it. He put the word around that whoever did it was a dead man. We've had no leads. We've had no indications that the uncle's made any progress either.'

'So what's the connection?' asks Roisin, giving a little yawn.

'I don't know yet. Too many coincidences. Too many unanswered questions. I just can't seem to get past it. I want to hear that she's alive. I don't believe that she is. I can feel her, Roisin. You know I'm not like that. I don't hear voices or believe in clairvoyants. I've never read my horoscope. It's not like that. It's just . . .'

'An obsession?'

He looks at his feet, chastened and ashamed.

Roisin changes her position and snuggles into his chest, poking a finger through the buttons of his shirt to tickle his hair. 'She might be having the time of her life somewhere,' she says. 'You don't have to think the worst.'

He reaches down and kisses the top of her head. Wishes he could convince himself that Hannah is just a missing girl and not a murder victim. It feels like when he was eleven – still trying to persuade himself of the existence of Father Christmas, the Tooth Fairy and God.

They sit in silence for a while, only rousing themselves when Lilah wakes and uses Daddy's leg to right herself and starts bumbling off down the slope to where her brother is running towards them, holding a branch as long as himself. From this distance, he's a kilted Highlander, charging through the heather and the thistles with a claymore in his hand: a miniature of his father.

McAvoy is about to stand up and charge towards the boy, pretending to be an English invader dead set on having his innards sliced open by the noble Scotsman's blade. He knows Fin will like that. Wishes only that the boy wasn't spoiling the overall effect by wearing a Ross County football shirt and a pair of Bermuda shorts.

'Your phone,' says Roisin, nodding at his pocket as she hears it ring. 'The work one.'

He answers with his name, rank and unit, briefly recalling the days when a call from work would set his heart racing with excitement. Here, now, he simply knows that something bad has happened and it is about to interrupt his day.

He nods into the phone. His eyes darken. The colour seems to leach from his skin. He looks up at the sky, at the blue overhead, and the grey to the east.

He takes his keys from his pocket and starts walking up the hill to the car.

Towards Hull.

And an appointment with another dead girl.

# DARK WINTER

## DS MCAVOY: BOOK 1

### David Mark

DS Aector McAvoy is a man with a troubled past.
His unwavering belief in justice has made him
an outsider in the police force he serves.

Then on a cold day in December he is the first cop
on the scene when a young girl is killed in Hull
Cathedral – and the only person to see the murderer.
A masked man, with tears in his eyes . . .

When two more seemingly unconnected people die,
the police must work quickly. Only McAvoy can see the
connection between the victims. A killer is playing God –
and McAvoy must find a way to stop the deadly game.

AVAILABLE IN PAPERBACK AND EBOOK.

MULHOLLAND
BOOKS
HODDER

# ORIGINAL SKIN

## DS MCAVOY: BOOK 2

### David Mark

Suzie Devlin lived for pleasure – until her best friend Simon
was murdered. Now Suzie seems to be in the killer's sights . . .

Who wants her dead? And why? She's done nothing wrong . . .
except, perhaps, get involved with the wrong person.

DS Aector McAvoy has been a marked man all his
life. He knows how one misstep can put you in
harm's way. He's determined to protect Suzie, even
if it means inviting danger to come to him . . .

AVAILABLE IN PAPERBACK AND EBOOK.

MULHOLLAND
BOOKS
HODDER

ALSO AVAILABLE

# SORROW BOUND

## DS MCAVOY: BOOK 3

### David Mark

Philippa Longman did what we all aim
to do. She did the right thing.

She's about to pay for it with her life . . .

DS McAvoy has spent his career playing by the
rules. He has the scars to show for it.

And his latest case will take him into a world
in which good intentions make no difference
to those with a thirst for revenge . . .

AVAILABLE IN PAPERBACK AND EBOOK.

MULHOLLAND
BOOKS
HODDER

# You've turned the last page.

# But it doesn't have to end there . . .

If you're looking for more first-class, action-packed, nail-biting suspense, join us at **Facebook.com/ MulhollandUncovered** for news, competitions, and behind-the-scenes access to Mulholland Books.

For regular updates about our books and authors as well as what's going on in the world of crime and thrillers, follow us on **Twitter@MulhollandUK**.

# There are many more twists to come.

MULHOLLAND:
You never know what's
coming around the curve.